THE ZOMBIE CONSPIRACY

Parts 1-3

The Population Control Bundle

By Jeremy McIlroy

The Zombie Conspiracy Parts 1-3

The Population Control Bundle

© 2016 Jeremy P. McIlroy

- This is a work of fiction. Names, characters, businesses, places, events and incidents are either the products of the author's imagination or used in a fictitious manner. Any resemblance to actual persons, living or dead, or actual events is purely coincidental.

- This novel contains graphic violence, sex, coarse language, and politically incorrect viewpoints. It is not intended for consumption by children or anyone else.

ISBN-13: 978-1533035028
ISBN-10: 1533035024
Library of Congress Control Number: 2016907936
CreateSpace Independent Publishing Platform, North Charleston, SC
First Printing, May 2016   Printed in the USA

This book is dedicated to my lovely wife Stephany and to my three sons: Patrick Henry, Jeremy PQ, and Bryan.

Special Thanks to Brian McWilliams and Brenda Pemberton. You each helped just when I needed it. Devon and Thomas, thank you for the encouragement. Phil, sorry, no hover tanks or rail guns (yet), but thanks for being my sounding board and inspiration.

Works Published By Jeremy McIlroy

Finding Sanctuary: A Novel of Alternate History
Falling Star: A Dystopian Short Story
A Husband's Revenge
Get Out Of Debt: Financial Freedom Fast
The Z.A.P.S. Gear Survival Grenade User's Guide
The Zombie Conspiracy Parts 1-3 The Population Control Bundle
The Zombie Conspiracy Part 1- Undercover
The Zombie Conspiracy Part 2- D.A.R.P.A. Dangerous
The Zombie Conspiracy Part 3- Going Home

The Zombie Conspiracy Parts 1-3
The Population Control Bundle

Table of Contents

Preface

A friend of mine has been a big fan of zombie fiction for as long as I've known him. He had just finished reading my first novel, *Finding Sanctuary*, when he told me I should write a zombie novel. At first I thought the idea was absurd because I didn't know the first thing about zombies. I had never seen a zombie movie or read any zombie fiction. The Walking Dead TV show hadn't been made yet. I told him as much.

He then proceeded to tell me all about the commonalities and differences within the genre. Things like: zombie are undead and can only be killed again quickly by destroying the head, they don't attack other zombies—usually just humans and contamination is usually spread with a bite, some are slow while some are fast, a zombie apocalypse would mean a complete shutdown of modern society while everyone runs away from hungry corpses, etc. I asked questions and took note of his answers.

I must admit that I didn't really intend to write any zombie fiction while we were discussing zombie characteristics, but the more I thought about it, the more the idea grew on me. As a mental exercise I tried to think of how a zombie apocalypse, while staying true to my friend's listed characteristics, really could happen in our world, in our current society where zombie fiction is popular.

The story idea that I came up with stemmed from my conspiracy theory reading (which makes life interesting and sometimes comical), and the 'how' of my zombies came from the technical research in other subjects for my previous novel, which has nothing to do with zombies but includes high tech science, drone warfare, and conspiracy theory related and unrelated to entities within the US federal government. I put the story idea down on paper, threw together a short outline, and started writing. What you are about to read is the result.

Fair warning: this is not your typical zombie novel. It doesn't start with the world falling apart and zombies everywhere in the opening scene. I build up to that. I explain where zombies come from and why. This is how I imagine a real zombie apocalypse could happen.

Phil, you asked for it. Here you go.

PART 1 – Undercover

Chapter 1: Propositions

King Philip raised his goblet.

"My friends," he said with a booming voice and a smile as he turned his attention to each side of the table in turn. "I thank you all for joining me tonight on this most joyous of occasions. It is not every day that a king finds a woman worthy to be his queen, but today I tell you, I have found my shining star.

"How was that for an opening?" he asked, lowering the cup and his voice and turning towards his friend. "Too thick?"

"No, I don't think so. I thought it looked and sounded pretty good for what you are doing," Jeff said from where he sat in the heavy leather chair a few paces away. A charred log popped in the fire behind him. "I especially like the costume. If you grew a beard you'd look a bit like Sean Connery at the end of Robin Hood Prince of Thieves. It looks pretty authentic...like realistic royal garb."

"Pfft, it better. We spent enough on it, and it is a tax deductible business expense, so why not."

Philip popped the top on his soda can and poured some Pepsi into the ancient-looking goblet.

Several staff members dressed in period livery whirled around the table, arranging everything for the upcoming dinner party. They studiously ignored their boss and his guest, completely intent on their own tasks, or so they would have liked him to believe.

"So what was so important that you needed to interrupt my speech rehearsal, Cur? I need to practice. I don't want anything to go wrong tonight."

Jeff chuckled.

"Relax, Phil. You already proposed, and she said 'yes.' Now it's just a celebration of that fact."

"Yeah, I know you're right, but this is where we go public with our engagement. I want it to be perfect for her. So seriously, what's up? I can tell you've been holding something back. What's going on? Is it spy stuff?"

Jeff winced slightly.

"Yeah, I guess you could say that."

Philip reached under the table.

"Hold on. Let me turn on the counter-surveillance white-noise generator so we can talk."

Jeff snorted.

"Ha-ha—very funny. But in all seriousness, if you actually had one, I'd say to go ahead and turn it on."

Philip raised an eyebrow.

"That serious, huh?"

Jeff nodded.

"Well, all right then," Philip replied, looking at his staff moving around them. "Let's go to the library. It's a bit more private." He emptied the goblet and placed it on the table for one of the "servants" to clear away then turned and walked out through the double doors.

Jeff stood and followed, bringing along a small briefcase that had rested on the end table next to his seat. On the way out he slowed, taking an extra look at the suits of armor that guarded the entrance to the dining hall. They were polished to a nice shine, but they also looked heavy as hell. Not for the first time, he wondered how they managed to wear them back in the old days.

Their footsteps echoed across the stone floor. Colorful banners hung from the walls. Recessed lights gave the appearance of sunlight streaming through the occasional break in the stone ceiling.

"Medieval Kingdom. So how has attendance been?" Jeff asked, catching up as Philip turned the corner into an adjacent hallway.

"Pretty good. I couldn't ask for more, actually. We've had a steady stream since we opened the castle. The tourists were already flowing in to see Yellowstone, and we've gotten a healthy percentage of them to stop in here and spend their money. Everyone seems to be pretty excited to visit. If we're lucky, we'll be able to draw in winter tourists even after Yellowstone closes for the season."

"Excellent," Jeff replied. "If we're doing that well our first season, I can only guess at how we'll take off when even more people find out about the new attraction in town."

Philip nodded then turned as he opened a door and swept his hand.

"After you, Sir."

"M'Lord," Jeff replied, tilting his head in mock deference as he stepped into the library.

The walls were floor-to-ceiling bookshelves, and the shelves were packed, a room in which any bibliophile could happily dive in and never come up for air. A fireplace was at one end of the room, not far from the door they had just come through, and at the opposite end of the room were tall, stylish windows of stained glass that wouldn't be out of place in a true medieval European cathedral. Small nooks here and there afforded additional privacy, and a few small anterooms opened to additional reading space off of the main chamber.

Philip followed and closed the door, turning the lock against uninvited intruders.

Jeff quickly walked around and peeked in to the extra rooms to check that they were alone.

"Better send Linda a text letting her know we'll be out of touch for a little while," he suggested.

Philip nodded. "Good idea."

He sent a quick message then turned off his phone and handed it to his friend. "Just like the old days, huh?"

Jeff nodded and took a pouch out of his cargo pocket. It was made of some kind of reflective fabric and was sealed with Velcro. His phone was already nestled inside. He dropped Phil's in next to his own.

"That's it?" Philip asked. "You're not going to pop the battery first?"

"Nope, this will do it, the latest in signal blocking technology. Copper, nickel, and rare-earth-metals-infused electronic forensics evidence bag—blocks all signals going in or out. The phones can't be remotely accessed, so their microphones can no longer be used for eavesdropping—as long as they stay in the bag. Even the radio feature inside is scrambled enough to prevent snooping or location triangulation. You can do the same thing by wrapping them in quadruple layers of aluminum foil, of course; but a government agent can't be seen doing something so cheap—you know how it is."

"Of course," Philip said, nodding his head and chuckling, as he leaned back against one of the small tables that rested in the center of the room. "So—spill the beans. What's going on?"

"First, let me just say that I really did come out here to wish you and my sister congratulations on finally deciding to tie the knot. I'm not just using it as a pretext to visit undercover; I really am happy for you guys."

"Ok, but—?"

"But," Jeff continued, "I also need to ask you for a favor."

Philip looked skeptical.

"I've got a job for you if you'll take it."

"Come on, Jeff. You know Linda doesn't want me doing that stuff anymore. We were this close to getting caught by the Iranians three years ago when we went off on one of your missions," Philip said, pinching his fingers together and holding them up in front of his face.

"I know, I know, believe me, I know. My ear drums are still ringing from the chewing she gave me. But this is important. And last time was a fluke. We weren't even supposed to leave the safe house. That was totally out of my hands."

Philip sighed and shook his head, looking up at one of the crystal chandeliers that hung at the level of the open second floor.

"Why me?" he asked, bringing his gaze back down. "Why not get one of the agency guys? That's what they get paid for, you know."

"I know, but, strictly between you and me, I think the agency might be compromised."

"What? Why would you think that?"

"Because some strange things have been going on lately—and not overseas. Domestically. Some previously sweet resources have all of a sudden dried up and gone quiet, and turning over new stones is producing nothing. Zero, zip, nada. Guys are going out and not coming back. It's like someone got their hands on our playbook and is running us in circles while feeding us a steady diet of bull shit and zero calorie soft drinks. And that only happens when the bad guys have someone on the inside or crack your codes."

"Well, that's a pretty vague explanation of why it's me you need," Philip replied. "In fact it's not an explanation at all. There's gotta be somebody on the inside that you still trust."

Jeff closed his eyes and pinched the bridge of his nose. When he opened his eyes, he looked about as serious as Philip had ever seen him.

"There are a very select few—but they aren't suited for what I need you for. I'm not positive we're compromised, but it sure feels that way lately. What I'm about to tell you is S-C-I level Top Secret. If the powers that be found out I was talking to you about this, we'd both be locked up in a secret prison where the sun doesn't shine and seeing the stars is pretty freaking rare too."

"Got it, sealed lips, never heard a thing," Philip replied, returning the serious look.

Jeff nodded then continued.

"After the debacle in Iran, the agency decided to put me on easy domestic cases, something I could work quietly while things blew over on Capitol Hill."

9

"Ok"

"I've been plugging away in the background, staying out of sight/out of mind, but then something came up, something big—even if it didn't really make much of an impact in the news. The director assigned me an investigation into something the Defense Advanced Research Projects Agency has been working on."

"You're investigating DARPA."

"Yes," Jeff replied.

"Why?"

Jeff sighed.

"Do you remember a while back, Science Digest had a special on military drones and special projects?"

"Sure"

"Well, there was an article in there about DARPA's top secret super soldier program, that wasn't vetted or cleared for print. It's spot-on-accurate from what I've been able to gather from my own inside source."

"Oh, crap."

"As eloquently put as usual; but, yes, in this case, 'Crap' is right. Certain members of congress flipped out when they read the article, not only because of the secrecy breach but also because whoever sourced the piece basically admitted that DARPA is engaged in researching some restricted areas of bio-engineering and human experimentation; the very thing the U.S. entered into multiple international treaties to prevent. So congress went on the war path and ordered the DIA to investigate. It's not Edward Snowden big, but it's big enough."

"So if you have an inside source what do you need me for? Why don't you just bust DARPA in a congressional hearing and be done with it?"

"Unfortunately, what I have hasn't been completely substantiated—not well enough to stand up in court, which is where this whole thing is headed. I don't have the physical evidence—yet. DARPA isn't playing ball with the investigation despite Congress's orders, and even more unfortunate…my inside source seems to have gone completely dark—no contact."

"And you want me to go in and take his—or her—place. You're not making a very convincing case for yourself here, Bud."

Jeff smirked and replied, "I wouldn't necessarily need you to take his place. We would be better served if you could go in, make contact, and start the flow of information again—through him if possible. And if he is unable, or unwilling, to continue, then, yes, I could really use your help getting me the information I need."

"And you said the director specifically chose you for this. Well, that sounds kind of good for your career."

"It could be, if it works out ok. The problem is that now I'm under intense scrutiny from some people I didn't even used to know existed, and they are pressuring me to downplay the whole thing. There are some major money players involved and they aren't above buying agents' loyalty. I've already been approached with bribe offers."

Philip shook his head.

"Very substantial offers," Jeff added. "Knowing that, and seeing what is happening on the operations side ever since this all broke, I need an outside investigator to go undercover while I manage the 'public' side of the investigation. In addition to the private bribes that have been offered, I've been pressured by certain opposing members of Congress as well. It's getting rough. I need someone I can trust not to be bought out from under me. Someone I can trust to get the job done."

"So you came to me," Philip replied.

"Yes…I know it puts you in a tricky position with my sister, but this is extremely important."

Philip sighed.

Linda definitely wouldn't like the idea, but he was a sucker for a friend in need. And this was Jeff. Loyalty to him went a long way.

"I'll think about it," he said. "But I need to know more about the mission. What it entails. How long you anticipate this thing taking. The risks. The rewards. Most importantly—how Linda will be kept safe while I'm not here for her."

"Naturally," Jeff replied. "I'll address the last two concerns first. I will have a few people here on the staff watching over my sister. They're old hands at the protection game, and they'll be undercover until there is a need. They'll blend right in, even here. She won't even know they're here. And, no, they aren't DIA.

"As for reward, well, I am authorized to pay out quite a bit of taxpayer money for this investigation, and the director did specify that, if necessary, I can appropriate additional funds from the black ops budget—as long as I can guarantee him deniability, of course."

"Of course," Philip replied. "So what exactly is the mission?"

Jeff nodded. "And that's where the classified info comes in."

Opening his brown leather briefcase, he pulled out a manila folder.

"If we didn't have history I wouldn't be showing this to you until after you signed another Non-Disclosure Agreement," Jeff said, holding the folder to his chest.

"Got it. Ultra top secret with no decoder ring, no talking about it—not even whispering."

"And no joking either."

"Got it," Philip said, smiling one last time before turning completely serious.

Jeff shook his head, pulled an 8 x 10 photo out of the folder, and slid it across the table.

"Memorize his face. This is Donovan Clarke. He is your mission."

Philip nodded and studied the photo.

It was a standard head shot of a man who looked like he could fit in comfortably in just about any corporate job in America. He was a balding Caucasian with corrective glasses on a thick nose over a strong jaw. The light reflecting off his glasses and the solid-colored backdrop showed that it was a professional photo not just a snap shot.

"Don has been working for the DIA for at least a year," Jeff continued. "I've been his case officer for the last three months, except I haven't been able to get through to him for the last month. He isn't responding to any of the usual ways we have set up to communicate with him. All flow of information from his side just stopped as if he has fallen off the planet.

"The last update he sent was corrupted. Most of the data was nearly impossible to make sense of. What I was able to salvage, with the help of an NSA reconstruction expert and his supercomputer, was this." He slid a stack of paper-clipped papers across the table.

"Looks like partial schematics," Phil said, scanning through the pages. "...and gibberish."

Jeff nodded. "The schematics are specialized nanotechnology designs based on Doctor Harper's patents, but our copy of the schematics *is* massively incomplete. Again, most of the file was corrupted before it reached me. Keep looking. I highlighted the most important piece we found that was readable."

Philip mumbled as he sorted through the lines and lines of seemingly random letters, numbers, symbols, and technical drawings. He flipped through and stopped mumbling.

"E-W-E-S-6 trials complete and successful. Z-S-1 trials commencing."

"Yes," Jeff replied.

"And what are E-W-E-S-6 and Z-S-1?"

"EWES we know," Jeff replied, pronouncing it "Use." "It is an acronym that stands for the Elite Warrior Enhancement Series, in this case: Series 6. That is the official name of the DARPA super soldier program. And, according to this, it is a success. Just one problem: Congress revoked their funding and shut them down two months ago when the article exposed their illegal research methods. At that time they were only on EWES-4, so they are getting funding from somewhere else, despite Congress's orders, and they are continuing their research—

14

in fact, accelerating their research, contrary to lawful orders."

"And Z-S-1?"

Jeff shook his head and shrugged his shoulders. "We don't know what Z-S-1 is. We have absolutely zero documentation on it. Judging by the 'S' in EWES we can bet that the 'S' stands for Series, but the 'Z'? Your guess is as good as mine."

Philip leaned back and closed his eyes, pinching the bridge of his nose and clenching his jaw.

"I have the inside scoop on EWES from one of the Special Forces commanders that I've worked with over the years," Jeff said. "He said that initially EWES was getting volunteers from the S-F community but that he and the other commanders were getting pissed that their guys were volunteering and never coming back. They'd get word back later that each and every one of the volunteers either had died in 'training accidents' or had ended up in military psych wards. Whatever EWES was doing was either killing our best guys or messing up their heads."

"But this says EWES-6 was a success," Phil countered, holding up the paperwork.

"So somewhere between EWES-4 and EWES-6 they made a breakthrough—maybe, if they're being honest in their internal paperwork," Jeff guessed. "But they're not doing it with military volunteers any more. None of that really matters though because the way they're doing whatever it is they're doing in there is against U.S. law as well as international law."

Philip nodded and wiped his eyes. This conversation really wasn't going the way he would have liked. He would rather have come in here to relax, smoke a nice smooth cigar, and talk about the "good old days" when they had been working together back in the Sandbox.

But that just wasn't going to happen right now.

"So what I'm thinking," Jeff continued, "Is that there are three possibilities for what happened to our asset. One: Don was compromised during his poking around for us and was killed and then disappeared. Two: he was compromised and then captured and locked away where he has been unable to reach out to us. Or three: he was either compromised or felt like he was about to be and went on the run or into hiding and has been unable to contact us."

"There's a fourth possibility," Philip suggested.

Jeff tilted his head questioningly.

"Maybe he got scared and just decided not to have anything to do with you or the agency anymore and is just working at DARPA as if nothing has happened. Maybe he is just ignoring you."

Jeff closed his eyes and rubbed a hand across the stubble on his cheek. Opening his eyes, he nodded.

"You're right. That is another possibility. None of them are very palatable, but we have to face reality, and if that is the reality then having you on the inside will at least show us where we stand."

There was a moment of silence between them.

A crowd out in the courtyard began cheering. A clock that hung on the wall in a gap between bookshelves told Philip that it was time for the daily joust, always a guest favorite.

"Phil, I wouldn't ask you to do this if I felt like I had other options. I have to find out what happened to my

16

asset, and if he is gone, I need you to get me the information he was after. I'll need you to look into Joshua Harper, the creator of these schematics. That is where Don left off. Something here," he said, holding up the stack of papers, "Was important enough for him to send it to me.

"Best case scenario, you won't have to do anything but walk up to Don's room, tell him why you're there, and he gets back to me. Then you're done. But I don't think that's going to happen. I need you in there. You're loyal. You operate well under pressure. You have a knack for this kind of work…You're loyal"

"Ugh—enough already," Phil said, dropping his head into his hands and pulling them down his face. "Linda is going to kill me."

"Yeah, but then she's going to marry you. And you'll have a chance to make it up to her for the rest of your life."

"And I'm sure she'll remind me of that daily."

Jeff chuckled.

"Well, the half a million dollars that Uncle Sam will pay you out of the black budget for your service, tax free I might add, will make sure that you can make it up to her in style."

"Make it a million," Phil countered.

"Deal. I think that's reasonable, considering what you'll have to do, the potential dangers involved—and there *are* some serious dangers with you doing this. And, of course, I have to mention the fact that you'll have to wait for about a year to go through with your current wedding plans."

"A year? Seriously?"

Jeff nodded. "Possibly. I hope not, but it could be. Your new name is Richard Dalton. I have a bio for you all ready to go with references, a social history, and an impressive résumé that will make you a shoe-in to the job I'm getting you at the DARPA facility where you'll be going undercover. But if the résumé is going to be believable, *you* have to be believable. You have to be able to talk the talk and walk the walk. You will be getting some concentrated intensive training from a few experts I've got lined up before you go in to get you up to that level, and you'll need to get yourself into better physical shape. You're supposed to be a former SEAL after all."

Philip shook his head.

"You had to name me 'Dick'?"

"Well, 'Dick' is an acceptable shortening of the name 'Richard', but you don't have to use the short version if you don't want to—Dick."

Philip laughed then thought it over some more before speaking.

"All right, but if I'm going to do this, I want half of the money up front in cash—and you have to be best man at the wedding."

Jeff smiled.

"I'll do you one better than that. *All* of the money up front, in cash, with a bonus to be added in later to pay for your honeymoon—and I'll be best man at your wedding and godfather to the many children you and Linda will spawn."

"You have yourself a deal, Brother," Philip said, and put out his hand.

Jeff shook the offered hand then reached into his suit jacket and brought out two cigars.

"Congratulations, Dick. You're hired. And Congrats on successfully proposing to my sister. May you grow old together in absolute bliss."

Philip laughed and looked longingly at the cigar that was extended towards him.

"I was beginning to worry that our meeting was going to be all business—and thank you."

"Well, now that that's out of the way, I still want to talk business. How about you tell me about *our* business? Medieval Kingdom seems to be everything you told me it would be and more, but I still haven't taken the time to learn all of the ins and outs of owning an amusement park. I've had so much going on."

Philip smiled and began to talk about their investment.

Chapter 2: Snooping and Pooping

Richard eased the door shut behind him and listened for any sign that his intrusion had been detected. He mentally counted off thirty seconds. The room was quiet. There wasn't even the small hum of a TV in standby mode. Turning on a small penlight, he flashed dim light around the room. To the left, the bathroom door was open to cavernous darkness. Ahead, the bed was empty, as he had expected it to be. To the right was a standard work station with which most of these dorm rooms were equipped. No other doors. No windows. The room was designed for privacy, less so for comfort.

He was alone.

Perfect.

He had just broken into Joshua Harper's sparsely furnished, undecorated dorm room. For being one of the leading scientists in the field of nanotechnology and a billionaire, he sure didn't live up to the lifestyle he could afford.

Strange

Casting his light along the wall for the light switch, he found it in the same spot as in all of the other rooms.

The temperature in the room was the usually comfortable 70°F, but his clothes were soaked through with sweat. Since he had been hired by DARPA, the US's premiere research and development agency for technology on the bleeding edge of science and warfare, this was his

I'll just take a quick photo, so I know everything is left as I found it. He pulled out a Polaroid camera and took a snap shot of the desk then set the photo off to the side to develop.

He was using old school technology for this job, but that was preferable this time. Newer tech, like the smart phone he'd left back in his room and some of the newer digital cameras, had features like GPS/Wi-Fi/Bluetooth connectivity, which were great for recreational applications, could very likely blow his cover here. The security office had signal trap hardware secreted around the facility with software programs that monitored which devices connected to which servers. So if he, an unauthorized user, happened to be in an area he didn't have good reason to be in, like right now, his newer devices might connect to servers he didn't want to connect to and then it would be game over, go straight to jail, do not enjoy one million dollars.

Putting the camera back in his bag, he grabbed his tool kit and set it on the desk. Then he turned off the computer and monitor and went step by step through the process of getting to the computer's motherboard safely and without leaving signs of tampering.

It was imperative that he gain access to Joshua Harper's hard drive. He'd been shown how to access a back door built into the DARPA Operating System by one of Jeff's training cadre, but they had warned that some of the higher clearance staff could have additional protective features on their equipment. So, of course, Harper had to have additional layers of security.

That was ok. Richard came prepared for that possibility. Instead of accessing the hard drive now, he'd have to wait a little while. When he had the motherboard in front of him, he pushed a small chip down into one of the free slots then began to reassemble everything.

The key stroke logger would record every entry Harper made, including the BIOS password. Richard just had to give Harper time to use his personal computer then he could come back, recover the chip, and use the information it held to access the hard drive.

He just didn't know how long he'd have to wait. Harper was a bit eccentric and spent most of his time in his lab at the other side of the facility, even sleeping there occasionally. But Richard had been told that Harper did go back to his room sometimes and sometimes accessed his lab's computer from the computer in his room.

That was the whole reason Richard was breaking into the dorm room instead of attempting a much more difficult infiltration into Harper's lab.

Just gotta be patient, he told himself. The keystroke logger was equipped with a second software program that, once activated with the reboot of Harper's computer and subsequent sign in to the DARPA OS, would send a short spam advertisement to a dummy email account using Harper's hardware, letting him know that he could continue his information and intelligence gathering when the room was once again vacant.

When he had everything reassembled and positioned correctly at the workstation, he double checked then triple checked that everything was as it had been when he had come in, using the Polaroid photo to verify.

greatness that he had turned Islam's enemies against themselves.

"Allah be praised. Surely you are the Most Praiseworthy, the Most Glorious," he said, finishing his prayer.

The target was coming into view.

It was a small white building with a cross atop its steeple. The nearby parking lot was packed. Local police cruisers and unmarked, federally owned sedans and SUV's lined the curbs within a block. Uniformed police officers stood around near the street, keeping the generally curious away. Men in suits milled about closer to the building, giving the pat down to anyone who was allowed entrance by the first ring of police.

A police car turned on its emergency lights and began to pull out into the intersection in front of his cargo truck to cut him off. It didn't matter.

Muhammad accelerated, and his adrenaline began to really flow. He smashed the truck into the car's engine compartment, flipping it out of his way. He lost some momentum but not enough to hinder him from accomplishing his goal.

He jerked the steering wheel to the left and then back to the right. The truck bounced up onto the sidewalk and then tore over the grass next to the side of the church. As the men guarding his target reached for their guns, he grabbed the remote initiator that hung around his neck, shouted "Allah huAkbar!—Allah is Greatest!" with his last breath, and slammed his hand down on the plunger.

Nothing happened.

He slapped it again.

Panic crept into his soul then a sharp pain in his chest blossomed outward into the rest of his body. He was vaguely aware through his disappointment that he had been shot. Fear and doubt flickered through his consciousness. He had failed, but he would die anyway. Would his brothers still welcome him? Would he still receive the virgins each martyr was promised?

As his breath, blood, and strength leaked from his body for the final time, he made one last desperate attempt. He depressed the plunger with the last of his strength.

The payload in the back of the box-truck detonated.

The hallway was clear as he approached Harper's door. Holding his breath, he turned the master key in the lock. The deadbolt was sticking just like last time, so he gave the key more of a twist and pulled the door knob towards him. With a click far louder than he would have preferred, the bolt retreated into the door. He looked up and down the hall one last time and slipped into darkness, re-locking the door. If it had been loud enough to wake anyone, they'd find an empty hallway when they poked their head outside.

Pulling the Polaroid camera from his backpack, he walked towards Harper's workstation. He snapped a few shots of the computer desk's cluttered surface after he turned on the desk lamp. He set the shots under the light to develop.

Nothing looked to have changed from the last time he had been there.

Yesterday he'd finally received the message that Harper had accessed the computer. Richard hadn't been able to break in last night when Harper, true to form, was at work in his lab. He had been forced unexpectedly to cover a shift for one of the other security personnel who had gotten bed rest and pain killers after a rough tumble during hand to hand control tactics training. Tonight was different. He was going into his days off and wouldn't be needed for several days.

Moving as few of the objects on Harper's desk as he could get by with, he unplugged the desktop and pressed the power key to discharge any internally stored electricity. Then he used a screw driver to open the tower casing. He pulled on the keystroke logger to take it off of the motherboard, but it didn't pop off.

Wow, it's really stuck in there.

He gave it a little wiggle, and just as he started to pull on it again, he heard footsteps in the corridor outside.

Oh crap, he thought, yanking on it as he looked toward the door. It popped off into his hand, and he gripped it in a fist. *Please don't be Harper.*

With Harper being free to make his own work hours, it very well could be him heading back to his room. Richard began sweating anew as the footsteps grew louder. They slowed near the door.

Son of a bitch, he thought. *There's no way I'm going to be able to explain this. I am so royally screwed.*

Putting the keystroke logger into his pocket and leaving everything else where it was, he hurried over to the door and hid next to the wall where he wouldn't be immediately seen when the door opened. As soon as the door opened and Harper stepped inside, he was going to have to hit him on the head behind the ear with the lead-filled leather sap that he was pulling from his pocket.

Once Harper was unconscious, Richard could finish copying the hard drive and then leave. There would be a hellacious investigation afterward, but it was possible he might be able to keep off the radar, especially since he could very well be the one assigned to investigate the break-in and assault. That was certainly better than being seen by Harper and then everyone knowing he had been there.

All right, just one more thing to do tonight and then I can chill.

After making a connection to the internet, he went to a site using its numeric IP address. The domain name it used had too many randomly selected characters to remember. Accessing the site required entering a password and then answering a few questions that very few people, two to be exact, could correctly answer.

Jeff, back at the Defense Intelligence Agency was the only other person who knew how to access the site—or even knew about its existence. Since Guddemi was on the other side of the country, and Richard's cover job was inside a secure facility, they needed a way to pass information to each other without either one being caught or the information itself being compromised and falling into the wrong hands.

This site made that possible. He selected Harper's drive to upload and began sending the information into cyberspace.

He knew it would take a while, so he decided to take it easy. He went to his refrigerator and grabbed a bottle of orange juice. He guzzled a few gulps to quench his immediate thirst then poured a healthy amount into a glass from the cupboard. Then he went and plopped down in front of the television.

Watching an episode of Robot Chicken brought a few laughs, but he didn't feel like watching what came on next, so he flipped through the channels. He stopped on a news channel where the talking heads were discussing an outbreak of something as yet undetermined over in China that was claiming a lot of lives. They said it was so serious that the local Chinese officials had ordered the quarantine of entire areas and the burning of several towns. The talking head wondered when we would send aid to help those poor people.

Richard shook his head.

There's always some story of doom and gloom going on. We can't—and shouldn't, fix everything in the world. We've got enough of our own damned problems that need to be fixed first.

He changed the channel.

Another news network. Another dark-haired, news anchor—this time a man, wearing a solemn expression.

"...entire community of Amish folk in Berlin, Ohio have disappeared with no explanation. The local authorities are investigating the cause and..."

Maybe a rival sect kidnapped them all and cut off their beards. Maybe they'll show up in a few days and, he yawned. *Oh, who am I kidding? I couldn't care less if the Mennonites packed it up and went into hiding.*

His eyes were beginning to glaze over and their lids to droop.

Just a little bit longer. Gotta wait for the upload to finish, he thought and opened his eyes wider by raising his eyebrows.

He changed the channel and immediately felt a little refreshed when he saw a gorgeous blond with a British accent wrapping up a news segment on the G20 that had been in session over the last few days. He half listened to her talking about how it must have gone better than many had feared it might, since none of the world leaders had

Chapter 6: Trace Alert

Sitting at his desk, half asleep, Deron Brown jerked upright in his chair when the computer console in front of him began chiming a warning.

What the hell? He thought, as he looked at the screen.

He didn't recognize the alarm code the computer was showing. It had to be one of the alarms his supervisor had mentioned was only explained in the books up in the cupboard.

And that means it is some serious *shit*, he thought. *Oh boy.*

He grabbed the key from the hook on which it rested over the supervisor's desk, and opened the cupboard. Confirming the number sequence of the alarm again, he grabbed a binder with numbers across the bottom. Opening it, he flipped through the plastic protected pages until he found the sheet that listed his alarm.

When he saw the directions, his knees almost gave out on him.

He recognized the phone number he now had to call because on his first day on the job, his supervisor had told him to make sure he never called that number, not unless it was the end of the world. He'd memorized it. He knew that number better than he knew his own birth date.

Fingers shaking, he dialed the number. It rang twice.

"What?"

Deron swallowed.

"Um, Sir. I, um—that is, uh, the alarm went off, and…"

"Yeah? Spit it out."

"Sir, it's a five-nine-three, dash echo-one."

There was silence on the other end for a full second.

"Sir?"

"I will be right over. Make no other calls."

"Yes, Sir. I won't ma…"

Click

Deron looked at the phone then placed it back on the receiver.

When the door opened, Deron shot to his feet.

"Sit," the new arrival said, as he walked past Deron and went to the computer with the flashing screen.

"It just started going off about…"

"Don't talk."

Deron opened his mouth to acknowledge, but he caught himself and just nodded. He watched as the man's hands flew across the keyboard faster than Deron ever seen anyone type before.

The man's head never turned from the screen. Eventually the screen stopped blinking, and the alarm stopped sounding.

Before Deron had a chance to see what the man had accessed in the computer, the screen was blank again.

"If it happens again, you know what to do," the man said as he left.

Deron nodded his head and didn't stop until the door had been closed for several seconds. He shivered and sat back down in his seat.

He blew out a long breath.

Those damage control guys are spooky. He shivered despite the warm coziness of the room. *Not my problem. I'm not going to worry about it.*

He leaned back, closed his eyes, and tried to forget about what had just happened.

Chapter 7: A Toast

Each year the President of the United States hosts a dinner party at the White House for the governors of each of the fifty States. He gets them together to talk about the different issues he would like them to concentrate on within their States to help the federal government achieve its goals, and he listens to what they have to say about the needs of their constituents.

President Nelson had the governors and their wives waiting down on the State Floor, where most dinner parties and special events at the White House were held. The Marine Corps band, also known as "The President's Own," kept them entertained with instrumental music, and the residence staff walked paths through the crowd with trays of hors d'oeuvres and glasses full of several selections of wine from the President's Napa Valley vineyard and winery.

Nelson stood at the top of the Grand Staircase with Marlon Dunwoody.

"Are they all here?"

"All but Alaska and Texas—Alaska had something come up with the new Denali pipeline at the last minute..."

Nelson shook his head and muttered something derogatory under his breath about the polluting oil companies and their greed.

Marlon nodded and finished what he had been saying. "And Texas had to cancel with apologies. Governor Haynes's nephew died over the weekend, so he is staying with his brother for a few days until after the funeral service."

The President nodded.

"We are almost there, Marlon," Nelson said with his chin up, as his man straightened his tuxedo bow tie. "The G20 went as well as we had hoped. There will be no turning back now and not very much longer to wait."

Marlon smiled and nodded.

"We have waited such a long time," Marlon agreed. "The pieces are all in place. China has already hushed their media around the Premier. They haven't figured it out yet. The rest will follow. Now there's just tonight. Go knock them dead," he said, giving the President an encouraging slap on the shoulder.

Nelson laughed.

"Oh, you can be sure of that, my friend—that you can."

"I'll go see if Diane is ready," Marlon said.

The President nodded and turned to look at himself in the mirror, while he waited for his wife. He stood tall, admiring himself. He had taken care of himself over the years, and he liked how young he still looked—even if he didn't feel so young. No matter. Harper had promised something that would make him look and feel young for as long as he liked.

Marlon returned with the First Lady at his side.

"Sweetheart," Nelson said. "You look ravishing, as always. You'll make every woman down there jealous."

"Thank you," she said, smiling.

She wore a red dress that highlighted the slimness of her hour glass figure. White pearls were strung at her neck and a matching set of pearl earrings framed her elegant cheekbones.

"Shall we?" Nelson asked, offering his arm.

She nodded and slipped her arm into his.

They descended the red-carpeted Grand Staircase and emerged onto to the State Floor, where the President's Own stopped the song they had been playing and began "Hail to the Chief," the traditional song of serenade to the President.

"Thank you, thank you," Nelson said, holding up a hand and waving to the crowd.

The First Lady was all smiles, as she stood by her man.

"Thank you for coming tonight," the President said. "I know we all thought President Zimmerman would be doing the honors tonight. He was a good man, a righteous man."

Several in the crowd clapped their hands, and a few said, "Hear, hear."

Marlon appeared at the President's side and gave him a portion of wine. The flute was a little more decorous than the others that floated around the room. The wine had been poured by Marlon's own hand from one of the bottles Nelson kept upstairs, separate from the rest. Tonight only Marlon, the President, and the First Lady would drink from this bottle. It was special.

Nelson raised the wine for all to see.

"A toast," the President said. "To President Zimmerman—a man who cared for and served his country like few have before. May he and his family rest in everlasting peace."

"To President Zimmerman," the room repeated.

As one, everyone in the room raised their glasses and drank.

"And to our boys in the military who are going to hunt down the damned terrorist bastards who are responsible for taking him away from us," one of the governors added.

There were cheers and the room drank again.

President Nelson and Marlon mingled into the crowd to talk to a few of the more influential governors, and the First Lady, always the perfect hostess, went to talk to some of the wives.

Chapter 8: Alcoholic You Say?

Dressed in a white tuxedo, like all of the other White House staff who walked through the crowd serving hors d'oeuvres and flutes of the President's wine, Antoine Davis carried his empty tray back into the kitchen to get more refreshments. Several of his coworkers bustled past with their own newly filled trays, and he stepped out of their way.

Events like this were always busy, and he had learned to work hard, go with the flow, but also to get a few bites and swallows in for himself throughout the night. And if he happened to drink a little more alcohol than the others, well, it wasn't a big deal. He was a bigger guy than the others. He deserved a larger share for his larger frame. At least that's what he told himself.

Anything to keep from admitting to himself that he had a drinking problem. Deep down he knew it was probably true, but he never let himself entertain such thoughts for very long. There was always a rationalization for why he should allow himself to drink a little more.

Tonight, the staff had been very clearly told that the wine was for guests only. Anyone caught drinking the wine could face suspension if not termination from employment. Pretty serious consequences for something so simple. Some grumbled that it was unreasonable, but only when their supervisor wasn't close enough to hear.

Antoine didn't grumble. But he didn't fully agree with the order either. Normally he would go along with that kind of directive because he understood that sometimes the supplies the White House ordered were in short supply elsewhere, so it made sense if there were limited quantities. The guests should enjoy the best before the serving staff. That was just common sense.

But in this instance there were cases upon cases of the wine that the President had ordered delivered to Washington DC from his Napa Valley vineyard.

A tray of fluted white wine rested on the counter a few feet away from the table that should have held hors d'oeuvres.

He knew that very shortly one of the kitchen assistants would bring up another cart on the elevator from the kitchen. There was not yet anyone else in the lesser kitchen with him.

Without even thinking about it, he snatched up a flute of the white wine from the tray, downed it in two quick gulps, and tossed the empty wine glass onto a growing stack in the trash.

Not thirty seconds later the elevator door opened and a cart came rolling off the elevator.

"There you are," Antoine said. "They're really scarfing them down tonight, hey?"

"You're telling me."

Antoine grabbed enough to fill his tray and then snaked his way back out into the crowd of governors.

Hours later the party had wound down and the staff had cleaned most of the mess that had remained afterward. They knew they were required to be right back in for work in less than six hours. Most of them lived too far away to make leaving for their own beds worth the trip.

After events like this, with so little time before coming back to work, it was customary for the staff to be offered the opportunity to sleep on cots specially set up in spare conference rooms next door at the Eisenhower Executive Office Building.

Tonight their supervisor practically insisted that nobody leave, saying that it wouldn't be safe for them to drive after such a long day and with so little time before they were required to report back in. A few tried to argue that they lived only fifteen minutes away and that they would rather drive home to their own beds and drive back in in the morning.

Not too long later Antoine saw them setting their bags of sleepover gear under cots a few rows over from the one he was already lying on. He ignored their quiet complaints. His stomach felt a little funny, and he was tired, more tired than he thought he should be.

Rolling over onto his side away from the grumblers, he pulled the gray military issued blanket over his head and closed his eyes to seek a few precious hours of sleep.

Chapter 9: Wake Up Call

Joshua Harper was not your typical geeky looking scientist in a white lab coat. No, he was actually quite handsome, according to the ladies, being tall, with dark hair, sparkling eyes, and a charming smile—when he did smile. And he was rich—filthy rich, having successfully patented several very useful and thus valuable inventions in the new but growing field of nanotechnology.

Presently, Harper was tired. He would have slept on the cot in the lab, but he knew the smell of something he had just burned would prevent him from getting any rest. The bed in his room was more comfortable than the cot, and it had been a few days since he had slept in it.

His thoughts whirled and tangled in his head. There was so much going on, and his associates still had so much they expected him to do before the end. He wondered if he should just take the plunge with his most recent batch and hope for the best.

Stupid! It could still go wrong. I still have to check to make sure they will deactivate under the controls. If they don't, there could be some serious side effe…

A knocking at the door interrupted his thoughts.

He looked at the clock hanging on the wall.

Who the hell would disturb me here at nearly two in the morning? he wondered. *I'm going to light a fire under someone's ass.*

He walked over to his door and unlocked the deadbolt. He was about to open it and see who wanted to be transferred to Antarctica for penguin duty, when the handle turned and the door opened without invitation.

"Do you mind?" he asked, his voice rising an octave. "I don't know who you think you are—" he began, but stopped when he really saw who it was. His eyes went wide. "Brandon Brock. What are you doing here?"

"Sit down," Brock ordered, as he stepped further into the room.

Harper backed away from him. Fear began to creep into his soul, as he sat down on his bed.

"And Tim Mercer too," he whispered, when he saw the second man come through the door.

"Did you miss us, Doc?" Tim asked, as he closed and locked the door

"Not really," Harper said. "I've been too busy to really miss anybody."

"That's what I like about you, Doc," Mercer said with a chuckle. "You speak your mind, regardless of what anyone else thinks."

Brock ignored the banter and went to Harper's computer desk.

"What are you doing?" Harper asked at Brock, who ignored him.

"What is he doing?" he asked again, this time to Mercer.

"Well, Doc, we've got ourselves a little problem," Tim replied. "It seems someone accessed this computer right here in your room and then sent some very secret information to a website online. That's a big no-no, you know. We can't have you sharing our secrets now can we?"

"What? That can't be; I've been in my lab all night, and no one else..."Harper began but drifted off, his voice growing quieter and his eyes dropping to the floor. "I didn't do it," he said, looking back up. "So why are you here?"

Mercer nodded, his eyes boring holes into Harper's skull.

"We're here to find out if your system agrees with our information. If it does, you get to go see a mutual acquaintance of ours, so you can explain yourself.—Relax, Doc, we're not here to kill you, if that's what you're worried about."

Harper didn't say anything, just leaned back, understanding clearly visible in his eyes.

Mercer shrugged his shoulders then continued.

"If the system info doesn't match, we'll have to go look somewhere else for the culprit, and you can go back to whatever our acquaintance has you doing here…For your sake, Doc, I hope our information is wrong. That nano-shit you put in us has really helped."

Mercer actually looked sincere.

"What is your first password?" Brock asked, making the room feel cold.

Harper swallowed as he looked at Brock. He was afraid to look the man in the eye all of a sudden. Curious, he had never felt that way before with any of the men he had tested and improved.

"B-u-c-k-m-1-n-5-t-3-r-f-u-l-l-e-r-e-n-3," Harper spelled.

"What the hell is that?" Mercer asked, as Brock typed it out.

"Buckminsterfullerene," Harper replied. "It's the most stable fullerene with sixty carbon atoms in the shape of…"

"Whoa, never mind," Mercer said, chuckling. "That stuff is way over my head. Sorry I asked."

"What is the next password?" Brock asked, in his chillingly monotone voice after BIOS began booting the DARPA operating system.

"3-n-d-0-h-e-d-r-@-l-F-u-l-l-3-R-e-n-e," Harper spelled again.

Brock typed the characters into the prompt box, and the DARPA operating system decrypted the drive contents for usage.

"Endohedralfullerene," Harper said to Mercer, needing to say something to ease his nerves. "It's a hollow carbon molecule with an atom of metal or a noble gas trapped inside. They can be used…"

"Doc, really, it's Greek to me, and I don't care," Mercer interrupted. "I was just making idle conversation, while Brock searches your usage history logs. I'm being somewhat friendly because I don't want to believe that you would betray us and the whole organization after all that you have accomplished."

Harper nodded, as Mercer maintained eye contact.

"But don't get me wrong, Doc; if the man orders it, I will put a bullet right between your eyes, and I won't lose a lick of sleep over it. Got me?"

Harper leaned back, a little shocked at the directness of the statement, but he knew these men's capabilities. He hadn't ever worried that their special talents for violence would ever be directed at him, but now he could imagine the possibility.

He nodded his head again and pulled his hands closer to his body. They had started to shake, and that was just too damned embarrassing to live with.

Mercer sighed.

"All right, Doc; look, I'm sorry. Our friend just wants to make sure…"

"Why can't you just say his name?" Harper interrupted. He didn't like being scared, and right now he was scared shitless.

"Because we both already know who I am talking about," Mercer replied. "And if you have betrayed us, he doesn't want to risk further exposure to himself or to the group.

"Now, as I was saying, he wants to make sure you are not the bad guy here. You are a valuable asset to the group's goals. He doesn't want that brain of yours falling into the wrong hands. If our information is incorrect, we'll call him and let him know. He mentioned having some instructions for you if you haven't turned."

"I swear, I would never go against the group—or our friend," Harper pleaded.

"We'll see, Doc," Mercer replied.

Brock cleared his throat, getting Mercer's attention.

"Look at this," Brock said when his associate walked over to join him.

Mercer read the log entries, and nodded then turned back to Harper.

"It was this computer all right. You said you were in the lab all night."

Harper nodded.

"What were you doing?"

55

"I was running projections for endurance on one of my latest batches of nano…"

"Were you logged into your lab computer while you were running these projections?" Mercer interrupted.

"Of course, the computations would take forever if I had to do them long hand. The only reason I came back to my room tonight is that I had to do a heat test on one of the filaments in—something I am not really authorized to talk to you about, and I accidentally caught the—um, accessories on fire when I pushed too far past the rated heat limits."

"Good," he interrupted again. "You come with me," he said to Harper. "See what else you can find," he said to Brock.

Brock nodded his head, already focused back on the computer.

"Where are we going?" Harper asked.

"If you were logged into your lab computer then there will be a record of it there too. If it shows you were logged in there, then your story is probably true."

"And?"

"And assuming you are telling the truth, this facility has a mole—a spy, who broke into your room, accessed your computer, copied your drive, and then sent it to someone online. Whether it was you or someone else, that cannot be tolerated. The trace program that was inserted into your operating system can't activate itself except in very specific circumstances—like when someone sends it to the internet."

"Oh my god," Harper said, as they walked out of his room toward his lab. "Someone copied my hard drive? Oh my god."

"Come on, Doc," Mercer said, as Harper began to fall behind. "We have to really move on this. No time to waste."

Harper walked faster. He knew very well what kind of damning information was stored on his computer.

Brock studied the usage log again. He had a feeling the Doctor was telling the truth.

Harper was obviously an idealist. If you were a member of the group, you had to be. And no way did someone bribe him into betraying the group. He already had more money than most people would see in a hundred life times.

Which meant that an outsider was probing. *And they just got more than they bloody well bargained for*, he thought.

He knew the high security BIOS on these computers were outstanding. That's why they used them. If somebody wanted to break into it, they pretty much had to be present to do it.

So if Harper was telling the truth, someone else had been here.

He thought about how he would break into the system if he had been doing the probing. A few thoughts entered his head, but were quickly rejected. Then another came.

He snorted.

Maybe.

He logged out and turned off the computer then unplugged it and discharged any internally stored electricity. He removed the tower's outer case then slipped some latex gloves on over his hands.

Inspecting the motherboard for anything that didn't belong, he found something that made his suspicions all the more probable.

A bent gold-covered, copper prong was still attached to the motherboard right where he knew a keystroke logger would have been placed, had someone been using one.

The Doc's clean. That's good, at least, he thought and sighed. *That will definitely make Benson happy, but this won't*, he thought, as he removed the abandoned prong.

Setting the motherboard aside, he pulled a phone out of his pocket and dialed a number from memory.

"Put him on the phone please," he said when the call connected. "Good morning, Sir. Doctor Harper is clean. There is a mole in Spokane.—Yes, Sir; I am sure. There is evidence that a keystroke logger was secreted inside his computer. Has there been anything new about the site the information was sent to?—I see. Yes, Sir. We'll be in touch."

He put the phone away.

It didn't take long for Mercer to confirm Harper's claims in the lab or for them to return to his room.

"He was telling the truth," Mercer told his partner.

Brock nodded.

"I know; look what I found," he said showing them the metal prong and then explaining where he found it and what it was for.

"So someone really is spying on me," Harper said.

"Sure thing, Doc," Brock said, in a much less hostile voice than he had used when they had first arrived. "And may come back. That's why our mutual friend has ordered the two of us to stay here with you and provide 'round the clock protection. Like Mercer said, we don't want you to fall into the wrong hands."

"I'll stick to the doc like glue, so he can continue his work in the lab," Mercer volunteered. "How about you stay here in his room, and catch the mole if he pops his head back in while we're away."

Brock thought about it for a few seconds then nodded his head.

"That will work just fine. I'll start searching the room for other signs of surveillance. We could already be on video or audio."

Mercer nodded and looked thoughtful.

"Yeah, you'd better get on that right away."

Harper yawned. He had been tired before all of this had started, and the recent stress had depleted his energy reserves.

"That's fine, Gents," he said, before another yawn broke through. His fear from earlier was gone. Now he just wanted to sleep. "I'm sure I can find an excuse for having you follow me around like lost puppies tomorrow, but right now—I am exhausted; I'm going to bed."

His visitors nodded and let him go do what he needed to do.

A few hours later, after Harper had already crawled into his bed and fallen fast asleep, Brock's phone vibrated with an incoming call.

"Yes, Jax?" Brock said, his voice as quiet as he could make it.

"The site is hosted by the DIA. We will know soon who is working it for them. Another team is already being tasked to take care of the receiving end. I'll have the location to match the IP address the copy was sent from and then you or another team can go find the asshole that did this. I should have that soon too."

"All right, thanks," Brock replied. "Anything else I need to know?"

"Yes," the voice on the other end replied. "We were told to treat this as exposure. We're going hot with Project Wildlands. The boss has some new instructions for Harper. I just sent them to your email. Good luck."

"Thanks," Brock said, and the connection ended. He walked over to where Harper lay sleeping, and laid a hand on the scientist's shoulder. "Doc, wake up."

"Whaaa—"

"Wake up, Doc. Our friend has some things he wants you to start doing," Brock said.

"What? Right now?" Harper asked, bleary-eyed.

"Yes, right now," Brock replied. "We need to get you over to your lab."

He made sure Harper was up and getting ready before he went and made sure his partner was up and ready to go as well.

He hung up on Brock and dialed another number.

"What is it, Jax?"

"Frank, I've got a job for you and your team. You are needed at the Pentagon. We found the recipient of our stolen data. The name is Jeffrey Guddemi. He's D.I.A. According to a source inside the agency, he was put in charge of the DIA's investigation into the DARPA shadow programs that twisted the congressional oversight committee's panties into a bunch a while back.

"My trace program indicates that the DARPA mole sent the data to a private server located at Guddemi's private residence. We need you to pick him up at the Pentagon, interrogate him, and then make him and his server disappear."

"We'd better get moving then."

Frank's phone vibrated in his hand and then chimed.

"That should be the email I just sent you," Jax said, after hearing it from the other side. "Address and target information—everything you should need."

"Got it."

"Make it quick. I should have a location for the sender soon. Their physical location was cleverly concealed, but I'm narrowing it down by process of elimination. They're definitely in the Spokane DARPA facility. We'll need you to get him as well, and we are now on a time line. Project Wildlands is hot. The boss wants this hushed quickly, so our voice is the only one people hear when the shit comes out."

"Roger that. We'll do the grab at the Pentagon and interrogate him in the air as we head west to Spokane."

"Sounds good. Keep me informed."

Chapter 10: Called To the Principal's Office

Jeff had a habit of shaking his pen between two fingers when he was nervous, and at the moment it was blur of rapid motion. The newly appointed Director of the Defense Intelligence Agency had demanded his presence at DIA headquarters within the Pentagon as soon as he had arrived at the Arlington, Virginia satellite office—not a good sign. He knew it had to be related to his investigation into DARPA. That was the only thing he had on his plate.

Normally he lived by the saying "Out of sight—out of mind," but with him working such a high profile case, that just wasn't an option this time.

He sat on a leather-upholstered chair outside the Director's office, staring blankly at the photo of President Nelson hanging on the wall near the door. He had taken notice of it fifteen minutes earlier when he had first sat down and had thought how quick they had been to remove the picture of President Zimmerman for that of the new President, but then his thoughts had gone back to questions of why he was being called in front of his new boss.

"Director Borrenpohl will see you now," the Director's secretary announced, interrupting his thoughts.

Jeff stood and cleared his throat.

"Thank you," he replied and stepped up to the door. He realized that he still had his pen in his hand, so he hid it in the inside pocket of his suit jacket before he opened the door and stepped inside.

This was his first time in the new Director's office.

A quick glance around showed that all of the

furnishings, even the layout had changed—except for the desk. *He would keep that.*

The desk was huge and made of mahogany, a clear display of power to anyone invited to appear before it. Vertical blinds over the window behind the desk were closed, but enough sunlight to clearly see still filtered through and gently permeated the room. There were frames with art and photographs hanging on the walls, but Jeff didn't look at them.

At that moment he only had eyes for the Director, who was sitting behind the power desk already glaring, practically burning holes through Jeff's skull.

This can't be good, he thought in dismay.

"Jefferey Guddemi reporting as ordered, Sir."

The Director glared at him for a second longer then barked, "Sit down!"

Jeff barely kept himself from collapsing into the chair across from the man who controlled his paycheck.

"Who gave you authorization to put one of our clandestine operatives inside DARPA to act as a mole?"

Oh crap, Phil. What happened? Jeff thought, as he swallowed hard and sat up straighter.

"No one gave specific authorization, Sir," he replied.

"Then why the hell am I finding out that you did just such a thing?"

"Sir, as you know, I am heading the investigation into DARPA's research methods. Part of the investigation includes using undercover investigators. Because of the sensitivity and classified nature of the issues involved, certain predecessors put procedures in place that would allow these kinds of operations while also affording the agency and the Director, in this case you, deniability should one of our contractors be discovered in the course…"

"I don't care how the last Director ran this agency, Mr. Guddemi," the Director interrupted, slamming his palm down on the desk. "This is my agency now. My predecessor may have wanted deniability for your incredibly stupid actions, but what I want is an agency that keeps to a specific chain of command, a chain of command that answers to me."

The Director was red in the face. Rumor had it he was a strictly by the book kind of guy who liked to step on anyone who showed an ounce of initiative, the exact opposite of the man who had given Jeff this assignment.

"How do you think I felt this morning when DARPA Director Mangano called my office to complain that you have spies secreted in their midst, as if we can't trust them? Huh, Mr. Guddemi? It couldn't have been anyone else because, as you already pointed out, this is your investigation."

Jeff was speechless. He opened his mouth to respond, but he couldn't think of anything.

He called? How the hell could they have possibly found out? He wondered.

"Director Borrenpohl, I—I don't know what to say," he finally stuttered. "Richard is one of our top operatives. He knows how to stay under the radar and…"

"Under the radar? He sure as hell isn't under the radar now!" the Director yelled, interrupting yet again. "You want to know why? Because he transmitted top secret documents onto the world wide web, and those documents had a trace program secreted in them. And do you know where those documents ended up on the internet, Mr. Guddemi?"

"Yes, Sir, I have a pretty good idea," Jeff answered quietly. "We set up a DIA hosted site."

Director Borrenpohl glared at him and shook his head.

"You did not follow DIA guidelines. You used a private server out of your home, even if it was DIA issued equipment. You realize you are going to do time for this don't you?"

"What?" Jeff shouted. "Any files that were transferred were from one federal computer system to another.

"We had to do this. For months now no one in the Spokane DARPA facility has submitted to the congressionally mandated inspections. They have been working in some extremely sensitive areas without oversight for too long. Richard has been there to see to it that whatever the hell they are hiding from congress is not prohibited under law. He's there to make sure that their work is still in the best interests of the US government."

Jeff's face turned red. Anger was boiling to the surface. So much was invested into this investigation at the behest of the former director who had died recently under, to Jeff at least, suspicious circumstances. And now this fucking bureaucrat was trying to get information that for security and integrity reasons he shouldn't have.

"What is the name of your asset inside DARPA?"

"He goes by Richard, Sir."

"His real name"

"I can't give you that information, Sir. It would jeopardize our man's health, and I won't do that unnecessarily."

"How noble," the director said, sarcastically. "Who else knows about this little operation you initiated?"

"Just me, Richard—and former Director Tilton," Jeff admitted, feeling slightly guilty for bringing his prior boss into it.

"Good," Borrenpohl said. "This is going to be hell on wheels if anyone else finds out."

Jeff nodded in silence.

"Now, is 'Richard' currently employed with D.I.A.?"

"He is a private contractor, and part of his contract is that he remains anonymous until he has completed his job," Jeff said.

Director Borrenpohl stared him in the eyes, studying him. He shook his head and sighed.

"You...are a hard-case. I can see that right now. Well, protecting your asset is admirable, but this is something that needs resolution right now. Last chance: who is Richard?"

Jeff clenched his jaw, saying nothing. Whatever the Director thought he could threaten him with, it wouldn't work. No way in hell was he going to give up his best friend to this untrustworthy bureaucratic political appointee.

The resolve in his eyes was clear.

Shaking his head, the Director stood and walked over to the office's side door and motioned for someone to come in.

Two large men in suits entered the office, one shorter man between them.

"There he is," the Director said.

Jeff stood.

"I want to talk to a lawyer," he blurted, as the big men yanked his arms behind his back and threw cuffs on him.

"You don't get it, do you?" the Director said. "You aren't under arrest, and you aren't going to jail. We have the authority to hold you for transmitting classified information over unsecure lines—in essence: espionage, which now falls under the USA Patriot Act. You are being *detained* as an enemy combatant. You have no Constitutional rights now. You are going to disappear."

"Bullshit!" Jeff shouted, as he shook his head and kicked his feet and tried to keep the big men from dragging him away like a criminal.

But it was too late to resist. He was already restrained, and Frank's grip was hard as steel. Quite unexpectedly, they also gagged him with a cloth and then slipped a black bag over his head, taking away his ability to see or talk.

"You should have told me his name," Borrenpohl said at his back. Then, turning to the shortest of the three men, "Do you have what you need, Mr. Keyser?"

"Yes," he replied.

He had a scar on one of his cheek bones and another across the top of his head and forehead; his nose was crooked from having been broken and reset numerous times; and his eyes were like cold steel—unflinching, unfeeling. His hands, sticking out of nicely tailored suit sleeves, were also a mosaic of scars.

"We have what we need." Even his voice sounded like it had been through the grinder. "I'm sure the list of employees named 'Richard' who was picked up or transferred to Spokane DARPA within the last six months is fairly short."

"About Mr. Guddemi," the Director said hesitantly.

Frank smiled an Arctic breeze.

"We'll take care of it."

The Director nodded, his eyes downcast. Then he looked up and met Frank's hard eyes.

"Tell Mr. Benson it was an honor to be able to provide this small measure of help for him in his time of need."

Frank snorted as he shook his head and walked away.

The Director went to sit behind his desk, as the men left the way they had come in. He checked to make sure the door was all of the way closed and then breathed out a sigh of relief.

Even if he too occasionally worked for their boss, those men scared him. He tried not to think of what they were going to do to Jeff Guddemi. *He shouldn't have poked his nose where it doesn't belong. Hopefully, for his sake, they kill him quickly. No one messes Bruce Benson and lives.*

It was not a common sight to see someone being escorted through the halls of the Pentagon in cuffs with a black bag over their head, so their procession drew a few looks.

Frank's glare made most of them return to whatever they had been doing. Those brave few that didn't look away didn't concern him. In a week or two they'd all likely be dead anyway.

Jeff still tried resisting even though he couldn't see, but Frank and his partner were more than enough to keep him in line. They were freakishly strong. They could literally pick him up with one arm each and calmly walk him out, squirming and kicking and all, which they ended up doing as soon as they hit the steps leading out to the loading dock in a rear parking lot away from the main entrances.

A plain black suburban waited for them.

They tossed Jeff into the back seat and climbed in, sandwiching him between them.

"Go," Frank ordered.

The suburban accelerated quickly, circling around the Pentagon and heading south into Crystal City. Reagan National Airport was less than ten minutes away.

"Did you find the server?" he asked the driver.

"I did," Wagner replied. "Down in his basement. Fragged it with thermite. That bitch ain't bein' read by anyone ever again."

"Good."

He pulled his phone from a pocket and dialed home.

"We've got him and the server has been destroyed," he said, as soon as Jax answered. "We'll be in the air in ten minutes. And I've got a name for you. Richard."

"Excellent! That will speed up the personnel elimination process significantly. I'll send you a list of questions to ask him during your interrogation and anything else I come up with before you land in Spokane."

"Roger that."

"Oh, and, Keyser."

"Yeah?"

"The boss wants him to suffer, and he wants to watch, so make sure you get video."

"Understood."

Chapter 11: Go Home; Doctor's Orders

It wasn't unusual for Stanley Witmer to wait on Antoine. They lived just a few blocks away from each other in Annapolis, Maryland, so they took turns driving each other to work at the White House. Stanley knew Antoine had a bad habit of oversleeping. It was about the only point of contention between them in an otherwise peaceful and beneficial carpool.

Neither of them had had to drive in this morning because they had both slept on a cot in a conference room next door to the White House. And still he waited on Antoine.

"Come on, Tony," Stanley grumbled from the cot next to the one where Antoine lay, still covered by the blanket. "You're going to be late, buddy. We have to be across the street in half an hour. "Come on, or you'll be working on an empty stomach."

He reached over and shook Antoine's shoulder.

A miserable groan wafted up through the blanket. It sounded like it had come from a dry, scratchy throat.

Stanley didn't like the sound at all. He leaned over his friend and ever so slightly lifted the blanket off of Antoine's head.

Antoine looked like he had lost several pounds overnight. His normally fully fleshed cheeks, a little closer to pudgy cheeks actually, had a sunken, grayish look to them. His body was covered in sweat, and when Antoine opened his eyes they were more bloodshot.

"Damn, Tony. You look like shit."

Antoine's eyes fluttered a bit, and he began to shiver and groan some more.

Stanley could tell right away that his buddy was in no condition to work today. He looked up and caught the eye of one of the other staff.

"Hey, Joe. Give me a hand would you? Tony don't look too good. I want to take him down to the medical unit."

"All right."

They lifted him up and got him to his feet. When the blanket fell to the floor, they saw that Antoine hadn't even bothered to undress last night before sleeping. At least that saved them from having to dress him before taking him downstairs.

Coughing in the elevator drew some concerned looks. Stanley was sure everyone was wondering if poor Tony was contagious and if they'd have to worry about catching it in the elevator. Heck, he was wondering the same thing himself.

"Hang in there, Tony. We're almost there."

Antoine nodded his head weakly and coughed into his hand.

When the elevator stopped, they let everyone else off before they tried getting off themselves. Stanley caught several that had ridden down with them glance over their shoulder to look back at them and then get hand sanitizer from automatic dispensers that were installed every so often along the hallway walls.

Not a bad idea, he thought.

"Thanks, Joe," Stanley said, as they sat Antoine in one of the seats in the medical unit waiting room.

"Sure, no problem. Hey, I'll let the supe know what's going on. I'm no doctor, but I'd say it looks pretty clear that they're going to send him home today. He's in no shape to work, an' I doubt they're going to want him around the rest of us if he is contagious."

"Thanks"

Joe nodded then tried to get Antoine to look him in the eyes. It didn't work. Tony had his head down.

"I hope you feel better soon, Tony," he said.

Antoine bobbed his head a bit and groaned.

Joe's head was shaking as he left the medical unit.

They didn't wait long. The duty doctor came out of a back room where he had been stocking supplies and took them in right away.

"Fever, cough, raspy throat, and a touch of dehydration. You've got a flu," the doctor informed them after a quick inspection. "I'll get you a few meds to take home with you, but you'll need to drink plenty of fluids, and I would recommend you up your vitamin intake for a few days to help your immune system fend off this bug."

"Thanks, Doc," Stanley said, as he wheeled Antoine out of the medical unit in the wheel chair that was offered.

Traffic on the drive home wasn't as bad as it normally was on the way in, since they were going the opposite direction of most of the rest of the people on the roads. It still took them close to an hour, and in that time, Antoine only seemed to get worse, despite the meds the doctor had given him in the office. His groaning seemed to increase in intensity, and Stanley worried some more for his friend.

Something just wasn't right.

In the last ten years that they had been driving to work together, he could only remember one time when Tony had called out sick, and it hadn't even been for him. It had been for his mom, as she lay on her death bed.

"Come on, Tony. Let's get you inside."

He wheeled his friend up to the front door then took the house keys from Antoine's pant pocket. He took him inside and got him to the bedroom where his friend collapsed onto his bed.

Stanley called back to work and let them know that he wouldn't be coming back for the day because Antoine was in bad shape, and he just didn't feel right leaving him alone, as incapacitated as he seemed to be. It was going to cost him at least a day of vacation time and some overtime that he otherwise would have worked, but he accepted that as inevitable and focused on taking care of his friend.

Chapter 12: Wakey, Wakey

Richard woke and groaned. His bladder was painfully full. He knew he shouldn't have had that glass of orange juice so close to bedtime last night. He stumbled out of the cozy bed, hugging himself a bit in the cold of the room, and walked through the dark into the restroom. After a hot summer, these autumn morning were beginning to feel downright cold. After relieving the pressure that had woken him, he shivered and made his way back to his bed. He flopped back down to relish in the warmth under his sheets.

He really didn't want to get out of bed. It wasn't often that he had the chance to sleep in. *Just another hour*, he thought, as he cracked an eyelid barely enough to see the time displayed on his alarm clock. *Way too early!*

Two hours later, he woke again feeling refreshed and ready to start the day. A glance at the alarm clock showed that if he hurried, he'd be just in time for the tail end of breakfast at the cafeteria.

I could really go for pancakes and eggs right now.

He flipped the lights on and yawned, as he pulled clean clothes over his muscular frame and slipped into a pair of comfortable boots. His breath wasn't kosher, so he made another trip to the restroom for mouth wash.

While he was there, he splashed some water on his face and looked at himself in the mirror. His hairline was receding faster than he had thought it would. Both of his parents' fathers had gone mostly bald, so he knew that his time would eventually come too. He planned to shave his head and keep it shaved before his hairline crept too much farther back on him. He certainly didn't want to look as old as he felt.

That's me—Mr. Vain.

His stomach grumbled, reminding him that he was hungry. He dried his face and turned off the bathroom light.

"Better pick up the pace, *Richard*, or you'll be eating breakfast in town," he said, as he stuffed his pockets with his wallet, phone, keys, and other every day carry items. Lastly, he pulled back the unbuttoned Hawaiian that he wore over a white T- shirt and clipped his worn leather paddle holster into his waistband and over his belt.

He never went anywhere without his issued Springfield XD(M) .40 and a few spare sixteen round magazines. He had learned that lesson in the Marine Corps years before when he had walked around with a different name.

Mr. Murphy, of Murphy's Law, always seemed to pop up when you are least prepared for him.

His stomach grumbled again, as he reached for the door handle on his way out.

Enough already. I'm on my way.

He turned the handle and pulled the door inward with one hand and flicked off the light switch with the other.

Mr. Murphy decided to visit.

Framed in the doorway of the room opposite, a man dressed in black with cauliflower ears looked Richard in the eye and began raising his hand toward him, almost as if he were offering a handshake.

Who's this guy? Oh, shit!

But that wasn't a finger that was about to be pointed at him.

Richard recognized the fat cylinder attached to the end of a Walther P22. He had used one a few times himself. Because of its reliability, ease of acquisition in the Western world, and decibel reduction when fired, the pistol/suppressor system was one of several weapons used regularly for close in work by assassins the world over.

His natural reaction saved his life. His body flinched back and curled in on itself to present the smallest possible target to this new threat. At the same time, his arm shoved the door closed. If he had taken the time to think about what to do instead of just reacting, he would have been dead.

Before the door slammed shut, the assassin got a shot off. The bullet impacted the metal door with a louder ping than the sound of the shot itself. Since it hadn't completely lost its energy and the door was at an angle to its trajectory, the bullet skimmed across the door, grazed Richard's right arm, and made a second impact sound as it hit the face plate of his government issued sheet metal dresser drawer, deformed completely into a pancake of lead, and fell to the floor.

Richard jumped forward to the closed door and turned the deadbolt to the locked position just as the door handle turned and the door was jarred in its framed from the impact of the assassin's shoulder. He stepped back away from the door as it shuddered from another impact that connected with the door, this time the assassin's size ten boot.

He took his Springfield from the holster at his hip, brought it up towards the center of the door, and then shifted his aim by roughly a foot towards the door handle. He let loose with three rounds. The sudden loud noise in the close confines of his room made his ears ring enough that he could barely hear the curses from the man out in the hallway.

His vision swam with fuzzy little balls of colliding red and white ghost light, the after effects of the muzzle flash imprinting on his retinas. The only other illumination in the room were his glowing tritium night sights which were currently bobbing slightly up and down with his breathing and accelerated heartbeat. The lack of light coming through his door told him the rounds he had fired had not penetrated through the door.

The cursing was followed by bullets impacting the door from the other side. The small projectiles from the assassin's gun weren't penetrating through either. Richard moved out of alignment with the door anyway, just in case.

The man yelled in frustration and began kicking the door again. He was making a lot of noise, but the steel door and frame held. How long it would stay that way, Richard didn't know.

He kept backing up, his body and gun pointed toward the door in case the assassin broke through. His butt bumped into his computer desk. The sudden stop surprised him. He was concentrating on the door and on his gun's sights. He tried to catch his breath.

The door was holding. He had a few seconds to act. He switched the XD to his left hand and used his right to fish into his pocket for his phone. He found it then switched the gun back into his primary shooting hand.

Even in the dark, it was a cinch to press the buttons to unlock the phone. The display screen glowed to life, temporarily restoring his normal vision, and Richard pressed the speed-dial button to Mack, his security supervisor.

Nothing happened.

He brought the phone up into his line of sight without bringing the gun down from its aiming point.

No signal.

That's impossible. I always have a signal here in— oh shit! He's gotta have a jammer. Radio!

He dropped the useless phone into his pocket and put both hands on his weapon. He sidestepped in the dark until he made it to the foot of his bed and the nightstand. A quick glance in the dark showed him what he wanted. The LED on the radio's battery charger glowed green, indicating a fully charged battery but also letting him know where to find the radio. He reached down and across his body to grab the radio with his left hand, keeping the gun pointed at the door with his right.

The door was still being assaulted, but thankfully it held.

He turned the power knob on top to the "on" position and listened for a second and a half. No one else was broadcasting. He keyed the transmitter microphone.

As soon as he began speaking, the radio let out a low, continuous tone. He released the transmit button and then tried again. He got the same tone.

Damn it!

Either Murphy was playing with Richard's radio, or the radio had been dropped from the encrypted security system. Regardless, it was worthless to him now.

The pounding on the door stopped.

"Come out and play, Richard," he heard from the other side of the door.

He didn't respond.

Why is this asshole trying to kill me? He thought. *Shit! I'm trapped and I can't call anyone to help me.*

There was only one way out of the room, and the would-be assassin began kicking away at it again.

Think! Think!

He took a deep breath, held it, and then let it out slowly. He willed his heart beat to slow down.

He replayed the incident in his head. His attention had focused on the gun that was being raised towards his face. The face behind the gun went blurry during the adrenaline spike he had experienced as soon as he had realized what was happening, but he recalled that brief second when the other man had made eye contact.

Target identification verification. Wouldn't want to take out someone other than the intended target. I saw him just like he saw me—only I don't recognize him, and he clearly recognizes me. He can't be one of the staff or security; I would know his face, even if I didn't know his name. That makes him someone from the outside. How could someone from the outside know about me? Only Jeff knows why I'm here. Jeff wouldn't...He was right outside my door just waiting for me, and he knows my cover name. There was recognition in his eyes—but not instant recognition. There was too much of a gap in time. He

81

should have raised the gun as soon as the door started opening. So he knows me, but not well—Jeff wouldn't betray me. He wouldn't—not after all we've been through together. What the fuck is going on?...My cover is blown. Somehow, someone found out, and they didn't like it, so they called in a pro. Who? Damn it!

He caught his breath speeding up again, and he forced it back into submission.

The incessant pounding on the door stopped.

Maybe someone complained and security showed up to investigate. Yeah right. Who's going to complain, Richard? You're the only one who takes time off on week days around here. Everyone else is already at their work station well into their work by now. Why did he stop? Duh, because it's not working. So what else is he going to try? Is he just going to wait? Would I?—No. what would I do? Fire axe? No. Battering ram? Where the hell is he going to get a battering ram? Explosive entry charge? No, he would have already used it. Think.

It doesn't fucking matter what he is going to do. I need to concentrate on what I'm going to do. How do I get out of here without getting shot?

Then he remembered the layout of the rooms in this wing of the facility. His room had a concrete floor and overhead, and three of the walls were made of steel reinforced, concrete-filled cinderblock. The fourth inner wall, the one that he was forced to share with his sometimes loud next door neighbors, was made of timber and drywall. So the assassin was facing a nearly impenetrable shell of hardened walls and steel doors, while

Richard could break right through the drywall of the next several rooms with hardly any effort at all.

His neighbors would be pissed when they came back to their rooms and found huge holes in their walls, but it was his life on the line. If he could make it through a few rooms before the assassin broke in the door, he could leave out of one of the front doors that faced into another corridor. The assassin would be banging away in the other hallway and wouldn't see him leave.

Like all good spies, Richard had contingency plans should he need to leave in a hurry. They hinged on him being able to leave his room, but he had plans. And he had everything he needed to go on the run already packed and pre-staged at a safe house in the city—if he could get there.

The only things he couldn't leave without now were his tough-book laptop computer and the external hard drive that he had saved files on last night. He made his way back to the computer table, felt around until he touched the external hard drive, and then stuffed it into his pocket. The tough-book was already in its shoulder bag, which he quickly slung over his back.

Then he sidestepped to the back of the room away from the front door until he bumped into the wall. He moved forward until he found the drywall then backed up one deep step. He timed his kick into the drywall with the thump of the impact into his front door.

No need to let the assassin out front know that he was doing anything inside other than cringing in fear.

"Go away!" He yelled, giving his voice a hint of fear. "I'm calling security!"

He broke through into more darkness. Light wouldn't be a danger in this other room. Having the larger, double-sized unit on the end, he was neighbor to two back-to-back rooms, each with its own separate entry corridor. He debated breaking through another wall into another room or just going out into the corridor from this room.

He paused and listened.

The impacts on his door continued.

Screw it! I'll take speed over stealth right now.

He raced to where the front door should be—and tripped over something hard and low to the floor. He heard the crunching noises of several things breaking, at least one of which sounded like glass.

"MMMMmmmm!" he stifled a yell of unexpected pain.

Murphy strikes again!

From the floor he saw a thin, horizontal bar of light under the door where the weather stripping had worn away and an area of darkness where another obstacle waited to nail him on the way to the door. He pushed himself off of the floor, dodged around the obstacle, grabbed the door handle and yanked.

It was locked—of course.

He slid his hand upward and felt for the deadbolt, found it, and finally managed to open the door. He stumbled out into the light and immediately brought his gun up to shoot anyone coming at him in the corridor.

It was empty—in both directions. Maybe he had finally outrun Murphy.

He turned left into one of the three exit halls on the ground floor, each the length of one room's width—and ran right into the back of a large man silhouetted against the light coming in through the glass door.

The man grunted in surprise then saw who had run into him and began raising a gun, suppressed like the assassin's at Richard's front door.

How many appearances can Mr. Murphy make in a day?

Don't ask.

This time Richard didn't have to react in complete surprise. He was already past that stage and was well into combat mode. His gun had barely lowered from where he had been carrying it since he had come out of that neighbor's door.

He was so close he didn't even need to bother with his sights; the second assassin took up most of his forward field of view. He squeezed off two rounds so fast that it almost sounded like one shot.

He watched his rounds take effect. The assailant crumbled inward on himself and fell backward to the floor, dropping the gun from his hand—another suppressed Walther P22. Blood began to leak onto the floor from beneath the body fast enough that there would soon be a puddle of it. Blood had already spotted the front of the man's shirt where the bullets had connected. They had shattered the man's heart.

Unfortunately, Richard's handgun did not have a suppressor like those connected to the assassins' weapons. He knew assassin number one would have heard his shots and would be responding forthwith—with more help if this goon on the floor was any indication of their modus operandi. He took a good look at the dead man's face, while he reached down and grabbed the suppressed handgun that could have punched his ticket. He tucked the unfired weapon into the waist band at his back and turned to leave.

The bullets that had taken down assassin number two had been fired at such close range that they had torn right through his back and gone through the glass door he had been guarding. Now the door was a mess of blood-splattered, spider-webbed glass, and Richard was careful to only touch the metal bar that ran across the frame as he pulled the door inward.

Out he stepped and began running. As he crossed the wide road that separated the dorm building from the adjacent buildings in the maze that made up the DARPA facility, he heard the door behind him slam shut and its glass face fall to the ground. He didn't turn to see if he was being pursued; he just ran and prayed that he wouldn't take a stream of bullets in the back—or run into Murphy again in front of him.

Chapter 13: Kick It!

Frank Keyser kicked the door for what seemed the millionth time. The door frame was stubbornly solid, and had yet to open for him despite his above average strength and the pounding he was giving it. Maybe if he had had the larger bulk of either of his teammates, Nate Wagner or Scott Davies, he might have already caved the door in and shot this lucky "Richard" bastard. *You were lucky this time, asshole; but luck has a way of turning.*

While the rest of the team changed out of business suits into their tactical gear, Davies had beaten Richard's last name out of Guddemi on the plane ride to Spokane, though that was about all he'd been able to get out of him. The information had gone straight to Jax, enabling him to separate this Richard from the other twenty-some-odd Richards that worked at the Spokane facility. Also, the new information enabled him to procure a photo of the correct Richard from the DARPA personnel files, which he then forwarded to Keyser and his team. But there was enough of a difference in appearance between Richard's photo and Richard now that Frank had hesitated for a fraction of a second too long to verify that he had the right target before bringing the gun up to shoot. It was just enough for him to miss a body shot.

He lined up for another kick when he heard the shots from somewhere else in the building. *Shit! Same floor, inside...bastard was trying to sneak out the back— unless—other security personnel? No, McCann said all of his other people were warned away from this side of the facility for our "training exercise." We'll see.*

"Report," he said into the throat mic he wore below his jaw as he sprinted down the corridor.

"Jackdaw clear"

Davies

He waited to hear from Wagner. Seconds passed. He rounded the corner to the left and continued down a shorter corridor.

"Magpie, report," he called.

Silence

"Magpie, report"

He turned left again and saw light spilling into the otherwise empty corridor from the exit hall ahead and to the right. Seconds later he turned into the light and found Wagner flat on his back, blood pooled out to either side and oozing towards the shattered door, like angel wings of blood.

"Magpie down; hold position"

Keyser continued to the door frame and ducked through it. He scanned left and right, his handgun pointing everywhere his eyes went. He didn't see a sign of Richard.

"Target loose; no visual," he said, as he ducked back into the dorm building. "Creeper, do you have a track on his cellphone?"

"That's a roger, Raven. Cell is mobile. Current location four hundred sixty meters south-west of your current position and increasing."

"So he has it with him," Keyser said. "Excellent. Continue to monitor and keep me informed, Creeper. Out."

"Creeper copies. Out."

Keyser sighed and stretched his neck before straightening and calling for his other team mate.

"Rally on me—north entrance."

"Jackdaw copies"

Keyser waited until Davies showed up to provide security for the team before kneeling down next to Wagner. He tore the man's shirt open and poured a vial of grainy powder into each of the bullet holes. Then he slapped a pair of adhesive patches over the holes, both front and back, and turned to Davies.

"Your turn"

Davies shook his head but didn't complain otherwise as he reached down and grabbed the man's meaty palms. He stepped over the body to straddle it and then lifted and hefted it over his shoulder in a fireman's carry.

"Now what?" Davies asked. "You want to go get him now or wait until we have better numbers?"

Keyser stared through him in thought.

"We'll wait for Wagner," he replied a few seconds later. "I'll go recover all of the electronics in Richard's room, so we won't have to worry about other copies getting out, and we can see what Mr. Richard has been up to. You go ahead and get him to the suburban. We're going to have to rely on Jax's tech skills to track him down now."

Davies nodded and began carrying the body of their fallen comrade the two blocks to where they had left their black Chevy Suburban. He opened a rear door and unceremoniously dumped him into the back seat. Then he climbed into the front seat and dialed a number into his phone.

Keyser showed up fifteen minutes later.

"I talked to Jax," Davies said. "He's got a good lock on Richard's phone."

"Good," Keyser said.

"What about him?" Davies asked, nodding to the back seat.

"Throw a blanket over him. We'll get rooms in town, and he can join us once the bugs do their thing."

Davies nodded then leaned over the seat and put a finger to Wagner's neck.

"He's got a pulse again, so it's working. He's going to be hungry as a hog when he wakes up."

"Yeah," Keyser said with a smirk. "We'll just have to find a grocery store after we wrap up our little Richard situation."

"We oughtta start making him wear a vest."

Keyser laughed.

"With his luck, it would just mean the next time he gets shot—it'll be in the head."

Davies snorted.

"He has had some bad luck lately."

They drove away from the facility, a cloud of dust following behind them.

Chapter 14: Grand Theft Auto

Richard was sweaty and winded when he stopped running. He had made it out of the DARPA facility without having been seen or having set off any intruder alarms. Once outside the fence and into the tree line, he had turned toward Spokane and run.   Spokane was the city closest to the facility and the most likely place for him to go. His attackers had to know this too, so he was determined to be very careful not to be spotted by them. He stayed off of the road into the city and away from the occasional houses that lay between him and his destination, keeping instead to the forested sides.

Constantly expecting a vehicle from the facility to catch up, full of pursuers out to kill him, he decided to steal a car the next time an opportunity presented itself. Opportunity came at a gas station just a few miles outside the city limits. He had just skirted another house and walked half way into a cluster of trees when he found it. He stayed hidden in the shadows as he crept closer and watched the area.

Several cars were sitting at the pumps with people filling up. A few more were parked in front of the merchandise area doing their normal business. He wouldn't risk the cars in front. There was too much traffic in the area. The probability of an owner coming out or anyone else finding his behavior suspicious while he tried to break in and start the engine was just too high.

There were two cars around the back. One was a truck. He thought the other was a Honda Civic, but he couldn't tell from where he was hidden, so he moved further around to that side, careful to still stay hidden in the trees.

He was partly correct. It was a Honda Accord, and the owner had left the window down.

Paydirt!

Because the Honda Accords and Civics were made with widely interchangeable parts, they had the unfortunate honor of being the most stolen cars in America. Chop shop money makers.

He would feel guilty later for stealing it, but right now that Accord could be his life line. He stalked through the trees to the point where he judged that he would be exposed the least then walked toward the car.

The door wasn't even locked.

As he sat in the driver's seat he reached into his pocket for keys out of habit. There were no keys, but he felt his phone and then realized he had made a huge mistake.

Shit! Shit! Shit! He thought. *How could I be so stupid? Remember your training, dumbass.*

He pulled the phone out of his pocket and placed it on the dash. Then he popped the catch on his shoulder bag and opened a side compartment. He withdrew a flat, grey bag. A "Paraben's StrongHold" logo was imprinted on its surface every few inches.

The bag was sealed with Velcro, which made its usual tearing sound as he pulled the sides apart to access the inner compartment. Grabbing his phone from the dash, he fit it into the inner compartment and sealed the inner and outer Velcro.

His hands were shaking from the surge of adrenaline that had jolted his system when he realized that someone could be tracking his phone. Now that it was safely in the signal-blocking bag, he breathed a sigh of relief, shook his hands to stop some of the trembling, and set his mind on the car he was sitting in.

It took him a few minutes to hotwire the engine. He was sweating bullets that someone would come out the backdoor and catch him at it. No one did though, and as soon as the engine was running and the steering column bypassed, he buckled up and drove away.

He glanced in the rear view mirror as he left the gas station, half expecting to see someone running out of the store and chasing after their car. No one did, but a black Chevy suburban pulled in rather quickly just as he was leaving. Seeing it nagged at his fear. It looked suspiciously like a vehicle out of a federal agency fleet. Between that and having just recently shielded his phone, he felt spooked. He settled a little more weight on the gas pedal and glanced up into his rear view mirror every couple of seconds.

Chapter 15: Guns Hot

"Signal lost"

That was not what Keyser wanted to hear.

"Last known location, Creeper?"

"Five point two miles ahead of you. It looks like it's at a FasTrak gas station."

"Copy that," Keyser said then stomped on the accelerator.

There was a groan from the backseat and the blanket rose into view in the rearview mirror.

"Welcome back, Sugar," Davies cooed.

Wagner showed him his middle finger.

"What the hell happened?" he moaned.

"You got shot is what happened," Keyser answered. "That's twice now you been a fatality. You're slowing us down. From here on out, you need to wear a vest, Big guy."

"Aw, come on, Frank," Wagner pleaded. "You know I hate those freaking vests. They're too freaking small, and they're too hot. I get rashes in places…"

"That's an order, Nate," Keyser interrupted. "Quit being such a pussy; you're a SEAL damn it. Start acting like one. Suck it up. Just be glad I'm not making you wear a helmet too."

Wagner, who had been sitting there with his mouth open waiting to plead his case as soon as his team leader quit talking, shut his mouth and sat back with his head down.

"Roger that," he mumbled.

Keyser shook his head.

"There it is," Davies said, pointing.

Keyser slowed just enough to pull into the parking lot without running into anything or losing control then he stomped on the brake pedal. The suburban slid to a stop directly in front of the front double doors.

"Stay here, Nate," Keyser ordered, as he and Davies jumped out of the front. "Watch our six."

The two of them stormed into the FasTrak with M4 carbines ready, prompting a few screams from female customers. The man behind the counter let out an "Oh shit!" before he realized that they weren't there to rob him.

They cleared the three aisles of merchandise in the front of the store then went into a hall to the back. There was a single storage room to the left, which was full of merchandise and clearly wasn't hiding anyone—they checked it anyway, and a restroom to the right with light showing under the door. All that remained down the hall was a door with a red "exit" light mounted above the door frame.

Keyser aimed at the door of the restroom. Davies went around his back and grabbed the door handle. With his free hand he turned the door knob. It was locked, so he backed up, raised his rifle, and waited.

Keyser stepped back, tensed himself, then lunged forward and planted the bottom of boot against the edge of the door, just above the door knob. The wood of the door frame was reduced to splinters as the deadbolt easily sheared through it, and the door crashed open. Keyser stepped in ready to shoot; Davies squeezed in next to him.

Before the screaming started, a woman had been bent over the sink, her dress splayed up to her waist, while a man was behind her thrusting away.

It wasn't Richard.

"Damn it!" Davies yelled. "Where is this guy?"

"Let's search the grounds," Keyser said, as he backed out, keeping an eye on the two love birds who were now cringing against the back wall trying to cover themselves.

They went back out of the front of the store then turned left and left again, searching the side of the parking lot. Another left turn put them behind the gas station.

Davies hopped up to check inside the cab of the truck that was still parked there, while Keyser kept an eye on his partner's back as well as the area a little further off to their right in the open, unsearched area.

Just as Davies stepped down, the back door to the gas station popped open in a hurry.

Both men pivoted and aimed their rifles at the person in the doorway.

It was the man they had caught in the bathroom.

"Don't shoot!" he yelled and raised his hands, turning his face away as soon as he saw them.

"Get the fuck back inside," Davies snarled.

The man moved to comply but then froze again.

"Hey, where's my car?" He asked. "I left it right here."

Keyser turned to make eye contact with Davies.

"That's him. He stole the car. Grab this dumbass, and let's go. He can tell us the descriptors on the way."

Davies nodded and grabbed the man by the back of his shirt at the neck.

Chapter 16: Safe House

Richard drove into Spokane faster than he would have any other time. He was taking a chance that there wouldn't be any speed traps between him and the city limits. He felt the risk was warranted. Seeing the black suburban pulling into the gas station rather quickly had set off alarm bells in his head and spooked him.

As soon as he made it into the city, he found the bus station, and parked the Accord. He rolled the windows up and locked the door before going over by the bus terminal. He was sure the police would find it within the next few days.

Instead of buying a bus ticket, Richard jumped into the first taxi he found and had the driver take him to a hotel on the other side of the city. He paid the driver and walked towards the lobby of the hotel. Once the taxi had driven away and was completely out of sight, he pretended to throw something away in the trash can in front of the hotel and began walking. He kept his eyes open for any signs that he was being actively followed or watched, and he changed his direction several times.

A mile later he walked into a mom and pop diner with a direct view into a local residential neighborhood. He took a booth with a view of the street leading into the neighborhood. There weren't many customers inside. He must have arrived right between the heavy breakfast and lunch crowds a diner like this could expect. He'd be able to watch his new area of operations without being remembered by every working Joe who stopped in for a bite to eat.

Perfect timing.

A television was playing near the bar. Only one patron was watching. Richard recognized the news anchor as Jamie Davis, one of the locals at KREM channel 2. She was cute, as the young ones usually are. She was talking about a story from Wyoming—something about the governor, but he could barely hear any of it, and he became distracted by movement in the corner of his eye.

A middle-aged brunette woman walked toward his table and gave him a menu to look at. The tag on her blouse named her Marie. Up to that point, he had been so worried about evading whoever these pros were that wanted to kill him that he had forgotten that he was hungry.

"Thank you but, no, I'll just have water," he said when she offered him coffee, and after a quick glance at the lunch menu, he added, "And I would like the grilled chicken sandwich meal."

"Ok," she said and took the menu back.

"Is there any way I could substitute apple sauce for the French fries?" he asked.

"Sure, that's not a problem at all," she replied. "I'll go put your order in with the kitchen, and I'll be right back with your water."

"Thanks," he said and smiled.

He watched her walk away then turned his attention back to the neighborhood out front. Every once in a while a car would drive up or down the street. It wasn't busy. Kids would be in school, and adults would be at work or on their way back to work from their lunch hour.

Richard sighed and shook his head.

What the hell happened, he thought. *What did I do wrong?*

Nothing came to mind. The idea that he might have been betrayed kept sneaking back into his thought process, but he didn't want to entertain those thoughts. That would mean that his best friend had turned against him.

Jeff was the only one who knew I was there. Even Director Tilton didn't know who the operative would be when he authorized the mission—just Jeff.

He closed his eyes and shook his head.

Footsteps caught his attention, and he looked up.

It was the waitress. She had his glass of water.

"Thanks," he said when she placed it on a napkin in front of him.

"Your sandwich will be ready soon," she said before leaving him to his thoughts.

He nodded and looked back outside. Nothing looked to have changed in the neighborhood, and no one was out of place on the street. He was close to his safe house. That was why he had chosen this diner. It would allow him to get a feel for the area again, before going to ground.   Running directly to the safe house in a panic was a sure way to raise the suspicions of those he would need to blend in with if he were to stay alive and out of enemy hands.

He would have loved to try to contact Jeff, but he couldn't risk using his smartphone. He would just have to wait.

There was a phone at the safe house that couldn't be connected to Richard, Jeff, DARPA, or the DIA. It was completely clean. He would use it as soon as he verified that the safe house was still safe.

"Here you go, Sir," Marie the waitress said, placing a plate in front of him. "A grilled chicken sandwich and a side of apple sauce. Is there anything else I can get for you?"

"No, this is good, thanks," Richard replied.

She walked away, and he tore into his meal. It tasted so good after all that he had been through that morning. He just hoped it wouldn't turn out to be his last meal. A lot could go wrong. He didn't know who he could trust, or even why, now of all times, he was being hunted.

It must be something to do with Harper's hard drive, he thought, as he finished his sandwich. *Well, it's time to find out what's on there that's worth killing for.*

He put a twenty dollar bill on the table to cover his meal and Marie's tip and then left. Nothing outside had changed. He hadn't seen any particular car drive by more than once. If he had, he would have been more worried that someone was driving circles around the block, surveilling the area. He waited on the traffic light at the intersection then crossed the street and walked into the residential neighborhood.

He felt out of place wearing the colorful Hawaiian shirt, but he hadn't seen a clothing store in which to buy a replacement during the walk from the hotel to the diner. At the safe house, he had clothes he could wear without standing out at the safe house, along with a selection of hats, sunglasses, and a few different disguises he could wear to change his appearance if needed.

Strolling along the sidewalk with his hands in his pockets, he did his best to look like he belonged there. He didn't hurry, didn't keep looking back over his shoulder. He was just there, one more person in a world that hadn't gone crazy, hadn't fallen apart all around him.

The neighborhood was just like thousands of other neighborhoods around the country, one house indistinguishable from the others around it except for the number out front on the mailbox or maybe a different kind of car in the driveway.

A perfect place to blend in and disappear.

The safe house driveway was empty, just like most of the other driveways in the neighborhood at that time of day.

He walked up the drive to the side of the house where the air conditioning unit rested. He was out of view of the street now, and he pulled open the maintenance panel on the AC unit. The house key was waiting for him, right where he had left it.

He unlatched the gate to the back yard and closed it behind him. Walking up to the back door, he brought his handgun out and prepared to use it if necessary. Very little of the inside was visible through the window in the back door, but he could see that the security system keypad mounted on the wall showed that the house was secure.

Now it was time to test the theory that his buddy Jeff, unlikely as he believed it to be, might have turned on him for some reason. If anyone else was in the house waiting for him, he would have his answer.

He was extra cautious as he unlocked the door and stepped inside. He went to the keypad and entered his security code before the system called home to its parent security company.

The house was quiet.

Systematically, he walked through the house, room to room and bottom to top, checking for signs of intruders. When he was confident that he was alone, he went through a second time with specialized equipment, checking for listening devices and spy cameras. That turned up clean as well.

For the moment, he appeared to be safe. He felt confident now that he could rule out the possibility that Jeff had deliberately outed him. It felt like a weight off of his shoulders, but he knew he wasn't "out of the woods yet," so he determined not to grow complacent.

His next step was going to have to be getting out of Washington and going back to the Arlington, Virginia DIA office. After what had just happened at DARPA, he wouldn't be surprised if he were ordered to respond to DIA headquarters at the Pentagon for a major ass-chewing.

Thinking about Virginia brought Jeff back into his thoughts.

Time for a little chat, old buddy.

He went upstairs to a room that was stuffed to the gills with metal equipment lockers and a sizeable wardrobe. Unlocking the lockers, he found the untraceable prepaid phone that he had been thinking about earlier and several cards with extra minutes.

And it's urgent enough that I can call you directly.

He punched in Jeff's number and listened to the dial tone. While it rang, he set up and turned on his tough-book computer. Jeff's voice mail came on. It was a generic message that didn't name any names—just repeated the number that he had called and told him to leave a message.

After the beep, he left his message.

"Hey, Jeff, it's Tommy out in Seattle. I ran into one of our old friends today, and he told me you are moving up in the world. He gave me your number and said you might want to catch up. Give me a call at 206-555-9555. I have a lot to tell you."

He disconnected the call. Giving a different name and location was a standard precautionary measure. Jeff would know his voice and know exactly how to contact him. Using the 9555 ending on the fake phone number would let him know it was of the highest priority that they make contact.

Setting the phone down within easy reach, he turned his attention back to his computer and made sure the screen capture software was recording, so he could add audible notes during the initial viewing. Then he reached over to a shelf with computer accessories and grabbed a pair of headphones with a built-in mic. He put them on, keeping one ear uncovered, so he'd be able to hear the sounds of the safe house and the neighborhood. If a suburban pulled up, loaded to the gills with the guys he'd just escaped from earlier, he'd need to know *before* they kicked the door in.

Now let's see what is so damned important about Harper's drive, he thought, as he opened the separate partition in his drive to access cloned drive folders.

What the hell?

Every folder and every file he opened in the separate partition was corrupted—damaged. He couldn't make sense of anything. He went back to his system

103

settings and tried a system restore. Nothing happened. The files remained corrupted.

That's just great, he thought. *All of this cloak and dagger bullshit for files that are now worthless.*

He wanted to pick something up and throw it, but there wasn't anything in reach that he could afford to damage. Then he remembered the external hard drive he had originally copied to. He needed to check there too. He turned off the screen capture program. No need to leave notes on a video of garbled pixels.

Thinking about countermeasures that could have been built into Harper's drive to corrupt the data without him realizing it, he decided to try something. He closed the partition on his tough-book so that any corrupted files with a built-in anti-piracy virus routine wouldn't cross contaminate any files on the external drive. He kicked himself for not thinking about the possibility sooner.

Without opening the folders on the external drive, he dragged and dropped the contents of Harper's drive onto another external drive so that he would have another, hopefully uncorrupted, copy. Then he unplugged the copied drive from the computer and opened Harper's folders.

Oh thank goodness.

The files were fine.

He wondered why there was a difference between the files in the separate partition on his computer and those on the external hard drive. He analyzed what he had done differently between the two.

I copied the contents from the external to the computer. That shouldn't have triggered anything; Harper would have to back up his files too, so it can't be that. Then

I uploaded the files from the partitioned copy, but I didn't from the external. I had already unplugged the external. I haven't touched either one again since then. That's the only difference then. It must have a built-in program that destroys files uploaded to the web without authorization. Shit! That means Jeff won't have a clue of what is on this drive.

He looked at the phone, wondering if he should call again, but only a few minutes had passed. He had to be patient. Who knew what Jeff was busy with?

I need to make sure he can see this right away in case anything happens to me. I can't risk corrupting the files again by sending it directly. Sending the video file of opening the original should be fine though.

He restarted the screen capture software program that would make a video log of everything he saw while perusing Harper's drive.

Yes, that should work.

"Examining the contents of Joshua Harper's personal hard drive, taken from his room at the Spokane, Washington DARPA facility. I'm Richard Dalton, deep cover sub-contractor working for the Defense Intelligence Agency."

He rattled off the time and date so they would match what was shown on the task bar at the bottom of the screen then began concentrating and trying to figure out what Harper had been up to.

He looked into a folder labeled EWES. It contained a text document and several video files. He opened the text document first. The title at the top was revealing: Elite Warrior Enhancement Series.

DARPA's Super Soldier Program, he thought. *This is what Don was looking at before he disappeared... But what is Harper hiding?*

It wasn't a long document, so it was a quick read. Based on the way it was worded and on its length, he surmised that it was a promotional piece that someone had put together for the generals at the Pentagon in a push for extra funding.

Why didn't Harper just use his own money if it was such a big deal to him? Richard thought. *But then again, why spend your own money, if the big wigs will throw taxpayer money at you?*

The document didn't tell him anything he hadn't already been briefed on before he infiltrated DARPA, so he closed it out and opened the first video.

Another funding promo.

He closed it out and flipped to another video further down the list. Again, it was another promo video.

Geez, how many of these damned things do you need?

He scrolled to the bottom of the list and decided to try one before moving on to another folder. He needn't have bothered.

As he was about to close the folder and try another, he noticed a folder he hadn't seen while looking through the videos. It was labeled 'P'. Upon opening it, he found that 'P' was for Personnel. There were two subfolders labeled 'A' and 'D' respectively.

He opened 'D' to find a long list of files, each labeled alphabetically with a person's name. He double-clicked the first.

Carl Andersen, US Navy, SEAL Team Two, Volunteer. Below was an official military picture of the seaman, "Deceased" stamped in red across the bottom. At the bottom of the page was a footnote: "Series 4 unsuccessful."

Richard opened another file with similar results: Jim Auston, US Army, 10th Special Forces Group, Volunteer, Deceased, Series 2 unsuccessful.

File after file, each showed basically the same results: Special Forces volunteers from the different branches of the military—each deceased because series 1-5 were unsuccessful.

That's a lot of dead volunteers, he thought, looking at the subfolder's metadata at the bottom of the screen. *One hundred and thirty-eight good men gone.*

He shook his head and went back to look in subfolder 'A'.

Interesting, he thought, as he scrolled down the list. *Only seven this time. I guess they started running out of volunteers.*

Instead of scrolling back up to the top, he opened the last file.

Nate Wagner, let's see who you are, he thought, as he double-clicked the thumbnail.

"Oh…my…god," he said out loud.

The file had opened to a picture of a man with a face that Richard would never forget. It was the same man he had shot and killed just a few hours before.

"This is one of the guys that tried to kill me this morning. I shot him dead in self-defense."

When he was past the initial shock of seeing one of the assassins that had been after him, he realized that assassin number one could very well be in there too. He clicked quickly through each file, until he made it to "Frank Keyser." He instantly recognized that face as well.

"Mr. Keyser, here, shot me at my door step. He was using a suppressed Walther .22. I am very lucky to be alive right now," he said for the benefit of the screen capture software.

So I have at least one active super soldier after me, trying to kill me, he thought. *This is just great—just freaking, fantastic. And there are five more on the list. Geez, could it get any worse?*

Maybe it was the cosmos' idea of a sick joke, but, apparently, it could get worse.

After looking through each of the active super soldier files and memorizing each face, he dug deeper into some of the other folders. In one he found more video files, and what he saw sickened him.

The video had been labeled "ZS3." It had been filmed in a prison and shortened for length. The camera showed two men in a prison cell, facing each other, each shackled at the wrists and ankles. The shackle cables of the man on the left were loose at first allowing him a few feet of movement if he desired. He held his hands close to his chest, and he looked to be trying to stay as far from his cell mate as possible. From the quick rise and fall of his chest, it was clear he was the one whimpering in the audio. He was looking away from the camera, so his face wasn't fully visible.

The other man's shackles were fully retracted, keeping him pinned to the wall, but he leaned forward as if trying to be as close to his cell mate as possible. He had longer hair that hung down, hiding most of his face—all but a portion of his heavily bearded chin. *He must be the source of the moaning.*

A line of prison guards arrived at the cell door, their footsteps echoing in cadence. The cables attached to the prisoner on the left retracted into the wall, forcing him spread-eagle against the wall, just like his bearded mate. The cell bars obstructed part of the view but not enough to matter.

The fear on the face of the inmate on the left was plain as soon as he looked towards the guards, and he looked familiar. The cell door slid open, and one of the guards stepped inside. The man shackled on the left side of the frame began crying and shaking his head. The guard turned to the crying man, reached up with his right hand, and tapped the man consolingly on the face with his fingertips.

Richard could just barely hear the guard saying, "Hey, don't worry; you'll get your chance at the afterlife soon enough, traitor."

"What the hell is this?" he muttered, shaking his head.

Traitor?

Whatever the hell this was, it wasn't right.

Who is this guy?

The man's expression changed, and suddenly Richard knew exactly who this was.

"That's Donovan Clarke," he said.

Donovan Clarke. Holy shit! Jeff's inside man. This is why he wasn't heard from.

The guard turned away from Donovan, toward the other shackled man. The guard's head tilted to the side, as if he were studying a curious new insect, then his hand fell to his side and came back up abruptly with his sidearm. Three quick shots into the man's chest—and the man no longer leaned into his restraints; he slumped, not quite able to fall to his knees. A glistening stream of blood flowed down his chest to the floor and began to trickle toward a drain in the center. Donovan was now screaming and jerking at his shackles.

"Oh my gosh."

Richard felt like throwing up the chicken sandwich that he had eaten. Executing a prisoner as the just punishment for crimes committed was one thing; whatever was going on here was quite another. This clearly wasn't something that was sanctioned by US law.

The prison guard stepped out of the cell, the barred door slammed shut with a bang, and the bleeding man's restraints were loosed completely, dropping him in a heap on the floor. He twitched a little at first but then didn't move at all.

The guards crowded around the bars, murmuring among themselves; but one of them pushed the others back and gestured towards the camera. Several of them looked up into the camera and smirked then made room so it could capture all of the action.

The video jumped ahead by over thirty minutes. This was the part that scared Richard the most.

The inmate on the floor began moving, little spasms at first but then wide swinging of his arms and legs and shaking his head back and forth. The moans that came through the speakers sounded unearthly.

Donovan was clearly flipping out, terrified. He had a large wet stain in the crotch of his bright orange jump suit.

Most of the guards appeared to be plenty entertained, but a few of them were beginning to look disgusted as well.

Bleeding man gained his feet after much jerky motion, but his balance appeared precarious. He stumble stepped toward Donovan and fell on him.

Donovan did his best to get away from him, but there wasn't much he could do, since he was shackled tight and the other man was not. He kept crying for help, but the guards just laughed.

Bleeding man fell on his shackled mate and started biting. He bit at the chin, and a chunk of flesh fell away, blood dripping in its place. Next a part of cheek and then a part of nose fell to the floor. The screams changed pitch and sounded louder.

"What the hell?" Richard said, but he couldn't look away. "Is this for real?" He added, but he knew it was.

The guards backed away some, as blood and bits of torn skin and muscle were flung about.

Crazy, Psycho, Cannibal man didn't just bite. He bit, really latched on, and then shook his head, like a dog intent on tearing something apart for the fun of it.

Donovan stopped resisting as much and began to slump in the restraints. The guards still moved around a bit, and Cannibal man was drawn to the movement—or maybe the noise; Richard wasn't sure.

The same guard that had shot him in the chest earlier walked closer to the bars, aimed his gun at Cannibal man, and blew a hole through his head. His target slumped to the floor, and the guard backed away again.

Cannibal man didn't get back up.

The video jumped forward again.

Donovan leaned in his shackles towards the guards, his face a frozen snarl. He looked and acted the same as his cellmate had before being loosed to attack him.

Oh, God, what has Harper created? I have to get ahold of Jeff. He needs to see this for himself. This is going to be huge. He's going to have to bring in outside investigators. This has gone beyond just me and my discreet investigation, while he wrangles in the corridors of power. This has to end before it gets out of hand.

"This is really bad," he muttered before pausing his recording.

Chapter 17: Library With a Side Of Head

Jeff hadn't answered his message in over three hours, and Richard was beginning to worry. If the program embedded in Harper's drive was not just a program to prevent transmission online but also a trace program, then his friend might soon be in trouble.

If Jeff had covered his tracks well enough when he had created the website, then he had time; if the people who had tried to kill Richard were able to find out who had created the site, Jeff was screwed.

Richard tried calling Jeff's phone one more time, but there was no answer—just the voicemail again. This time, he didn't leave a message.

What's going on, Jeff? Why haven't you gotten back to me? he thought. *Could they have already found out that he created the site and then gotten to him first? What if he has been calling my phone trying to warn me? I know it's against the rules we set, but if it were urgent, he would contact me directly.*

He ran a hand through his thinning hair.

Well, I can't turn on my smart phone anymore; it would be foolish to give them something to track and pin point my location. Why wouldn't he call this phone? Maybe he forgot the number off the top of his head and isn't in a position to go looking for it. How else would he contact me? There's the website. He wouldn't forget that...I can't sign on here, though; not with these guys having access to the tracking equipment they must have. They'd have my IP address and location as soon as I signed in to Jeff's page.

The safe house would be compromised, and then they would have me.

He tried to remember where in town the library was but it eluded him. Since he wouldn't be going online to their site, he wouldn't have to worry about being traced if he just went online to find the local library. That's what he decided to do, using his tough-book.

He found the address to the library and checked out the surrounding area using Google maps. If he ran into trouble, he wanted to be able to leave in a hurry...and he might want to eat somewhere over there too.

Before leaving the house, he showered and changed his clothes. He wore tan slacks and a polo shirt under a blue windbreaker that wouldn't look out of place. The weather was cool but not cold, and he still needed a way to conceal his handgun. A heavier coat might be a bit too much. To top off the new look, he picked a crimson and gray ball cap with a howling, white cougar on it, the colors and mascot of the Cougars of Washington State University.

There was a shed in the backyard where he kept a mountain bike. Since he didn't have a car anymore, the bike would have to work until he was ready to move on.

He didn't want to take the chance that the men after him might show his picture around to taxi and bus drivers for them to report back if they saw him. They would say that they were cops and that he was wanted for something really bad but that they didn't want to panic the public—the usual BS deception.

With the tough-book in a book bag over his shoulder, he hopped on the bike and rode away from the safe house. He had memorized the directions to the closest library, and he followed the turns where they would take him.

When he arrived, he locked the bike in a bike rack and went inside. He walked around until he found where to sign up to use one of the computers. There was an opening for the top of the next hour, so he put his name on the list.

While he waited, he browsed through the books on display. A copy of *Finding Sanctuary* stood out among the other books around it. He read the back cover.

Sounds interesting, he thought, putting it back.

He wouldn't be checking out any books—not without the library card that he *wasn't* going to sign up for.

Sanctuary—I wish I didn't need sanctuary right now. This whole situation is such a mess...I hope Jeff is all right. Who the hell do I take all of this to if he isn't?

He shook his head and moved on. There were a few chairs open in the periodicals section, so he went and sat down. He saw that he still had a few minutes before it would be his turn at a computer, so he looked at the magazines on the shelves around him and waited for one of them to grab his attention.

It was a Time magazine commemorative issue that did it. The cover was of President Zimmerman.

Richard had seen a little of the news coverage after the assassination, but at the time, he had been fairly busy and hadn't taken much time to pay attention. He had time now, so he stood up and grabbed the magazine. Opening it to the table of contents page, he sat back down.

Finding the story about the assassination itself, he began reading. He wasn't that interested in the stories on

Zimmerman's past. He had already looked into that before he had voted for the man in the last election.

It was not at all surprising to him that Muhammad, the assassin, had known where to find Zimmerman on a Sunday morning. This President had been predictable that way. What was surprising was how close Mohammad had been able to take an auto-borne explosive to a US President.

Zimmerman may have insisted that he attend Sunday services, but the secret service should have been able to insist on a larger perimeter, he thought.

The final article was a small piece on, then, Vice President Nelson and the challenges that he would face in finishing out the term of the Presidency. It said that he had a tough schedule ahead of him, if he didn't cancel anything, but that he was in a good position to make things happen. The Republicans were said to like him because of the wealth his family had earned with the wine business they had built from scratch. The Democrats were said to like him for the leftist environmental views that he espoused and supported with the family cash.

Richard's watch beeped an alarm, letting him know that he was scheduled for a computer in five minutes. Putting the magazine back on the shelf, he walked over to the attendant's desk and was given a numbered and laminated note card that had the computer log in information he would need.

He logged on and went directly to the internet. First he pulled up a website that he could click on and browse quickly if someone walked up on him while he was looking at the DIA sponsored site. Then he accessed Jeff's site.

It was mostly the way he had last seen it. The corrupted copy of Harper's drive was gone now though, and he noticed a new icon in the top left corner of the page. Without clicking on it, he hovered the cursor over the new icon. The file descriptor that popped up showed that the file was in a video format.

The computer was equipped with an earphones headset, so he put it on over his ears and made sure the volume was low enough not to blast his hearing. Hoping the video was his friend giving him alternate contact instructions, he double-clicked the file icon.

Jeff's face was the first thing that came into view when the video began. A surge of hope flooded through Richard but subsided just as quickly when he saw that his friend was bloody and battered. Hair was plastered to his forehead, sticky with blood. An eye was puffy and purple. His nose looked like it had been broken, and a small trickle of blood was submitting to gravity.

Split lips opened, and Jeff coughed. A muffled droning sound in the background made it a little difficult to hear, even with the headphones on.

"Richard," Jeff croaked. "Richard, they want me to tell you to give yourself up. The files you took will...hmmppff"

Jeff's head jerked back. Someone had him by the hair on top of his head. A shiny metal object entered the frame—a great big bowie knife blade.

The blade went into Jeff's neck, all the way up to the brass hilt. The person doing the stabbing pulled back more on Jeff's hair and pushed the edge of the blade forward in a sawing motion until it cut clean through the front.

Richard watched in horror and disgust as his best friend was mostly decapitated. Blood sprayed everywhere. A few drops hit the lens of the camera and then trailed downward.

The camera panned down with Jeff's body as his murderer dropped him to the metallic floor. His eyes were beginning to glaze over, and the sloppy sound of blood bubbling in his final exhale made Richard want to vomit.

His palms were bleeding from where his nails dug into them as he made fists with his hands. Tears came to his eyes. His jaw clenched so hard he knew he would have a headache later. He wanted to turn away, but he couldn't. That was Jeff, not some nameless stranger in a sick snuff film.

"Richard," said a gravelly, electronically disguised voice.

The camera panned back up to the mask-covered head of Jeff's killer.

"I'm going to kill you next, Richard. You got lucky earlier. I won't miss again," he growled, pointing the big bowie at the screen. "You can't stop what's coming to you—coming to the world. You're mine."

Then light flooded the scene, washing out the camera view at the same time the microphone picked up a torrent of sound, as if it were at the edge of a hurricane. When the camera's sensor adjusted to the changed condition, Richard saw that the view framed an open doorway in the side of an aircraft, military by the looks of it.

The masked man reached down, grabbed a handful of Jeff's button-up shirt and picked up Jeff's body with one hand. He held him in place for a moment, giving Richard another quick glimpse of his friend's lolling head and glazed eyes before tossing him out the door. The camera panned down and caught Jeff's body flopping head over feet as it plummeted towards the ground thousands of feet below.

The video ended to the sound of the masked man's laughter, and the computer's default media player began replaying from the beginning. Richard closed the window and sat back, as tears threatened to blind him. He took the headset off and set it on the table. Feelings of guilt began to build inside of him along with the grief. He swept them aside and let rage build instead.

Super soldier or not, the asshole that killed his friend was going to die…and so was the scientist that had started it all, he decided. There was no way Harper could be innocent in this.

He turned off the computer, so no one else could see what had happened to Jeff and then he left in a daze. He was still in a daze when he rode away on his bike. Car horns honking after he had cut into traffic, snapped him back to what he was doing and where he should have been going.

Chapter 18: Trace Alert 2

Deron sat in front of the bank of televisions and computer monitors. Various lines of numbers and symbols with the occasional intelligible sentence scrolled up the screens.

He couldn't kick his feet up and relax just yet. His supervisor might walk out of the office and catch him at it.

He had decided to accept the overtime that the scheduling office had offered because there was a beautiful motorcycle he had his eyes on. Another few months of overtime and he would be cruising.

The man he had relieved told him about the new code that had been entered into the monitoring system that morning after Deron had left. It was another code with the response action written only in the binder in the supervisor's office.

Sometimes he wondered what the coded alarms actually monitored and protected, but the one time he had asked, he had been told not to ask.

It was good money, so he didn't ask again...but he still wondered.

"All right, Deron, it's all yours," the supervisor said, emerging from the office with his lunch box and book bag in hand. "I'm going to head out for a drink and then some shut-eye. I will see you tomorrow."

"Ok, Mr. Gibson," Deron replied. "You have a good night."

Mr. Gibson nodded his head in acknowledgement and then walked out of the monitoring station. The door automatically closed and locked behind him.

Standing, Deron stretched and yawned. This really was an easy job with easy money.

He went over to his backpack and retrieved a portable DVD player and a pepsi. He had a few movies to watch and then he would nap for a little while. If he was needed to answer an alarm, the speakers were set loud enough to wake him.

An hour later he put the Transformers 4 movie on pause and walked over to the small restroom to take a leak. He left the door open, so he would be able to hear the alarm if one went off.

Soda had the tendency to go right through him. It was so predictable, he could almost set a clock by it. It usually took forty-five minutes from the time that he drank one to the time he had to go.

He was mid-stream when an alarm went off.

Cursing and swearing about the timing, he pinched it off, did up his pants, and went to see to the alarm.

"Son of a bitch! Why me?" he said when he saw the code.

It was the new one that had been entered into the system just that morning. Below the code, an IP address appeared, followed a few seconds later by a physical address somewhere in Spokane, Washington.

He wrote the information down then went into the supervisor's office. He unlocked the book cupboard and found the correct binder.

"Of course," he said when he saw that the response action called for phoning the same number he had called the night before. "I just hope spooky dude doesn't have to come in here again," he muttered, shaking his head.

He dialed the number.

"Hello," spooky dude answered on the third ring.

"Sir, we just had a code seven-one-eight-dash-zulu-seven at monitoring station bravo delta."

"There should have been other information with it, yes?"

"Yes, Sir;" Deron answered then gave him the IP address and the physical address.

"So he is still in Spokane. Very good, Mr. Brown. Clear the alarm and go back to watching your movie."

Deron swallowed hard. He wasn't technically supposed to have been watching anything but the work monitors, but spooky dude knew.

"Y-yes, Sir," he said and put the phone receiver back in its cradle.

Deron hadn't known that someone was monitoring him while he worked. He knew now that they could see what he was doing, but he wondered if they could hear what was going on too.

He shivered, though it wasn't cold, and hoped the damage control guy wouldn't take offense at him having called him "Spooky Dude" out loud.

Chapter 19: Again?

The black suburban skidded to a halt in front of the library, and two men jumped out. They sprinted into the library and climbed the stairs three at a time to the computer section. Looking at each face, they scanned the small crowd looking for Richard.

When they didn't find him, they began a top to bottom search of the entire library. Again they didn't find him.

"Turning up nothing in here, Raven," Davies said into his throat mic.

"Keep looking," Keyser ordered from the vehicle.

"Jackdaw copies"

They were too slow. Richard got away again. He just knew it. Keyser punch his fist into the dash board.

He wanted to curse and swear, but if he did, it might draw undue attention that would slow them down. Instead, he kept the curses inside, took slow deep breaths, and imagined his hands around Richard's throat, slowly squeezing the life out of him. He grinned.

A pedestrian walking by saw Keyser's face. She thought he was snarling at her, but then she saw the badge that he held up. It still didn't comfort her, and she hurried to get away from the area.

Keyser watched the woman leave and thought about the fun he could have with her if he should ever find her alone one night in a dark alley.

"Still nothing," Wagner called out.

"Fine," Keyser said. "Rally on me; we'll start searching the streets. He has to be close."

An hour later they had found no sign of their quarry, though they had driven up and down all of the main streets and side streets within three miles of the library.

"He's gotta be around here somewhere," Davies said, breaking the silence that had prevailed inside the suburban for the last fifteen minutes. "We've been monitoring the police band all day. He hasn't stolen another car. The taxis and bus drivers would report him for how much we offered as a reward."

Keyser shook his head.

"This guy's either exceptionally lucky or he's had some top notch training. Clearly, though, he wants something here. He should have left the State when we missed him this morning, but now we know that he didn't. So he's after something here—we just have to figure out what it is and then get there before him."

"Do you think McNeil would know?" Wagner asked, pulling down on the neckline of his ballistic vest. He was still trying to live down having been killed by their target.

"The security chief?" Davies asked.

Wagner nodded.

"He might," Davies replied.

"It's as good a place to start as any," Keyser said, and he made a turn at the intersection. He stepped heavy on the gas pedal, as he drove back towards the DARPA facility.

"You shouldn't have killed Guddemi," Wagner added. "We might have gotten him to talk, and then we wouldn't have to mess with all of this running around."

"Fuck you," Frank said. "He was done talking…And he pissed me off."

"Benson is going to be pissed that we keep missing this guy."

"Well, fuck him too. He doesn't even know how to catch an STD, let alone an operator who doesn't want to be found. I'm sick of his shit. We're doing the best we can with the intel we're given. That's what we tell him. Plain and simple."

"You got it, Boss," Davies said.

Wagner nodded but kept his mouth shut.

Out of the corner of his eye, Frank saw him rubbing a hand over the scar at the base of his skull.

Fuck Benson, he thought. *Fucking asshole.*

Chapter 20: Singing In the Shower

Stanley had fallen asleep while he waited in a chair by Antoine's bedside. He had made sure his friend took the medication the White House Medical Center doctor had prescribed that morning and had made sure he had consumed plenty of fluids to go along with it, but the quiet of his friend's house and the complete lack of anything else to occupy his time had quickly made him bored and drowsy. He drifted into sleep without realizing until his phone had chimed, reminding him that he had one more day to take advantage of a special offer from one of the applications installed on his smartphone.

He put his phone back in his pocket and looked around. The bed was empty.

Standing up, he stretched and then went looking for his friend. He hoped it was a good sign that his friend was up on his own again, but he worried that he had maybe gotten up and then not been able to return on his own.

He poked his head into the other rooms along the hallway but didn't see any sign of Antoine.

Then he heard a thump ahead.

It sounded like it had come from the bathroom at the end of the hall, but he could see from the crack under the door that the light was turned off in there.

"You all right, Tony?" he called.

A groan came from the bathroom.

"I'm sorry, buddy; I fell asleep. I would have helped you," he said, as he took the last few steps to the door.

"Do you need help?" he asked with his head close to the door.

Another groan came from the other side.

Stanley paused.

Was that a groan or a growl? He thought.

There was another thump from inside.

"I hope you're decent because I'm coming in. I can't tell what you're saying, so I'm coming in to check on you...doctor's orders," he added, as he turned the door knob and open the door a crack.

The smell that came out with the opening of the door almost made him gag. It smelled like something had died inside.

"Oh, god, Tony, is that you? Ah, man, it smells bad in here."

Stanley fumbled around on the wall for the light switch.

"Oh, my god, Tony. Are you all right?"

Antoine was sprawled on his back in the tub, facing away from the door, his arms swinging erratically.

"Oh my gosh. I am so sorry, bud," Stanley said, as he rushed to the bath tub. "Here let me help you up."

He grabbed ahold of Antoine's closest arm, right under the armpit, where he would enough leverage to, hopefully, lift him up and get him to his feet.

Antoine jerked his arm towards himself so quickly and unexpectedly that Stanley lost his balanced and tumbled forward over the tub. He threw his other arm up and caught himself on the wall before he fell in on his sick friend. His friend reached up and grabbed his arm with surprising strength.

127

But then Antoine turned his face towards him, and Stanley knew he had made a huge mistake.

This wasn't his friend Antoine. It was some demon out of a grave. Its face was contorted in a hideous snarl, and its eyes were shot through with spider webs of black.

Stanley barely had a chance to scream in terror as a mouth full of slimy teeth sank into his arm, and he tumbled down into the tub on top of his doom, bringing his face and neck closer to those evil teeth.

Part 2 – D.A.R.P.A. Dangerous

Chapter 1: Diary Dump

After locking away the pain of seeing his best friend brutally murdered and then finding his bearings, Richard rode his bicycle for the safe house. When he arrived, his legs were burning from exertion. He barely registered the fact that there were quite a few more cars in the neighborhood driveways. Once again, he entered through the back door.

Upstairs in the equipment room, he began prepping the gear he would need to break back into the DARPA facility.

After agreeing to the take the assignment, Richard had been sent to Brent Salazar for some intensive security and breaching training.

Salazar had been one of the original members of the Red Raiders, the US Navy's top secret counter-terrorist team whose cover mission was US military base security testing. Each member of the Red Raiders had been recruited from among the various SEAL Teams.

Salazar had been a member of SEAL Team Six prior to being recruited. SEAL Team Six was high-speed; the Red Raiders were high speed but "didn't exist." It was an easy choice to join when he was approached by the unit's commander.

During his time with the Red Raiders, Salazar had travelled the world, testing military bases' security by acting out the terrorist role of infiltrating the bases and creating chaos for the base security personnel. After each infiltration, the Raiders had explained to the security personnel exactly how they had exploited the base's weaknesses and how those weaknesses could be fixed. It had been loads of fun, though it had also pissed off and embarrassed the base commanders.

That had been their cover mission, in case anyone ever found out about them. Their real mission had been infiltrating into the terrorists' back yards and assassinating them before the terrorists could ply their trade on innocent Americans.

Unfortunately, the Red Raiders were eventually disbanded because they had embarrassed one too many base commanders. One of the commanders had raised hell in the ranks of ring knocking naval officers after they had created mayhem on his base, and the brass had hung the officer in charge of the Raiders out to dry.

Each of the members had been sent back to one of the SEAL teams, but the brass had made sure that they were kept separated from each other so that they couldn't cause any trouble in the teams.

Unable to get a transfer back to SEAL Team Six, Salazar had finished out his time with SEAL Team Two and then left the Navy. After his experience, he wanted nothing to do with military officers who were more worried about their promotion opportunities than they were about the lives and safety of the men and women in uniform who served under them—which amounted to about ninety percent of the officers he had contact with.

When Jeff Guddemi, who had had a security clearance that made him privy to the personnel files of each of the former Red Raiders, had approached him and asked him to train a Defense Intelligence Agency contractor in security procedures and how to get around them, Salazar had cooperated.

So Jeff had brought Richard to him and left it in his hands.

The first thing Salazar had done was take Richard to a bar, get him drunk, and then pick a fight with the locals. The locals, of course, had risen to the occasion and tried to rearrange their faces. Richard had proven himself to be capable in a fight and got both of them out of there with their facial features intact, without killing any of the locals, and before any of the local cops had shown up.

After that, Salazar had said he would show Richard a few tricks. "A few tricks" turned into a grueling three month boot camp in which Richard learned more than enough to pass as a former member of SEAL Team Six, as Jeff ended up putting on Richard's resume for the transfer into the DARPA security officer job.

"A few tricks" also gave Richard the knowledge and experience he needed to put a plan together to break back into the DARPA facility. One of the tricks Salazar had taught him involved creating diversions and finding ways to wear down the patience and resolve of the base's security personnel.

He remembered something Salazar had told him about how the Red Raiders would throw a rabbit over the fence to trip a base's alarms. The security personnel would respond, check the area, find the rabbit, and declare the alarm area clear.

When the personnel had gotten rid of the rabbit and then left, the Raiders would throw over another rabbit, repeating the process and taking note of the security personnel's response time. They would repeat the process over and over; each time the base personnel would take a little longer to respond and show less and less interest in the alarm area and the rabbits.

Usually after or four or five times of responding and finding a rabbit, the base personnel would turn off the alarm and stop responding. Then the Raiders would sneak onto the base undetected and create havoc for the security responders.

Remembering the rabbits gave Richard another idea. He would use animals as a distraction, but he would also use them as bait for the real distraction.

Using the secure connection on his tough-book, he went online and found some animal rights activists. Initiating a conversation with one of their members, he told them that a shipment of animals slated for cruel experiments and product testing would be arriving at a location outside of town later in the evening.

They were furious and wanted to know more. He told them he had to wait to give them the exact address, but that he would get back to them as soon as his sympathetic friend in the company doing the testing got back to him with the exact location and time of the shipment's arrival.

In the meantime, he suggested, they should round up as many of their members and followers that they could get to go protest, and if they had anyone with a sympathetic ear in the local press, they might want to bring them too. They agreed and said they would wait for him to get back to them.

He could have told them exactly where he needed them to go, but the timing had to be right. If they went out earlier than he needed, not only would they have fewer people for a smaller diversion, but the DARPA security personnel might have already dispersed them by the time he made it out there to begin his infiltration. By waiting, he gave them more time to gather more people for a larger diversion, and it enabled him to attempt infiltration under the concealment of darkness.

He was seriously outgunned and needed every advantage he could make for himself.

He had several hours before he needed to begin his return to the facility. He decided to use the time learning as much as he could about Harper's plans and what Harper had already accomplished.

He restarted the screen capture software and went to work.

One of the folders on Harper's drive was labeled "Diary."

That looks like the perfect place to start, Richard thought, clenching his jaw tight enough to hurt. Anger still boiled through him. He began telling what had just happened and what he had learned into the mic. The recording would no longer be going to Jeff, but someone out there would need to know, and he felt the need to tell them while it was still fresh in his memory.

There were hundreds of subfolders, each labeled with a date. Richard didn't know how long Harper had been working on "ZS3," so he started at the most recent entry and worked his way backward through the subfolders.

Much of what Harper entered in his personal diary was in such specialized scientific jargon for nanotechnology that Richard didn't understand what he was reading, but there were parts that were written in plain English, with which he had no trouble at all.

I've successfully created a hybrid series that uses the best features of the EWE-S7 and ZS3, so far without any of their shortcomings. Testing is as yet incomplete, but this new series looks promising. Test results so far have shown that they are very resistant to dangerous outside stimuli.

Post-Mortem vivisections of the first four baboon test subjects showed that the new strain regenerates damaged tissue that would otherwise be terminal for the subject and without the aid of additives the likes of which EWE-S7 is reliant upon. Each was healthy when it was put down, though they had been submitted to sarin gas poisoning, irradiation, extended asphyxiation, and the introduction of massive amounts of cancer cells, respectively. Two were male and two female, so we know gender is not a factor in this series.

Each of the four exhibited a dramatic rise in measureable muscular strength levels after introduction of the new series. I was forced to put them down one after another, after one of the males began to bend the steel bars enough to make escape possible. The others observed and repeated his attempt in their own cages. Each of them bent the bars as if they were minor obstacles. They had not previously been able to damage the steel that had held them prisoner.

This is quite promising for the life extension and enhancement properties I have been pitching to the other Infinity Group members. I think I will call this the "Harper Series;" since without my ingenuity, the others would probably succumb to ZS3 eventually. I still haven't told them—or even Benson about the protective properties of my watches. If this series works out as hoped, the watches will become obsolete anyway.

The initial subjects also exhibited other traits that are very interesting but that I will not go into here. I need to investigate more with additional subjects before I will even dignify my suspicions by putting them to paper, suspicions that open an entirely new line of study above and beyond the current intended life extension and enhancement goals.

I still have more testing to complete before I present the new series to the Group as a finished product, but once it has been successfully tested on multiple human subjects and results have shown to be within safe levels, I will make the amount required by Benson. I think he plans to keep the others in line by keeping the initial batch in hand, until they are ready to declare him Grand Master. He knows I will go along with whatever he decides; that is his ace in the hole.

Why he decided to initiate the final phase of the Wildlands Project before I have completed testing this first hybrid, I do not know. Hopefully, there will be no need for an HS2. Now that the G20 is over and Nelson will be hosting the governors tomorrow night, there is very little, if anything, that can be done to reverse what is coming and little time for me to perfect anything that might be wrong with this first series.

Richard furrowed his brows at reading the last paragraph.

"What is coming"—he thought, repeating the line from the diary. *That does not sound good at all—not after watching the ZS3 videos and hearing him imply that someone might want to stop "it" from happening, whatever "it" is. What is this Wildlands Project that Harper thinks this Benson person should have waited to initiate? Is the Wildlands Project the "it" that people might want to stop? And why is the G20 and something to do with the governors important for the Infinity Group's timeline?—whoever the hell they are. He's got to be talking about* President *Nelson if he's talking about the* official, international *G20 and the* State *governors.*

There was so much information in the last diary entry that built on information Richard didn't have. He supposed that if he had read from the beginning of the diary, he would know right away what Harper was talking about, but he just didn't have time to read the whole thing.

He wished he had Harper tied down to a chair right there, so he could ask him all kinds of questions before he inevitably killed him for his involvement in Jeff's murder; but then, if that were the case, he wouldn't have needed to plan an incursion back into the lab in the first place.

Richard scanned over the last entry again to more firmly embed the details in his memory, before leaving that entry and skipping backwards quite a few. He sighed, as he opened another entry and began to read.

As usual, Jason and Hanna requested to have Saturday off and invited Shelley and me over for dinner and a movie. Though I don't have to give them Saturday off, I usually do. I had turned down their requests to have us over for dinner and watch movies for the previous several weekends, since Shelley has been away. Now that Benson has let her come visit me again—he's a nice guy, but he is too protective of his daughter—I decided to take them up on the offer.

We had dinner with them, and it was great. Jason really knows how to grill a steak, and Hanna's mashed potatoes were the perfect complimentary side dish. Afterwards we were all kicked back on the couch, watching Day of the Dead or Dawn of the Dead—one of those.

I didn't really pay attention, so I don't really know which one it was, and I don't really care. I'm not interested in horror flicks. I just know that it was a zombie movie and that the survivors ran to and held out in a shopping mall, of all places. Not important—what is important is that while we were watching, Jason said, "It's a shame we can't just make our own controllable zombies with our nanos instead of wasting the lives of so many Special Forces volunteers,"—or something to that effect.

The three of them laughed it off, but it really started me thinking about the possibilities having something like that would present. It would allow the Infinity Group to accomplish at least some of our goals—and possibly to do so several generations ahead of schedule. I know I would certainly like to be around to see completion.

I'll bet Benson would jump all over it, if I could make a series of "Zombie Nanos" that the Group would be safe from. If I could create zombies, we could eliminate over ninety percent of the humans infesting Gaia, and we wouldn't have to worry about contracting ebola or whatever other virus Benson has others working on.

It all hinges on whether or not we can have a proven cure for whatever we unleash on the rest of humanity. I think I can get Benson to see things my way. After all, ebola can mutate, making our counter-measures less effective or not effective at all—nanos cannot mutate.

I am almost positive I can make a workable series of zombie nanos and a safe guard for all Group members.

It's a shame the McIntyres aren't in the Group. Jason and Hanna both could really help a lot, if only they weren't so damned prejudiced in their favor of humans over all of the other organisms on the planet.

Gaia will decide.

"Harper is insane," Richard said when he finished reading the entry. "Absolutely, fucking nuts. Wipe out ninety percent of the human population? Who the hell does he think he is?" *And not just him—who the hell does this Infinity Group think they are*? He thought.

He mulled over what he had learned from this entry and put it in perspective of what he had read in the final entry. What he came up with didn't look good at all.

They wanted to cull the human population, themselves excluded. The G20 and an event with, presumably, President Nelson and the governors were somehow seen as a point of no return for the Infinity Group's plans to be successful. Someone named Benson was the leader. And if the reverent use of the word "Gaia" was any indication, they were earth-worshipping environmentalist whackos.

Richard shook his head.

This can't be how we end. It can't. I'm going to stop this sick bastard tonight—or I'm going to die trying.

"I'm going to kill this prick," he said.

Richard looked at his watch. He still had a while before it would be time to move. He skipped forward a few subfolders and opened another file in the diary.

After Jason gave me the idea to create zombies I began looking to the animal kingdom because I remembered hearing something about a parasitic fungus that takes control of ants in the Amazon and makes them leave their typical habitat on the forest floor to scale a nearby tree. Near the top of the tree, the ant latches on to a leaf or stick and then waits to die. The fungus eats away at the ant until the ant overflows with fungus spores and bursts, raining spores down onto ants below to begin the process all over again. The fungus turns the ant into a zombie.

And it seems the fungus is not alone in nature in its ability to turn a living creature into a mindless zombie. The jewel wasp, for example, can take complete control of a cockroach. The wasp stings the cockroach, injecting it with a mixture of different chemicals. It actually snakes its stinger into the roach's brain, feeling out the regions that initiate movements. Then it douses the neurons with neurotransmitters which have the effect of psychoactive drugs. The cockroach is still perfectly capable of movement, but it has lost the will to move. The wasp then walks the roach to a location of its choice and lays an egg on the roach's underside. The roach just stands there as the

140

egg hatches and larva wasps burrow into its belly to feed and grow larger. The roach ends up dying and the new wasps go out looking for more cockroaches to take control of.

*There are numerous other examples of similar natural zombies which I am not going to list, but I did study as many as I could find in the research of colleagues. It was inspiring. Without their research I may not have had the breakthroughs that I've had with the ZS nanos. **It's all about the neurons!** Credit given where credit is due. I will ensure the Infinity Group's posterity will learn the names of these unknowing contributors to my research and thus to Project Wildlands and honor them even after these first researchers into zombie science have become my zombies.*

Richard shook his head and scanned through more.

Jason has been growing suspicious over what I've been doing in my lab. Since our labs are separate but connected, he can sometimes see what I am working on. I haven't brought the McIntyres in on the Zombie Series, since they aren't Group members. Any advances in technique I have come up with in the zombie series, I am passing on to him under the guise of working on the Elite Warrior Enhancement Series. Still, I feel like I am losing his trust.

Our testing facility in Alaska has been testing ZS3 on prison inmates that have been sent to the facility for being, what one of the previous Presidents has deemed, "incapable of rehabilitation due to political views" and have been made ineligible for parole or pardon. The series appears to be working perfectly.

The series does not require an internal power source, as the nanos are powered in the same manner as those in all of the previous series—through the reception of ambient electromagnetic energy. The small antenna at the tail of each individual nano picks up energy broadcasted from, say, the local radio station or the electromagnetic fields surrounding power and telephone wires. The energy travels up the antenna to the nano body, providing enough power for the nano to carry out its programming.

The left over energy inside the nano is then released in a small energy discharge pulse, which is also picked up by surrounding nanos. This has created an effective way for nanos inside one organic host to "ping" or communicate their collective identity to those in another nearby organic host. In all tests to date, the nano-infected hosts, upon reaching optimum nano saturation within the host, have completely ignored other hosts and have focused their aggressive replication drive on uninfected humans.

The replication drive is programmed into the nanos at creation.

This series of nano has been designed to focus concentration on the host's brain and central nervous system. Once the CNS is saturated, the nanos can, within limits, control the host's body by controlling its urges. The nano replication drive triggers the host's urge to feed itself meat. This causes the host to bite any human that does not have enough of the nanos in its system to be able to communicate through "pinging."

The tests that have been conducted so far show that from the time of the first bite, the nanos introduced through the saliva can require about half an hour before the host *has enough nano saturation to effectively" ping," at which point they will begin to hunt down others to infect. In some, the effects have been much faster...as early as three minutes from bite to aggression. Complete saturation in a newly infected host can take anywhere from twelve hours in your average adult to thirty-six hours in larger adults, much faster in children. At complete saturation levels, the nanos stop replicating, directing all of their energy into maintaining the host body's current level of health and hunting...*

I'll need to find a way to slow down the reproductive rate of the ZS3 we're going to put in the wine so that it will not cause the leaders of this world to turn too quickly. They need to make it back to their countries and states before they turn if this whole plan is going to work. If I can't slow it down enough, it might not work. They'll discover the cause and shut it down before we can make this a real global pandemic. The timing has to be just right...

Well, I guess the bastard figured out how to do that, Richard thought, remembering one of last night's news reports of Chinese towns being quarantined and burned to the ground. He went back to reading the damning confession of a madman.

Without an uninfected human in range to draw their attention, the hosts appear to go into a type of stasis in which they mull about. The sensitivity of the nanos' receptors appears to be fairly acute. Several subjects have been blinded and made deaf prior to introduction of ZS3 into their system, but once the nanos have reached a level of saturation, they have still been able to detect the presence of uninfected humans. I believe the reason for this is that the nanos can detected the small electrical impulses of a beating human heart and possibly even the electrical impulses of an active human brain.

I suppose I could be mistaken, but I don't think so. We have tested the hosts' senses.

Their sense of smell seems to disappear sometime after infection. Either that or they have no repulsion to the smell of decomposition as their bodies do begin to rot to some extent after infection.

Their sense of touch seems to be unimportant to them, as they have been poked and prodded through automation in an attempt to gain their attention, with and without a potential feeding source in front of them, with no visible external reaction.

Taste doesn't matter at all; they will eat human flesh that has been doused in all sorts of repugnant contaminants.

I've already mentioned some of the hosts having been blinded. Some hosts were not blinded, but showed no reaction to the introduction of uninfected within normal visible range for humans but outside of pinging range for nanos. One curious characteristic that has developed in a fair number of ZS3 saturated hosts that has not been seen in any of the EWE candidates is the development in the eyes of a black web-like lattice structure. The webbing mirrors the convex exterior of the eye, and upon further investigation, I have found that it is composed entirely of communications nano materials. These webs appear to enhance the broadcast range of the nano's ID ping. Removing the host's eyes does diminish the nano's ID ping range, but it does not eliminate it entirely.

The sense that they seem to retain most strongly after infection is their sense of hearing. They do seem to be drawn to loud noises if no human is within pinging range.

Hosts do not seem to be drawn to non-human meat. I'm still not sure for the reason for this, but it has been observed numerous times. Accessible goats, rabbits, horses, cats, dogs, are completely ignored whenever a human is present, even if the human is detectable but inaccessible. Even when a human was not present, the animals were ignored. I do not currently have a theory to explain this, unless I am mistaken about a host's sense of smell. I suppose it is possible that the host smells a different neutrino than those present in humans.

Regardless, it appears Group livestock should be safe from zombies, even if kept in open pasture outside of Group strongholds, so our continued sustenance is nearly guaranteed barring any other outside threat.

Richard couldn't go an entire page without shaking his head at how stupid and foolish these people must be to be willing to do something like this.

The information he was reading was plenty interesting, if downright scary, but he wanted to know how to stop it and how the Infinity Group members planned to survive the apocalypse they planned to unleash—and apparently already had. Surely they did plan on surviving it.

He thought about the news report he had heard the night before, about the G20 being finished and the national leaders going back to their home countries. Then there was the magazine article he had read at the library that had mentioned that President Nelson was scheduled to host a dinner party for the State governors. It tied in with Harper's earlier entry about needing to slow down the nano reproduction rate for the world leaders.

Oh, my god, he thought. *That's how they are going to spread it. The members of the G20 will take it back to their native countries, and the governors will take it back to their States. And Harper already mentioned that Nelson is somehow involved too.*

He tried to remember when the article said the dinner was going to be.

The 17th—damn, that was last night, he thought, looking at the date on his wrist watch. *Whether the President is involved or not doesn't matter anymore. If he is involved then he is a traitor and won't do anything to help the Americans; if he isn't involved then it is too late to save him anyway because he would already have the ZS3 crap in his system and so would all of his staff that attended with him.*

If the ZS3 takes over a host within thirty-six hours of being introduced, the national leaders at the G20 should already be showing signs of infection. It would be on the news by now, wouldn't it?

Turning on the television, he flipped through the channels until the   British Broadcast Channel came on. They were talking about rugby.

No

He flipped through more news channels. The American news channels were as oblivious and locally focused as usual—nothing about the President being sick or about anyone biting those around them.

No

The Russian news seemed to be talking about wheat production and drought.

No

Just as he was about to change the channel to check the Japanese news station, the Russian channel changed stories and showed a photo of a young Asian female nurse wearing a medical face mask, the Chinese flag in the background behind her.

He didn't understand what was being said, and they didn't have any accompanying video footage for the new story, but Richard remembered the news report about an unexplained breakout in China from the night before. He also remembered hearing somewhere that the Chinese delegates had left the G20 a day earlier than everyone else.

Son of a bitch, it's already gone global. Harper wasn't kidding when he said the G20 was the point of no return. The US is going to go nuts when this breaks.

Richard caught himself trembling.

How the fuck do they plan to survive this?

His anger was turning into frustration at not knowing what he could do.

The story changed again to something irrelevant, so he changed the channel back to BBC, where at least he could understand what the talking heads were saying. Now they were talking about the bailouts Spain was requesting after the economic default their government was facing.

Richard shook his head. Economic collapse seemed like a walk in the park when faced with the prospect of an impending zombie apocalypse. He turned back to Harper's diary and opened a new subfolder.

Benson flew me out to his ranch in Jackson Hole, Wyoming for the weekend, so I could spend some time with Shelley. It was great. We took some horses out to Yellowstone and rode around. It was wonderful to have a taste of how empty of human contamination Gaia will be once we bring the Wildlands Project to fruition.

I had an interesting talk with Benson last night after dinner. As always, we talked about the future and what Gaia has in store for us after we free her from the scourge of human over-consumption. It is a grand idea, but so far no one has laid it all for me exactly how it would all be brought about. I'm sure there are a million factors involved and many things that could prevent our ambitions from being realized.

When I brought this up, Benson at first seemed hesitant, but, now that I have confirmed the viability of ZS3 for the role he has envisioned, he trusts me completely, so he explained it for me.

As the scheduled G20 approaches in a few months, it will be necessary for Vice President Nelson to take on more responsibility. Benson has contacts who have arranged for Zimmerman to be assassinated.

Richard's jaw dropped.

These were the fuckers responsible for Zimmerman's death? And Harper knew about it ahead of time? Anger grew even hotter inside of him. *I swear I am going to hurt him before I kill him.*

"President Nelson is working for these people," he said.

He continued reading.

I'm not sure how it is to be done or when exactly, but with Zimmerman out of the way, Nelson will be able to carry out the Group's goals. The fat, lazy Americans will look to him for salvation, and he will deliver it. He will save them from themselves. The rest of the world will follow.

Benson explained that as President, Nelson will not fall under suspicion for attending the G20, where he will gift each attending national leader with a bottle of his family's famous wine. My ZS3 nanos will be in each bottle, and when they drink—hopefully on their flights home, they will be carriers and infect their home countries for us.

Likewise, the governor's dinner at the White House a few nights later will involve his family wine, and they will spread my ZS3 to each of the fifty States.

Nelson will have one more role that will be crucial to the Group. As President, he will hold launch authority to the US's nuclear arsenal. Once satellite imagery shows that a large enough percentage of the human population has been destroyed with ZS3, he will order a number of launches into the upper atmosphere.

When they detonate, they will be high enough that irradiated fallout will not present a threat to Gaia or to the Infinity Group. The resulting Electromagnetic Pulses will wipe out all communications and power on the ground.

Since ZS3 relies on these for its power supply, doing this will effectively turn the zombies off, and the human hosts can rot away to nothing.

I know the timing of all of this is important, but I think it would be better if Benson waited to make sure I am able to create the EWE-S7/ZS3 hybrid I have envisioned. With a successful hybrid we would be less vulnerable to damage by ZS3 infected. We might really also be able to achieve one of our ultimate dreams—indefinite life extension.

Unless I do finish the hybrid, we will be forced to live underground while we wait for the ZS3 to run its course and then for the EMP's to do their work. I know it won't be as bad as it sounds. The underground bunkers that an entire club of billionaires pay to have built will surely be as good as staying at any five star resort, but still, I'd prefer the ability to go out in the open if I tire of whatever entertainment my billions have bought me.

I've looked at the Post-Event Survival Network that Benson put together for the group, and it will be like being on vacation—all the food and fun we could want while we wait for Gaia to equalize. I do look forward to all of that. I'm not sure I look forward to what he plans for after.

He says he has built an army that the rest of the Group knows little about. Once we return to the surface, he plans on having his army round up all of the surviving humans on the planet and use them as slave labor to carry out the Group's needs. They will grow our food. They will make our clothes. They will provide entertainment. They will serve, or they will die.

"So much for life, liberty, and the pursuit of happiness," Richard murmured to himself.

Somewhere in the reading, depression at the enormity of it all rose up and began competing with his anger for top spot on the emotions podium.

He lowered his head into his hands and closed his eyes. He didn't want to look at the offending words on the computer screen any longer.

Where was his future now? What about his fiancé's future?

Rage flared in his soul again.

You took Jeff from me, Harper. You're not taking her too.

He looked at his watch. It was almost time to get going, but before he did, he needed to go public with this. He turned off the screen capture software and renamed the video file.

It was exceptionally disturbing that the President of the United States was not only knowledgeable of the conspiracy but also quite actively one of its key players. This meant that if Richard exposed the conspirators through the proper channels, the Infinity Group was likely to either accelerate their plan or obstruct any further investigation into the evidence he could bring forward or, more likely, a combination of both. Either way, it would require he expose himself and put himself at their mercy while hoping that the system would work correctly, something that seemed highly unlikely in this case.

There has to be another way, he thought. *There's got to be a way to warn people so that they can be prepared for the hell that is about to be unleashed and so they can know where to point the blame when it really does break bad. How do I blow the whistle on the most powerful organization the world has ever known and still not get myself killed?*

The first option that popped into his head was the press, televised news stations. The news could be broadcast immediately over popular TV channels and their websites, reaching the highest number of people in the quickest amount of time.

He did a quick search online, and saved the contact information for the top five news agencies in the US and abroad.

Next, he needed a backup plan in case the press corps blew him off or were somehow shut down.

He remembered a time years before when a federal contractor very publicly blew the whistle on what he believed was government overreach with its surveillance programs.

What was that guy's name again? Ah, that's right— Edward Snowden. I'll look up how he did it and maybe take a page from his book.

Once he had the contact information for a number of whistleblower organizations, WikiLeaks being probably the most well recognized, he opened a number of web browser tabs and began looking up their websites as well as those of the news networks.

He began uploading his video to each one as well as to YouTube and a cover Facebook account that Jeff had opened and maintained for him.

If ever a video needed to go viral, it's this one, he thought, as he finalized the uploads. *One last thing to try before putting the computer away.*

He needed to do something to protect his fiancé in case he wasn't able to make it back to her. He turned back to the computer and minimized Harper's diary window.

Harper may have been a nano-tech genius, but he was definitely an idiot when it came to security. Richard knew this from the experience of working near him for the last four months.

Come on, Harper, prove to me that you are a complete dumb ass, Richard begged, as he went to the tough-book's operating system and initiated a drive-wide search for "Post-Event Survival Network."

Several seconds went by as the laptop performed the search of Harper's drive.

A folder and numerous files popped up in the result bar, making Richard smile, as he notated each for closer inspection.

First he opened the folder dedicated to the topic. The first file was a generic text document labeled "Instructions." He opened the text document and scanned through the message.

Harper, you really are a bigger shit than I thought you were, he thought, as his grin grew wider.

Feeling less than confident in his computer skills with the unfamiliar operating system the Post-Event Survival Network used, Harper had left himself detailed instructions of how to open an administrative level account (the highest level possible) in the network, how to access the network once he had an account, and how to order

153

equipment and supplies he would need for the lab Benson had built for him in the Infinity Group's bunker resort.

Best of all, Harper had left a copy of his username and password because he had been afraid that he would forget them while he was busy with other things.

Richard printed off the directions and debated with himself over how to proceed. He could access the Group's network now and take a chance that it could be traced like Harper's drive had been; or he could leave it alone and make the attempt after he killed Harper and destroyed as much of the ZS3 that he could find in the lab. One left him open to danger; the other left his fiancé open to danger should he fail.

I'm used to risking my own life. I'll do this for Linda. This could be her only hope for survival.

He followed Harper's directions, and signed onto Harper's account using the username and password Harper had left. The user interface was fairly easy to navigate, so it wasn't difficult to find the supply and delivery section.

First he made sure a delivery could be made to the destination he had in mind. It would be a waste of time to order a big delivery only to find that the system would only allow delivery to certain sites.

There didn't seem to be any restrictions limiting order destinations, so he breathed a sigh of relief.

Going back to the supply inventory section, he entered "Rocky Mountains" from the options given when prompted to enter a regional location for delivery. A supply cache site within that region appeared on the screen, along with a full inventory of the cache.

The system was designed for large orders. All he had to do was pick a size of the container to be shipped and the number of supply modules to be included in each. The modules from each "department" included a full variety of whatever supplies would be appropriate. So, say, for "Food," a module would be full of an assortment of different freeze-dried and other long-term storage meals; and for "Maintenance," it would be full of cleaning supplies and the like. Specialized modules could be assembled from scratch, if the user so desired, but delivery time would be delayed, the interface warned.

Looking at his watch again, he realized that he was running out of time. Scanning the inventory lists for the different delivery modules, he chose the ones that he thought would be most helpful for his fiancé. He chuckled when he saw what was in the modules under the "Weapons/Armament" department.

Rock and roll, he thought, though he sobered up again when he realized that he would be facing down Infinity Group men who had the same weapons at their disposal—but in much larger quantities.

His mood was somber as he finished the order.

"One more thing to do," he muttered as he went to the account creation page. "Let's see if this works."

Once again using Harper's account and the directions he had left, he created another administrative level account for the network. He used a fictitious name for the account owner information.

If he was successful at taking Harper out tonight at DARPA, he wanted to be able to sign back into the network to order more supplies later, but he didn't know if Harper's account would be closed or frozen, once the Infinity Group people discovered that he was dead. He also hoped Harper's account wouldn't be too closely scrutinized later. If anyone noticed that Harper's account had just created an additional user and decided to look into the new user it would draw attention to actions and places Richard would prefer to keep hidden.

Time to go, he thought when he looked at his watch again.

He logged out of the network. Just to make sure his new account worked, he logged back in under the new username. It seemed to work just fine. He logged off for good and turned off the tough-book and packed it away for travel.

As he was walking down the stairs, an idea popped into his head. If it worked he wouldn't have to face as many of the super soldiers when he went back to the facility. He dropped his bags in the kitchen then went back upstairs to get it ready. Once it was complete, he jacked the temperature up as high as it would go on the central heat thermostat then grabbed his tools and left the house.

Riding a bike would take him too long to get out to the DARPA facility and wouldn't allow him to carry much, so he decided to steal another car. It would be faster, and he could carry more gear. This time he had brought a tool kit that would help him break into and hotwire a car without doing a lot of damage to it. It was too much to hope that he could find another vehicle with the windows rolled down and the keys inside.

Taking his bicycle around to the front, he looked around for anything suspicious then hopped on and rode out of the residential neighborhood.

He went back to the hotel the taxi had dropped him at earlier in the day. There were quite a few cars in the parking lot out front and quite a few in the lot in the back as well. He rode around the entire hotel, checking for people outside who could call the police on him and checking for a vehicle that would be easiest to break into and hotwire.

He found another Honda Accord, but after seeing the two car seats in the back for younger children, he decided to skip it and find another. He felt bad enough stealing someone's car. He didn't want the extra burden on his conscience that he knew he would have thinking about the possible single mother trying to get around with no car and two small kids. Especially since that car might mean the difference between life and death once the zombies were plentiful. She might make it somewhere safe, if she still had her car.

Sometimes he hated having an imagination.

The next best car he found was a Toyota Camry—no car seats or kid's toys, but it was tougher to break into. It was a newer model and had an antitheft system which took him a few minutes longer to circumvent and disable.

When he had it running, he hopped in and drove back to the safe house to quickly pick up the gear he would need before heading out towards the DARPA facility.

Outside of Spokane but not yet on the road that would take him to the facility, he pulled out his generic phone and dialed the number to the animal rights activist he had chatted with earlier.

It didn't ring for long.

"Hi, Beth; this is Gary. We talked earlier about the animal delivery that will be made later tonight but that I didn't have the specifics on. I have everything now. Do you have a pen and paper handy?"

Keeping the directions simple and to the point, he told her how to get her people to the facility, which side they would have the best chance of seeing the animals off-loaded from and of being seen themselves, and what they could likely expect from the facility security—if the security personnel followed their standard operating procedures and rules of engagement, all information acquired through his friend that works for the company, of course.

After breaking the connection with Beth, he called another number. He listened to it ring, hoping his fiancé would pick up. After seven rings he had a feeling she wasn't going to answer. He waited for the voice mail.

"Hello?"

Oh, thank goodness, he thought when he heard her voice.

"Linda, it's Phil," he said.

"Philip? Oh my God! Where are you?" she asked.

"I'm sorry, Babe; I can't get into all of that right now. I just called to let you know that after I take care of something tonight, I'm planning on going home."

"Really? Oh, that is such good news," she said.

He could tell she was excited. They hadn't seen each other in too many months.

"Is everything ok?" she asked, worry cutting into her voice.

"I wish I could tell you everything is fine, but it's not—it's really not," Richard replied. "There are some crazy things going on right now, and they're only going to get worse. I want you to promise me something."

"Ok..." She was beginning to sound unsure.

"Promise me that even if I don't show up any time soon, you will not come looking for me? All right?"

"But you just said you were going to be coming home," she said. "Philip, what is going on? You're not making any sense."

He sighed into the phone.

"I...ok, look; I know this is going to sound crazy, but I swear to you I haven't lost my mind and I am one hundred percent telling you the truth."

"All...right, what is it?"

"You know I agreed to go work under cover for Jeff."

"Yes"

"Well, I found out that some people hidden within the government, without government sanction, have been working on a project that will deliberately kill ninety percent or more of the human population by turning some of them into zombies and letting them loose on everyone else."

She laughed.

"Oh, Philip, you always were the joker."

"Linda, listen to me," he said, becoming angry. "I'm not joking. These people are trying to kill me right now. They already killed Jeff."

"What?" she asked, her voice growing angry.

"You know I would never joke about something like that. You know me," Richard pleaded. "I am not kidding; this is not a joke."

"Jeff's dead," she half said, half asked.

"Yes, I'm sorry; I know this isn't how you should have to find out about it, but there is so much going on right now."

He could hear her starting to cry.

"Linda, listen to me; this is important," he said, trying to get her mind away from Jeff.

Her cries turned to sniffles and dropped in volume.

"I ordered some supplies. I'm having them sent to the park," he continued. "It is absolutely imperative that you or whoever you have working inventory accepts the delivery. You will need the things that I am sending there, and the people who will be bringing them don't know that you aren't a part of their plan."

"But, Philip, if…" she interrupted.

"No, just listen; I don't have much time left. I'm about to go into danger, and I need to know that you have a fighting chance if I don't make it out of there alive."

She was silent. Good.

"In your bedroom, under your window—beneath the second floor tile in from the wall, I buried a lock box. I want you to dig it up and take out the cash. It's all that I had left after we invested in the park. Take the cash, first thing in the morning, and go to every store in town. Buy everything they have: food, tools, building supplies, gasoline, propane, all the lumber and concrete and bricks you can get your hands on, tents…batteries…lights and light bulbs, toilet paper. Just buy everything."

160

"But Phil why? And how am I going to get it all out here?"

"Buy their trucks too if you have to. Just buy up everything you can get your hands on as if it is going to be the end of the world at midnight tomorrow and you will never have a chance to have any of this stuff built or delivered again. Store everything at the park, and get as many people as you know to get inside the walls of the park. Our friends and family first. Cancel all of the shows."

"Philip, you haven't answered why," she argued.

"Because it is going to be the end, Linda," he said quietly. "It's moved past the point of no return. It's already gone global—just nobody knows what it is yet."

"Is that why the governor disappeared?"

"What? I don't know what you're talking about."

"It's been all over the news," she said. "Governor Collins came back from DC last night; at least, his plane landed. No one has seen him since."

"I don't know," Richard replied. "I guess it might be related, if he went berserk and they are just trying to keep it out of the news for now."

"Oh, and supposedly the wife of the governor of Florida got sick and started attacking her staff this morning. According to the news, hospitals in several States have begun talking about Pandemics."

"All the more reason for you to do what I've already told you," he said. "Buy up all of the supplies in town and get people out to the park."

"You have to tell somebody," his fiancé insisted. "If all of this is really true, you have to tell somebody. Call the

President if you have to. With your background, he'd have to listen."

Richard shook his head and pinched his temples with one hand.

"If what I have learned is accurate, he is a member of this group."

"What? Philip, are you sure someone hasn't just pulled your leg? The President? Come on."

"This isn't the result of a prank," he replied. "I know this for sure. Just promise me you will do what I've told you—please."

"All right, Phil; I promise," Linda said. "Now you promise me something."

"What?" he asked.

"Be careful; whatever this is that you've gotten yourself mixed up in, I want you to come home alive. You still owe me a wedding, Mister."

"I promise you I will be careful," he said. "Babe?"

"Yes?"

"I really am sorry about Jeff. I wasn't there to help him."

He heard her breathe heavily and try not to break into tears again.

"Just come home, Phil," she whispered.

"I love you."

"And you know I love you too."

"I do," he replied. "I have to go; I'm going to go kill the people that killed your brother."

She was silent. He hoped she would understand.

"I have to go."

Just as he was disconnecting the call he heard her yell, "I love you," one more time. He set the phone on top of the bag he had sitting in the front passenger seat and concentrated on making the turn in the road that he knew was coming up in the dark sometime soon.

Chapter 2: Scout

The DARPA facility relied on high tech sensors for most of their perimeter security information. Typically, the fence line surrounding the facility would be empty, without anyone around.

Simple laser sensors would trip if the beam was broken by anything passing through that area. Buried pressure sensitive cables inside and outside the fence would trip if enough weight came down on them. Any sensor trip would immediately alert the security personnel in the control center who would then direct a response team to check the alarm and surrounding area. The response teams could be anywhere in the complex within minutes on their four wheel ATVs.

The sensors were all-enclosing and overlapping, but because technology is fallible just like humans, a security team of two would drive around the inside of the fence line several times a night in a quiet electric vehicle similar to your typical golf cart but with a few upgrades. Maintaining radio contact with the control center the team would sequentially trip each alarm to ensure it was still functional, and they would look for signs that an intruder might already have bypassed the sensors.

On top of all of that, video cameras gave the control center immediate eyes on any area of the perimeter and in most places within the facility. It would be a difficult infiltration.

The night vision goggles that Richard had worn from the time he had driven off the main highway without headlights, before the long hike to where he was now, were no longer necessary. The facility was brightly illuminated before him, and he put the NVGs away in his backpack to instead use binoculars to see what he needed to see inside. It was refreshing to see the world without the green tint of the night vision, but the degree of depth perception loss was only slightly better with the binoculars.

The going was slower the closer he approached. It was important to make as little noise as possible. Richard knew that the security personnel regularly patrolled inside and outside the perimeter of the facility, and if he made too much noise, even from as far away as he still was on the opposite side of the hill, they would hear and send someone to investigate. The trees would do much to muffle any sound that he made hiking to the top of the hill, but they could also make noise if he broke a branch or dislodged a tree that was dead and already ready to fall. With no city noises to mask individual sounds, a broken branch might as well be a crack of thunder.

When he crested the hill the facility appeared on the plain below him. It was a maze of buildings surrounded by razor wire topped chain-link fence and high intensity lights.

Security liked to run drills, but not much usually happened at this facility out in the country away from the city activity and distractions.

He noticed immediately that there were additional patrols out.

Interesting.

He watched each patrol drive along the little dirt road just inside the fence. Each lap around the inside of the perimeter took about ten minutes, and each team always seemed to be in view of the teams in front of and behind it.

Hmm, are they expecting something to happen? Why the heightened alert? Why the extra men?

Shifting the binoculars towards the dormitories, he studied a bit more carefully. The first thing he noticed was that there were fewer lights on in the individual living quarters than was usual. Then he saw movement at one of the doors.

Someone was leaving the building.

What the hell? he thought, looking closer. *I shot him dead.*

It was Wagner, and he was alive, walking towards the black suburban parked a little further away from the dorm. He didn't look at all as if he had been shot through the heart less than twenty-four hours earlier.

Son of a bitch, he thought as Harper's diary came back to him. The super soldiers could regenerate thanks to the EWE-S7 nanos in their blood. *I'll have to make sure I take headshots from now on.*

After Wagner grabbed something from the vehicle and returned to the dorm, Richard went back to scanning the interior of the facility. Having super soldiers inside was going to complicate things. These guys were pros; there would be no room for error.

What are they still doing here in the first place? Still hoping to kill me? Do they think I would come back? Have I done anything that would give them reason to think that?

He couldn't think of anything he had done that would make them think that he would go back to the facility.

Maybe this isn't about me then. Maybe this is about Harper and his zombie series.

He had a feeling that before the night was through he was going to have to face some of these super soldiers. It wasn't a pleasant thought. He knew how good these guys were. He had worked with SEALs and Marine Force Recon bubbas before.

People outside of the Special Forces community often idolized the abilities of those inside the community, thinking them almost super men. With Harper's nano series flowing through their blood, maybe now that kind of thinking wasn't so farfetched.

Facing super men with superior training and possibly better weapons wasn't Richard's idea of a good time, but he knew Harper had to pay for what he had created and especially for Jeff's death. If that meant confronting super men then so be it.

Looking at his watch, he figured Beth and her activists would be arriving before too much longer. Before he had initiated contact with their group, he had found out online that some of the members had been arrested previously for violent activism. He hoped some of those that were coming tonight would a little violent. That would certainly be more of a distraction for the security personnel.

He heard them before he saw them. It sounded like a whole convoy of vehicles. He didn't hear car doors closing, but shortly after they turned their vehicles off, they started chanting.

"Animals are people too; No more experiments. Animals are people too."

Richard rolled his eyes.

Animals are people—what a bunch of nonsense.

But the nonsense was working. DARPA security began coming out of the buildings, and they were focusing on the side he wanted them to. The patrols that were already out began speeding towards that side as well.

Reaching into his front pocket, he pulled a new pre-paid phone that wouldn't be on anyone's radar. Taped to the back of it was another phone number he had jotted down before leaving the safe house. He pulled the paper off the back then entered the digits and pressed "send." After it had rung five times he pushed the "end" button, slipped it back into his pocket, and then began to approach the facility's fence.

Chapter 3: Activists

"Animals are people too! No more experiments! Animals are people too!"

"What is this?" Keyser asked as he walked into the security control room and heard the chants over the surveillance system's speakers.

"Animal rights activists showed up about ten minutes ago and started protesting outside the north fence," McNeil answered, turning away from the monitor screens that showed the protestors with their rather professionally made signs and their loud-speakers.

"Sir, Spokane PD is enroute," said one of the dispatchers who had popped up and was waving his hand to get some attention. "They will have two busses for prisoner transport and an unspecified number of officers arriving in marked and unmarked cruisers to effect the arrests."

"Thank you," McNeil said, nodding.

The dispatcher sat back down and immediately began chatting into his comm headset.

"Is this a common occurrence around here?" Keyser asked.

"Not at all. We've never had a single protest here before. Most people don't even know we are out here, and the few that do sure as hell don't know what goes on inside."

Keyser nodded and thought.

"This could be a distraction," he continued after a few seconds.

"A distraction from what?" McNeil asked.

Keyser looked at him. There was no way he was going to tell the man why he and his men were really there.

"Maybe a terrorist attack," he finally replied.

McNeil's eyes opened wider.

"If I were you," Keyser offered. "I'd have a few of your men keep an eye on these protestors, with a response unit in reserve in case things get out of hand. In the meantime, have your perimeter patrols step up their activity around the rest of the facility because that is where the actual attack is going to take place. I would also put out a general announcement to all staff that they are to hold their current positions until your men can contain and control the situation."

McNeil nodded and stepped over to the control center broadcast system to begin dispatching units to new locations according to Keyser's recommendations.

Keyser took advantage of McNeil's focus elsewhere and walked out of the control center. As soon as he heard the door close behind him he spoke into the microphone at his throat and began to jog down the hall.

"Jackdaw, Magpie, I have a feeling Richard is coming. I'm guessing he is going to use the protestors outside the fence as a distraction, so he can bypass the perimeter security systems. Jackdaw, I want you to…"

His phone vibrated in his pocket. He slowed to a walk.

"Standby," he said before muting his throat mic and answering his phone. "Keyser here."

"Frank, stop what you are doing and head back into town. Richard's phone just went active again. Its location coincides with an address we pulled from Guddemi's computer. I'm sending coordinates to the onboard nav system in your ride."

"You've had an address from his computer and you're just now telling me about it?"

"No, Frank; I was just coming down here from I.T. with the safe house location from encrypted files that we were just now able to get into. When I got down here, the alarms were going crazy because the trace on his phone has a hit again. I'm not keeping intel from you, Buddy. It's just the timing. It was out of my hands."

"Question...did the files they cracked have Richard's real name? That could come in handy if this safe house lead goes nowhere."

"Stand by; I'll find out."

The line went to annoying classical music as he was put on hold.

Keyser looked down at his hands, drew them into fists, and watched the numerous scars stretch or compress based on their geography. There was rage building in him. He let it grow, but he was doubly aware that until he found Richard he was unlikely to have a decent outlet to pour that rage into. This was the only target he had looked in the eye and pulled the trigger on who had escaped alive. He would soon fix that.

A scratching sound came to his ears as Creeper picked up and touched the microphone on his headset so many miles away.

"Frank, they do not yet have any additional information on Richard, but if any turns up I will notify you immediately."

"All right," Keyser replied. "Thanks for checking."

"You got it, Buddy. By the way, I was told to have you take Brock with you on this one."

"Will do. Out."

Keyser put the phone back in his pocket and reached up to restore his throat mic.

"Jackdaw, Magpie, respond to the suburban. We've been tasked. I'll brief you on the way."

"Jackdaw copies."

"Magpie copies."

Keyser turned around and jogged towards the dormitories.

Chapter 4: Lab Talk

Mercer picked up one of the glass vials from the laboratory counter, held it up to the light, and swirled the contents around. It was mostly clear but had a yellow tint to it—almost like urine.

"So this is what will do us all in, is it?"

Harper looked up from the task he was trying to complete in order to fulfill Benson's instructions and frowned.

"Only the feeders," he replied. "You and I and those aligned with us will be spared. I'll see to that. The human virus that infects mother Gaia will be eradicated, and she will restore herself to her former glory. Now, please, put that back down."

Mercer chuckled but did as Harper asked. He was dressed in a DARPA security uniform to minimize questions from the rest of the facility staff.

The speakers built into the walls crackled.

"All personnel are hereby advised to maintain their current positions until security advises further."

While the message was repeated over the sound system, Mercer frowned and pulled a radio out of his cargo pocket. He had turned it off and stuffed it in there hours ago after the mundane security traffic had begun to annoy him. Now he turned it back on, keeping the volume low, and clipped it to his belt.

It only took a few minutes of listening to figure out what was going on and to understand why the rest of the staff was on lockdown.

"Hey, Doc, I've got an idea. How about we field test these zombie bugs of yours? You haven't tested them outside of controlled conditions yet have you?"

Harper frowned, annoyed at the distraction again, but decided to answer.

"No, I haven't. But the tests conducted so far have been conclusive. They work, just as I said they would."

"Well, how about we do our own little experiment here?"

"I'm busy," Harper replied then paused. "Why? What did you have in mind?"

Mercer laughed.

"The curious scientist," he said and then laughed again. "Well, there just happens to be an overzealous mob outside protesting our existence. How about if I take some of these new bugs of yours and go make us some zombies?"

"Hmm," Harper grunted. "That's a good idea." *It will get you out of my hair, so I can actually get some work done*, he thought. "How are you planning on 'infecting' them? Do you think you could mix in with them and poke a few with hypodermic needles?"

"You can't weaponize a few of these vials real quick?" Mercer asked. He really had no interest in merging with the fanatics outside.

Harper shook his head and said, "I don't know about that. That isn't how they were designed to be spread. Person to person—that's how they work. I don't have anything to shoot them out of or anything like that."

Mercer pursed his lips and blew out a sigh. "All right, Doc. I'll go poke a few for the fun of it. It beats sitting here doing jack shit."

"There are needles over there in that drawer," Harper said, as he grabbed a few vials of the yellow liquid.

Chapter 5: La Cucaracha

Richard stalked down the hall, his gun up and ready to use. Somewhere behind him he could hear a vacuum cleaner being used in one of the offices on this floor. He wanted to put distance between himself and the overnight cleaners. He had no grudge with them, but they would certainly alert the authorities if they spotted him and didn't mistake him for one of the DARPA men.

He passed a maintenance closet on the left next to a drinking fountain and then a few dark offices on either side with open doors. As he moved forward, he heard the footsteps of several people walking towards him from a cross corridor farther ahead that branched off to the right. At least one of them was wearing high heels.

He stopped as several possibilities of what approached him and the variant outcomes flashed through his mind. They could be a group of admin types who had had to work late and were just now going back to their living quarters. Or, maybe one of the office secretaries was scared because of the rowdy activist crowd outside and had asked for security to escort her on an errand.

He wasn't here to assault the staff or to take prisoners. His only goal was to kill Harper. But he hadn't brought anything to use against innocent noncombatants without permanently hurting them should the need arise, and he mentally kicked himself for the oversight.

He wasn't going to turn the corner and shoot his way through them; though they were approaching from the direction he needed to go. His conscience told him that would be murder. He considered hiding in one of the open offices he had just passed and waiting for them to pass by before continuing on.

The echoing clack-clack of the high heels on the hard tile floor grew louder, and he ditched that idea. What if the woman was on her way to one of those offices for something? Murphy's Law dictated that he would probably choose the same one to hide in that she would end up going into and then all hell would break loose as soon as the lights came on. Or what if a cleaner walked in, saw him, and freaked out? Same result. Not something he was prepared for.

In the half second this all flashed through his mind, he chose to hide in the maintenance closet. The cleaners carried their supplies on a little push cart, and they were still in a room farther back down the hall. He judged it unlikely that they would choose just that moment to go to the closet for additional supplies. At least the people up ahead wouldn't even think of going into the closet. That would be above their lofty station in life.

Sprinting back down the hall, he turned towards the closet, banging his hip on the drinking fountain in the process. His eyes watered with the pain, but he ignored it. He had to hide. He opened the door and slipped inside.

Unlike the nearby offices with solid doors, the maintenance closet had a metal door with a big, wire mesh-filled glass window that filled the entire upper half of the door.

Richard scooted to the back. The closet was only about eight feet deep but afforded a few shadows he could conceal himself in while he waited. He stood against the wall next to a shelf of cleaning supplies.

Across from him was a wash basin that supported a damp mop. The musty, chemical smell emanating from the mop head told him the cleaners should have just thrown it away and replaced it instead of drying it for additional use.

Hmm, he thought. *The things we notice when it doesn't matter.*

He shook his head and listened for the high heels. They were getting closer. His eyes slid down across his body and double checked that nothing on him protruded past the plane of the edge of the shelf.

Through a gap between boxes of scouring pads he was able to see out the window. Two men walked past carrying open folders and talking in low tones. The woman wearing high heels was right behind them.

Richard stayed where he was until the sound of the high heels had diminished to barely audible echoes. Then he leaned forward from the shadows and stepped towards the door. As he reached for the door handle, he saw someone else walking by in the center of the hall. Despite a sudden spike of adrenaline to his system, he froze so he wouldn't catch their eye as they passed.

It was a man dressed in the black fatigues of DARPA security, but he only looked vaguely familiar. He was singing, "I'm gonna make some zombies. I'm gonna make some zombies," to the tune of *La Cucaracha*.

At least those were the words that Richard thought he heard the man singing.

He used the sleeve of his blouse to wipe beads of sweat from his forehead then looked left then right then left again through the window before opening the maintenance closet door. The halls were empty again, so he continued on.

The cross corridor that branched to the right came up and he turned into it. He followed it for another fifteen paces or so before making another turn, this time to the left. The door to Harper's lab was just a few doors down.

With his gun in one hand and an access card keyed to the lab in the other, he stepped up to the door and swiped his pass over the card reader.

Chapter 6: Makin' Zombies

Chaos

That was what registered in Mercer's mind when he saw what waited for him as he stepped out of the building. His own special version of La Cucaracha died on his lips. He stood in the doorway for a few seconds and took it all in.

Individuals in the crowd of animal rights activists outside the fence were crying and screaming and generally running around aimlessly like newly headless chickens, courtesy of the tear gas spewing from gas grenades which had recently been tossed among them by the DARPA security force inside the fence. The gas had caught the wind and quickly swept through the whole gathering. Even the newsies at the far edge of the madness were getting a heavy dose of the riot control agent. People were running into each other, slipping down the slope towards the facilty, and being trampled under the feet of their own people.

Adding to the pandemonium, one of the new pain-ray devices developed by DARPA was being deployed from a rooftop. The microwave beam emitted from it was being aimed at the activists at the top of the slope. The pain it inflicted was intense and unbearable, and the activists' quickest and easiest route of escape was downhill over their fallen comrades.

Mercer shook his head and smiled in amusement. He walked towards the fence, skirting around the ranks of DARPA men with their gas masks, clear plastic crowd-control shields, and wooden batons.

Idiots. All of you out there.

Some of the activists that had slipped down the slope went in exactly the wrong direction and stumbled into the chain link, unable to see through eyelids that were reflexively clenched tight in pain.

Mercer found one leaning against the fence. Long hair and part of a maroon sweatshirt were pressed inward through the gaps between links. He took a syringe and slammed it into the meaty section of the shoulder under the sweatshirt, depressing the plunger before the woman on the other side could jerk away from the fence. A second activist received an injection. Then a third. Within minutes, Mercer had found targets for each of the five syringes he had brought.

"Good work, Boys," he said, as he walked away from the fence and passed behind the rank of security men. They were giving him funny looks. Some realized that they didn't recognize him, though he wore the same uniform as they. Others were just shocked that he would approach the fence through the cloud of teargas without a gasmask and without showing any discomfort. None of them had any idea what he was doing to the activists against which they were protecting the facility.

"Keep at it," he said, leaving them behind.

Harper had told him that there would be observable effects from the injections very quickly. He couldn't say how quickly, but he had mentioned that a bite usually passed enough of the nano-infection to saturate the victim's internals inside of thirty minutes. The injections he had just delivered carried far more of the zombie-nanos than anyone would pass in a bite, so the transformation would be much faster. Mercer thought it prudent, despite his present proximity to the action and the chain link barrier between them, to watch the rest from inside, so he trotted back to the building from which he had exited just minutes before.

Setting a fast pace, he walked to the control center to watch the coming show on the security camera screens. When he walked in a few minutes later, the room was noisier than he had really expected, a constant din from several conversations between the dispatchers and the troops outside as well as various alarm tones and phones ringing at random making casual eavesdropping impossible.

He caught McNeil's eye as he stepped around a dispatcher's chair on his way to the camera monitors. He gave a head nod in lieu of a verbal greeting. McNeil returned it, though an upturned mouth corner hinted at some internal contempt. McNeil was busy and didn't want to be bothered by the guest muscle he had had to put up with for the last twenty or so hours.

Same to you, Buddy, Mercer thought, as he took his place in front of the screens.

Realizing that he wouldn't be able to hear anything over the background noise, he found a pair of unclaimed headphones and activated the bluetooth feature. His ears were assaulted by a more exciting kind of noise: screams of pain and fear. He turned the volume down and returned his attention to the scene outside.

The gas grenades had finished their spewing, and the gas had been carried away on the wind. The effects on the activists, however, were longer lasting. Many had fallen to their hands and knees and were groping along blindly, their bodies still jerking about with spasmodic coughs. Ropes of phlegm dripped from their nostrils.

His five test subjects were easy to pick out in the crowd. Their faces and clothing were already drenched in blood. Their movements within the crowd had visible purpose. They were the only ones who didn't seem to be in pain, but they looked to have gone totally feral. Anyone else that stumbled near them was quickly attacked. They were biting. Not just biting, they were tearing away strips of flesh like jackals on a kill. The effects of the injections had begun much faster than Mercer had expected.

The security detail was visibly shaken, their unbroken wall of shields dipping lower as they shook their heads in shock.

And so it begins, Mercer thought.

Chapter 7: Safe House Raid

Keyser parked the suburban in shadows a block away and around the corner from the address Guddemi's computer claimed was Richard's safe house and where "Creeper's" trace placed Richard's smart phone.

"Radio check," Keyser said into his mic.

"Loud and clear," Brock replied.

Keyser had dropped Brock and Wagner off on the opposite side of the block. They would cover the front of the house, while Keyser and Davies went in through the back—or vice versa if the situation dictated once they were closer.

Keyser and Davies quietly closed the doors and entered a narrow alley that was left between the fences of the neighborhood's back yard boundaries. Calf-high grass muffled their steps.

Lights were on in a few house windows on either side and on a few back porches, but none were close enough to illuminate them as they approached the safe house. The back was dark with no light coming out of the structure.

"Approaching the back," Keyser said. "All dark and quiet here."

"Copy," Brock replied. "We are in position. Quiet here, but we have one light on, north-west corner room, second floor. No visible movement."

"Copy," Keyser replied.

The back yard behind the safe house was surrounded by a privacy fence. Davies used a night vision monocular to inspect the back gate for traps and early warning devices and then the back of the house.

"The gate is clean," he mumbled, "but the house has a motion-activated flood light over the back door."

"Where inside the house is Richard?" Keyser asked.

"Hold on," Davies replied then reached into a pouch connected to the side of his load bearing vest. He pulled out another monocular and put the night vision in the pouch in its place.

"Give me a lift," Davies said then waited.

Keyser moved closer and knelt enough for him to step into his gloved hands. He raised Davies up above the fence, higher than he could have reached on his own.

Using the thermal imaging device, he scanned the whole house and grunted.

"Down," he mumbled to his mate.

Keyser brought him back down below the level of the fence.

"Well?" he asked.

Davies shook his head.

"I don't know; the house looks like a furnace inside. The internal heat is cranked—as high as it will go I'd guess."

Keyser breathed out a sigh of frustration.

"What does that mean?" Wagner asked.

"It means," Keyser said, "That unless Richard frames himself in the window for us, we won't be nailing down his position in the house. He turned on the central heat to mask his body heat."

"Oh"

"We'll just have to go in blind like we did in the good old days," Davies said, as he put the thermal imaging monocular back in the pouch.

Keyser nodded.

"You wearing your vest, Jackdaw?"

"That's a roger, Raven" Wagner replied, sounding less than thrilled about the fact.

Keyser nodded to himself and raised the suppressed pistol he had used earlier that morning. Aiming at the motion detection sensor on the back floodlight, he squeezed the trigger.

The gun coughed out a single round and hit the sensor dead center.

"Opening rear gate," Davies muttered, as he reached up. He inched the gate open, until both he and Keyser each had enough room to slip into the backyard. They closed it behind them and latched it shut. Staying in deep shadow, they crept towards the house, ready to shoot if Richard opened a curtain or a door to look out at them. The floodlight stayed off, so Keyser's shot had clearly done the trick.

Davies took out the night vision monocular when they reached the back porch and then scanned the porch for traps or sensors he would have missed from farther back. Satisfied that the area was safe, they stepped up onto the deck, avoiding the wooden steps which might creak under their weight. Then he inspected the door.

The outside of the door looked fine, no visible alarms or traps; so Davies pulled a small fiber optic surveillance device out of a pouch on his belt and snaked the cable under the door. As expected, the inside room was

186

dark. He switched the viewing mode to IR assisted night vision and the room became visible in shades of green.

It was a kitchen with no furniture to obstruct his view. A quick poke around showed no one in the immediate area, so he inspected the inside of the door. There were no wires showing or magnetic contacts attached to or around the door, so he felt confident that he could open the door without alerting Richard.

He took one more look around inside then removed the fiber optic cable and stowed it in its pouch. Keyser caught his attention with a head nod that implied the question, "What's up?"

Davies gave him a thumb up then pulled a torsion bar and lock picking gun out of his gear. He lined the pick up inside the lock's key slot then pulled the trigger. After several tries and just a few seconds, the pick successfully bounced the tumblers into place and the cylinder turned to the unlocked position.

Inching the door open even slower than they had the back gate, they waited to hear if the hinges would creak with the motion. It opened smooth as silk.

Inside, with the door closed again, Keyser made a double clicking sound with his throat that he knew would be audible over their communication system but not by anyone in the house, so Brock and Wagner would know that they were inside.

They walked slowly through the lower level without finding Richard. There were signs that he had been downstairs recently: wet dishes in the sink, bloody gauze in the trashcan, a suture kit on the table.

So I did get him, Keyser thought. *The question is: Where and how bad? Not bad enough. He made it this far.*

There wasn't a basement, so that left only the upstairs. They climbed the stairs slowly, keeping their feet to the outside edges of the stairs where they would be least likely to cause a floor creak.

The downstairs level was uncomfortably warm. The higher up the steps to upstairs they went, the hotter it became until at the top it felt like they were in a boiling cauldron.

What don't you want us to see, Richard? Keyser thought.

Two closed doors appeared to the right. The closer of the two was dark under the door; light escaped under the farther.

With the back of his hand, Davies wiped away a river of sweat that had been threatening to run from his forehead into his eyes. He watched Keyser take up a position right next to him, along the outside wall, covering the door to the lit room. Davies pushed his rifle around to hang behind him on its sling. He drew his pistol from the drop-holster at his thigh then went down to one knee next to the door frame of the dark room, staying clear of the center "fatal funnel" of the doorway.

With his handgun up, he grabbed the door knob with his other hand, twisted, and gently push the door inward. Then he returned to his two-handed grip and activated the flashlight under the barrel of the pistol. He swept the beam across the room.

There was a small bed, empty and unruffled, and a dresser next to an open closet with only a hand full of clothes hanging inside.

Behind him, Keyser made a soft "ssstt" sound to get his attention. He looked back and saw Keyser point at the door down the hall with his non-shooting hand and then bring it up to cup his ear. He had heard something from the other room.

Davies stood and poked his head back out into the hallway. Then he too could hear a voice. It sounded like a man, which they had expected, but they couldn't hear what he was saying or any replies from whoever he was speaking to. He put the pistol back in its holster and swiveled his rifle back up to the front.

"I hear a man's voice," Davies said in a low voice.

"Copy," Brock said from outside.

When he was ready, Davies stepped forward taking the point position, and Keyser followed. A few steps away from the door he looked to see that he had Keyser's attention and then pushed his rifle forward a foot then pulled it back into his shoulder.

Keyser nodded.

That was the sign. No more pussy-footing around; they were going to go in hot and heavy.

Davies sprinted forward, crashing into the door with his shoulder. It sprang inward, and he let his momentum carry him into the corner of the room. Keyser was a step behind him, but he button-hooked to the right and cleared the opposite corner of the room. Then they each turned towards the center.

In the center was a small table on which a metal box rested with the lid propped open by a wooden dowel attached to a contraption with a clock, a phone, a few levers, and lots of wires. Next to that was an audio player/recorder, the source of the voice they had heard from down the hall.

With plenty of experience under his belt, the purpose of the device flashed into Keyser's head. The metal box was a radio frequency shield. Visible under the propped lid was a phone, probably Richard's. The clock and lever contraption, with the attached external phone, had received a call, probably from Richard, and had then raised the lid of the metal box, allowing the phone inside to send and receive a GPS signal and thereby be picked up by Creeper. The audio device had lured them into the room, and he could see that the wires trailed off of the table to the floor and ended in a bundle of detonators which were inserted into a formed panel of plastique, which he recognized by smell as C4 explosive, which was in turn topped with hundreds of large steel ball bearings—the teeth of the trap.

In that final one fifth of a second before the explosives detonated, sending the ball bearings to pulverize through their guts, he saw the blue, 55-gallon water barrels that the explosives were propped up against and realized their intent. They were meant to tamp the explosive, so the destructive force would shred the entry team but not endanger the residential neighbors.

Genius

"Fu—"

The world disappeared.

Chapter 8: We Meet At Last

Richard swiped the ID card over the card reader and entered a four digit PIN on the key pad below it. The light on the reader turned green, and he heard the lock click back into the door. He turned the door lever and pushed in. The door was heavy and air-tight, the kind made to keep dangerous conditions locked down in lab emergencies.

He stepped into a small containment room with amber-colored windows, through which he could view the lab. Once he closed the door, jets of cool air sprayed from nozzles set into the walls on either side and from overhead, and ultraviolet lights came on bathing his entire body in radiance.

He closed his eyes against the light.

When the air stopped, the UV lights turned off and the magnetic lock on the second door deactivated.

In the lab proper, bright lights overhead and extra reflective white walls made Richard wish he had brought sunglasses. Bars of white and red afterimages glowed in his vision from the UV to which he had just been exposed. Polished steel tables and countertops gave the lab a sterile look despite the various microscopes and other devices he didn't know the name for that were in organized workstations throughout the room. Off to the right another door like the one he had just entered was closed, but more light pored through the circular window set in the upper quarter of the door.

When he closed the second door there was a loud clack as the magnetic locks gripped the door again.

Hunched over a workstation with their backs to him were two people in low level hazmat suits. The rest of the room was vacant. At the sound of the locks activating, they looked up and saw him. One was a man, the other a woman, and the look they shared when they saw him was one of annoyance. The woman turned towards him.

"You can't come in here like that. Protective suits are required at all times," she said. She started walking towards him. "Who gave you authorization to come in here?" she continued.

Richard said nothing but began walking toward her as well.

"What is your supervisor's name? You are not..."

Richard raised the suppressed .22 handgun and pointed it at the tip of her nose.

"Be quiet and stay right there," he said, using the most soothing voice he could manage. "You," he said, nodding to the man. "Come here, and you keep quiet too."

Annoyance had disappeared and now there was genuine fear behind those eyes.

"Be careful with—" the man began, but Richard interrupted him, swiveling the gun barrel in his direction.

"I said be quiet."

The man nodded his head and shut his mouth. He joined the woman.

"Now, turn around and put your hands on your head, and I want you to interlock your fingers for me...That's a good boy," Richard said, as the man obeyed. "Now you."

The woman obeyed as well.

"Good," Richard said. "Now don't move a muscle."

193

The man stiffened a bit, his back going rigid, but Richard ignored it. Instead, he stepped forward and switched off the communicators attached to the outsides of their suits. Then he backed away from them again.

"Now we can talk," he said. "Turn around, but keep your hands on your head."

The man and the woman turned to face him. Their lips were pressed tight, and their eyes were beginning to show traces of anger.

"Jason and Hanna McIntyre, am I right?"

Neither said a word, but they both frowned.

"You are Joshua Harper's assistants, so that would make you the McIntyres; am—I—right?"

The man looked him in the eye for a moment then nodded.

"Good," Richard replied, smiling. "That means you are the good guys. You may not believe it right now, but I too am one of the good guys; and your boss in there is one of the bad guys. And they are *very* bad guys."

The look on his captives' faces was one that questioned his sanity.

"I didn't think you'd just take my word for it. Unfortunately," Richard said. "I don't have time right now to spell it all out for you. As long as you are compliant, I will not hurt you; but I can't leave you unattended either, so—Jason, put these on your wife's wrists."

He slid a pair of handcuffs over to the man.

"Hanna, sit down on your butt and put your hands behind your back and on either side of that table leg there."

Neither of them moved.

Richard lowered the gun and pulled the trigger.

Both of his captives flinched at the quiet cough and subsequent ricochet that left a swollen bump upward in the surface of the steel table behind them. Jason looked down and saw that the tip of his shoe, just forward of his big toe, had a clean hole through the top of it and a ragged hole out the side.

"This isn't a joke," Richard said, his tone deadly serious. "Do what I tell you, when I tell you, or things or going to get very messy. Do you understand, Doc?"

Jason nodded his head and bent down to pick up the handcuffs.

Richard shook the business end of the gun up and down towards Hanna.

Keeping her eyes on him, she moved down to sit on her butt and put her hands on either side of the table leg down near the floor.

"No," Richard said. "Your hands go above the cross beam there."

She corrected herself, and Jason moved to put the cuffs on her wrists.

"They better be tight."

Jason looked at him and sighed then closed the links over his wife's wrists.

"Now you," Richard said, taking a second pair of cuffs from his backpack and sliding them across the floor.

Once Jason had joined his wife, Richard stepped closer, checked the cuffs, and removed the wires connecting the communicators to the microphones in their suits. Then he pulled the communicators themselves away from the suits and set them on the counter away from the table and out of reach.

"Keep quiet, and don't go anywhere," Richard said before turning to the other door.

The other portion of the lab visible through the window was equally well lit but was smaller and more cluttered with equipment. There was only one occupant, facing away from the door and dressed in the same fashion as the McIntyres. It made sense that this would be Harper.

But don't assume, he reminded himself. *We don't want to kill the wrong guy.*

The person was leaning over the counter, filling a syringe with a thick, golden solution from a large petri dish. When the syringe reached a level that satisfied the holder, he squirted the contents into a glass tube which he then stoppered and placed in an upright tube holder that was just in reach. That made two filled and stoppered tubes resting in the holder. Then he began filling the syringe from the dish again.

Richard open the door and stepped inside.

It was definitely him. He recognized the face he had come to hate over the last twenty-four hours, as Harper looked up from filling a third tube with the golden elixir.

"You're not Mercer," Harper said stupidly then recognition lit his face.

"No, I'm not Mercer," Richard confirmed. "But I see you know who I am now."

Harper's eyes were wide, and he looked like he had swallowed a particularly large bug. He turned his attention away from the gun in Richard's hand and focused on something over his shoulder, and Richard thought he saw a glimmer of hope in those eyes.

Keeping his gun pointed towards his prey, Richard glanced over his shoulder to see what the doctor had been looking at.

There was nothing there. It was the same empty wall he had seen before he had stepped into this part of the lab.

What—ah, damn; I should've seen that coming, he thought, as he turned back to see Harper swinging his arm toward the emergency lockdown button on the wall above the counter. He tightened his finger on the trigger and watched a bullet shatter the tube in Harper's hand and then poke a hole in the side of his hazmat suit.

Harper kept going for the button, so Richard kept shooting, his body swiveling to follow the desperate doctor. A bullet blasted through the edge of the steel counter. Another went through the tube holder, shattering those tubes as well. Finally a set of shots impacted Harper's arm, one in the triceps an inch above his elbow and the other grazing the top of his forearm.

But he was too late.

The button compacted under Harper's weight. A red light began to flash throughout the room and an alarm klaxon sounded.

"Damn it!" Richard yelled then stepped in and kicked his leg back, sweeping Harper's feet out from under him.

Harper latched on as well as he could with the hand that was now empty, catching Richard by surprise.

As Richard pitched forward off balance, he saw Harper's other hand come up and then swing down towards him. A sharp pain jolted through his shoulder as the syringe needle dug deep just behind his collar bone, going right through the thick nylon webbing of his pack's shoulder strap and then his clothes.

Then they were on the floor, Richard on top. Harper was kicking his feet and trying to stab him with the syringe again. Richard flexed his back muscles, arching away from Harper; rotated his wrist, bringing the mouth of the pistol suppressor up under Harper's chin; and squeezed off the remaining rounds in the magazine.

The top of Harper's head disintegrated under the onslaught of lead.

Richard rolled off and lay on his back.

"Son of a bitch!" he groaned as he tried to catch his breath.

"Hhnnnn," he wheezed, climbing to his feet. He looked around him, taking in the lab.

His mission was accomplished. Harper was dead.

But Harper's work remained.

He opened the door to the main lab and immediately had Jason's and Hanna's attention.

"Is this everything Harper has outside of his room?" he asked, leaning against the door frame. "I'll have to get over to his room too," he muttered, more to himself than anyone else.

"I don't know," Jason replied. "You realize we're locked in here now that the alarm has been hit don't you?"

"What?"

"We can't leave. The system won't let us. If they don't come let us out, we will die in here."

Richard stared at him.

He walked over to the lab's exit and pulled on the door. It didn't budge. The magnetic locks were on. Shaking his head, he remembered the card reader. Out of his pocket, he took the spare security card that had worked to get him into the lab and scanned it at the card reader.

The red light on the card reader blinked then stayed solid. He tried again. It stayed locked.

He shook his head and stepped back. Looking through the amber colored glass at the other door leading out of the interior of the containment room, he couldn't see anything through the outside circular window. Then he looked at the amber glass itself.

It looked pretty thin.

He took a few more steps away from the window then raised the handgun and began pulling the trigger.

"No! Don't!" he heard Jason yell over the cough of two rounds.

He quickly realized why and flinched in on himself.

"It's bullet proof!" Jason shouted. "Stop shooting; you're going to hit us."

Hanna was softly whimpering next to him.

Richard stood up straight and walked over to the window. There was hardly any effect on the glass; just the smallest little scratch was visible where he had shot.

"Geez! It doesn't look thick enough to offer ballistic protection," Richard said in frustration.

"We created it here at DARPA," Jason said, a touch of pride in his voice.

"Well, that's just great," Richard muttered.

He lifted the handgun and dropped the magazine to check how many bullets he had left. The magazine was empty.

"Damn it," he whispered.

All he had left was the round in the chamber, and he already had plans for it.

"Well, I'd better get to it while I can."

He walked back into Harper's lab, raised the handgun, and shot a circular device protruding from the ceiling overhead.

"Why are you still shooting?" Hanna burst out.

"Because I have to incinerate Harper's work," Richard replied when he stepped back into the main lab, "and I can't do that if the halon fire suppression system kicks in."

"Why are you doing this?" Jason asked. "What have we ever done to you?"

"You—nothing. It was Harper. Fortunately for you, I've read his diary, and he has confirmed that you know nothing about his work. If that wasn't the case I'd have put a bullet in you too."

Jason pulled back and looked as if he had been slapped in the face.

"We happen to be two of the most knowledgeable scientists in the nanotechnology field, thank you very much," he said.

"Yeah, I know, Doc. Regardless, you don't know jack shit about what Harper was really doing in his lab...The Elite Warrior Enhancement research?— Obsolete," Richard said. "I know that's what you are still working on—but not Harper. He had just finished working on, and actually deploying, a *third* Zombie Series; and he was close to being finished on a life extension project he was going to call the 'Harper Series'."

Jason looked surprised then worried.

"What? What are you talking about? He didn't..."

"Harper is a member of a billionaire club that worships 'Mother Earth' and collectively wants to wipe out the human race in order to save the earth. He made and tested several series of nanobots for that purpose."

"Oh, Sweet Jesus," Hanna cursed. She turned to her husband. "It makes sense, Jace. All those times he talked about the 'Green' movement—he was trying to recruit us."

Richard nodded.

"You knew him better than I ever did," he told them. "But because you didn't show any interest in his god, he didn't fill you in on his other project."

Jason shook his head.

"This doesn't make sense. What about oversight? Someone would find out. They would shut him down."

"Would they?" Richard asked. "Someone inside the agency I'm contracted with knew that something was going on, but they didn't know what. That's why they sent me in to investigate, under the radar so to speak.

"And Harper's diary points to upper level government officials having knowledge and giving support to the whole operation. Just this morning one of the super soldiers from your program tried to kill me because they found out that I stole a copy of Harper's hard drive with proof of their illegal plan and activities. And that's after they killed my best friend to get to me."

The McIntyres were quiet as they digested what he had told them. Just as Richard was about to go back to destroy the other lab, Hanna looked up at him.

"You said you have proof of all of this?"

"I did," Richard said, "And I do. It's all on the laptop in my pack,"

Jason looked at his wife then back up to Richard.

"Show us this proof. If what you say is true, we will help you try to fix whatever he has done. I'm assuming you…I'm assuming Josh is dead now?"

"Yes, I killed Harper."

Jason nodded.

"Then you will need our expertise in dealing with the rogue nanotech that you allege he has made."

Richard nodded.

"Yep, probably."

He turned and walked to the other lab, leaving them powerless to do anything but watch as he set about destroying Harper's life work.

The last thing Jason saw before the other door closed, separating them, was Richard dragging the limp body of Joshua Harper to the entrance and then taking a gold watch from each wrist and placing them in his own pockets.

Chapter 9: Say What?

Mercer watched in fascination as the activists into whom he had injected the zombie nano series bit gouges into the flesh of their fellow demonstrators. It seemed that they somehow instinctively bit for the neck and throat area of whomever they attacked. They didn't hesitate to bite and tear away any of the arms and legs that were thrust defensive at them, but they seemed to like the neck the most.

I wonder why that is? He thought.

"...cer! Mercer!"

Turning his head to see who was calling him, he saw McNeil approaching with a dirty look on his face.

Ah, shit. Now what?

"What's up?" he asked.

"Didn't you say you were supposed to be keeping an eye on Harper tonight?" McNeil asked.

Uh-oh

"Yeah—but he was fine just a bit ago, and he wanted me to leave him alone. Why?"

"Because his lab is in lockdown right now. Someone hit the contamination emergency button, but no one is answering on their comm."

Ripping the Bluetooth set from his ear, he started to leave.

"Stop," McNeil said, putting a hand out and stepping in from of him. "You're going to need this."

He handed Mercer a security card.

"The override code is 'seven-two-seven-two.' I'd go with one of my men normally, but the Spokane PD is pulling in, and I've got a million other problems to deal with right now."

Mercer snatched the card and took off at run. As he was leaving he heard one of the dispatchers.

"Oh my god! They're through the fence!"

Chapter 10: Tasty

In the fifteen years he had served on the Spokane police force, Officer Cardoza had never before seen anything as crazy as the cannibalistic riot that was unfolding in front of him.

He had arrived late on the scene, having become embroiled in separating two slap-happy screamers from a domestic dispute outside one of the newest nightclubs downtown before being dispatched to the DARPA facility. If it hadn't been such a high priority call out, the two clubbers would have spent the night in jail. Instead, he had waited until they were each in separate taxi cabs headed in different directions before driving out to DARPA.

As he was arriving, he had passed one of the Spokane PD prisoner transport busses headed back into town, loaded to the gills with prisoners who had just been arrested for trespassing. There had been a few garbled transmissions over their radios, probably because of how far away from town that they had had to respond.

At first the facility seemed deserted. There were plenty of buildings that looked like standard warehouses but no people, not even the other police cars. They were on the opposite side of the campus. He realized this when his radio filled with frantic cries from his fellow officers and then gunshots rang out and echoed off of the building walls.

Then they came.

People were running through the small streets that crisscrossed the facility, some chasing, some being chased. Most of the chasers had blood smeared across their faces, and were so intent on their prey that they ignored anyone and everyone else around them.

A few people tripped and fell in their attempted escapes and were set upon by the chasers. Cardoza could see some of them jerking and twisting after they were down, trying to get away while the others began biting and tearing away at any flesh that was exposed.

He almost lost his fast-food dinner when he saw a woman who had fallen, succumb to a biter, despite a last ditch spray of pepper spray to his face, and have nearly all of the flesh torn from her nose with a single bite. His training took over, and he sent several bullets from his service piece through her attacker's chest.

He rushed to her side when the maniac had fallen off of her, and he tried to render assistance.

Frantic and thinking she was still under attack, the woman continued screaming as she hit and kicked at him and jerked her head back and forth.

Nothing he said calmed her. He wasn't even sure she could hear him as panicked as she was.

She started coughing when the blood from her torn nose started leaking down into her nasal cavity and was sucked into her lungs between screams.

Not wanting to injure her even more, Cardoza backed off a bit and came in from the side. He rolled her over onto her side. That's when he noticed the plastic card that was at the end of a lanyard around her neck. He reached in and grabbed it, keeping away from her constant wild fist swings. It was a white, laminated ID card.

"KREM 2 Spokane (CBS news) Jamie Davis"

Cardoza let go of the card and shook his head. He'd seen her on the news before. Looking at her now, he doubted she would ever look the same as before the nose bite, and he was sure she would have mental trauma for the rest of her life—if he could keep her from drowning in her own blood.

"Dispatch, Cardoza requesting an ambulance for a white female, mid-thirties, bleeding copiously from the nose and multiple other wounds to the face and upper body."

Silence

"Dispatch, Cardoza, did you copy my last?"

He was about to call it out again when he heard quick shuffling sound on gravel. He turned towards the noise, but his view was blocked by the corner of a building and his police cruiser.

"Damn it," he said, standing from his crouch just long enough to see through the glass of his open car door. He really didn't want to let Miss Davis thrash about any more.

Coming around the corner was a sight that chilled his blood. It was one of the DARPA security guards, decked out in full riot gear—minus the helmet, dragging a clear shield as he staggered towards Cardoza, feral hate clear as day in his blood hazed eyes. What almost froze Cardoza's heart though was the complete lack of a lower jaw as if someone had shot it off with a shotgun at close range. He must have been shot in one of the legs as well because one of them had blood running in rivulets and wasn't bending properly.

The guard was giving him the willies.

He glanced down at Miss Davis. She had stopped her screaming and thrashing and now leaned forward on her knees with her head resting against the gravel. He thought he saw tears leaking from the corner of her eye, but it was hard to tell through her scraggly hair that draped down across her temple and cheek.

He looked back up at the approaching guard, thinking he might have to draw his gun and shoot him if he turned out to be as crazed as the other chasers. His hand floated down by his gun, but he kept his eyes up on the approaching menace.

That's when fire shot through his fingers, and he screamed in pain.

Looking down, he saw Miss Davis leaning forward with her mouth clamped down on his gun hand. She shouldn't have been able to contort her body the way she was. The human body just wasn't designed to twist that way.

He tried to yank away his hand, but she refused to let go. She started jerking her head back and forth, like a dog playing tug-o-war with a rope. Yanking and yanking away from her, he began to stop thinking rationally and went into a panic. She just wasn't letting go, and in his peripheral vision he could see the guard coming closer.

Finally, dreading the results that were sure to follow, even while believing it was the only reasonable thing left to do, he cocked back his left arm and gave the crazed Miss Davis a wicked uppercut, right into the underside of her jaw.

The pain was intense, and he found himself blinking back more tears than he could contain. Looking down at his shooting hand, he saw what he feared. He was missing the lower three fingers. They'd been sheared clean off by her sharp teeth. All he had left intact was his thumb and pointer finger. The rest were just bloody, little nubs.

But Miss Davis wasn't satisfied. She wanted more, and lunged at him, her mouth open in a snarl, blood dripping from her teeth.

He was already pushing himself to his feet. Her bulk crashed into him, pushing him up and back faster than he was ready to accommodate. The gravel slipped under his feet, giving him the extra distance he needed. He twisted to the side as soon as she had a grip on his arm, and it yanked her off balance.

She landed in the dirt at his feet.

He took the opportunity to run to his car, narrowly ducking under the outstretched arm of the guard who had finally made it within range. The guard changed his trajectory as soon as Cardoza had slipped around him.

As Cardoza managed to get the key into his cruiser's ignition and turn the car back on, he looked back up at the chasers. There were three now. He recognized the first one who had been chasing Miss Davis before she had gone mental. Apparently a few bullets to the chest weren't enough to put him down for good. How was that possible?

Realizing that the city lawyers were going to have a field day with what he was about to do, and further realizing that at this point he just didn't care anymore, he threw the car in gear and hit the gas. He jerked the wheel and let the back of the vehicle body slam all three of them.

A smile cracked his lips as he rushed away from DARPA, but it soon turned to a grimace as the throbbing pain broke through the adrenaline that had spiked in his system in the heat of battle.

By the time he had driven to the Kootenai Medical Center, the Eastern-most hospital in town, and stumbled out of his seat, he couldn't remember why he had driven there. By the time an ER nurse had come out to bring him in for medical attention, he was hungry.

She looked pretty tasty.

Chapter 11: An Awakening

The annoying klaxon horn had finally stopped sounding the contamination alarm inside the lab.

Richard felt his ears ringing and thought his head might explode from the pressure he was feeling inside. His eyes felt more tired than the rest of his body and they were burning. The lights in the lab suddenly felt too bright. He wanted to hide and sleep. It even felt like a tremendous effort just to breathe. He sensed his thoughts slowing down and in his sluggishness wondered if he was about to become a zombie.

Harper had stabbed him with the hypodermic needle. There had been a small amount of that golden colored solution still inside. Even if the amount had been miniscule, a "zombie" bite was the means of communication. There had to have been at least as much of the solution in the needle as in the typical amount of saliva that would be passed into a wound by a bite.

I have to warn the McIntyres. They are nice people. I should free them and give them a fighting chance against me before I fully turn. Then if someone comes to rescue them, they'll have a chance to survive the coming holocaust...Oh, Linda, I should have just said 'Screw Harper,' and gone there to protect you. Must I always be such a fool?

A picture of Jeff's face popped into his head, and he winced. Now Linda would lose both of the men she loved.

I need to release the McIntyres, he thought again.

But he didn't.

He felt so tired.

211

His head drooped to his chest.

He closed his eyes and sat down.

Leaning back against one of the counter cabinets, he let his head rest on his arms, which were in turn resting on his knees.

He didn't know how long he sat there before he heard Jason.

"Listen"

"Wha—" he started to say before realizing that he had heard perfectly well and didn't needed to have it repeated.

Listen to what? he thought.

At first all he heard was his heartbeat. Then he noticed the air filtration blowing through a vent overhead— a whiny torrent of air flow, louder than he remembered having heard it before. Distantly, he heard the fans turning, the slightest hint of metal on metal contact where the fan shaft needed some lubrication. Then he heard them breathing, both of them. It sounded loud, actually, and very slow. He almost felt like he could hear the air moving around the individual hairs in their noses. He chuckled to himself. That would just be silly.

What am I supposed to be hearing?

He strained his hearing as far he could imagine. His eyes were open, and he suddenly realized that they weren't hurting any more—even with the red light still flashing.

Footsteps. Distance footsteps.

At least that's what he thought they were. But that couldn't be. They were far enough away that they would be coming from somewhere outside the lab, which was hermetically sealed, drastically cutting out the amount of anything, to include sound, from the outside that could get through the walls into the lab and vice versa.

When he heard his heart beat again, he realized that his sense of hearing was more acute than it had ever been in his life.

And his vision—he looked around and found that he could read the fine print on a chart posted close to fifteen feet away.

"Do you hear it?" Jason asked, sounding excited.

"The air is on," Hanna replied. "Oh my god, the air is back on."

Jason smiled and bobbed his head.

"They're going to come get us out of here. We may be trapped, but at least now we won't suffocate."

Richard smiled back at him, but in his mind he felt a little worried. His gun was out of ammo. The people coming would have guns with full magazines. They were trying to kill him.

And he suddenly couldn't explain why everything seemed to be moving in slow motion except for the action in his head. It was like he could think faster. He felt more aware of his surroundings than he had ever been before.

Is this what it's like to be on speed?

He felt super-charged, like he had so much energy to burn, so much he could accomplish, but his body was calm. He had no idea what had happened to the fatigue he had been feeling just a little earlier, but he was no longer worried about it. In fact, he felt pretty good.

Another sound registered.

Someone was at the front door to the main lab. He could hear them pushing buttons on the electronic keypad connect to the access card reader. He heard the small beep the reader made when a card had been accepted and then heard the outer door begin to open.

Whoever was out there was coming in.

Richard dove out of sight, past the McIntyres, and crouched low. Steeling himself for a fight, he turned towards the inner door and blew out a few quick breaths.

Chapter 12: Get It On

Mercer swiped the pass McNeil had given him. The card reader display flashed red and showed a message.

"Warning: Fire detected in berth 23; Activation system malfunction. Halon extinguisher not engaged."

"Damn it," he muttered. "What is he doing in there?"

The light flashed red, indicating that he was running out of time to enter a PIN code.

Seven-two-seven-two

The card reader beeped, and the indicator light turned green.

He pushed open the door and stepped inside.

"Come on; come on," he said, bouncing with impatience, as he stood in the center of the containment room.

Closing his eyes, he waited for the UV lights to turn on and off and the small jets of air to do the same.

The magnetic locks on the inner door clicked open, and he pushed into the lab.

Harper, you had better not have gone and set yourself on fire... What the hell?

He stopped short when he saw the McIntyres sitting on the floor, their hands cuffed behind them to the steel table.

I am so screwed! Where is Harper? He thought, pulling his handgun from the drop-holster at his thigh.

Motion at the edge of his peripheral vision caught his attention, and he turned to see what—or who—it was.

Someone slammed into him before he had turned his head and gun far enough to get them in his sights. He toppled over and fell on his back, the added weight of his attacker knocking the air from his lungs and the gun from his hands.

Richard tackled Mercer as soon as the super soldier was through the door. The gun went sliding across the floor, and for the slightest micro-second he felt like going after it.

But he didn't.

He had the element of surprise, and he decided to exploit it to the fullest. He began raining down punches into the man on the floor.

Mercer quickly raised his arms to cover his face and shield himself from the blows.

Richard landed a few punches through Mercer's guard but then lost his balance when the man bucked his hips. He fell forward, and Mercer pushed against him with the enhanced strength of a super soldier.

Falling back and away from Mercer, Richard caught himself on another steel table next to the McIntyres, causing it to slide across the tile floor and then tip over onto its side. He gained his feet then looked back to find Mercer rolling off of his back and searching for his gun.

He found it and lunged.

Fortunately for Richard, he didn't make it far. Mercer slipped on some of the blood that had been beat out of him, and he came up short.

Without thinking, Richard slammed his fist down on the table leg, snapping it away from the table. He gripped it in his hand and then jumped at Mercer.

Mercer grabbed the gun and whipped around to find Richard, his finger already applying tension to the trigger.

Landing with his feet to either side of the super soldier, Richard slammed the hollow end of the table leg through Mercer's chest.

Mercer instantly deflated, but still managed to squeeze off a round, punching a hole through Richard's ear.

Richard registered the pain that sprouted in his ear but ignored it. He watched Mercer's hands fall to his sides.

He was dead, the table leg plunged right through his heart.

Remembering the regenerative capabilities these Wagner had demonstrated before, Richard decided to make sure this was one super soldier that he didn't have to fight again. Dropping to his knees, he leaned forward, grabbed Mercer's head between his hands, and squeezed with all of his strength.

The head popped like an over-ripe melon, blood spraying the wall behind them.

With the back of his hand, Richard wiped away the blood that had splattered up onto his cheeks and forehead and turned away from the deformed mass of pulp that remained of Mercer's head. He stood and flicked his hands at the floor. Pink and white matter fell off, but some of it remained.

He looked at his hands and shivered.

Adrenaline coursed through his body, leaving him feeling a little shaky. He stepped away from the body and staggered towards a wash basin. He washed the muck from his hands and face then took an additional moment to compose himself before turning back to the McIntyres.

"I'm sorry you had to see that," he said, his voice just barely in check enough not to crack.

They looked at him with wide eyes but said nothing.

"Here let me get you out of those handcuffs," he said, walking towards them. "We should go."

"We?" Hanna asked.

Richard paused. He had assumed he would be taking them with him, but now he reconsidered. He didn't intend to keep them prisoner, and he didn't want them to think that he did.

Bending down, he released Hanna and then her husband.

"If your offer to help fight the rogue nano-bugs is still good, yes," he replied. "From here on out, you are no longer my prisoners, nor are you the prisoners of the Defense Intelligence Agency—the agency I contracted with."

"You still haven't shown us proof that our colleague is the bad guy here," Jason said.

Richard nodded.

"Come with me, and I will—I promise," he said. "But right now we need to get the hell out of here. I just took out one of your Elite Warrior Enhancement Series guinea pigs. I don't know how many more are in the area gunning for me, but I'd be willing to bet there *are* more."

Jason nodded and looked to his wife. She nodded to him as well.

Richard swayed on his feet, but caught himself on the counter.

"Why do I feel exhausted all of a sudden? I feel like I haven't slept in years; and I'm hungry—so hungry," he said before his eyes fluttered and rolled up into his skull. Then he passed out and fell to the floor.

Chapter 13: Martial Law and Murder

President Nelson sat in a high-backed, leather chair in the Oval Office. His hands rested on the circa 1880 *Resolute* desk, his eyes were closed, as his makeup specialist brushed anti-shine powder on his cheeks, nose, and forehead. The soft bristles felt like angel kisses, supremely relaxing.

"That's enough. Sheila. Thank you," Dunwoody said, as he walked in from the adjoining office.

Sheila looked at the President's assistant and nodded. She swept her brush over Nelson's forehead one last time then straightened, gathered her cosmetics kit, and left the room.

Nelson opened his eyes and sighed.

He'd had to call an emergency press meeting because some clown out west had released a video, supposedly taken from Joshua Harper's hard drive, that outlined their entire plan, all of their players, even him. He had to nip this in the bud before this video gained too much ground online. It had already been viewed by far too many people. If it weren't for Benson's men monitoring the internet for just this kind of exposure, he didn't know how he would have caught it in time. Fortunately, this was a possibility for which they had a contingency plan.

"They're ready for you," Dunwoody said, meeting the President's eyes.

Standing, Nelson stepped out from behind the iconic desk. He wore a dark blue suit jacket over a white shirt and a red tie. His hair was perfectly combed, and his face was appropriately somber.

"That's the perfect look for the occasion," Dunwoody said, inspecting the President from head to toe. "Excellent expression. Now all you need to do is stick to the tele-prompters."

Nelson nodded and pinched his lips together.

"Don't worry," Dunwoody continued. "If you make any mistakes, we'll edit them out. The ticker at the bottom will still say 'Live' when the people see it, so no worries. You'll be fine."

Nelson smiled and chuckled.

"It does feel good to be in the final phase doesn't it?"

Dunwoody nodded and returned the smile.

The President sighed one last time, set his expression back to "somber," and stepped out of the Oval Office, Dunwoody following right behind him. He walked down the hall and through a sliding door into the press briefing room.

"Ladies and gentlemen, the President of the United States," said Press Secretary Humbolt, from behind the podium before stepping off to the side.

Nelson walked to the podium, put his hands on the rim of each side, and looked up to the teleprompter positioned in line with the press cameras.

"Good evening, America. I come to you with a heavy heart tonight. As you know, over the last few days our great nation has been under attack. Intelligence now confirms that the sporadically spaced biological attacks that have been deliberately targeted to infect our citizenry are the work of narco-terrorist groups operating out of South America.

"The method of initial delivery is believed to have been through the ingestion of tainted narcotics and recreational drugs smuggled into the country over our southern border. Further delivery is known to be through the bites of the initially and all subsequently infected."

The announcement raised the eyebrows of most members of the press who listened in the seats in front of him, but as they had been told before the President's entrance, questions would have to wait until after the speech. No one wanted to be ejected from such an important conference, so they each remained silent.

"These attacks are reported to be widespread on an unprecedented scale. To combat these heinous acts and to prevent any further attempts on the lives of our citizenry, it is my duty to engage in and direct an unprecedented response.

"I am hereby declaring a National State of Emergency, and I am authorizing FEMA, with the assistance of the US military, local law enforcement entities, and the CDC to implement and enforce Executive Order twelve-six-fifty-six. This is effectively a declaration of martial law."

Several members of the press gasped.

Nelson's eyes moved forward and back as he continued to read from the teleprompter.

"To keep the American people safe, I have issued orders to the commanders of each State's National Guard as well as the chain of command for USNorthComm to begin quarantining infected areas and limit travel in the areas surrounding these zones. They have already begun deploying. Their combined mission is to secure the homeland. They are further tasked with sealing our country's borders against further invasion by drug smugglers and the infected, as well as evacuating uninfected citizens from the zones surrounding the most infected areas to safe zones that are already being established. They are also tasked with taking the fight to the enemy.

"Our resolve is unmatched. We as a country will not be defeated. We will not allow these criminals to destroy our way of life.

"In order to facilitate the accomplishment of our objectives so that we can return to life as we knew it and to rebuild our great country, I am nationalizing all forms of transportation and communication. To prevent the further spread of panic-inducing rumors, I am temporarily shutting down access to the internet. Panic will only make a grave situation worse, so rumor-mongering will not be allowed. FEMA has people in place who will keep all of you in the public informed of what your government is doing to protect you. This situation is trying enough as it is. We don't need things to get out of control. There have been rumors online already about government conspiracies and finger pointing. Please recognize these for the frauds that they are.

"Just like after the attacks on 9-11-2001, the airspace will be restricted except for federally approved flights.

"There are infected among us. The CDC has already begun studying the infection and will, hopefully soon, have a cure. Until then, I must implore each of you to stay in your homes. Do not go into public any more than absolutely necessary. Food, water, and medical supplies will be distributed to those that need them.

"This will be one of the most difficult times in our history, one in which we will all need to pull together with determination and hard work to show these narco-terrorists that Americans don't break even in the face of supreme hardship. Let us not ever lose hope.

"We will succeed. We will survive. And when this trial of tribulation is over, we will be stronger than ever.

"Good night, America. Stay strong, and God Bless."

The President stepped away from the podium, and the press, sensing that the time they had been promised was about to slip away, could no longer hold their questions.

Nelson looked at them degenerate into a moving, shouting mass of unintelligible chaos and pointed to his press secretary. He kept his somber expression as he passed back out through the sliding door into the hall to the Oval Office. As the door slid shut behind him, the noise was reduced to a quiet rumble.

Dunwoody stepped to his side and chuckled.

"Poor Humbolt. He looked like he had been pole axed when you left."

Nelson laughed as he entered his office, giving his protective security detail a nod as he crossed the threshold.

"Let him deal with all the noise. That's why I hired him.

"So what do you think?" he asked, as he sank back into his comfortable chair behind the antique desk.

Dunwoody pursed his lips, tilted his chin up, and gave a slight shrug of his shoulders.

"I think the majority of Americans will obey long enough for the situation to get well and truly out of hand. By the time any of them act it will be too late. And I think the small percentage of those that don't follow directions will not be large enough or informed enough to make a difference. In less than a week the country's backbone will be broken and then it will just be a matter of waiting for its last dying gasps and spasms to pass. Then we can move on to our endgame. I'm sure Benson is quite happy with your actions so far."

Nelson smiled as he nodded and then leaned back in his chair and closed his eyes to imagine what the world would soon look like.

"But another matter warrants your attention before we can retire for the evening," Dunwoody said. "One I was hesitant to bring up before the meeting, for obvious reasons. A little less stress makes for better acting."

Nelson sighed and leaned forward.

"Now what?" he asked. "More threats from China?"

"No, something right here in our own neighborhood. Blake Howard is a journalist with FAUX news. I have given him preferential treatment in the past because he has worked with us to soften some of the harder stories to originate from this office in the past."

"Ok, so what's the problem?"

"It seems the time for softball is past. He started asking questions about the Governors. He began linking their reported illnesses with the annual ball you hosted here last week."

"Damn," the President swore, as he looked down at the surface of the desk. "Has anyone else asked about the connection?" he asked, looking back up to his assistant.

"So far, no. If we can keep this quiet for a little bit longer then it won't matter if the rest of them find out. We will have complete control of the airwaves, so they won't have a platform to shout from."

"Meaning until we do have total control, Mister Howard and his ilk are going to have to be disappeared."

Dunwoody nodded in agreement.

"Where is he?" Nelson asked.

"Just down the hall. A few of your more trustworthy agents are sitting on him."

Nelson stood and exited through the same door he had entered just a few minutes before. Turning, he walked down another hallway. His security detail followed.

The hallway ended at the office he had occupied as Vice President until just over a month ago. Another of his agents waited outside the door. As he approached, the agent turned the door handle and opened the door for him.

Nelson stepped into the small office where the Vice President's secretary would greet VP guests then crossed to another door that led to the actual VP office. He entered to find Blake sitting in a chair in front of the VP's desk and an agent in front of and behind the desk, effectively keeping Mr. Howard detained.

Blake looked over his shoulder as the President entered and began to stand up.

"Sit down," the agent behind him ordered, as he pushed the reporter forcibly back down into the chair.

"So Blake," Nelson said, as he walked around to stand behind the VP desk. "You don't mind if I call you Blake do you?"

Blake shook his head, but the President had already continued as if his answer didn't matter.

"I didn't take you for one to cause trouble, Blake. I guess I was wrong."

"Mister President, unlike some of my associates, I am normally all about going easy on Republican administrations, but this is just too much," Blake said, finding his courage. "Of the fifty state governors, only the two that didn't make it to the Governor's Ball that you threw have not become ill with this weird disease that is starting to go around. The other forty-eight all got sick at the same time…after attending your event. Don't you find that even a little strange?"

Nelson shrugged.

"Not really," he replied. "I didn't realize you were such a follower of conspiracy theory. Talk like that will only make matters worse you know."

"The American people have a right to know what is going on," Blake said, giving the President a look of pure disgust.

"Not anymore they don't," Nelson replied. "At the press briefing that you just missed, I declared martial law. Those freedoms of speech and of the press that your type is always using to defend your annoying meddling, well, they're gone. I abolished them."

"What? You can't just order—"

"Max," Nelson said, interrupting the livid reporter and looking to the agent standing behind him. "Dispose of this would you?"

"Yes, Sir, Mr. President," the agent replied. "With pleasure."

Max reached into his suit and pulled out his issued handgun.

"Too noisy and too messy," Nelson said, shaking his head.

Max nodded and put the gun away. He looked up to his fellow agent and gave him a quick chin lift. The other agent looked at what Max was indicating then nodded and stepped forward.

"You can't do this to me," Blake was saying, as Max stepped up behind him and put a massive arm around his throat and the other behind his head. The other agent slammed his hands down on Blake's keeping them pinned to the VP's desk.

Max tightened his grip on Blake's throat until the reporter screeched out a final whimper then went still. With a little more pressure, there were some bone-popping crunches as his esophagus gave way.

"No trace," Nelson said, as he left the room.

The agents nodded and watched him shut the door.

"We're going to need a mop and bucket," Max said.

The other agent looked at him quizzically.

"He pissed himself."

They both shook their heads then went about making the corpse disappear.

Chapter 14: Wrong Kind of Dream

Time passed in a void of darkness and haze. At one point Richard thought he heard screaming somewhere nearby, but he couldn't see anything and it faded away.

And he dreamed.

Strange dreams that made no sense.

He was flying below pink clouds in a small, single-engine airplane. Out the passenger window, an enormous paper coffee cup was a mountain resting on blades of grass that were like redwood giants. It was urgent that he reach his destination, but he couldn't remember why—or even where. He didn't know how long his journey would take now that he was the size of a mosquito. He just knew that he had to make it and that time was against him.

At one point his eyes fluttered opened, and though his vision was hazy, he thought he recognized the person leaning over him, blocking the light.

"Linda, is that you?" He tried to ask, but the darkness returned before he regained enough consciousness to be coherent.

He was in a city he hadn't been in since he was a child. Everything looked as he remembered. Why he was down by the river, he didn't know, but he wasn't worried because he could see the usual afternoon traffic headed home just a stone's toss away. Beyond the road was a stone wall surrounding a nice gated community. Even further back was a small hill covered in green grass and more empty land.

A gentle breeze caressed his face. He closed his eyes and turned into the wind, enjoying its silky touch.

A flash of light dazzled him through his eyelids, and he realized that he was dreaming a scene he has had in his head several times before. He was afraid to open his eyes but knew that he must.

There it is, just as he remembers having seen it uncounted times before: A mushroom cloud rising into the sky, threatening to blot out all life in its wake.

He runs.

He hasn't died every time in this dream, hasn't had his flesh scoured from his bones by an enormous wave of fire. Sometimes the blast passes over him as he reaches a drainage ditch just in time. He can see that life-saving depression in the ground ahead of him. He pushes himself even more.

A mechanical scream comes from off to his right. Without slowing down, he looks over to the source of the sound and sees a helicopter falling out of the sky, its rotors tearing into the tree tops that line the river, black smoke trailing away behind it. The pilot is trying to regain control with no success. The nuclear detonation's electromagnetic pulse effect has crippled the electronics that are required to fly the complex aircraft.

It is drifting toward him.

Would it be better to be chopped to bits by the helicopter's rotors or burned to a crisp by the approaching wave of thermal nuclear energy?

He jumps for the ditch.

Heat and thunder rushes by overhead. He turns over onto his back and sees the blast wave rolling by.

The helicopter crashes into the ground close to him and he looks at it. It is too close. The rotors are still moving. One of the jagged stumps of metal spins toward him, and he knows it is going to cut right through his face.

Well, this is a new way to die…

Flash

He sees the prison cell that holds a zombie in shackles against the wall. It's the video from Harper's hard drive again. The zombie is thrashing against its restraints trying to get at its cellmate. In the deepest recesses of his mind he knows without a shadow of a doubt that Donovan Clarke, Jeff's informant, is supposed to be shackled in the cell with the zombie; but for some reason he looks different.

He wills himself closer for a better view, even though he knows he doesn't really want to see what is about to happen to Don.

Long hair covering the face…

That's not right. Don was balding.

Skinny…feminine frame… What? That can't be right.

The hair shifted as the head turned up to face him.

Linda!

The zombie's shackles fall to the floor.

Linda screams as its jagged teeth tear into her neck, spraying blood all over the cell.

No!

Chapter 15: Proof

"Richard, wake up."

He opened his scrunched eyes and immediately experienced such clarity of vision that the feeling almost took his breath away. He saw mountains and valleys in the minute texture of the surface of the ceiling panels, and all of the colors in the room were so vibrant—as if they were bleeding color. He also differentiated immediately the dream he had been having and the real world.

"You are feeling the enhancement effects, aren't you," Hanna said.

Richard looked at her and nodded.

"This is so weird," he said. "It's like I've been living in analog and now all of a sudden I'm not only living digital but digital high def."

Hanna nodded and smiled at his wide eyes as he looked around the room and even raised a hand to look at it up close.

"We have heard that before from some of our subjects."

"Your super soldiers."

"Yes, they have been called that a time or two," she replied. "Their physical attributes have been enhanced, but we can't change the laws of physics. We can't make them fly like Superman."

Richard laughed.

"I almost feel like I could fly though," he said.

"And you're not bulletproof either, hotshot," she said.

Richard smiled at that.

"Come on; get up," she ordered. "You owe us an explanation. You promised us proof."

He nodded, turning serious again.

"How long have I been sleeping?" he asked as he tossed back the covers and sat up. Looking down he saw that he was dressed in sweat pants and t-shirt.

The look on his face must have conveyed some of his thoughts because she didn't answer his question right away.

"No, I didn't undress and redress you. Jason did. And before you go any further you should know that Jason and I are not just married. We are happily married. Ok? So don't try that road."

Richard looked at her in surprise and shook his head.

"I didn't mean…"

"Two days," she said, interrupting and changing the subject.

"Two days?" he almost yelled. "Why have I been out for two days? There's no way it takes that long…"

"We sedated you," she replied.

"But"

"We kept you under after you passed out because at first we weren't sure we should really trust you at all."

He was silent as she paused.

"And then we saw the people you claimed were going to be infected with a nano-series created by Josh Harper. There was definitely something wrong with them. Their movements were jerky and disjointed, as if they were marionettes being bounced around on strings by a puppet master. As if each of them had become Bernie from that old movie Weekend At Bernie's—only far more aggressive and violent and blood thirsty.

"We laid you down here in our home away from the labs where you would be safe while you recovered and then we went out and captured one of the slower, more injured of the infected. We took her to our lab and ran some tests."

Richard listened as he watched her sight grow distant. She took on a thousand yard stare.

"What we found explained a lot about their characteristics, but raised a whole slew of other questions—questions we wouldn't be finding answers to in the lab."

She turned towards him, and she looked like she came back to herself.

"And that's where I come in isn't it?" he asked.

She looked him in the eyes and nodded.

"Yes, that's where you come in."

Richard turned the laptop towards them and opened the folder that contained Harper's digital diary.

"Here you go. In Harper's own words. See for yourself. And while you're verifying my claims, do you mind if I use your phone to call my fiancé? She's gotta be worried sick by now."

"You can try," Hanna said. "We've been trying the phones for the last two days and haven't been able to get through to anybody."

Richard picked up the receiver and dialed the number from memory. Instead of ringing, it automatically went to a recorded message.

"We're sorry. All lines are currently busy. Please hang up and try again later. If you have an emergency, hang up and dial 9-1-1. We're sorry. All lines are currently busy."

"Damn it," Richard whispered.

Jason looked him in the eyes, shook his head in a way that told Richard he was sorry the phone wasn't working, then turned to the Toughbook. Hanna joined her husband, and they read the damning evidence for themselves.

As usual, Jason and Hanna requested to have Saturday off and invited Shelley and me over for dinner and a movie. Though I don't have to give them Saturday off, I usually do. I had turned down their requests to have us over for dinner and watch movies for the previous several weekends, since Shelley has been away. Now that Benson has let her come visit me again—he's a nice guy, but he is too protective of his daughter—I decided to take them up on the offer.

We had dinner with them, and it was great. Jason really knows how to grill a steak, and Hanna's mashed potatoes were the perfect complimentary side dish. Afterwards we were all kicked back on the couch, watching Day of the Dead or Dawn of the Dead—one of those.

I didn't really pay attention, so I don't really know which one it was, and I don't really care. I'm not interested in horror flicks. I just know that it was a zombie movie and that the survivors ran to and held out in a shopping mall, of all places. Not important—what is important is that while we were watching, Jason said, "It's a shame we can't just make our own controllable zombies with our nanos instead of wasting the lives of so many Special Forces volunteers,"—or something to that effect.

The three of them laughed it off, but it really started me thinking about the possibilities having something like that would present. It would allow the Infinity Group to accomplish at least some of our goals—and possibly to do so several generations ahead of schedule. I know I would certainly like to be around to see completion.

I'll bet Benson would jump all over it, if I could make a series of "Zombie Nanos" that the Group would be safe from. If I could create zombies, we could eliminate over ninety percent of the humans infesting Gaia, and we wouldn't have to worry about contracting ebola or whatever other virus Benson has the others working on.

It all hinges on whether or not we can have a proven cure for whatever we unleash on the rest of humanity. I think I can get Benson to see things my way. After all, Ebola can mutate, making our counter-measures less effective or not effective at all—nanos cannot mutate.

I am almost positive I can make a workable series of zombie nanos and a safe guard for all Group members.

It's a shame the McIntyres aren't in the Group. Jason and Hanna both could really help a lot, if only they weren't so damned prejudiced in their favor of humans over all of the other organisms on the planet.

Gaia will decide.

"I'm responsible for giving him the idea for this madness?" Jason asked, horrified.

Hanna shook her head and grabbed her husband's arms.

"No," Richard replied. "They had plans for exterminating most of humanity already. You just started the spark of thought for something they are hoping is more controllable than Ebola."

Jason breathed out heavily before speaking again.

"You know, Josh used to be a really nice guy— none of this save Gaia bullshit. He didn't starting talking like that until after he met Shelley. She changed him."

Hanna nodded her agreement.

"Shelley was his rebound girl after his wife Patricia died," she added. "We invited them over fairly often because we were trying to reach out to him. Patricia was a wonderful woman. Josh was torn up after she died."

"How did she die?" Richard asked.

"She was trampled," Jason replied.

"What?"

Hanna nodded.

"Yeah, she was trampled by Black Friday shoppers. Josh claims she was in line waiting to buy a game console that was on sale. It was for her younger brother for Christmas. But something went wrong, the crowd turned nasty when the store didn't open their doors fast enough, and she ended up falling and being walked all over in their rush to get inside."

"I guess that makes a kind of sense," Richard said.

"What does?" Jason asked.

"Why he seems to have had a deep-seated hate for consumers in his diary entries; why he would be willing to kill off ninety percent of the world population and enslave the rest. He made billions of dollars off of his patents in nanotechnology, and he ended up despising anyone else who was a taker and not a maker."

"I wish we could have talked to him before he completely lost it," Hanna said. "I mean, I wish we had known."

She shook her head as she finished.

"I lay blame for my best friend's death at his feet," Richard said quietly. "That is why I came back to kill him. I might not have gone all the way if it weren't for the fact that in his diary here, he claims that their plan is beyond the point of no return. And if that's true—and it sure as hell sounds like it from what he put in there—then there won't be any courts left to try him in. We're talking complete breakdown and annihilation of society because of this stuff being introduced into the population.

"It might not be much, but at least I was able to see a little bit of justice meted out."

"I'm sorry for your loss," Hanna said.

Richard nodded.

"Now all I have left is my fiancé. She should be ok where she is at—for now anyway."

Jason shook his head.

"I don't know. The scenes that have been unfolding on TV look pretty bad. The big cities that have been hit are in chaos, and no one seems to know what to do about it, so the authorities everywhere are trying to lock down everything in their areas."

"Where is your fiancé?" Hanna asked after her husband had finished.

"She's out in Wyoming," he replied. "Cody, Wyoming," he added when he saw a weird look of worry cross her face. "Why that look?"

"I'm sorry," she replied, shaking her head. "It's just that the local news was saying how bad things were, and I heard them mention Idaho and Wyoming being bad in some places—not as bad as cities on the East coast, but still bad for this area."

"The State capitols seem to have been hit the hardest," Jason added. "But there is chaos everywhere."

"The governors," Richard said.

"What do you mean?" Hanna asked.

"I read in there," he replied, pointing at the laptop and Harper's diary that was on the screen, "that one of the events that signified a point of no return was the Governor's ball hosted by the President at the White House. And that was less than a week ago."

"So Josh found a way to have the each of the State governors contaminated with this new series and then take it back to their respective States," Jason said, finishing the line of logic that Richard had begun. "That would give the President a damn good reason to declare a national emergency and begin a martial law crackdown on the entire country without the citizenry resorting to armed resistance."

"Oh my god," Hanna said, bringing a hand up to cover her mouth.

The room was quiet for a few heartbeats, until Richard shook his head and broke the silence.

"I have to get to Wyoming. Linda is going to need my help. I already told her I would be going there as soon as I finished up my work at the lab."

Jason raised a single eyebrow at the mention of lab work.

"I've already been here too long," Richard continued. "I should have left the other night as soon as I finished dealing with Harper."

Jason and Hanna were silent as they watched an inquisitive look come over Richard's face.

"What happened to me that caused me to black out?" He asked, realizing that neither of them had mentioned anything about that part of the night.

"Well," Jason said, looking to his wife.

She nodded.

"We have seen something like it before," he continued. "In our volunteers for the E-W-E-S...some of them blacked out after they first received the series."

"Ok," Richard replied. "Why?"

"We believe," Hanna jumped in. "Mind you it isn't proven; we're just speculating here."

"Ok"

"We believe the nanos cause it when they first integrate with a host body. We think they take micronutrients from the cells in the body to replicate themselves faster than with the added raw materials that we usually have the volunteers ingest in tandem with the series injection."

"So, what? You're saying the little bugs are destroying my cells to make more of themselves?"

"Yes," Hanna replied. "At least they were. They injured your healthy cells because they provided the fastest source of needed materials.

"Well, that's just great," Richard said.

"They repaired the same cells that they injured," Hanna added reassuringly. "They just needed a deposit of raw materials to repay the loan they took out."

"Which we already gave you," Jason added. "While you were unconscious, we gave you supplements that we began giving to our volunteers with their first series of injections after we found out about the black-out side effect. You shouldn't have to worry about a repeat performance now."

"By now," Hanna interjected. "The series that was injected into you has already reached a saturation point. They won't need to replicate much more to accomplish whatever tasks Harper designed them for."

"But we don't know much about this new series he created because he kept us out of the loop on this one," Jason said.

"Well, let's hope everything I need to know is on there," Richard said, pointing to the computer.

"We can tell you everything we know about the E-W-E-S series of nanotech that Josh worked on as well. I'm sure much of his work on this new series is based on our combined original work."

Richard nodded and looked at him.

"I meant what I said about going to Wyoming. Did you mean what you said in the lab about helping me? Because if you did, that means you are coming with me."

The couple nodded.

"We meant it," Jason said. "We would rather stay here where we have access to a full lab to work on a possible cure or counter series to the zombie series, but I can see that it would be impossible for us to keep you from going to your fiancé. I'm a commissioned officer in the navy. I've seen plenty of your type. Men of tremendous resolve. Men who wouldn't quit even when they know they're beat."

Richard clenched his jaw. The man could just as easily be saying he was stubborn or a fool.

"But we will go with you," Jason continued. "Josh designed a mobile lab with nearly all of the same amenities as the lab we were working in when you broke in the other night and then he had DARPA build it."

"And it's parked right over there on the restricted level of the underground garage," Hanna said. "You do still have access to the garage don't you?"

"I'm pretty sure I can get us in there," Richard replied.

Jason nodded, and Hanna grinned.

"That's good because there is something we haven't told you yet," Jason said.

"And what would that be?" Richard asked.

"Well, you know how I said we have access to the lab here?"

"Yes."

"That's not entirely accurate anymore."

"Why not? What's the problem?"

"Zombies," Hanna replied. "And quite a few of them."

Chapter 16: Food and Friend?

Richard pulled back the curtain and looked outside. The first thing that struck him was that he was several stories above ground level. That shouldn't have surprised him, but it did. He hadn't given much thought to what floor the McIntyres lived on. He was familiar with the facility and the dorms, having lived there—on the ground floor, and until he looked out the window, he naturally thought of himself as being on the ground floor.

The second thing to impress itself upon him was the crowd of no longer totally human bodies that were milling around down below seen through a cloud of strange smoke. Most had wounds where they had been attacked and turned by other zombies. Their clothing was spotty with dried blood, and dirt was caked in some of the blood stains. Their faces were expressionless, their eyes sometimes rolling up into their skulls, unseeing.

The stench they had to be putting off was thankfully not penetrating through the moisture barriers built into the building's walls. Then he realized that what he had thought was smoke was actually swarms of flies flying above the bodies of the reanimated dead.

"Damn" he muttered. "How long have they been down there?"

"Since the other night when we first brought you up here," Jason replied. "I think we might have drawn them here when we returned from the lab after we caught and studied one of them inside."

"Why haven't they left though?"

Jason shrugged his shoulders.

"I don't know. They were pretty aggressive that first night. They've calmed down quite a bit since then, but I don't know why they still hang around right here. Maybe they can smell us."

"No," Richard said, turning his gaze back to the crowd outside. "Harper put in his diary that smell isn't a trigger for them. He felt that they lost their sense of smell after they had that crap put into them. I don't see how they could possibly smell us through their own stench."

Jason shrugged his shoulders and shook his head.

"Their hearing is pretty good, but their sense of smell and their sight are pretty crappy. The scary part is that they sense our bodies' electrical impulses and could follow us with that as long as we are within range."

"Within what distance?" Hanna asked, a worried look on her face.

"I don't know. That wasn't actually specified," Richard said, meeting her gaze, "But Harper said it wasn't as far as the eye can see, so there is the possibility that we can see them from far enough out to avoid them before they can detect us. Assuming, of course, that we are able to get away from these ones, get to the mobile lab or another suitable vehicle, and move out without being turned into one of them in the process."

Do you think they know we are up here right now?" Hanna asked.

Richard sighed and shrugged his shoulders.

"I don't know. Maybe there's just enough material in these walls to hamper their detection abilities so that they know there is something in the building without realizing it is us. Maybe there are others in their rooms that they are detecting. Who knows?"

"Do you think there are others?" Jason asked.

Richard snorted.

"You didn't check? I couldn't possibly know. I just woke up. Remember?"

Head down, Jason replied, "Right. No, we didn't check. We had a lot of other things on our minds."

Richard nodded his head.

"All right," he said. "No need to get bummed out. I'm not blaming you or anything. I'm just a little surprised. We'll just have to check before we leave. All right?"

"Yeah," Jason whispered, nodding in agreement.

Looking out the window, Richard could see the other dormitory buildings. One was where he had had his own rooms before this whole mess had started. A good thing too he realized, remembering the shattered glass door he had left behind him after bumping into Wagner. He wondered how many zombies had wandered into the other building.

"How safe is this building?" He asked. "I mean: were any of the doors left open when you came in? Were there any of these zombies inside that you know of?"

Jason shook his head.

"We haven't seen any of them inside the building, so far. They were right outside last we looked, but nothing made in yet that we've seen."

"Well, that's good, at least," Richard said. "We should still proceed under the assumption that some of them might have gotten in. We certainly don't want one of those things surprising us."

245

"It may have been cruel of us, but we chained the doors shut once we made it back from the lab," Hanna said, her voice somewhat subdued. "Those things were out there running around, attacking anything that moved."

She shook her head.

"We didn't want to take a chance that one of them might remember how to open the doors."

Richard nodded.

"That was smart. We don't know these things' capabilities. If one of them *had* remembered how to open a door and you *hadn't* locked them, we might not be having this conversation right now."

Hanna nodded and wiped away a tear that had begun to form in the corner of one of her eyes. She sniffed.

"I just can't stop thinking that maybe one of those poor people who were being chased out there might have survived if we hadn't locked them out."

"I can see how you would think like that, but you can't beat yourself up over this. This is one of those end of the world scenarios that no one ever thought could possibly happen, but it did. The normal rules for civilization no longer apply. You have to consider your own survival now above all else. The rest will come later after we have had a chance to adapt to this new reality, but for now—we survive."

Both of them looked at him and nodded.

He experienced a moment of déjà vu, as he looked at them looking up to him. He almost felt like he was a sergeant of marines over in the sandbox again with a squad of young men counting on him to lead them to safety.

"Anyway," he said, breaking the moment of silence. "Let's get ourselves together, so we can get out of here."

"Right," Jason replied.

"I would like one of you to come with me and together we will check the rest of the rooms in the building. See if we can find any other people who were holed up. The other of you would need to stay here and pack supplies."

"I'll go with you," Jason said. "I'd rather Hanna didn't face any more exposure to those things than can possibly be avoided."

"I think it will be safe enough inside the building, Jace," Hanna protested.

"Besides which," Jason continued, raising his voice a little louder, "I am absolutely horrible at planning and packing for trips."

Hanna laughed.

"Well, you're right about that. Fine, I'll stay and pack, but, Jason, you'd better be careful."

Jason smiled.

"Like you said, Sweety, it should be safe enough inside the building."

Richard looked up and down the hallway before stepping fully out of the safety of the McIntyre's living quarters. Jason followed right behind him.

Since he didn't have any of the guns he had brought back to DARPA with him, Richard carried an aluminum baseball bat that Jason had pulled out of the bedroom closet.

247

Jason also carried a bat, but his was wooden, and it was autographed by Barry Bonds. Up until this crazy week had started, he had actually been proud of the sports collectible and wouldn't have even thought of walking out of the room to potentially use it as a weapon. He still hoped he wouldn't have to use it. It was in mint condition. Inwardly he had cringed at the thought of Richard using it to bash some heads. He could just see someone's teeth scratching the finish or even becoming embedded in the wood. That was why he had handed over the aluminum bat first.

Jason shook his head at the thoughts that were going through his head. He wouldn't be retiring on his eBay sports memorabilia sales now. eBay was history.

Richard rested the bat on his right shoulder as he walked to the next door down the hall and raised his master key to the lock with his left hand. Turning the key and the knob, he pushed the door open and raised the bat to a more ready position.

"Hello—oo," Richard called softly. He didn't want to startle whoever was supposed to live there and in the process end up with a face full of buckshot. "Anybody home?"

No one answered.

He flicked on the lights and crossed the living room to look down the hallway to the bedrooms. The kitchen was to his right, and as he leaned over to get a more unobstructed view down the hall, he heard movement in the kitchen, like a cupboard opening on dry hinges.

The kitchen was somewhat dim, the window having a shutter to block outdoor light.

He thought he could see something lying on the floor in the corner. Was that big enough to be a person? He leaned forward a little more.

A crash sounded beside him, and he jumped. He instinctively brought the bat forward a foot to swing at whatever had scared the crap out of him, but then he stopped as he saw the flippant flick of a hairy tail as it went around the corner.

Jason blew out his breath.

"Oh my god," he choked, clutching the bat handle to his chest. "That damned cat almost made me piss my pants."

Richard responded with a nervous laugh, but he didn't say anything. He was intent on the lump that he could still see in the corner on the floor. He inched forward, raising the bat to strike should the lump lunge for him.

The light came on overhead and he flinched to strike, but then saw what he was stalking and laughed. It was a big bag of potatoes on the floor with an apron hanging from the counter, partly covering it. One of the apron strings was caught on an upturned edge of the wooden trim that bordered the tile counter top.

"Geez," he said. "We're only in the first room, and I've already got the willies."

"Me too," Jason replied. "Let's just do this and get out of here."

Richard nodded.

"You're right. Anyway, at this pace it will take all day."

Jason nodded.

"We ought to skip opening all of the doors and just take a look in through the front. If nobody answers after we poke our head in and shout then we should just move on to the next one."

"Yeah," Jason replied. "It will be safer that way too. If one of the zombie things charges you, you can just slam the door in its face and lock it. Right?"

Richard laughed.

"Exactly. A lot safer."

He laughed again and shook his head.

"What's so funny?"

"Oh, nothing," Richard said. "I just realized how foolish I've been. Here I was thinking Marine Corps style—clear every room, don't let a threat come in from behind. These things aren't going to be shooting at us. They'll be trying to bite us. You're right. We'll just close the doors in their faces."

Jason smiled and nodded.

"Come on, let's get out of here."

They closed the door behind them and painted a big "X" on the outside to show that they had already been there.

They moved on to the next room, and Richard unlocked and opened the door enough to yell inside. No one answered the call.

After a third room with no answer, Richard turned to Jason.

"McNeil put the facility on lockdown right around 9, 9:30 right?"

"I wasn't paying attention to the time," Jason replied. "Josh had us looking at how the molecular chain of crystallized…"

"Jason," Richard interrupted. "Not to be rude, but a simple 'yes' or 'no' would be great. I don't understand all of the scientific jargon that comes out of your mouth, and at the moment it isn't pertinent to the situation."

"Right, sorry. I don't know. Why do you ask?"

Richard nodded.

"I only bring it up because that's about the time, in my experience, that most of the staff that aren't still working are over at the rec center."

"You're right."

"So if McNeil put everyone on lockdown at about that time, most of the people we could potentially save would be over there."

"Yeah"

"Which also means there are going to be a lot fewer people to be found here."

Jason nodded his head.

"Sounds about right."

"Good. That should make this that much faster."

They moved on, knocking and poking their heads into the subsequent rooms on that floor. Not a single one showed any signs of life after their initial cat scare.

With one floor above them and three more below them, they decided to search the topmost floor before moving downward.

As they closed the fourth door on the top floor, a door just a little bit further down at the end of the hall closed shut. Instinctively they raised their bats to swing and looked up to see a chubby, bald man staring back at them in surprise. He wore a t-shirt and shorts but had leather work gloves on his hands. He had scratches and scabs on his scalp.

"Hi," Richard said, when he saw fear and intelligent thought in the man's eyes. He lowered the baseball bat and walked slowly towards the new arrival.

The stiffness that had taken over the man's body at suddenly finding them in front of him melted away at the sound of Richard's voice, and he took a breath.

"Hi," he answered. "Who are you?"

"I'm Richard, and this is Jason. We've been looking for survivors before we leave."

"I live downstairs on the fourth floor," Jason added.

Richard nodded.

"And I lived on the ground floor of the dorm across the street."

"Nice to meet you," he said guardedly. "I'm Scott. I live on this floor."

"Where are you coming from just now?" Richard asked, realizing that the door that had closed behind Scott accessed the stairs.

Scott didn't answer and appeared conflicted about whether or not to answer at all.

"I only ask because we want to make sure the building is secure and stays secure as long as we are inside. We don't want any of those things outside getting in."

Scott nodded.

"I was up on the roof," he offered. "I never went below this floor."

"Good," Richard replied. "So if any of them are in the building, it won't be because of you."

It was more of a question than a statement.

Scott nodded.

"And what were you doing up there?" Richard continued when Scott didn't say more.

"In case you hadn't noticed, the phones and the old internet are down now. The TV's are still receiving news broadcasts because the networks are sending the signals out via satellite, but nothing new is coming through. They're broadcasting the same footage from yesterday's recordings on a seventeen hour loop. I was just up there wiring in to some of the DARPA hardware, so I can use it with my system. I would like to know what is really going on out there. If the whole country looks like what we have downstairs then we are seriously screwed. If my modifications work, I should be able to find out more than what's being shown on the boob tube."

"Ok. You know, I don't remember seeing you around here before. What is it that you do for DARPA?"

"Well, you wouldn't have seen me much because I generally don't leave my rooms very often. People annoy me, and when I get annoyed I start itching like crazy. I don't like itching, so I stay away from other people."

He tried to keep a straight face, but Richard's eyebrows rose in surprise of their own accord.

"I write code," Scott continued, ignoring Richard's look. "Security software programs for some of DARPA's unmanned drones, and I can do that from my rooms."

"O-k," Richard replied. "Well, it wouldn't be very nice of us not to offer you a ride out of here when we leave, so I'm offering."

"Where are you going?"

"Wyoming"

"Why?

"Family and, hopefully, some level of stability that we won't be able to recoup here."

Scott nodded and itched his nose.

"When are you leaving?"

"Hopefully today. There are some things we need to see to before we get out of here, but they shouldn't take long."

Scott nodded again.

"I'll think about it," he replied. Give me a few hours ok?"

Richard pursed his lips and then nodded.

"Ok. Room 407 when you make up your mind…But don't take too long; we should leave before we lose daylight."

Scott nodded and itched at his earlobe.

"Already find us annoying?" Jason asked.

Scott realized what he was doing and put his hand down.

"Nah, I'm just a little hyped up right now," Scott said, looking down. "Surrounded by zombies," he muttered. "I'll be in my room. 519—back down there and around the corner."

Richard and Jason watched the man walk past them, head down, and turn the corner.

"Weird," Jason said.

Richard nodded.

They heard a door close from the vicinity of where Scott had said his room was.

"Come on, let's check the rest," Richard suggested, raising the bat to rest on his shoulder again.

Chapter 17: Drone

Scott Lewis sat heavily into his chair, popped a roasted vegetable Ritz cracker into his mouth, and began crunching away, as he typed the names of the two men he had just met into a special software program he had created. The program scoured the DARPA database as well outside agency databases for whatever information he requested.

"Let's see who you are," he said, accidentally blowing a few cracker crumbs onto his keyboard.

He frowned then grabbed an aerosol of canned air and blasted the offending organic matter away from his hardware. Putting the can down, he went back to the keyboard and hit the "Return" key. His program began crunching data, and he ate another cracker.

Swiveling around in his seat, he turned to another computer and began typing commands. Several lines of text appeared in response, and he pushed his chair away, swiveled around again, and picked up a game controller and a TV remote.

He turned on the TV, hit the "menu" button, and scrolled down to change a few of the settings. When he was finished, the TV showed a live view of the dormitory roof.

What he hadn't told Richard was that in addition to wiring into some of the hardware on the roof, he had also fueled up a drone helicopter and made it ready for flight. Now, with the drone controls in hand, he sent the helicopter into the air.

He kept it in a hover three feet over the roof, while he tested the controls. He didn't want to send the drone out untested only to find that one of its servos had broken since its last use and he would have to go get it through zombie infested territory or abandon its use altogether. No, testing beforehand was much smarter.

The computer chirped behind him. He glanced over his shoulder to see that the query on Richard and Jason had returned results. He considered putting off the drone flight to read through whatever his program had found, but quickly decided to forge on and read the results later.

The controls responded well, and everything seemed to be working the way they had been designed, so he sent the chopper over the edge of the building and flew a quick circuit around the facility scanning each of the building rooftops. He didn't find anything new, so he brought the drone back to ground zero and lowered it down to within a few feet over the heads of the zombies below. Slowly and methodically he flew over the crowd and captured images of their faces. He flew the drone in a slow circle around the building until he was confident that he had captured each face. Then he expanded outward through the facility.

He kept an eye on his fuel level which was displayed as an animated gauge icon on the lower left hand corner of the screen. Other icons gave him the drone's speed, direction of travel, altitude, time in flight, etc. but he mostly ignored those. He primarily focused on capturing faces on the drone's camera, his remaining fuel, and where he had been versus where he still had to go.

He was looking for one face, the one face that had eluded him since this nightmare had begun. As long as that face didn't appear among the zombies, he would continue to search. If he found it among them, his time would have been for nothing, and his heart, he was sure, would break.

Melany Garcia

He remembered the first time he had seen her. She had stepped off the DARPA bus just inside the gate along with a handful of other new staff members. The bright sunlight had accentuated the slight brown tint to her dark hair. She had smiled at something one of the other new arrivals had said.

Feelings of regret formed in his chest. He had never spoken to her. Off and on for the last three months he had watched her from various cameras around the facility and occasionally from one of the drones that he handled. He knew everything about her that could be found online or in any of the various databases around the country that could be accessed remotely. He had read her University of Florida transcripts, become familiar with her social networking friends, even taken a virtual tour of the house her parents had put up for sale in Tampa.

But he had never worked up the courage to go talk to her. He condemned himself for being a coward.

His scalp felt itchy, but he couldn't get to it properly with his hands on the drone controls. He resorted to bringing the controls up and wiping his forearm across his head. The friction helped a little.

Sighing, he watched as gravel streets passed relentlessly across the TV screen. He was almost finished with his daily search of the facility grounds when he spotted a door open in one of the buildings that hadn't been open the day before.

It was a building that he had only circled around before because it hadn't previously been open and because it wasn't one of the areas staff were allowed. It was where the unmanned ground assault vehicles and other dangerous machines were kept.

He brought the drone to a hover several feet from the open door and looked at the image that was relayed to his TV. Blood was splattered all over the floor just inside the door. There wasn't a body anywhere in view that he could see. He had been into that building a few times to manhandle some of the UGVs before the world had gone to hell, so he knew it was largely an open room about the size of a standard school gymnasium. He couldn't see far into the room because of the lack of light inside.

If he could get the drone into the building he could switch to the night vision settings and easily see the inside, but the rotors were wider than the door. If he pushed forward too much more he would incapacitate his drone.

He considered what to do next. He thought about putting the drone as close to the door as possible and turning on the night settings anyway just to see if he could see anything more inside. The drone's fuel level decided it for him. It was running too low. He brought it back and landed it on the roof.

Once it had touched down and he had confirmed that it was running its deactivation for servicing sequence, he set the controller down and slid his chair over to one of his computer desks.

The first thing he did was activate the facial recognition program on the computer to which the video data was being streamed from the helicopter. Then, logging into an administrator account that he had set up for working within the DARPA intranet system, he pulled up the specs on the building he had just been observing. It was listed as an UGV storage area as he had expected, so he left that page and accessed the building's inventory record. He found the location of a model he could work with and exited the system.

Using another program he had written without DARPA's permission or knowledge, he remotely activated one of the smallest UGV drones in the other building. He chose one of the three Dragon Runners on loan to DARPA from QinetiQ North America's Technology Solutions Group. It was an electric model that didn't require him to be physically present to activate. Weighing in at just over twenty pounds, it was only slightly larger than some remote controlled race cars that were popular among hobbyists.

Once the Dragon Runner was on, he picked up the controller he had used for the helicopter drone and ran the UGV through a series of tests. The battery icon showed that it was fully charged and, in fact, still plugged in. He did a quick nomenclature information search and found that the charger should slide right out of the female charging slot, since it did not have a small bend in its design like some other small electronics do.

The Dragon Runner rolled off of the table it had been stored on and bounced, its night vision settings painting the scene in shades of green and gray. The view as it rolled along on rubber treads wasn't as smooth as that seen from the helicopter, but it wasn't bad enough to make Scott sick.

He double checked that the power cord was no longer plugged into the charging slot then directed the UGV towards the open door where he had seen the blood. As it approached, he slowed down some to absorb as much information as he could.

The open door was a beacon of bright light outlining the shapes of the larger canvas-covered UGV weapons platforms. The model he had chosen was designed for reconnaissance and surveillance missions, whereas the models before him were designed for actual combat missions. They could carry machine guns or rocket launchers, or in times of need they could be outfitted to carry wounded troops out of harm's way.

He picked up motion near the edge of the screen, so he rotated the camera to get a better view.

A person was walking towards the UGV. Even before he was able to get a clearer view, he could tell it was a zombie by the way it swaggered along with a painless limp, its arms hanging—not being swung slightly for balance. Dark streaks of what he guessed was blood made lines down the pale flesh of its arms.

Scott shook his head and sighed when it came close enough that he could see the face. The area around the mouth was smeared with blood, and it looked like it had been bleeding from the corners of its eyes at one point. He didn't recognize the person that the zombie had once been and after a moment of disappointment, he chided himself and told himself that he should be happy. At least it wasn't Melany.

He backed the small drone away from the zombie then directed it through a small maze of obstacles until he had it right in front of the open door. He found the blood on the floor and began following its path through the building. He almost hoped it would only lead to the zombie he had just seen.

The blood trail led to a set of stairs that went up to a loft area. He hadn't ever been up there himself, but he knew some of the security guys liked to hang out up there when they were tasked with perimeter security instead of one of the interior posts. It was supposed to be used for extra storage space, but he knew the guards like to have their "out of sight: out of mind" places.

He directed the UGV to the foot of the stairs and eased the control forward. The rubber tread on the UGV tilted upward into view on the screen, and he saw the rubber grip the wood. A little more pressure on the controller joystick, and the UGV began its climb up the steps.

His pulse quickened and his hands shook when the drone began to slip backwards on one of the steps, but he calmed when the tread found grip again and returned to inching its way upward. On the next step he saw that the edge of the tread was now covered with blood that he had driven it through without seeing. That would make the remaining steps a bit more of a challenge.

The last few steps did take longer, but he managed to direct it up without any mishaps. At the top of the steps he set the control down in his lap and wiped sweat from his face and head with a towel that he kept draped nearby for the purpose. Then he blew out a deep breath, picked up the controller again, and went back to surveilling the inside.

What he found once he rounded the corner was not at all what he had expected. Instead of a dark, dusty area with maybe a small table for playing poker or a chair to kick back and relax in, he saw a clean room with a bed against one wall, a table and chairs in the middle, and a storage cabinet set against the far wall. Someone had left the desk lamp on top of the cabinet turned on, so he could see well enough without needing the night vision settings on the robot.

The room was laid out as if someone had turned the loft into their own little studio apartment. All it lacked that he could see was a refrigerator and a computer. As a getaway it was about perfect.

Once he had taken in the layout of the room, he went back to looking for the source of the blood trail. It led right to the bed. He could just see the top edge of the comforter-covered mattress. A blood stain ran down the fabric to where blood had dripped and puddled on the floor.

His heart began to beat faster. He felt his fingers tremble. He wasn't sure he really wanted to know what was on top of the bed now. He found himself shivering and mentally kicked himself.

Knock it off, Scott. It won't be her. She wouldn't be up here. It's not her. This area was for the guards.

Setting the controller in his lap, he freed his hands and gave them a shake to get the blood flowing again. Tilting his head to the sides, he popped his neck then picked up the controller again.

Ok, here we go.

He set the brakes on the rear treads and hit reverse on the forward treads, causing the Dragon Runner platform to angle upward a few inches. Then he extended the boom on which the camera was mounted.

The top of the bed came into view. The sheets were rumpled and pushed together near the edge. Dried blood was everywhere.

Not a good sign.

Then he saw an ankle. Its olive skin was perfect and he felt his heart sink. The ankle was attached to legs that were beautiful despite the occasional little patches of dried blood that remained from contact with the bloody bed. The knees were almost blood free, but the thighs were completely covered in it.

He shook his head as his view moved up the torso. The body was naked, and it matched what he had visualized under Melany's clothes. The cleavage between those beautiful breasts no longer held any warmth for him, having served as a perfect valley for the river of blood that had flowed from that delicate neck that was now just so much meat resting in tattered strands against the bones of her exposed spinal column.

Scott's eyes went back to the breasts and spotted the little blue butterfly tattoo sticking out from under the upper edge of the dried blood line. He began to tear up, his vision turning blurry. He had seen that little tattoo a hundred times from the various camera vantage points that he was used to using when he had watched her move around during the day.

"No," he whispered in defiance. "No," a little bit louder. "No, goddamn it! No!"

He was on his feet and threw the controller against his sixty inch, LED HDTV. The glass screen cracked but continued to show the feed from the Dragon Runner. Sinking to his knees, he vomited then coughed and began sobbing into his hands.

"Goddamn it," he moaned over and over again.

The fantasies he had indulged in over the last few days ran through his head mocking him: fantasies of finding her alive, trapped and surrounded by a horde of hungry dead, waiting for rescue and of him saving the day with a fully loaded SWORDS combat drone blasting the horde to bits, walking up to her over the crunching bones of the recently fallen, and carrying her out to the safety of his room, where she would undoubtedly show him the gratitude and devotion he so desperately craved from her. He'd had plenty of fantasies of how she would show her gratitude.

And none of it would ever happen now.

At an intellectual level he knew he was exceptionally shallow, but he also knew that deep down inside he really did want a meaningful relationship with a woman, who needed to be beautiful, of course. He was tired of feeling lonely, tired of masturbation and pornography, tired of being tired.

For several more minutes he cried on floor, curled up in the fetal position. He deliberately kept his eyes closed. He didn't want to see the image on the TV screen. Never again. Then, gathering himself again, he crawled over, eyes down, and unplugged the TV. The Dragon Runner would just have to stay where it was. He wasn't going to use it again.

Now what? he thought. He needed something to fill the emptiness he was feeling inside. His thoughts wandered. Since it had been unsafe to leave the building for days, he had mostly concentrated on looking for Melany. Now that he had found her and no longer wanted her because of her transformation, he didn't know what to do.

He had also been doing daily searches online, looking for information on what was happening on a larger scale, but with the President's recent declaration of martial law, the internet had been shut down and many of his usual sources along with it. He knew the problem was a lot more widespread than it should have been if it were a natural outbreak of a disease. It had gone global and was completely out of hand in a matter of days. Nothing natural worked like that.

Remembering the two men he had met in the hall earlier and their offer to take him with them, he wondered what they were running to in Wyoming. Richard had said family. Did he really believe his family hadn't turned into those monsters?

He had at least a month's worth of food in his cupboards and maybe a week's worth of water and sodas if the power and water stopped working, which logic told him was bound to happen sooner or later, maybe not before he ran out of food, but one could never know.

And if the other staff that had been living in this building had stocked their kitchens like he had before they all went out and turned into zombies, then he could use their stocks as well. He could last here for a possibly a couple of years—well, maybe not that long. DARPA had their own power service, but would it last that long? He didn't know.

Whether I could survive here on my own or not, the issue is whether or not I want to. Do I really want to stay here and see Melany every time I see the drone controller or one of those things outside? Do I really want to think of her that way?

He shook his head.

I'd rather just forget. Richard believes there are people waiting for him in Wyoming. Really? Wyoming? Screw it. I'm tired of being lonely...and I can't stay here. Not anymore.

Walking to the closet in his bedroom, he moved aside the one suit he owned and several long sleeved shirts that he kept for the winter months and grabbed a backpack his mom had bought for him for Christmas two years back, her way of encouraging him to get out away from his computers and electronically dependent life.

Thanks, Mom. I'm glad you died without seeing this hell.

He packed a few changes of clothes then went back to the kitchen to pack the canned goods he kept in the cupboard.

Chapter 18: Hungry

The rest of the building was devoid of human life. They didn't find any undead inside either. They had seen a good number of zombies pressed up against the glass doors at the ground level, but the doors hadn't budged. The chains that Jason and Hanna had put in place were thick and unyielding. The door handles around which the chains had been wrapped and the frames in which the doors were set were all made of steel, and the tempered and laminated glass of the doors themselves was fairly strong as well.

As long as the zombies surrounded the building in an even press and didn't concentrate their efforts to get in on any one door, Richard thought the door would likely continue to hold. To be on the safe side, they tied the ground floor stairwell doors shut with the canvas fire hoses they found on spools set into glass-covered recesses in the walls.

If the doors into the building did shatter, and the zombies did come inside, they shouldn't be able to go any farther up into the human sanctuary. To be even safer, the men brought couches and other furniture from several of the second floor living rooms and piled them in front of the doors, which would have opened into the stairwells.

The elevators were a bit of a challenge at first. Richard didn't have the keys with him to lock them in place or to prevent them from going to go to the ground floor. Jason had the idea to just fill them up with furniture as well. If they could be filled up to capacity with, say, entertainment centers and bookshelves and dressers, there wouldn't be any room for the zombies to take a ride.

By the time they had searched the whole building, secured the stairwells, and filled the elevators, they needed a break.

"Well, I feel a little better knowing Josh's pets can't get in," Jason said, as he opened the stairwell door that accessed the fourth floor hallway.

"Me too," Richard said. "I just hope we won't have any trouble when it's time for us to go out."

Jason nodded.

"Yeah, I've been thinking about that. Do you think you can shoot enough of them to clear a path for us?"

"How? I ran out of ammo in the lab, and I haven't seen any of the guns or gear I was carrying then anywhere in your place."

"Right," Jason muttered. "I forgot. Look, I'm sorry for not bringing your things. It was just the two of us. You were out cold, and we were having a hard enough time carrying you without your gear. And then they came, and we didn't have time to go back for anything."

Richard nodded.

"I guess I can forgive you, since you did take me to a safe place, and I am still alive."

Jason laughed.

"I guess you have a point, but still we'll have to come up with something. I really don't want to end up as one of those things."

"Me either. Me either."

Jason unlocked his front door and walked in ahead of his guest.

"We're back, Babe," he called.

Hanna walked into the room and smiled at seeing them. She stepped up on tippy toes and kissed her husband.

"Good," she said. "I heard some banging, and I was beginning to worry."

"That was us," Richard said, a little embarrassed at the display of affection. "We decided to fill up the stairwells in case any of the stinkbags outside make it inside. It'll give us a little bit more of a buffer—just in case."

"Good thinking," she replied then turned back to her husband and smiled again. "Ready for lunch?"

"Definitely"

"We can have peanut butter and jelly sandwiches or a mixture of canned peaches and canned pears or spaghetti without sauce."

Jason grumbled and frowned.

"That's it?"

"That's it," she confirmed. "I told you we should eat up here more often and at the cafeteria less. Maybe then we would have more than a week's worth of groceries, most of which is gone now that we've been cooped up for a few days."

Jason grumbled again.

"I'm fine with any of the above mentioned delicacies," Richard said, interjecting himself into the conversation. "A week's worth of food mostly gone in just a few days, huh?"

"Well, a week's worth if we had continued working at the lab for most of that time like we usually do—did," she replied.

"I see. Well, I guess we'll have to find some food before we head out too."

"Where are we going to do that?" Jason asked and pointed to the bread and condiments for Hanna, who had stepped away and was holding up options for their lunch.

"Well," Richard replied, giving Hanna a thumbs up gesture as well, "The exchange carries some groceries, and it should have been closed up before the outbreak the other night. I guess we can try there before we leave—if we can get to it. We may have to just do another search in this building though. That would probably be the safest for now."

Jason sighed and shook his head.

"So I guess we won't be able to just poke our heads in and yell after all."

Richard laughed.

"Not unless your food usually answers back when you talk to it."

Jason shook his head.

"And if it does," Richard continued with a chuckle, "I really don't want to know about it."

Chapter 19: Sit Rep

They ate their meager meal in somber silence as the reality of their situation pressed on their minds. They were running out of food and they were surrounded by flesh-eating zombies of their own colleague's creation. Getting to the vehicles they would need in order to leave for somewhere more promising was not going to be an easy chore.

As he took another bite of peanut butter and jelly, Richard wondered if any of the other rooms in the building might hold a contraband firearm or two. He determined to keep his eyes open for the possibility when he and Jason went back out to look for food. Thinning the horde outside would increase their odds of survival when the time came to leave.

"Hanna, you..." Richard swallowed and took a drink of water. "Excuse me. Sorry, some of the peanut butter stuck to the back of my throat."

Hanna nodded and smiled, waiting for him to complete what he had started.

"You said the news mentioned that parts of Wyoming were pretty bad," Richard continued.

"Yes," she replied. "And Idaho was mentioned as well."

"I need to know how bad and where. Can you recall exactly what was said?"

"Well, I remember they mentioned Cheyenne and that there was rioting and looting after the initial outbreak there because a lot of people weren't prepared to stay in their homes indefinitely like the lieutenant governor was recommending. They said a lot of shops tried to stay closed when the news came out, but people needed food and water. They predicted that some areas would lose services because the workers would be sent home if they showed up to work."

"Did they mention Cody, Powell, or Worland?"

"I don't think so. Those names don't sound familiar at all."

Richard nodded.

"What about Idaho? Where are things bad there?"

Hanna shook her head and frowned.

"I don't know. It was a few days ago, and we didn't know then that we would end up trying to go through that area to go find your fiancé. I'm sorry. I should have paid more attention, but we had different priorities then."

"Boise," Jason offered. "I heard them say Boise was bad."

"That's far enough south that we shouldn't have to drive through it, I would think," Richard said.

Jason shrugged.

"I haven't tried it yet, but that guy we found up on five said the internet is down, so I think our phone navigation apps and mapquest is out."

"What guy?" Hanna asked.

"We forgot to tell you," Richard said. "We did find one other person in the building, right upstairs," he said, pointing up at the ceiling."

They then proceeded to tell her about Scott, how they had met, what had been said, and their offer to let him go with them when they packed up and left.

"And he said he would get back to you?" Hanna asked.

"Yeah," Jason said. "He seemed kind of weird to me though."

"He said he writes software," Richard said. "A lot of guys that do that see the world totally differently than the rest of us do. That's probably why he seemed weird to us."

"Hmm, maybe."

"Anyway, we'll need directions before we leave. Do you happen to have a road map of the western States?"

Jason shook his head.

"I used to have one in my car, but I don't know if it's still there," Hanna said.

"We'll have to see if we can find one; either in your car or in someone else's nearby," Richard said.

Hanna nodded.

"That sounds like a lot of little things we need to do before we leave," she said. "And you want to get it all done today and leave today or tonight?"

"I'd like to," Richard replied. "But if we aren't ready until tomorrow then we'll be leaving tomorrow. That's just how it is."

"Well," Jason said. "I've eaten enough. How about we go find some food for the road?"

Richard nodded and stood.

"The sooner we're done, the sooner we can leave."

"Be careful," Hanna offered, as the men walked out the door. She sighed as the door closed behind them. This was a nightmare she wasn't prepared for.

Chapter 20: Background Check Interrupted

Turning to the data his program had dredged up on Richard and Jason, Scott began reading about the men he was about to spend more time with.

Starting with Jason, he looked through the DARPA personnel file, saw that he had a PhD in nanotechnology from the University of North Carolina at Greensboro/NC A&T State University Joint School of Nanoscience & Nano-engineering, was married to Hanna McIntyre, and worked with Joshua Harper, DARPA's star nanotech guru. He had published several papers on subjects within the nanotechnology field, and there were also the transcripts from several seminars that he had spoken at dealing with the same subjects and material. His old Navy service record and medical records turned up as well. There was also a list of interactions with the police. It looked like Jason liked to drive faster than the posted speed limits and had one time gotten caught driving through an intersection at a red light.

His credit reports were good. He didn't have a lot of debt compared to his DARPA salary, and he hadn't ever been late making his payments.

Current medical records showed him to be in good health. He had a family history of diabetes but was not showing any tendencies in that direction himself.

Looking through the rest of the information his program had found, he determined that there really wasn't anything that interesting about Jason other than his current work, and even that didn't really interest Scott, but it gave him an idea of who he would be dealing with when they hit the road.

He moved on to Richard's information.

Again, he started with the DARPA personnel file. Richard had a hire date just six months prior. He hadn't done much at DARPA. He had only one personnel assessment review under his belt. His supervisor had given him good marks, and was recommending him for a monetary bonus for security upgrade recommendations that he had made. His Knowledge, Skills, and Abilities narratives said that he had leadership skills and experience from the Navy SEALs and the Red Raiders.

Interesting, Scott thought. *You don't hear much about the Raiders anymore.*

He skipped the rest of the DARPA folder, which was pretty boring stuff in most cases and this was not an exception, and went to Richard's Navy service record. He scanned through it and was surprised at how little was actually in it. There were brief mentions of the Teams and a small blurb on the Raiders, but there was almost nothing about actual missions.

Scott leaned back and thought about why that would be the case. The Navy didn't exclude much from service record books. If there was something that a service member became tangled up in that they didn't want the public to know about, due to the situation's or mission's sensitive nature, they tended to just make the record classified and inaccessible to those that didn't need to know. Well, this record was accessible, but there was next to nothing on operations he should have been on.

He also noticed that there was no listed credit report, which was a little odd.

Something didn't feel right to him about how small this guy's personal bio file was. Everyone had huge amounts of data in their bio files these days...unless they'd lived totally off grid their whole life, which was nearly impossible. DMV records, social networking site histories, credit card statements, phone records—and that was just the tip of the ice burg on most people. But Richard had very little of any of that stuff. It was like the guy had been born an adult just five years ago and hadn't made any friends.

An idea occurred to him, so he copied the picture from Richard's DARPA folder and signed into an old National Security Agency employee account he had created ages ago when he had been more involved in penetration testing than in programming drones and had maintained various government accounts for his own occasional little research projects. They weren't that hard to fudge. The NSA had access to far more electronic resources than DARPA, and he knew how to put them to work for him. The NSA didn't know that he still had access, and as far as he was concerned, they didn't need to.

He pasted Richard's picture into a facial recognition program and activated the search.

He had told Richard and Jason that the internet was down with the President's declaration of martial law, and for all intents and purposes it was a true statement. What he hadn't told him, was that only the civilian internet was down. The series of electronic networks that the Department of Defense had linked together for national security were still up and running. You couldn't order a pizza using it, but you could still find plenty of information and relay communications if needed—and if you knew how to gain access.

While he waited for the NSA to do their magic, he did a quick search on Hanna McIntyre. Her DARPA material came up fairly quickly, and the contents were not surprising.

Her background was just like her husband's minus the military start. She had her PhD in nanotechnology from the University of Washington. She had been noticed by DARPA after she had postulated a way to use nanotechnology to derive electricity from natural photosynthesis in plants and had explained how it could be approached. Now, she too worked with Joshua Harper.

Scott scanned through her folder, which turned out to be pretty boring stuff—just like her husband's, until his other computer chirped. He glanced over and saw that the NSA had performed for him as usual.

"Ok, what have we got on Richard?" he asked, rolling his chair over to face the other monitor. "That's what I thought," he said when he saw the name associated with the new pictures the original picture had been associated with. "So 'Richard' might not be Richard at all. Who is this Philip Quinio then, hey?"

He minimized Hanna's folder to access his search program and entered the new name. Once the computer showed that it was running, he rolled back over to study the NSA photos again.

"Richard" and "Philip" was the same person.

He leaned back in his chair and wondered why the subterfuge.

Clearly he is a spy, Scott thought. *The question is: Who is he spying for?*

He considered the numerous assorted entities out there that would pay big bucks for even a little of the information that could be found behind the scenes at DARPA then sighed when he realized that there really wasn't anybody left that he could tell that would matter.

At least not locally.

Standing and stretching, he decided to keep his findings to himself until he could use the information to his advantage.

I'll have to take everything he says with a grain of salt.

Looking at the light outside, he guestimated that the sun was about an hour from setting.

I'd better get my things down to the fourth floor before they decide to leave without me.

He sat again and went to the start menu to shut down the first computer. As soon as he had clicked the mouse to initiate shutdown, his second computer chirped an alert.

Now what?

Sliding the chair over, he tapped the spacebar on the keyboard to stop the screen saver and reveal the alert message. It quickly became apparent that the message was a communique that was not intended for him but that had been picked up by one of the intercept programs he had concealed in the DARPA system software.

Message text: Richard Dalton no longer primary objective. Contact lost with Alpha Team. Re-establish contact with Alpha Team. Recover Joshua Harper and his work. Acquire possession of McIntyres. Richard Dalton reclassified as secondary target of opportunity. Relocate Harper and McIntyres to the Ranch. Highest Priority. Eliminate all potential witnesses. Do Not Fail.

Scott furrowed his eyebrows. The message didn't make sense. He looked up at the source of the message.

What the hell is this? He thought, seeing the sideways 8 symbol for infinity.

Then he looked at the intercept time and compared it to the time displayed in the bottom right corner of the computer screen.

Nearly three hours had passed.

So why am I just receiving this alert now? He thought. *Unless…*

Minimizing the message window, he pulled up another window and scanned down the log entries.

"There it is," he muttered when he found the line of text. "Damn!"

The message had been sent in an encrypted format. His system had intercepted it, recognized that it was encrypted, and routed it to an NSA server he was always connect to. The NSA server had begun the decryption process, found a solution that its algorithms said was correct, and returned the decrypted message which he then found displayed on the screen. Only then had his system alerted him to the intercept.

And the reason it had only taken a few hours was that the message had been sent using US military encryption to which the NSA already had keys. Otherwise it could have taken days, weeks, even years.

He reread the message. It still didn't make sense to him. But the line that couldn't be misunderstood scared the crap out of him.

Eliminate Dalton and any potential witnesses.

And that means me too.

And that's when he heard gunfire downstairs.

Time to go. But first, a little something for later, just in case.

He took a few precious minutes to enter some commands on his desktop and left it running as he left the room he called home.

Chapter 21: Meal Interrupted

"So have you come up with anything doable that gets us to the mobile lab without any of us becoming one of those *things* outside?" Jason asked. "We haven't got much time left if you still want to leave before tonight. I'm not going out there after dark."

Richard nodded.

"I don't want to be out there after dark either. And yes, I have been giving it some thought. We're surrounded, we have no guns, and I want to leave tonight."

He shook his head.

"It might not be possible," he continued. "I thought about maybe finding something flammable like charcoal lighter fluid or a lot of hairspray...whatever we could find in the dorms and burning them out enough that we could get past them; but we're just as liable to burn ourselves to the ground in the attempt."

"That's all you could think of?" Hanna asked. Her facial expression said she didn't think it was such a good idea.

"Well, no that's not all," he replied, turning towards her. "But the other idea I had carries some pretty heavy risk too, and neither one is really doable in the time we have left before dark."

"What's the other idea?" Jason asked.

Richard took a long breath and sighed before answering.

"We just spent a couple of hours securing the bottom floor, so that we could feel a little safer while we looked for supplies for the ride out of here."

"Right"

"My other idea was to set up a barricaded kill zone on one of the floors right in front of the elevator. Then we go down to the bottom floor, make another barricade that channelizes the zombies right into the elevator from the front door. Then we undo the chains on the front door enough to allow them to push in eventually but not right away, so we have time to take the elevator back up to the kill zone we set up. Then we send the elevator back down, call it back up, and head-whack whatever zombies have gotten into it. We could use your baseball bat and whatever else we can come up with."

"Are you serious?" Hanna asked.

"Honey," Jason said.

"No, Jay," she replied. "This is a crazy idea. All it would take is one little bite that you might not even feel in the heat of the moment, and then you turn, and we are all compromised."

"Like I said," Richard replied. "It carries its own share of risk. We would have very little control over how many we would face at a time, though it would be fewer than if we tried to take them all on at once.

"We also wouldn't know if we had gotten all of them, even if we did manage to kill all of the ones that manage to make it up in the elevator. We could very well go down only to find plenty more waiting for us bottom."

Hanna shook her head.

"I didn't say it was a good idea or one that I liked. I just said I thought it was doable."

"I don't know," Jason said. "It does seem pretty risky. I think I would almost rather risk burning the building down trying to catch them on fire than have to get that close to them."

"I know how you feel," Richard said. "I'd rather not get that close either, but we've got to do something. And I hate to say it, but we might *have* to wait until tomorrow to do it. I want to leave right away and go to my fiancé, but it won't do us any good to hurry now if we don't have a workable solution to getting out the front door without getting bit.

"If we wait until tomorrow, we will be more rested and less likely to make life-threatening mistakes. Plus, we might come up with something that we haven't thought of that will work better."

Hanna nodded.

"That sounds smart," Jason said.

"So I guess I'll go look for food," Richard said. "The peanut butter and jelly sandwich was good, but I really feel like eating something else for dinner."

Hanna smiled and nodded her head.

"Well, that's something we can all do together don't you think?" she asked.

Richard nodded and opened his mouth to comment.

But was cut off by machine gun fire coming from below.

"Get down!"

Jason and Hanna obeyed immediately, dropping to the floor and climbing under the kitchen table.

Richard crouched lower and stalked toward the window. He had to stand a little taller than he liked to look out through the narrow slit he made by pulling the blinds away from the window, but it was the only way he could see the ground level.

The shooting was all down below and didn't seem to be impacting anything near them. He followed the sound to the source and saw two men in military uniform, shooting M4 rifles into the horde of zombies as they walked towards the building. Then one of them turned to get some other zombies that were getting closer, and he raised his cheek off of the stock.

It's hard to forget the face of someone you've killed at point blank range, and with his newly enhanced neuro-system, Richard instantly recognized Nate Wagner.

He dropped the blinds back into position and dropped into a leaning squat against the wall.

"What is it?" Jason asked in almost shouted whisper.

Richard looked him in the eye then shook his head and grinned a sardonic smile.

"Your super soldiers have come to kill me."

Chapter 22: Gotta Go

Looking out through the blinds again, Richard watched body after body drop lifeless to the ground after rounds from the men's machine guns tore through their skulls. The zombies had turned away from the building and were swarming towards the two super soldiers. They weren't making much progress. The soldiers were precise with their shots, and the zombies were too slow and too few in number to overwhelm them...so far.

There was a loud banging on the door.

"Open up!" they heard from the hall. "It's Scott Lewis from the fifth floor. Open up!"

"Should I?" Jason asked.

Richard thought about it for a second then nodded.

Jason got out from under the table and went to open the front door.

As soon as the door opened a crack, Scott burst in.

"We've got to get out of here right now," he said, waving his arms to emphasize his words. "That's a hit squad down there. They are here to take the McIntyres and kill Richard and everyone else that could be considered a witness. I don't want to die, man. Let's go."

Take the McIntyres?

Richard wanted to ask how he could possibly know what he was saying, but he knew it didn't matter at the moment. What mattered was that the hit squad *was* there to kill or kidnap them and that time was officially short.

"You're right," he said. "We do need to go."

Jason, you and Hanna grab the supplies we've already got packed. Scott, I hope you have everything you need as well."

Scott nodded.

"Good. I recognized one of the guys down there. I didn't see the other's face, but guessing by the company he keeps, they are *both* very good at what they do, very dangerous men. Ok, here's what we can do: While they are busy taking out the zombies and drawing them towards this side, we should slip out the opposite side of the building and make our way to the garage where you said your mobile lab is waiting."

Scott nodded his head and said, "That might work. Here's their message."

He handed Richard a printout of the message his system had intercepted.

Richard read it quickly, noting the infinity symbol at the top as the point of origination. They were trying to evacuate their assets, he realized. As soon as they realized that Harper was dead and his new nano series was missing, they'd begin actively looking for a signal on the frequency in Harper's diary. That signal would lead them right to him.

"The nanos that were injected into me are active. They're broadcasting on a trackable frequency, and these guys are going to be looking for it soon," he said, turning to Jason. "But Harper created a counter for himself. His watches...I slipped them into my pockets in the lab. Where are they?"

"I've got them," Hanna replied.
She ran around the corner into her room and emerged a few seconds later.

"Here," she said and tossed them to Richard.

Richard caught them and slipped them over his wrists, one on each arm.

"What are those supposed to do?" Scott asked.

"Block most, if not all, of my signal," Richard replied. "Now let's go while we still have time."

He slipped out into the hallway and began leading them towards the stairwell at the opposite side of the building.

Scott shook his head but followed. He had no idea what the hell Richard...no, Philip, he reminded himself, was talking about.

By the time he reached the ground floor in the stairwell, Richard's vision had gone back to what he had earlier described as analog. Colors weren't as vivid; details weren't as sharp; it was like he was looking at the world through a layer of oil-smeared plastic wrap. His hearing sounded muffled as if from liquid in his ear canal. His thought process also seemed to have slowed down. He knew it was the same as what he had lived with for all of his life, but compared to the boost he had been getting from the active nanos in his system all day, it felt almost crippling. He felt heavy on his feet.

The door at the bottom was still tightly tied shut with a length of fire hose, so he untied it after looking through the small window to make sure no zombies or soldiers waited on the other side. The others were slower coming down the stairs, since they were carrying most of the supplies.

He held the door open for them then grabbed a suitcase from Jason.

"Jason, you lead. You know where the mobile lab is," Richard said. "I'll bring up the rear and make sure everyone makes it."

Jason nodded and hurried down the hall to the side door. Hanna followed behind and then Scott.

They hurried into the street and jogged along the sidewalk, watching for zombies at every corner. The streets seemed to be mostly clear, the soldiers' machine gun fire on the opposite side of the dorm building drawing them away.

Along the way they passed a security check point booth. It was vacant, so, watching to make sure the others didn't get too far ahead, Richard stepped inside and used his keys to open the gun locker. Four shotguns with slings stood in their cradles next to three MP-5 submachine guns and a number of handguns. Spare magazines, loaded to capacity, and bandoliers of shotgun ammo were stored on a shelf below, and in the space below that were several green military ammo cans.

With some effort, and a few jabs into his ribs as a result, he managed to sling all four of the shotguns and two MP-5's over his back. Then he looped the bandoliers over his back as well. He managed to stuff six of the handguns into his waistband after loosening his belt some, and then he filled his cargo pockets with spare handgun magazines.

He realized he would move considerably slower carrying all of the extra weight, but he wanted some firepower in his corner if he did end up having to face off against the super soldiers. Even though the others in his group didn't have the firearms training he did, he hoped having guns in their hands would make the difference in their survival.

Grabbing a spare shotgun sling that someone had left in the locker, he made a make-shift carrying strap for the ammo cans. He looped it through their metal handles, tied it off, and then doubled it up twice to make a small coil that he could more easily grip. Lastly, he grabbed the suitcase Jason had been carrying and left to follow the others.

He could barely move.

The magazines in his cargo pockets dug into the sides of his legs, and the charging handles on the MP-5's bore holes into his back. He'd grabbed too much.

"Screw it," he muttered to himself, as he set the suitcase and ammo cans down. He grabbed the suitcase's drag handle and extended it until the pins locked into place. Then he set the ammo cans on top of it, looped the makeshift carrying strap around the handle, and began to roll the suitcase along behind him.

This freed up his right hand, so he grabbed one of the handguns from the front of his waistband, pulled the slide back a half inch to do a brass check, then released the slide and tapped the back of the slide to make sure it was all the way forward, fully in battery. Then he grabbed the suitcase handle and followed down the street.

As he had feared, the suitcase made plenty of noise as it rolled down the hard pavement. He only hoped the zombies didn't notice it over the thunder of the guns that his group was running from.

He made faster progress, but it was still a painful process.

For several long seconds he was alone on the street. He had seen Scott turn the corner around a building up ahead to the left. He followed as quickly as he could.

When he made it to the corner, Scott was waiting there for him, watching Jason and Hanna as they walked a little further ahead. They had slowed down when they realized he had been slowed up.

"You good, Mate?" Scott asked.

"Yeah," Richard gasped. "Here, take one of these."

He grabbed another handgun from his waistband and handed it to towards him.

"It's loaded. The safeties are all internal, so you pull the trigger it's going to go off."

"Got it," Scott replied, taking it. "Come on."

"Right," Richard said then stepped off behind him.

They made it up to where Jason and Hanna waited, looking anxiously around. Jason was pushing his shoulder against a door, but it wasn't budging.

"I don't have a key."

"Hold on," Richard said. He let go of the suitcase and handed Hanna the handgun. "Hold this please."

He reached down to his belt loop and pulled up on the paracord braid to which his key ring was attached, pulling the key from the bottom of his pocket. Two spare pistol magazines clattered to the ground before the keys came into sight. He looked at the lock to see the name of the manufacturer engraved on the face plate then picked a key from among many and slid it into the lock. It turned smoothly, and he pushed in as he turned the door knob.

While Richard was opening the door, Scott bent down and retrieved the magazines full of ammo that had fallen.

"Here, you dropped these," Scott said, as he extended them forward.

"Keep 'em," Richard replied. "Before this is all done with, you might need them."

Scott nodded then dropped them into the pockets of his long shorts, which, Richard suddenly realized, were totally inappropriate attire for this little excursion they had begun.

None of us were really prepared for this, Richard thought, shaking his head.

He followed Scott into the building, dragging the suitcase behind him and getting caught up in the door jamb when one of the shotguns caught on the frame. When he had sorted himself out inside, he turned and looked up and down the street one last time and then closed the door. He made sure it clicked shut then turned the deadbolt into place as well.

"Coming?" Jason asked tartly from in front of the door to the elevator after he pushed the "down" button.

Richard shook his head and smiled.

"Yeah, be right there."

The elevator arrived at their level with a ding and the doors slid open. Jason and Hanna were right there, and Richard watched them step forward, stutter to a halt, then launch themselves back out of the entrance. They both ended up sprawled on their butts, crab-walking backwards to get further away and shrieking in fear.

He quickly saw just what they were backing so desperately away from. One of the infected limped out of the elevator, one arm raised. Something had been gnawing on its other arm and legs and face. Its body was covered in wounds where gouges had been stripped of its flesh and muscle. It had been half scalped as well. So much missing flesh made it difficult to tell what its gender had been.

Dropping the suitcase, he reached for the handgun in the side of his waistband, cursing himself for not having gotten one out immediately after he had given the other to Hanna. The shotguns on his back impeded his range of motion, so it took some jerking and elbowing to get it out. He ended up taking his eyes off of the elevator scene in front of him in order to see what he was doing. As he finally managed to clear the barrel from his pants, he heard a gunshot then another.

Of course, Scott had done some backpedaling as well. Fortunately for Jason, who had been closest to becoming a zombie snack, Scott was a gamer with good reflexes. While Richard was struggling with his pants and everything he was carrying, Scott had stepped back, dropped the things he carried, and raised the gun he had just been given. His shot went right through the side of the zombie's skull.

The dead zed went limp and dropped to the ground.

The second shot came from Hanna. When she had landed on her butt, she had started scrambling backwards then realized that she had the gun Richard had given her. With a snarl of fury and fear she leaned back flat on the ground, raised the gun, and squeezed the trigger. She was startled when she heard the first shot but didn't feel any movement in her hand, so she looked up at the back of the gun. And then her gun went off, blowing a gouge out of the zombie's shoulder as it was already tumbling towards the floor. She was so surprised that she dropped the gun.

"Oh shit! There's more!" Scott yelled, bringing his gun back up.

Hanna rolled, fumbled across the floor, reaching for her gun. It slid across the smooth tile.

Richard, gun out and ready to shoot, couldn't take a shot because Scott was in his way, and he couldn't slide to the side for an angle quickly enough because he was still weighed down by the shotguns and submachine guns on his back.

Three more shots rang out before Scott lowered his gun a bit. He peeked around the shallow corner of the elevator. The two zombies he had shot were down, and there were no others for him to shoot.

Richard stepped up beside him and looked around at the mess they had made. Three zombies down with head shots on each, and he didn't recognize any of them.

"Nice shooting, Scott," he said. "I'm impressed."

"Thanks," the younger man replied. "Back in the day I used to be pretty kick ass at Resident Evil."

"Hmph, well, I'm glad to see you were able to take something useful away from it. You probably just saved Jason's life and maybe Hanna's too. With the outer door locked I really didn't expect to see any of these things in here."

Richard turned to Jason and Hanna and helped each to their feet.

"Ok?" he asked.

They each nodded and thanked him, still looking shaken.

As the elevator descended, Richard passed a shotgun and bandolier of shells to Jason. He gave another to Scott. Hanna decided to stick with the handgun, and he gave her a few extra magazines, which she slid into the back pockets of her denim pants. For himself, he chose to use the MP5 submachine gun, mostly because of the higher magazine capacity and the dual mag clamp that kept a second magazine attached to the one already loaded, effectively doubling his already large ammo load.

"All right," Richard said. "Guns up and ready as soon as the doors open. We don't know what is down there, if anything. We can't rule out the possibility that those things managed to get inside. Not after what just happened upstairs. If they did, we'll have to take them out. We have to make it to the vehicles. I'll lead. Be aware of where your muzzle is pointed. I'd really rather not be shot in the back."

The elevator dinged and the doors began to slide open.

"Here we go; everyone stay close."

The doors opened, and immediately Richard's eyes began to sting. His nose caught the foul scent of death, and he felt like retching his guts up right then and there, but movement in front of him forced him to control himself or possibly die.

Someone behind him lost it and began puking onto the floor of the elevator. He ignored the sound of their retching, as he took in the scene before him.

Turning toward him, probably from the sounds made by the elevator, were hundreds of corpses in various stages of decomposition. Blood was splattered against the walls, and there were puddles on the cement floor.

"Oh shit," Scott said behind him.

The sound of moaning quickly overpowered the curses that began spewing from Jason's mouth, like the vomit that was still dripping from Hanna's.

The zombies began stumble stepping toward the quartet, as Richard pulled up the slack on the MP5's trigger. It was set on semi-auto, one bullet per squeeze of the trigger. He didn't want to waste ammo, especially not when bullets might soon be very hard to come by.

The gun went off, and the zombie closest to them fell to the floor, its head a hollow melon. The resulting thunderous echo brought the others into action. Guns discharged their merciful lethal payloads. Corpses fell to the floor, but more kept coming.

Sometimes their shots missed the cranium, and the zombies stumbled but either kept walking towards them or began crawling towards them if they could no longer gain their feet.

The tempo of their shots rose and fell, as, one after the other, they were forced to reload their weapons as they ran dry. Richard's shots were by far the most accurate, but Scott's were making a difference as well. Jason was beginning to slow down as the constant hammering at his shoulder from the shotgun began to wear him down. Hanna decided to stay close to her husband and shoot when he was reloading, since he had to do it a lot more often, having only five rounds at full capacity.

Shooting those that were closest first, Richard shot as fast as he could move the sights and aim in on another. He tried counting his shots to have a general idea of when a reload was forthcoming, but the rapid push of mobile corpses towards their position had his mind jumping on other thoughts.

He began to wonder if maybe they should pull back to the elevator.

The next time he pulled the trigger, he caught the dreaded click of an empty chamber. Training kicked in, and he dropped the magazine, shifted the new one to position, pushed it up into the magazine well, and slapped the charging handle down. Then he re-aimed and squeezed the trigger.

The zombie in his sights dropped for good.

After a few more shots he found that he had time to breathe as their lethal wall of lead had taken down those closest. More zombies still filtered towards them, but they were slowed by the parked cars that they were forced to stumble around before having a straight path at the live humans.

"There it is!" Jason shouted, pointing towards a large vehicle at the back of the garage.

It looked like a gray RV, only bigger. Its windows had bars protecting them on the outside, and if it weren't for the big "DARPA" painted on the side in block letters, Richard would have sworn it was some new military communications vehicle that hadn't yet been revealed to the public that had paid for it.

There were a lot of corpses between them and the mobile lab. If they moved up the center towards it, they would be putting a lot of potential bites on either flank.

Richard looked to the right and made a quick decision.

"This way!" he yelled.

He moved to the wall to their right, shooting a few zombies along the way. Following the wall they would eventually make it to their getaway vehicle and keep the zombies to their front and left instead of being surrounded.

Jason's shotgun blasts were deafening, but they were effective. Richard wondered if he had been a skeet shooter in a past life. Hopefully, they would have a chance to discuss it in the future.

Scott's shots were even more accurate. The young man was devastating, dropping anything his sights rested on. Thank heaven for first-person shooter video games.

They used the vehicles for cover, as much as possible keeping the obstacles of metal and glass between them and the zombies. They made nice little channelizers as the group passed them, leaving narrow gaps between the cars and the wall for the zombies to try to fit through in their efforts to attack the quartet.

As they turned to continue following the wall at the corner, they lost their cover of vehicles, and were forced to compensate with more rapid gun fire.

After what felt like hours, they came within lunging distance of the back of the mobile lab

"Jason, get up here!" Richard yelled. As he waited for the man to respond, he took a few more shots, dropping zombies with each shot.

"Yes?" Jason asked.

"Hold on," Richard replied. "Scott take our six."

Scott nodded and dropped back behind Hanna. Almost immediately his shotgun began blasting holes in the zombies that were coming up, unrelenting, behind them.

"Jason," Richard continued. "Open it up for us, while we cover you."

"You got it," Jason said and moved to open the side door.

"Hanna, make sure none of those things crawl underneath."

She nodded and crouched down.

As the vehicle's door opened, a hand reached out and grabbed the edge then pulled back, opening the door even more.

"Ah crap!" Richard yelled then leaned over and kicked the door, throwing the zombie off balance. He followed through with a shot into the zombie's skull. Stepping to the other side of the door, he began picking off targets at a faster pace to create a small buffer of space, so they wouldn't get so close again.

As he blasted a few more, the headlights to the lab came on, and another second later the engine rumbled to life.

"Hanna, get in!"

He glanced over his shoulder to see that she had heard him then he stepped back a few steps and tossed the MP-5 into the RV behind her. He unslung the rest of the bandoliers of shotgun ammo and the other two shotguns and tossed them in as well. Pulling the last MP-5 over in front of him, he racked the charging handle. A live round flew out and bounced off the wall. Good, it was already loaded, and now he felt considerably lighter.

Scott was blasting away as he backed towards the door.

Richard checked around the front of the vehicle again. The closest zed was still a good fifteen feet away. He let loose and dropped it along with a few of its closest buddies.

Scott's shotgun went quiet, and he began yelling, "I'm dry!"

"Get in!" Richard yelled in reply, and shot at a few more in the front. He glanced back to see Scott lunge into the vehicle.

A few zombies were in the space between the wall and the vehicle.

Richard pivoted and took them down with shots to the head.

"Let's go!" the others were yelling from inside.

Richard took two more shots as he walked to the door then he stepped inside and slammed it shut.

"I sure hope you know how to drive this thing," Scott said, looking to Jason.

In response, Jason shifted the gear lever and mashed down on the gas pedal, sending the lumbering vehicle forward and swerving to the left, narrowly missing the big truck parked in front of it. The sudden move sent a music CD that hung from the middle console above the windshield to swinging wildly back and forth.

Almost immediately after Richard closed the door behind him, the zombies stopped moving toward them and began to just stand around. As the RV turned to follow the lane to the garage exit, Richard noticed and pointed it out to the others.

Jason nodded but focused on driving.

Hanna spoke.

"We thought Josh was just being paranoid. He knew all along, the bastard. He built this thing to block electromagnetic waves from coming in or going out."

That's when Richard noticed the metal screen embedded in the glass windows, like the screen in the window of a microwave.

"A faraday cage on wheels," he replied.

Hanna nodded but didn't speak again. She lowered her head into her hands and began crying. Her hands shook, and her back heaved with sobs.

Richard looked around at the interior. Again, it was similar to a recreational vehicle, having a small table and bench seats in one section behind the two front seats, a reclining middle chair next to a small sofa, with cupboards, a small stove area, a refrigerator and sink taking up the rest of the front. Towards the back, the similarity ended with a blank wall inset with an almost oval-shaped, pressure-sealed door like in the lab back in the building. One major way that it differed from an RV though was the large bank of television screens built into the dashboard and center console. They showed a 360° view around the outside of their lab on wheels. A very cool feature he was sure would come in handy later.

Then he realized something else.

"Uh, Jason?"

"Yes?"

Take us back over by the elevators."

Jason glanced over his shoulder then back to his driving. He turned the wheel ever so slightly and smashed a zombie against the front corner of the vehicle, but he didn't slow the RV.

"Why?"

"I realize none of us want to go back out there with those creatures, but we left all of our supplies right outside the elevator. I dropped mine when I started shooting."

Jason glanced down and saw the pile of guns and ammo sitting on the floor. What he didn't see were all of their suitcases with food and water. He sighed and slowed down.

He was shaking his head as he turned left towards the elevator instead of going up the ramp that led to the upper levels and the exit.

"Scott, I'm going out," Richard said. "Will you cover me, or would you be more comfortable passing the baggage in to Hanna?"

"Ahhh," Scott said, thinking. He looked back and forth from Richard to Hanna.

"I'll cover you," he finally replied.

Richard nodded.

"All right. Thank you. I'll pass Hanna the baggage. Hanna, when I give it to you just toss them back there. We can arrange them in better places after we are all inside safe."

"Ok," Hanna replied, nodding.

"Jason, it would be best if you stayed at the wheel with the engine running. When we need to leave in a hurry, you'll be ready."

Jason nodded as he turned the wheel again, bringing the RV around towards the elevator. He managed to bring it around so that Scott and Richard could get out and still have the RV between them and most of the zombies. The zombies were still standing relatively still, but that would change as soon as the RV door opened and they detected the electromagnetic waves generated by the humans and the electronic equipment inside the vehicle.

When the vehicle stopped, Richard looked out through the window in the door and checked the floor space in front of the elevator. It was clear of threats at the moment.

"How are we looking, Scott?" he asked, lifting his chin towards the window opposite.

Scott ducked down and looked out.

"None are coming this way; they're just standing around."

"All right. Let's do this. You've got the weapon on semi?"

Scott looked down at the MP-5 he had picked up and checked the selector switch on the side.

"All set for single fire," he replied, sounding almost sad.

Richard nodded and gave him an understanding smile. The MP-5 was a fun gun to shoot on full auto, but they didn't have the ammo to spare for such a luxury just now. It was better to be sure they could hit their threats and get back in the RV safe and sound.

"Ok, here goes," he said, swinging the door open and stepping out.

Scott followed right behind him and stepped out a few more paces. Richard began grabbing bags and tossing them inside to Hanna.

"Here they come, guys," Jason hollered.

The bags flew into the vehicle faster. Richard decided to save the suitcase he had dragged for last because of the heavy ammo can that was still tied to the top.

The gun blast assaulted his eardrums as Scott engaged the first of the zombies coming around the back of the RV. He stepped closer to the back to get a better angle on them as they came around the corner.

"Hurry up!" he yelled before blasting a few more.

Richard ran to the last suitcase and dragged it towards the RV. Pulling it up, a corner hit the edge of the first step, and the ammo can on top clattered to the ground, popping open and spilling magazines and a few stray rounds.

"Damn it!" he cursed.

"Leave them!" Jason yelled. We're about to get swamped. Just get in!"

"Scott!" Richard yelled, as he tossed the suitcase up to Hanna.

Scott came running and vaulted into the RV, over Richard, who had knelt down to pick up as many magazines as he could.

"Come on, Richard," Hanna shrieked.

Richard picked up one more magazine and snatched his hand back just as Jason pulled the lever to shut the door. As soon as the door slammed home, several dead bodies slammed into it and pawed at the reinforced window, leaving streaks of putrid looking blood and speckles of rotten flesh on the glass.

"Geez, that was close," Scott huffed, rubbing his stomach where he had landed on the MP-5 after his dive.

Richard nodded.

"Don't take stupid chances!" Hanna yelled, still looking somewhat frightened. "You endanger us all."

"You're right," Richard replied. "I'm sorry. It was stupid, but this ammo could save our life further down the line."

Hanna sighed heavily and shook her head before turning to hug her husband. Jason hugged her right back and patted her back, whispering in her ear so the others couldn't hear.

"Look at them," Scott said, eager to change the subject.

Richard looked out the window at the zombies to see what Scott was talking about.

Once again the zombies were back to milling around, nothing of particular interest giving them reason to do anything else. Some could clearly hear the RV, but they did not sense it as a threat or a target.

"Poor bastards," Richard muttered. "Let's get out of here.

Jason nodded, gave Hanna a final pat on the back, and turned back to the steering wheel. Driving over a few of the dead on his way, he turned left up the ramp. At the top a metal door rolled up allowing them access to the next level and closed as they passed through, once again trapping the lost souls in an eternal grave.

The other levels were empty as far as they could tell, likely because there were no cars for the fleeing staff to go to at the outset. A few DARPA vehicles were parked on the opposite side, but they saw no movement or signs of life from that direction.

Back at ground level in the room they had started from, Jason stopped the vehicle. The metal door to the lower levels rolled shut behind them.

"As soon as we go out there we're going to have to worry about the hit squad again. You realize that right?" Jason asked.

"Yes," Richard replied. "So it might be a good idea to reload all of the guns now while we've got a second to catch our breath."

"I agree," Scott said. "But let's not take our time. Right now there are two guys out there that we know of. Within the next half hour or so there will be quite a few more. That's what the message I intercepted said."

"Hopefully they're busy searching the dorm building top to bottom, since my signal dropped off their radar."

"Hopefully, yes, but what if they're right outside in the street just waiting for us? They had some serious firepower on them, enough to chew a hole right through the crowd of walking dead that surrounded the building."

Richard nodded.

"I noticed, but if we're lucky they'll be professional about it and search the other buildings. Maybe they'll wait for the rest of their guys to show up before trying to really secure the whole freakin' base."

Picking up an MP-5 and the ammo can, Richard began loading the side by side magazines to full capacity.

Scott began loading his as well.

"See that?" Richard asked, pointing up to the skylight.

Everyone looked up.

"I've got an idea."

Chapter 23: Let's Drive

The mobile lab inched its way out of the garage door into the street and made a tight turn to avoid the building across the narrow street. Jason and Hanna kept their eyes peeled for any sign of the two super soldiers they knew were somewhere in the area.

"Do you see anything, Babe?" Jason asked.

"No, this place is like a ghost town."

Jason drove in silence for another block then made a turn at an intersection.

"What's that sound?" Hanna asked.

"What—oh crap! Someone's shooting at us!"

"Drive faster!"

He stomped on the gas pedal and held it to the floor, thinking about the turn that was coming up before they would have a straight shot at the facility's main gate.

Richard lay on his belly facing forward on the roof of the mobile lab. He scanned the streets and the windows as they drew closer. Scott lay behind him, checking the back area.

They knew at least some of the hit squad was in the area. With as much firepower as they had been seen to have been carrying, it was unlikely that the zombies would have been able to get within bite range to disable one of them.

They agreed only to shoot if they were discovered and pursuit looked likely—or if they were attacked, obviously.

A few zombies picked up the men's EM discharge and began their staggering walk in pursuit, but the vehicle easily outdistanced them and their ghastly moans in no time.

They held their fire.

It seemed strange to hear the birds chirping, the bugs humming, and the wind blowing in the trees, signs of the world moving on, as if no life ending apocalypse had begun just days ago. For most of the world, life did go on.

Richard was struck with how beautiful the world was at that exact moment. The sun was setting, casting shades of rich orange on the big, puffy clouds that were lazily drifting along. The hills around them were blanketed in a covering of trees in various shades of green that were just on the verge of turning to the new season's lighter yellows and oranges. Just looking around he wouldn't have been able to guess that humanity was in turmoil.

But then Scott's gun went off behind him, shattering the moment and reminding him that humanity really was screwed. He did a quick scan of his area of responsibility to their front, saw no threats, and turned around to join Scott.

Walking towards them in the middle of the street, like cowboys coming to a showdown at high noon, were Wagner and another super soldier whose name he couldn't remember from the files. Both were in full combat rig, and both were now carrying General Electric miniguns.

Holy shit! Richard thought, and took aim at Wagner.

Scott continued to fire as the super soldiers advanced. They were walking slower than the mobile lab was driving, but their machine guns were just beginning to spin up, fire belching from the wheels of barrels, and the rounds they were spitting out were beginning to impact close to the lab.

As Richard squeezed off his first round, the incoming bullets began to chew into the armor at the back of the lab.

I'm going to die, Richard thought.

But then Wagner's partner fell flat on his back, and a line of tracers from his still whirling machine gun arced up into the sky.

That must have been Scott's shot.

He aimed in at Wagner's head one more time as the bullet impacts climbed their way up the back of the vehicle towards them. Squeezing the trigger, he focused on the MP-5's front sight and tried to hold it centered on Wagner's nose. He didn't even feel the recoil in his shoulder as a 9mm round the left his barrel and went home to its target.

Incoming bullets whizzed by his head, snapping the air with fury, but then the stream chewed into the building to their right and finally ended up piercing the sky with phosphorescent tracers as Wagner too fell to the ground.

Richard's heart raced a marathon in his chest, and he caught his hands shaking with the influx of adrenaline in his system. In the deafening quiet following the thunderous gun fight, he realized that the vehicle was moving faster.

Jason had finally figured out that they were taking hits.

Just before the RV turned the corner around some buildings, Richard saw a swarm of zombies surround and fall upon the two down super soldiers.

Good riddance, he thought.

"Now what?" Scott asked.

"Now we go back down inside and get the hell out of here before the rest of the hit squad gets here," Richard replied. "I doubt we'll get so lucky again. If they've got snipers with them, we won't be able to count on the others to spray and pray like these two just did."

"Maybe they would have taken better aim if they had known our ride is armored."

"Maybe, well thank goodness they didn't. Come on."

Scott dropped back down through the skylight first.

"We got them," Richard said after he was back down inside.

"Oh, thank God," Hanna replied.

Jason nodded his head and wiped the sleeve of his shirt against his forehead.

"Wyoming here we come," he croaked.

Neither of the men that had been up on the roof mentioned the large elongated number eight that was painted in black on the roof of the lab. It didn't occur to them that it might not actually be an eight.

Chapter 24: Suppressor

As they crossed the State line into Idaho, the road was open, devoid of any traffic or signs of life. The trees that lined the highway on either side swayed gently in the evening breeze. There was little to indicate that a major breakdown of society had occurred, other than the lack of the usual traffic.

As Richard came down off the adrenaline rush he had experienced during the shootout, he began to look around at the interior of the mobile lab, taking mental stock of the resources the group now had available to them. There really wasn't much that popped out at him as being immediately useful, but a few things caught his attention and gave him an idea.

It was the scouring pad by the sink and a small note written in permanent marker on a piece of duct tape that did it. Opening the door below the sink, he rooted around until he found a mostly full box of metal scouring pads. Then in one of the small drawers next to the sink he found the roll of duct he had suspected was still around somewhere.

"Hey, Jason, do you have any tools in here somewhere?" he asked when he couldn't find any at hand in the drawers or cupboards.

"I'm not sure, but if we do, they'd probably be in one of the lockers back in the lab area."

"All right, thanks."

"What are you looking for?" Scott asked, as Richard went towards the back of the vehicle.

"Well, I figure since noise attracts the zombies, it might help to have a quiet, or at least *quieter*, gun for when we have to go back out there. I'm going to see if I can make a sound suppressor."

"Cool," Scott replied. "Show me how, and I'll help you."

"Come with me."

The door to the lab was heavy with a wheel lock that secured the air-tight environment just like a compartment door on a submarine. Overhead fluorescent lights came on, illuminating the small room as soon as they stepped inside. Compact as it was compared to the lab Josh had enjoyed back at the DARPA facility, it was still at least as large as the rest of the combined forward sections of the vehicle.

Several of the instruments and the general layout of the lab now looked familiar, since he had seen them in the DARPA lab. Others he didn't recognize, but he could tell they wouldn't be of any use to him with his current project.

"So what exactly are we looking for?" Scott asked.

"I'm going to need either metal or plastic tubing that I can fit over the barrel of one of the MP5s, probably a saw for cutting the tube to the right length, and a drill."

"Ok," Scott replied, sounding like he doubted they would find everything.

Richard couldn't blame him for the negative outlook. The lab didn't look like the kind of place they'd find those items. So far everything looked to be too high tech for their needs.

They looked through cupboards and drawers without any luck. There were plenty of tools, just not very many that either one of them knew how to use.

Eventually they did see the row of lockers set into the wall the entry door was part of, and inside one of them, they hit pay dirt. They found hammers, wrenches, sockets, files, saws, and then power tools. They even found nails, screws, bolts, and nuts which Richard didn't think they could use at the moment, but it was nice to know they had them if they did end up needing them. In the same drawer he found some hose clamps which would come in handy but that he had forgotten to mention needing.

"Now we just need some tubing," Richard said, as he rifled around some more.

"I don't see any," Scott replied, looking through a locker containing medical supplies.

"Whoa, hold up," Richard said, looking over at the open medical locker.

"What?"

"I'll bet one of those aluminum crutches would work."

"Ok," Scott replied, shrugging his shoulders and grabbing the first crutch. "Just one?"

"For now, yes. Let's see if it works before we go destroying all of our resources...It would be nice if there were a vice here, but I haven't see one, so I guess we'll just have to hold it by hand to keep it from moving around too much while I cut it."

Scott was silent as he looked around at what they had.

"I've got a better idea," he said a moment later.

"Yes?"

"There are C-clamps in the tool box, and the counter tops aren't very thick. We can clamp the crutch to the counter top, and if we need to keep the clamps from crush the tubing, we can use that technical manual over there for padding."

Richard thought about it.

"You're right, that is a better idea. Let's get started."

Using the drill, they removed the rivets holding the center bottom piece between the side support pieces.

Richard clamped the tube to the counter top as Scott had suggested and used a hack saw to cut off the plastic-capped top end. Then he cut off the bottom six inches, leaving them with a foot long length to work with.

At one end he made two three-inch parallel cuts down the long axis of the tube. Then, with pliers, he bent the upper and lower sections towards the outside, leaving the remaining side pieces in place. Finally he cut away the bent pieces.

"So explain to me why you just did all of that," Scott asked.

"Sure," Richard replied. "This is about the maximum length we are going to want sticking off the end of the MP5 or the likelihood of it growing cumbersome increases, especially if we use it to clear the inside of a building."

"Ok"

"I put the groove in there so that after we slide that end over the barrel, the hose clamps will be able to tighten down on the tubing and the barrel, not just the tubing. That tension is what will keep the suppressor attached to the gun."

"Ah, I see. Very good. I want one too."

315

Richard chuckled.

"Well, we've only got the one box of steel wool, so I don't think we'll have enough materials for more than one right now, but if we *can* find more, or even a few rolls of window screen instead, we'll make another one for you too."

"Cool," Scott replied. "So what else is there to do?"

"Now we just drill a bunch of holes down the sides of the tubing so the gases made by the bullets' burning propellant can vent out to the sides. We should file off the external burrs made by drilling. Then we'll tape all of the steel wool around the diameter of the tubing and finish it off by capping the business end with duct tape. If we had window screen, we'd just wrap that around the tubing before the layers of tape. Either one will work.

"The gases and burning propellant coming out of the end of the barrel should bleed off into the steel wool, reducing the amount of noise we make with each shot and pretty much eliminating the muzzle flash, which will help when we're using the night vision goggles," Richard explained.

"Excellent," Scott said. "I've always wondered how silencers work. I just never took the time to do the research. I've always been busy gaming or hacking into systems."

Richard nodded.

"That's the down and dirty. Hey, uh, will you hand me the drill, and I'll need a quarter inch drill bit?"

"Sure"

Richard was pleased to see that Scott hadn't itched or scratched the entire time they had been in the lab together.

Twenty minutes later they had an ugly but, they hoped, functional suppressor attached to the end of their submachine gun. They didn't have anywhere to test fire it, but because it went over the barrel instead of being matched directly in line with the bore of the barrel, which would have required significantly more work and better resources, Richard was confident that their hodge-podge creation would indeed work as desired. The suppressor didn't interfere with the weapon's sights, so he'd be able to make well-aimed shots without drawing more distant zombies towards them with each shot.

Chapter 25: Fuel

Jason slowed but didn't stop when they began to see cars pulled off of the side of the road. At first there were only a few here and there. They were abandoned, and still they didn't see any other signs to indicate that there were other people in the area. Several of the cars had the hoods propped open, as if they had overheated or had had engine trouble. Others looked like the owners had left them in a hurry, leaving bags and luggage strapped to the tops and car doors open.

"That doesn't look good," Richard commented, seeing a line of dropped baggage and assorted fallen clothes leading into the trees.

The others were silent as they imagined what could have led to the people fleeing into the woods. What had scared them from the safety and mobility of their vehicles? Was it zombies all the way out here? That didn't seem likely. Bandits? Had they run out of gas?

After a few miles of passing sporadic derelicts, they spotted a truck on the side that had run into the back of another smaller vehicle. Both looked unserviceable from the crash and were riddled with bullet holes. There didn't appear to be any intact glass left in them, and a human corpse hung limp half in and out of one of the windows. The side of the car door where the body slumped was streaked with dried blood.

The crows that had been pecking at the dead flesh didn't even stir as they drove past.

"Now that definitely doesn't look good," Scott said.

Richard nodded and turned to Jason.

"It's almost dark enough to use the headlights, but I think it might be a good idea if we did without them for as long as possible. Who knows what kind of attention we will draw to ourselves out here? I have a feeling live humans are going to be more of a worry on this road than zombies."

"The night vision goggles I told you about are in a drawer back there," Jason replied, gesturing behind them. "If we are going to drive without headlights, I will need a pair in a little bit once it gets too dim out there."

"Ok, good."

"And we have an infrared spotlight up top that we can use to illuminate the road if there isn't enough starlight for the NVG's."

"Even better," Richard replied, "But let's hold off on the spotlight until absolutely necessary. I realize most people out there won't be able to see that spectrum of light, but if any of them have night vision devices also, our goose is cooked...so to speak."

Jason nodded his understanding and went back to concentrating on the road.

"I'll go get the NVG's," Hanna offered, finding herself becoming anxious after seeing the derelict vehicles. "Do you want something to drink while I'm up?"

"No, thanks, Babe. I'm fine."

Hanna nodded then got up and touched his shoulder.

Jason reached up and patted her hand then sighed as she went to the back.

"The world's gone to hell," he muttered under his breath.

Hanna came back with a bottle of water and the pelican case that held the night vision. Plunking down into her seat, she put the bottle in a cup holder then opened the case, removed the goggles, and looked at them dubiously.

"Uh…"

She looked at Jason, but she knew he couldn't help her without taking his attention off the road, so she turned to the back.

"Could one of you help me with this?" She asked.

"What's up?" Richard responded, going closer.

She held them up.

"What do I do?"

"Oh, here," Richard offered with an extended hand.

She put the goggles in his hand and handed over the case as well.

Richard reached into the case and took out the head harness and the batteries. He put the batteries into the compartment on the side of the goggles, sealed it up, and then attached the goggles to the harness.

"Here you go," he said, handing them back. "Just pull the straps here to tighten it down once it's on his head. You can swivel them up out of the way if we come to a place with enough external light to see by. Just take the lens cap off when you're ready to use them. Oh, and the power switch is right here," he said, showing her each of the features.

"Thanks"

He nodded and turned to go back to his seat.

"Richard," Jason said, keeping his eyes on the road.

"Yeah?" he asked, turning back.

"We're down to a quarter tank of gas. Nobody topped it off before we left, and this thing was designed to be part of a convoy, a convoy that would carry its own extra fuel."

"So we need to find somewhere to fill up."

"Right, and I don't know how far we will have to go before we find any place suitable. Coeur d'Alene is sure to have fuel, but they are sure to have zombies in the streets as well and maybe looters."

Richard nodded and looked back to see Scott reach for and open a road map book of the United States that they had found in the storage area under the bench seats.

"I'll see if we can find a gas station on the maps somewhere between here and Coeur d'Alene," he replied then went back to join Scott.

"Good," Jason said, "I'd really not like to go for a stroll out there if we go dry."

"We'll find something," Richard added reassuringly.

Minutes later, just as the last light of the day was beginning to fade, they were forced to go off the shoulder of the road into the grass to bypass a multi-car pile-up that completely blocked the lanes. The remains of several bodies were nearby and had clearly been ravaged by something that had been hungry. They hoped it was wild animals. Once past the pile-up, the road opened up again.

The interior was dark. They left the lights off inside and out to keep from attracting attention as they drove. Jason wore the night vision goggles, and up to that point had had enough external natural light for the NVG's to amplify that they had not needed to resort to the IR spotlight.

For the others without night vision, the dark, combined with fatigue from earlier stress, began to make the fight against sleep a losing battle.

Jason needed to keep his eyes on the road or he would have glanced back to confirm what his ears were telling him: that either Scott or Richard was snoring. Even from the seat next to him, he could hear Hanna's soft breathing as she submitted to the sandman as well.

He sighed heavily and began to wish that he could join their slumber. Then something flashed in front of the vehicle. He yelled in surprise and was late in slamming his foot on the brake. The mobile lab shuddered as it ran over whatever had gone in front of it. It came to a halt and rocked on its shocks.

"What happened?" Richard asked, just barely above a whisper.

Jason jumped in surprise. He hadn't heard Richard approach.

"I...I don't know. I just ran over something. It came out of nowhere. I just...I didn't see it in time. I..."

"It's ok, Jason. Take a breath. We're all ok in here," Richard said comfortingly. "Was it a deer?"

Jason let out a strangled sigh.

"It looked more like a person," he replied, sounding miserable.

Richard couldn't see his face but he imagined the tortured look Jason must have been making.

"Ok, well, it doesn't look like there is anything showing on the camera, so I guess I'd better go take a look around. I'll be right back. Leave the lights off."

"All right"

He went back to his seat, where Scott had stopped snoring, and grabbed the second pair of NVG's that he had already had out and prepared, just sitting on the table.

"What's going on?" Scott asked.

"Not sure. We ran over something. I'm going to go take a look."

He went back to the front. Jason and Hanna were whispering to each other. They both sounded uppity, like they were working each other up.

"I'm telling you I don't know. It came out of nowhere," Jason tried to explain. "I didn't get a good enough look to be able to tell what it was."

"Hey, Hanna," Richard interrupted.

"Yes?"

"Do you mind if I take that seat for a little while?"

"Oh, ok, I guess," she replied, before going back to join Scott.

Richard took her seat and put on the night vision goggles. When he turned them on, the nightscape outside became illuminated in shades of green. He didn't see any signs of whatever Jason had just run over or narrowly missed. In the distance, just at the limit of the NVG's illumination range, he saw something else in the road. The slow, jerky upright movements made it clear that it was no longer anything human.

"How far are we from Coeur d'Alene?" he asked.

"We passed a sign a few miles back that said ten miles, so about six, maybe seven miles."

"And we're already seeing zombies. Damn. This is going to get nasty. But it also means we're close to a possible source of fuel. There should be a small town just a mile or two ahead. We should be able to fill up there."

Richard flipped the NVG's up and massaged his temples with his fingertips.

"We have to keep going forward. Just slow it down some so if you run over any more of the dead, we won't take any damage."

"You got it," Jason replied and put the vehicle back in gear.

Richard went back to his seat at the table, and Jason began driving again, albeit a bit slower than he had been earlier. Hanna reclaimed the front passenger seat.

"What's wrong?" she asked, seeing her husband shake his head in the dull glow from the vehicle console.

He sighed.

"All of this destruction and mayhem." He sighed again. "And all because our worked helped a damned madman."

"I think you're being a little too hard on yourself. Don't you? We were trying to help people with our research."

Jason shook his head.

"Maybe in time, but we were making a better killer for the military. A 'super-soldier.' What the hell were we thinking?"

They sat in silence for a few moments.

"Oh my god," Jason said, dragging the words out as he slowed their vehicle.

"What is it?" Hanna asked, fear creeping into her voice.

"Look out there," he whispered, pointing out through the windshield.

Even without a night vision device to enhance her sight, she could see hundreds of people in the street, blocking their progress as they walked slowly towards the mobile lab. They looked slouched, heads tilted mostly down. The full moon reflected off of their faces and, in a few places, bald heads. Almost every one of them had plainly visible blood stains on their clothing and multiple gashes and bite marks somewhere about their body.

They were definitely infected.

"Just don't stop," Hanna said. "If you do, we might have trouble going again."

"Richard, we've got infected."

Richard left the table and went back to the front, taking his NVG's with him. He put them on and looked out through the front.

The closest of the crowd really stood out to him. The man's eyeballs each dangled by the optic nerve about an inch out of their sockets, as if he had been smacked in the back of the head with a length of two-by-four lumber. If that had been the case, it clearly wasn't enough to scramble the brain matter because he was shambling along just like the others, blood stains and gore coating his waxen skin and what clothing he still wore.

Richard felt bile rise in his stomach and sting his esophagus. Closing his eyes, he swallowed it down and let it pass. When he reopened his eyes, he forced himself to not focus on any particular infected and to keep his eyes moving.

They looked even worse on the camera monitors in the center console. He kept his eyes away from looking at them.

While their numbers were certainly intimidating, they didn't seem to even register the presence of the vehicle that was beginning to roll through their midst. As Jason rolled right over the zombies in the front, none of whom moved out of the way, crushing their bodies below the mobile lab's oversized wheels, Richard kept his eyes on the infected not immediately in front of them, off to the sides. They just kept walking down the road, oblivious to the faraday cage on wheels that passed through them. Some of them glanced towards the source of the sounds created by the bones of their fellows being crushed against the asphalt, but they didn't stop moving with the flow of their pack.

Jason kept the lab moving, and within minutes they had passed through the mob. A few stragglers remained here and there, but they weren't close to the vehicle. They were off on the shoulder of the road, and they were moving very slowly with a kind of jerky, rigid rhythm.

"Why would they move like that and not like the others?" Richard asked.

"My best guess is that they were damaged enough fighting humans after they were infected that the nanos in their blood released a coagulating agent to prevent catastrophic blood loss, so they could continue to infect more humans," Jason replied. "We came up with that idea years ago, the coagulating part I mean. The blood gels, and the limbs holding it lose most of their maneuverability and flexibility, but they can continue to move enough to keep going."

"And why haven't I heard anything about this before?" Richard asked. "Something like that could have saved a lot of guys on the battlefield."

"Sure, if it actually worked the way we wanted it to. The problem we kept running into was keeping the effects localized to just injured parts of the body. We didn't want immobile jelly men that were just barely alive, but that's what we kept getting. We ended up giving up on the project. It looks like Josh found a use for it after all, that bastard."

A few minutes later, they passed a sign that read, "Post Falls, Population 28,651." Another minute later, Jason saw something that raised his spirits.

"Oh, thank goodness," he said.

"What is it?" Hanna asked. "What do you see?"

"A gas station," her husband replied.

Once again Richard left the small table and went to the front.

"A gas station," he parroted, looking outside. "Good, but will we be able to get gas? That's the question. It's awfully dark out there."

"Too dark," Hanna replied.

"That's why we have night vision," Scott offered.

"I'll go out and scout around," Richard said. "See if there is still power to the pumps and make sure we won't be bothered by anything that might want to hurt us while we fill up."

"I'll go with you," Scott said.

"Bad idea, Scott," Richard replied. "I appreciate the offer, but there are only two pairs of NVG's, and one of them needs to stay here."

"But why? If we both go, we can cut our time outside in half. We can get out of here sooner."

"True, but if one or both of us are injured in such a way that we can't make it back, how are either Jason or Hanna going to find us? How would they be able to drive undetected in the dark?

"If I go alone and then get hurt or trapped, you all will still have a pair to keep you going. And it's definitely too dark out there to be fumbling along without them. Sure, the lab has cameras, but their range sucks."

Scott sighed and itched at a scab on his elbow.

"Yeah, you're right," he said, after a few moments of hesitation. "Well, at least take a radio with you, so we'll know to come looking for you if you do get hurt."

Richard nodded.

"Yes, that is a good idea, but I'm going to keep it turned off unless I need to talk to you. Remember, radio waves and other electrical signals attract and power the infected."

The others nodded.

"Be careful out there," Scott said. "None of us want to have to go out there looking for you."

"Thanks. I'll be careful. You all just stay put until I take a look around."

"No argument there," Jason replied.

"That guy either has massive balls or he is nuts," Scott said after Richard had stepped out.

They locked the door behind him.

"You're telling me," Jason replied. "I'd be scared shitless to go out there alone."

Outside, Richard took three steps away from the mobile lab and then went down to rest on one knee.

"What is he doing?" Jason asked, as he watched with the other set of NVG's.

"Why are you asking us?" Scott replied. "You're the only one that can see anything in the dark. What do you see?"

"He's just kneeling there. He stopped moving."

"It sounds like he is taking in his surroundings," Scott replied. "What the ground-pounders call a 'security halt'."

"Hmm, that makes sense."

Moments of uncomfortable silence ticked by inside before Jason spoke again.

"There he goes. He's moving."

Richard's mouth hung open, his jaw slack, enabling him to hear better than he otherwise would have been able to and to taste what was on the slight breeze, enhancing his sense of smell, a trick he had picked up in the Marine Corps. He heard some distant crickets serenading and smelled and tasted faint traces of gasoline as well as the distinctively putrid stench of rotting flesh.

The traces of gasoline lent him hope but the other smells worried him. He scanned the area around him with the night vision but didn't spot anything moving. Checking behind him, he saw blood and gore covering the tires of the mobile lab. The smell was awful. Hopefully it was the only source of what he smelled. He turned his head back forward.

The gas station was the only building in the immediate area, but it looked to also have service bays connected to it that indicated it had also offered vehicle repair services. A small fenced area behind it looked like the resting place for a pair of dumpsters. An icebox was outside next to the front doors. A single car was parked next to the service bays and another was parked in front of the store area. Dense trees stood as a backdrop to the scene.

Scanning to his right, he saw the gas pumps. Two islands, each holding two pumps, stood under the typical shelter designed to keep travelers dry in inclement weather while they filled their tanks with fuel. The pumps were deserted now, though a pair of plastic owls still kept watch from the rafters above.

Moving on, he looked farther to his right and saw a fuel tanker. Parked at an angle to his position as it was, he couldn't see much beyond the truck, but on the facing side it appeared to have its fuel hose still connected to the station's underground storage tanks. By the looks of it, they wouldn't have a problem getting fuel for their trek. He even considered maybe, after they were done filling up the mobile lab, seeing if the truck would start and taking it with them. It had been a while since he had driven anything requiring a Commercial Driver's License, but he still remembered how to do it.

Like riding a bicycle, he thought.

He pushed those thoughts away and focused back on the task at hand.

Beyond the truck was the road they had just come in on.

He stood up from his kneeling position and walked towards the left side of the gas station where there were the vehicle service bays and the dumpsters. Moving slowly, heel to toe to make as little noise as possible, he concentrated on what was around him.

It was difficult to determine if the dark stains on the pavement were from vehicles leaking oil or from the blood of zombie attack victims. He hoped it was just oil. The service bay doors were closed.

Several times he had to zig and zag around loose gravel that would definitely crunch underfoot if he walked on it.

He turned the corner and walked up on the car that was parked next to the service area. It was one of the small, two-door varieties. It was empty of anything substantial. Judging by the selection of clothing that was strewn willy-nilly in the backseat, the car belonged to a female, probably in her late teens to early twenties. Wherever she happened to be, he hoped she was safe and not walking around trying to bite people.

The air tasted and smelled slightly fresher away from the pumps, though the smell coming from the dumpster area wasn't much better. The woods were closer and seemed more sinister, though the logical side of his brain told him he likely had more to fear here, near the man-made structure, than he would if he were in the heart of the forest.

The dumpster area was clear, so he moved on.

The back door to the gas station was locked and felt pretty solid, but there were dark stains on its surface that were clearly congealed blood. Somebody had been beating on the door, trying to get in. It didn't look like they had succeeded.

Walking around the rest of the building's perimeter, he didn't find much else. There weren't any other entrances into the station. He didn't find any bodies, mobile or otherwise. He did find a handprint on the wall that was probably made in blood. He guessed that whoever had been beating on the back door had finally given up and stumbled away, using the wall to support themselves at some point and leaving the print in the process.

So far his scouting mission wasn't turning anything up, and that was a good thing, but he reminded himself not to grow complacent. There could always be something waiting for him at the corner up ahead. He looked over his shoulder to make sure nothing was sneaking up behind him.

Clear.

A crinkling noise came from just around the corner, and he found his heart rate pick up the pace. Easing a look around the edge, he spotted...nothing, nothing threatening anyway.

A large propane tank was nearby, and at its base a plastic grocery bag had caught on a protruding piece of metal. A breeze blew and the bag snapped in the wind, making the crinkling noise again.

He took a calming breath and checked around the back side of the tank, just to be safe, then moved on.

As he moved up, he found himself back up at the front of the station. Looking around, he saw nothing in the trees to his left or near the tanker truck ahead of him, so he inspected the vehicle in front of the station.

It was a light-colored SUV. The driver's side door was open, and blood was pooled on the ground below it. There wasn't any noticeable smell coming from it, but he looked in through the windows anyway. Empty.

He turned away from the SUV and focused on the gas station. No movement was visible inside the store section, but even with the NVG's on, he had trouble seeing all the way inside. There were blood stains on the glass, but reaching up and touching, he found that they were on the outside.

The front doors were locked together, and, upon closer inspection, he saw that there was a chain wrapped around the interior handles and secured with a padlock.

Maybe someone is still inside, he thought.

Putting the pieces together of what he had seen so far on his little walk about, he deduced that maybe the female that owned the car parked around the corner had locked herself in for safety and hadn't been able to leave. But then, it also wasn't outside the realm of possibility that she had locked up the station and then left out the back door, likely with someone else.

Even though they were there for gas and not to look for survivors, he decided to risk looking a little deeper into the station. Not a huge risk he told himself, just enough to satisfy his conscience that he wouldn't be leaving behind a maiden in distress.

He reached up and switched on the infrared light source that was integral to the NVG's. The resulting beam of light allowed him to look deeper into the building through the glass, but it wouldn't be visible to anyone without night vision capabilities.

Just outside of his normal range of NVG vision, he now saw that there was a body lying on the floor inside. Much of it had been torn apart, as if it had been mauled by a wild animal, and the back of the head appeared to be caved in. Blood and gore coated the floor around it. It looked like it had at one time been the cashier, a hairy cashier with a beer belly.

Not the girl, at least, he thought. *If there even was a girl. Maybe dead cashier dude had a teenaged daughter, and that's his car out there.*

He inspected the rest of the store through the glass. It had the usual shelves with candy bars and a few canned goods and convenience items for travelers who didn't want to take the time to stop at a real grocery store.

Finally, he saw another person inside. They were standing in the back corner looking up the ceiling and kind of swaying back and forth from one foot to the other. It was a man. A man in a dark-colored jumpsuit.

Auto-mechanic, he realized. *And he's infected. Damn! What is he doing?...Well, whatever, it doesn't matter—at least he isn't trying to get out.*

If there was a girl inside she was likely dead or a zombie. The proof was in a dark jumpsuit.

Richard switched the IR off and walked silently away from the station towards the fuel tanker and the pumps. That was the last place to check before he would feel comfortable making the noise that pumping gas would surely make.

He winced as a patch of gravel that he hadn't noticed crunched underfoot, but he froze in place and listened to see if he had attracted any attention.

The seconds ticked by.

Nothing presented itself as a threat, so he resumed his path to the truck. Having already seen one side when he first left the mobile lab, he went around the opposite side. The driver's side window was rolled down halfway. That didn't bode well for anyone who might have hidden inside if the infected had come through since then.

Moving as slowly and silently as possible, he climbed up the step and peeked into the truck's cab through the mostly open window. At any moment he half expected an infected horror to lunge for him with a growl, but there was no one there.

He blew out the deep breath he had been holding and stepped down and away from the truck. The only other area for him to check was the fuel pump pad right next to the truck, but he could see right through the area. There was nowhere for a zombie to hide, and the area was clear.

He walked over and began looking at the pumps. Like the station, they had no electricity to power them, either deliberately for safety or due to a local power outage.

Damn, he thought. *I guess we'll just have to pump it directly out of the fuel truck.*

As he walked towards the mobile lab, he reached up to turn on the two-way radio he had been carrying and let the others know that he was going to come in so that they would unlock the door for him, but before he could, the door swung open a few inches. Clearly Jason had been watching his progress.

"Good news," he said, as he stepped inside and sat down.

The others were silent as they waited for him to elaborate. Scott turned to face him after he relocked the door.

"There is fuel that we can use," he finally continued. "The station itself is locked up tight, and it doesn't have power anyway, so there's no need to bother going in to try to get the pumps to work from inside. There is food on the shelves, but there is an infected hanging out right by them. At least one. It is possible there could be a few more where I couldn't see. I'd rather not take the risk when we have enough provisions already to get us home.

"Now, while we can't power the pumps here or from inside the station, we should still be able to get plenty of fuel. Judging by the smell of gas outside, there's plenty available in the truck. Even if this lab is a beast on gas, there should be enough in the truck to get us the rest of the way home."

"That is good news," Hanna said. "But are you sure there are no more of those *things* out there?"

Richard sighed.

"Other than the one I saw locked up inside the station, no, I didn't see any more of those *things*."

He wanted to tell her to just call them zombies and be done with it, but he kept his irritation to himself.

"I'm thinking," He continued, "that the mob, or herd, or whatever you want to call it that we saw a few miles back, is what's left of the people from around here, and they were headed exactly opposite and away from us. So, I think we should be ok. I'll still want someone else out there to watch my back, while I concentrate on getting the fuel from that truck into our tanks."

"I'll do it," Jason volunteered.

A worried look flashed across Hanna's face, but she didn't say anything.

Richard could understand how she felt, but times were dangerous and everyone needed to contribute to their survival.

"Thank you," he said. "Scott, be ready to let us back in in a hurry if we come running, and, Hanna, be ready to drive us the hell out of here if things break bad. We'll have both pairs of NVG's with us, so if it comes down to it, turn the headlights on and go—after we're back inside."

Both Scott and Hanna nodded their understanding.

"All right. Jason, park this thing over there by the truck. If we make sure we are close enough now, we can limit out exposure time outside."

There was just barely enough room to squeeze the lab in under the pumps' overhead shelter. Jason parked it about twenty feet away from the derelict fuel truck then stood up and accepted the newly suppressed MP5 that Richard offered him.

"You ready?" Richard asked.

Jason nodded.

"All right. Just like we talked about."

Jason nodded again and gave a thumbs up, but his movements were jerky and forced. He was scared.

Can't blame him for that, Richard thought then gave a single nod to Scott by the door.

Richard stepped out first and looked around at the NVG green-tinted world. It looked as dead and as quiet as it had when he had first gone out. Moving to the front of the vehicle, he knelt down to a knee and relaxed his jaw, listening, listening.

Jason stepped out behind him, went to the back of the vehicle, and took a knee, holding the MP5 tight to his chest.

Richard heard the door click shut behind them then did a slow thirty count in his head as he scanned the area, paying particular attention to the closest shadowed areas on either side of the gas station. When he was satisfied that their exit from the vehicle hadn't drawn any attention and that no zombies had approached since he'd been out the first time, he stood and walked over to the side of the fuel truck.

When Jason saw that Richard had moved, he too stood up and walked to the side of the truck. He looked back and forth from the gas station to the road, watching for any sign of movement, while Richard inspected the truck. He found himself panting for breath and tried to force himself to breathe slower. Then his hands began to shake, so he gripped the submachine gun tighter. It felt like this was taking forever. His mouth was dry, making it difficult to swallow, and his sphincter had squeezed itself so tight he doubted he'd be able to squeeze out even a teeny tiny—well, never mind. He didn't want to think about his bowels.

One of the gauges indicated that the fuel tank was empty. Richard looked at how the hose was connected to the truck and spotted the lever nearby that should control the flow of fuel. He moved the lever and heard nothing. He moved the valve again and realized that it had already been open.

Damn it, he thought. *The fuel truck operator left the valve open. It all just leaked right out.*

Stepping up behind his sentinel, he grabbed Jason's shoulder and squeezed then leaned forward to get as close to his ear as possible.

"The truck's empty," he whispered.

"What? You said it had fuel. What are we going to do?" Jason asked, a hint of desperation creeping into his voice. "We're just about out of gas. We have to do *something.*"

Richard nodded then looked around again and sighed.

"Is there a siphon pump or anything like that in the lab?"

"I don't think so, but if there is it would be in the back with the tools."

"Damn," Richard muttered. "Then there isn't. Scott and I went through all of those lockers and drawers, and we didn't see anything like that back there."

He sighed again then squeezed his eyes tight as if he had an ocular headache.

"There is something else we can try, but it's going to make more noise than we would like, and I doubt it will be fast."

"Oh, great. What is it?"

"The truck puts gas in the underground reservoirs through gravity feed, but sometimes the driver has to pump some of the fuel back out. So what we can do is turn on the truck's pump to pull the gas out of the ground and then put it into the lab from there."

"You said it's slow. How slow?"

"A couple of minutes to pump it back into the truck and another couple of minutes to put it into the lab. I know it doesn't sound like a long time, but with the noise drawing anything hostile in the area towards us, a couple of minutes times two will seem like a hell of a long time, especially if we have to start fighting."

Jason was silent for a second before replying.

"Why not put the other hose into the lab's fuel tank then turn on the pump? The gas goes into the truck and then gravity feeds right into the lab. Cut the time in half. Less exposure. Less risk of a drawn out fight."

Richard blinked and processed the suggestion then felt pretty stupid for not seeing the simpler solution himself.

"Yeah, that's good," he replied. "I'll get to it. Keep a close watch. The noise is liable to draw a crowd if there's anyone or anything left in the area."

Jason nodded and hefted the MP5 a little higher.

After stretching another hose from the truck to the lab and inserting it into the lab's fuel tank, Richard went back to the truck's pump control, primed it, and flipped the switch that should turn it on.

The little motor sputtered, making Richard worry that it wouldn't work and they'd have to find another way, and then it kicked in strong, and L.E.D. lights on the side of the truck and along the spine of the fuel tank itself flickered on with it.

It was considerably louder than he had expected it to be. With the rest of the town having no electricity and no vehicular traffic and thus being very quiet, the motor sounded like an ear splitting concert in volume.

He cringed inside, as he imagined the hordes of undead that could have just perked up and turned their way, hungry for living flesh.

Come on, come on, he thought.

He felt the fuel flowing through the dredge line into the fuel truck, and the smell of gasoline became stronger.

Come on, Baby. As fast as you can now.

He walked back to the lab and checked the hose there as well. The flow was slower, but the gas was moving. It was working.

A scream broke through the din of the truck's pump, and Richard turned towards it, unholstering his pistol and bringing his sights up.

"Look out!" A feminine voice called out from above the gas station. A woman was watching them from on the roof, one hand covering her mouth, the other arm outstretched and pointing.

He turned his gaze in the direction she indicated and saw Jason looking over at her as well. She was pointing at Jason. No, that wasn't right. She was pointing above him.

Oh shit!

He started turning towards his friend, and his mouth began forming words of warning, but he was too slow.

A dark shape fell on Jason, seemingly from out of nowhere, and knocked him to the ground.

A few suppressed shots went off as Jason instinctively jerked the trigger on the MP5, but the bullets hit the ground several meters behind the lab—not the zombie on top of him. He thrashed and jerked and jerked the submachine gun this way and that trying to keep the metal weapon between him and the jaws that would bring death with a single bite, jaws that were snapping at his face with determination. He yelled for help, both in fear and in pain.

Richard's couldn't shoot. He was just as likely to kill Jason as stop the zombie, so he ran towards them instead.

The two seconds it took to reach his friend felt like the longest of his life. In that time, he could see that the zombie used to be the fuel truck driver and that he had already torn a gouge out of Jason's left bicep with a vicious, shaking bite.

The zombie turned its head for a bite at Jason's neck just as Richard arrived.

Even as he did it, he knew it was a bad idea, but he didn't want to risk the neck bite on his friend. He punched his arm under the zombie's head, so he could lift the head away from Jason and get a shot off with his gun.

As he lifted the zombie's head and brought his gun up to its temple, he felt an intense pain in his forearm, as the putrid corpse bit into his flesh. Yelling in pain, Richard pulled the trigger and watched the side of the zombie's head shatter outward to follow the path of the bullet that ended it forever.

The unsuppressed shot was loud. If the motor on the truck's fuel pump hadn't drawn distant zombies towards them, that shot surely would.

The driver's corpse collapsed on Jason, pulling Richard with it.

Jason groaned.

"Hang in there, Jason," Richard mumbled, as he sat up and rolled the zombie truck driver off to the side. "Come on. Let's get you back into the lab."

Blood ran down Jason's arm. It looked bad.

"Oh, my gosh, it burns," Jason croaked.

"Yeah, I feel it. The sorry bastard got me too."

They left the fuel pump running and stumbled over to the lab supporting each other.

Richard reached up and pounded his fist against the door.

He heard cursing inside.

The door remained closed.

Inside the lab there was an uneasy silence as Hanna and Scott tried to watch the men outside without the benefit of night vision optics.

Hanna's heart was pounding. Continuing a bad habit that she had given up seven years prior, she brought her hand up to her face and began chewing on her fingernails. She knew she would regret it later, especially after she could see the damage she was doing in the dark, but she was worried sick about her husband.

"What is taking so long?" Scott asked.

He drummed his fingers on the table.

"Stop. Did you hear that?" Hanna asked.

"Yeah. I'm not sure what it was, but I heard it."

A few seconds later they heard the fuel pump kick on.

"Oh, good, they got it working."

"It shouldn't be long now," Scott said, as he resisted the urge to itch his scalp.

The lights on the fuel truck lit up and cast a dim glow on the pumps and the men.

"I wish I could go in the station and grab some snacks. I'd kill for a Suzie-Q right about now."

"Shush. What was that?" Hanna asked.

"What was what?"

"I thought I heard a scream...from over there," she said, pointing towards the gas station.

Scott shook his head and sighed. The light from the tanker was just too weak to see beyond the pumps. The two men outside could obviously see something because they were looking towards the gas station. He began to get a bad feeling welling up inside of him.

Then they both saw something fall on Jason.

"Oh, no," Hanna gasped.

"Get ready to drive," Scott ordered as he stepped over to man the entrance. He held his hand up in front of him, so he wouldn't bump into anything. It was still too dark to see anything inside the lab.

Come on, guys. Don't get bit, he thought. *Don't get bit.*

Hanna wasn't quiet as she bumped her knees and shin getting situated into the driver's seat.

They heard a loud gunshot from outside.

Shit. Shit!

Scott wanted to just open the door and usher the guys in if they were ready, but he couldn't see well enough, and it was driving him nuts. He knew it would be foolish to open the door just to have a couple of zombies waiting right there for him.

Flashlight. Where's the flashlight?...On the table.

He stepped back to the table, felt for the light, turned it on, and grabbed his handgun.

By the time he was back at the door, someone was on the other side banging on it.

"Scott, it's us. Let us in!" Richard yelled, as he banged a fist against the door.

The door cracked outward and his vision went white as the night vision goggles flared in the wake of Scott's flashlight.

"Here, take Jason. Get him to the lab," he ordered, pushing Jason up the step into the vehicle.

"Oh my god; he's bleeding," Scott stammered.

"Get him back to the lab!" Richard repeated.

"Did he get bit?" the younger man demanded as he tapped the gun in his hand against his thigh.

Don't even think about it, kid, Richard thought, seeing the gun in Scott's hand twitching towards them.

"Later, Scott! Get him to the lab *now!*"

Scott relented and threw an arm around Jason.

Richard stripped the MP5 off of Jason's shoulder before he was out of reach and checked the chamber. It was ready to go.

"What happened?" Hanna asked, the fear and worry in her voice just barely held in check.

345

"I'll explain in a minute, Hanna," Richard replied, "But we need to get out of here. Start the engine. Don't turn on the headlights. As soon as the fuel gauge shows full we'll leave. Right now, I have to go back out there. There's a survivor on the roof."

Hanna blinked away a few tears and nodded her head as Richard stepped back outside. The door clicked shut behind him.

Richard holstered his handgun and brought the MP5 to his shoulder. The NVG's brought the world back into illuminated green clarity. He scanned the area, keeping the MP5 pointed everywhere that he looked.

The damage was already done with the gunshot he had made earlier. Any zombies still in the area would be coming. The suppressed MP5 would give him more bullets in the fight, thanks to the high-capacity magazines, and the quieter shots would not speed even more zombies his way. They'd still have to hunt him.

He walked closer to the gas station building.

"Hey! Lady! On the roof," he called, trying to be quiet and yet loud enough to be heard at the same time.

He heard some scuffing from above.

"Go away," she warned. "You'll just bring more of those things."

"I can help you escape," Richard offered. "You can't survive long up there. You're trapped. You'll be safer with us."

He listened for a reply but didn't hear anything for a few short breaths. Then he heard scuffling, stumbling footsteps.

Crap!

Looking to his left, he saw them, a crowd of the undead. They'd found him. After another second of looking, he realized that they weren't coming towards him; they were going towards the lab.

The fuel pump is drawing them now. Damn! They're going to cut off my escape route.

Aiming down the sights of the MP5, he shot the three in the lead and then a few more that were a little further behind.

"Last chance, Lady. More are coming, and we're leaving. Last chance to free yourself."

He didn't wait for a reply. Instead, he turned back to the advancing horde and brought down one after another with shots to the craniums.

But they just kept coming. There were certainly more of them than he had bullets.

A loud thump sounded behind him, and he checked real quick to make sure one of the zombies hadn't snuck up on him while he was distracted by the large group.

It was a duffel bag. The girl had dropped it and was now easing herself over the edge of the roof to follow it.

She slid down until she was hanging by her finger tips and then dropped. She landed with a grunt then grabbed her bag and sprinted towards the mobile lab.

Good girl, Richard thought and looked back towards the advancing mob. He had time to take a few more shots, kill a few more undead permanently, but he decided to conserve ammo instead. There would be safety enough inside the vehicle, so he ran.

The area around the bite on his forearm felt like it was on fire. He shrugged it off and tried to ignore it as he ran to reach the lab.

The girl from the roof made it to the door and began knocking, the strap of her duffel bag held tightly in her other hand. She looked like she was ready to swing it at anything that approached.

A real fighter, Richard thought. *That's good.*

Passing her by, he went to the fuel hose that was inserted into the fuel tank. Gasoline was overflowing and spilling onto the concrete. He jerked the hose out of the mouth of the tank then twisted on the fuel cap.

Then he was back at the door, pounding on it with her, and a second later it popped open.

The approaching horde was just coming under the pumps' overhead shelter.

"In you go," Richard said to the girl.

"Without any hesitation, she jumped inside.

Scott's flashlight illuminated the entry, causing Richard's NVG's to flare in his vision. Ignoring his temporary blindness, he jumped into the lab, smacking his shoulder on the door frame.

He turned and slammed the door closed once he was inside then turned the deadbolt to be extra sure nothing would be coming through behind him.

"Go, Hanna," he urged, as he brushed the NVG's up and off of his head. He checked to make sure the tube was turned off, since batteries could very well soon be irreplaceable.

The lab lurched into motion, and he stuck an arm out to grab the dinette counter to help him keep his balance.

He bent over and tried to catch his breath. His bite wound was beginning to intrude agonizingly on his senses again.

He clenched his hand into a fist then released it.

Other than his rapid breathing and the revving of the engine as Hanna tried to bring the lab up to speed, the interior was quiet.

When he looked up, Richard saw that the girl from the roof had moved up to hide behind Scott. Silhouetted against the glow of the headlights that Hanna had turned on, Scott stood a few feet away, his feet spread for balance in the swaying motion of the vehicle, a shotgun pointed right at Richard's head.

Richard froze, giving Scott no excuse to shoot him.

"You're bit," Scott snarled.

Richard saw Scott's finger hovering over the trigger.

Aw, shit, he thought.

Chapter 26: Triage

In a calm and soothing voice Richard said, "Scott, stop aiming the gun at me please, and let's talk like adults."

"You're bit, Richard! Or should I call you 'Philip'? Philip Quinio."

His eyes seemed to reflect a look of triumph.

"Call me whatever you like, but please put the gun down. I need to save Jason. There is a lot going on here that you don't know about."

"Oh, yeah? Like what? Like you spying for the Chinese? Or is it the Koreans...the Russians?"

The shotgun didn't waver.

Richard took that as a good sign, despite not wanting to be looking down that barrel. It showed that at least Scott was in control of himself.

"Like, there is a cure for what is happening out there. Like, I know who is responsible for all of this *shit*, and I plan on making them pay. And if you give me a few minutes, I can go back there into the lab and save Hanna's husband before it is too late."

The look on Scott's face told Richard that he was at least considering what he had said.

"Scott?" Hanna said. "Give him a chance. What Richard is saying is true as far as we can tell. He..."

"He's lying. His name isn't even 'Richard,' Hanna," Scott interrupted, never taking his eyes or the gun off of Richard. "His name is Philip Quinio, and he is a spy. I learned that much before we left DARPA. You can't trust him. You can't believe what he says."

"Scott, I can explain all of that rather easily," Richard said. "But right now Jason needs me. He doesn't have much longer before I can't help him."

"You've both been bitten. You'll infect the rest of us."

"This isn't a video game, Scott! This is real life, and in real life there are rules. Do you really think the man who put this together was so suicidal that he would make this zombie shit without having a way to counteract it? Do you? There *is* a cure.

"You're right, my name isn't Richard. It's Philip Quinio, that's 'kin-you' not 'kwin-ee-oh.' I was spying on Josh Harper, the creator of the zombie series nano. I was working for the Defense Intelligence Agency—the *United States* Defense Intelligence Agency. Not the Chinese or any other foreign government. You could say I was acting like an undercover internal affairs officer, under orders, but working across agencies within our government instead of within a single police department.

"You got me. You figured it out. But I already told Hanna and Jason all of this before we left Spokane. Now can I go save Jason before he has a chance to turn?"

"Fine," Scott relented. "Go, but leave your guns."

Richard gritted his teeth, but unslung the MP5 and put it on the counter. Then, slowly, he grabbed the handgun from his holster, and placed it next to the MP5.

Turning away from Scott, he walked the last few steps to the hermetically sealed door to the lab, hoping the whole time that Scott wouldn't shoot him in the back. Opening, the door and stepping through, he breathed a sigh of relief and closed the door, happy to be in one piece.

The lights came on as he turned the locking mechanism on the door. He had told Scott that he could save Jason, and, with the Harper Series nanos floating around in his own system, he hoped he wouldn't succumb to the Zombie Series either. But if he were wrong, he didn't want to put the others at risk. He was putting faith in Harper's work and in his diary claims. He had no other choice, unless you counted Scott's solution.

Jason was sitting on the floor, leaning against the base of the counter, cradling his left arm in front of him with his eyes closed. His eye lids fluttered as Richard approached.

"How are you doing, Jason?"

"My arm burns like hell," he replied, with chattering teeth.

"I see you did a little bit of self-aid," Richard said, gesturing towards the belt he saw wrapped tightly around Jason's arm just below the armpit. "That was smart. Slow that blood flow down."

"I don't think it will matter. I can feel the burn moving up past the tourniquet."

"Well, maybe I can take care of that," Richard said, as he went down to one knee in front of him.

He unclasped the snaps on both of the watches he was wearing and slid one off of each wrist.

"Here, let's get these on you," he said, as he slipped them onto Jason. "These were Harper's. Remember?"

Jason nodded.

"I'm in pain, but I haven't gotten amnesia."

Richard laughed.

"Good. In his diary, Harper said he created these to limit the amount of nano replication inside the body as well as to block the signal his new Harper Series gives off which can be tracked, just like the GPS on a phone. You'll be hidden from the zombies with these too. You'll have your own little invisibility cloak."

Richard worked quickly, talking to keep Jason focused.

"So these are supposed to stop the bugs in me, huh?"

Richard raised an eyebrow in surprise that the scientist would use a layman's slang term for the nanos and wondered if it was a sign of degradation of Jason's brain integrity.

He looked into Jason's eyes, not only to show him that he meant what he was about to say but also to check on his progression. His eyes were clear of any nano traces.

"Harper said they would stop his bugs. He trusted them enough to wear them himself," he replied.

Jason nodded.

"I guess they will have to be good enough for me too. I saw you take them off of him after you killed him."

"Sit tight," Richard ordered, as he stood and walked over to the lockers.

"Poor Hanna," Jason muttered. "I've put her through so much. She's a good wife. She doesn't deserve this."

"Hey, no more talk like that. You're not going anywhere. You're going to beat this, and you're going to help a lot of other people beat this, Hanna included."

He knelt back down in front of Jason and set the large medical kit from the locker on the floor beside him, along with an unopened five pound bag of sugar.

"We can take this tourniquet off now. The watches will either work or they won't."

Jason nodded and lifted his arm with a wince to give Richard access to the belt.

Richard released the buckle and unwound the belt from Jason's arm.

Jason looked like he was anticipating a more intense burn, but he relaxed when nothing happened. He clenched his hand into a fist several times to ease the needle pricks that he began to feel in his previously numb hand.

"Now, this is going to hurt too," Richard said as he lathered his hands in sanitizer and then slipped on a pair of latex gloves. "But if we don't do it, things will be bad."

He opened a foil packet of sterilized water and flushed Jason's wound, careful to also get the flap of skin that hung out like a half-peeled banana skin.

Jason gritted his teeth but said nothing.

"Yuck," Richard said, when he looked at the puddle on the floor. "I don't even want to think about what nasty shit was growing inside the mouth of the guy that bit you."

Jason closed his eyes and leaned his head back against the counter with a sigh.

"Sorry. I should have kept that thought to myself. Here, this is going to burn."

Jason clenched his jaw and nodded.

Richard dowsed the wound in Betadine from the first aid kit.

Jason flinched and groaned but took the pain in stride.

"Have you had a tetanus shot in the last five years?"

Jason nodded.

"Yeah, I got one last summer after I got cut up on some old, rusty barbed wire in a muddy field full of cow pies and an angry bull."

Richard stopped.

"What? How did that happen?"

"It's a rather embarrassing story that had to do with a dare that I'd really rather not like to repeat."

Richard chuckled and shook his head.

"I bet it's a good story too."

Jason grinned and raised his eyebrows as he nodded.

"Damn but we can do some stupid things to impress a woman."

Richard laughed.

"Yep, we sure can," he replied. "All right, enough said. You've got plenty to worry about here without adding wounded dignity to the list. You should be safe from tetanus, at least."

Jason pursed his lips and nodded.

"You're not going to like this next bit," Richard said, pulling the suture kit out of the medical bag and resting Jason's arm on his knee.

Jason let out a heavy breath and then wiped the sweat from his forehead with the back of his good hand.

"I'll like it a lot better than an infection," he replied. "Let's get it done with."

Richard nodded and threaded the needle.

"All right, now. Hold still," he said, as he transferred the suture needle to his left hand and reached into the plastic bag on the floor with his right. When his hand reemerged, he was holding a plastic scoop full of white granules.

"Is that sugar?" Jason asked.

"It sure is," Richard replied. "I wouldn't put salt on an open wound, now would I?"

"Damn, I hope not, but why sugar?"

Richard poured the sugar directly into the open bite wound and onto the inside of the flap of skin that jutted out below.

"Packing an open wound like yours with sugar before stitching it up allows the wound to breathe, which is a must, while also lowering the pH balance of the wound, which enhances the bacteriostatic effect, so bacteria won't grow inside and cause infection, along with other benefits like promoting dilation of small blood vessels, so you heal faster."

"That's good, I think," Jason said. "What? You're a doctor now? Can you say that again in layman's terms?"

Richard laughed.

"That *was* in layman's terms. OK. The sugar prevents infection and speeds recovery. If we sewed you up nice and tight without the sugar, bacteria that are already in the wound would multiply and eat you alive. Better?"

"Much"

Richard smiled and poked the suture needle through healthy flesh above the wound.

"Mmmmm!"

"Sorry," Richard said, as he pierced the flap of skin then drew it tight. He tied it off then snipped the needle free.

"One down. Quite a few more to go."

Jason groaned.

"I'm not a doctor, no, to answer your question," Richard said as he worked. "But I have had some pretty extensive medical training in treating wounds, a prerequisite, unfortunately, to going to some of the worst places on earth to hunt some of the worst people on the planet. A friend of mine made sure I got the training I'd need if I ever have to patch myself...or him up. You can't count on having all the newest advances in technology and medicine when you're knee deep in the shit. You gotta have the ability to fix things when you're in the middle of the poorest countries—or, apparently, when you find yourself in a zombie apocalypse."

Jason snorted at that then winced as the movement caused more pain.

"Almost done."

When Richard finished, Jason's face was covered in sweat.

"Done. You'll have a pretty impressive scar to show the grandkids someday."

"I sure as hell hope so, but I gotta work on having kids first."

Richard nodded and smiled then took off his gloves and popped the top of a medicine bottle. Nudging two pills out in a swaying motion, he gave one to Jason and swallowed the other himself.

"Cipro?" Jason asked.

"Yes," Richard replied. "Bites can leave some nasty bugs of the natural variety. This should keep them from messing us up any worse than we already are, and it will help your body kill off whatever bugs the sugar doesn't." He picked up his mess and started to walk away.

"What about a bandage?" Jason asked.

"Not on a wound like yours. It needs to breathe. Just make sure you keep it clean and dry, and don't put too much stress on it yet."

"OK," Jason replied then yawned. "I'm so tired."

Richard kneeled back down next to him. "Open your eyes; let me see."

Jason opened his eyes wide. Black lines had begun to form, just little hairline fractures of metal, but it was visible, even without his enhanced senses.

"You need to rest. Go ahead and get some shut eye."

Jason nodded and rested his head forward on his forearm and closed his eyes.

I hope these watches start working fast, or we're going to have a problem, Richard thought.

He walked over to the wall locker and sat down on its lip just above the floor. Folding his legs under him, he opened the medical bag and put on a new pair of latex gloves.

Opening another bottle of sterile water, he rinsed his own bite wound then flooded it with Betadine. The dark brown liquid mingled with the water on the floor and looked somewhat similar to old blood. He shook off the loose drops, dried the skin, and poured a scoop of sugar into his wound.

A loud buzzing from the lights over his head combined with the pungent smell of the Betadine on the floor was beginning to annoy him. Other sounds and senses began to intrude on his consciousness. Jason's breathing seemed louder. He could hear the crunch of pebbles under tire below him. He could smell Jason's wound and the not too pleasant odor of his own unshowered body. The light seemed brighter than it should be.

The Harper Series was clearly active again inside of him, he realized. Looking down at his wound, the pain receding more and more with every passing second, he saw that the gap between the skin was already starting to close and heal. He marveled at how quickly his body was fixing itself.

Then he noticed something that surprised him even more. With his renewed enhanced eye sight he could clearly see little black specks of metal smaller than the individual skin cells. They were being ejected from the bite wound, carried by only slightly larger silver specks.

He was surprised that he could see something so miniscule but also that the Harper Series was actively working against the zombie series. It was very encouraging.

It figures, he thought, shaking his head. *This stuff might make me immune to zombie bites, but now I'll have to worry about being tracked down by freaking super soldiers. It would be nice if I could wake up and find that this is all just one big fucked up dream.*

He sighed and clenched his fists, reveling in the feelings of strength deep within.

He knew he should feel exhausted with all that he had gone through, but he found that he was quite the opposite. He felt energized in a way he hadn't for as long as he could remember.

The lab bounced over a pot hole in the road, and it made a loud bump. The sound was loud enough to Richard's enhanced ears that it caused discomfort, and he reached up to cover them with his hands. He was hearing every creak and pop made by the shocks and shifting metal pieces that made up the frame of the mobile lab.

I've got to find a way to dial this down, or I'm going to go crazy with sensory overload, he thought. Trying to breathe as shallow as possible to limit his sense of smell, he wiped up the puddle of water and Betadine and then placed the wet cloth in a hazardous waste receptacle.

The door to the lab had a round window made of some kind of tempered glass or plastic and was about the size of a standard dinner plate. After putting the medical supplies away in the wall locker, Richard found himself standing in front of the door window looking out into the passenger compartment.

The lights were out up there, but still he could make out Hanna in the driver's seat, roof girl in the passenger seat, and Scott behind them, shotgun in hand, by the dim illumination provided by the different LED displays in the dash.

When he concentrated on ignoring the sound of his own beating heart, the lab's air purification fan, and the noise of the back wheels rubbing against the road, he found that he could hear the voices on the other side of the door.

It sounded like Hanna was just wrapping up an explanation of what a Faraday cage was and how it blocked the electromagnetic signals from powering the several series of nanos they had created at DARPA.

"So if you shut off all the electricity inside the cage, the nano things won't work anymore?" roof girl asked.

"Theoretically. I don't know everything about this new series my old boss came up with. There might be new features, if you want to call them that, which makes the new ones more versatile. I just won't know until I get a chance to do more research and tests."

Richard had been standing motionless long enough, with Jason already sleeping, that the automatic lights in the lab turned off overhead.

"I still say I'll shoot them both at the first sign that they've already turned or are about to turn," Scott said. "That's the mistake they always make in the movies and then—BAM! They infect the whole group."

"Richard said Harper..." Hanna began.

"His name is Philip," Scott interrupted.

"Fine, Scott. *Philip* told us that in Harper's diary, he talks about another nano series that is supposed to make whoever takes it immune to the effects of the zombie series as well as enhancing certain of the body's physical and immunological characteristics."

"So there is a cure?" roof girl asked.

"Yes, Erica. We believe there is a cure, and the only sample left is in Rich—I mean, Philip's body."

"Is there or isn't there?" Scott demanded. "You keep saying 'We believe' or 'Richard says this' or 'Richard says that'."

"Until I am able to do controlled tests in a controlled environment, or until I see everyone cured from

361

it, then I can't make definitive claims like that," Hanna replied. "I just don't have the data yet, and your attitude isn't helping anything."

"So Philip could be making all of this crap up," Scott said, his demeanor changing little.

"He could," Hanna agreed. "But I don't think he is. Back at the lab…"

Richard chose that moment to very noisily open the lock on the lab door and then the lab door itself. Until Scott could be convinced that he wasn't a bad guy or going to turn into a mindless zombie, he felt it prudent to leave him in the dark about his enhanced capabilities, and Hanna was getting close to spilling the figurative beans.

Scott jumped towards the door, grabbed the guns Richard had left on the counter, and retreated to stand between him and the women.

Richard sighed and shook his head. He closed the lab door then turned to the breaker panel and turned off all power going to the lab except for that of the air purifier. If for some reason Harper's watches didn't stop the zombie series, at least the lack, mostly, of electromagnetic signals in the lab would retard their rate of replication.

When he turned back towards Scott, instead of going up close to talk to them and risk a negative reaction from Scott, he sat at the small dining table at the midpoint of the vehicle, a safe distance away for Scott's feelings.

"What do you want?" Scott barked.

"Oh, Jason's fine now. Thanks for asking," Richard replied. "Hanna, you'll be glad to know that your husband's wound has been disinfected and sutured and that he now wears the watches Harper made specifically for preventing zombie series replication inside of their sphere of influence."

He didn't mention the black lines that had started in Jason's eyes.

"Oh, thank you, Richard," Hanna replied.

"Philip," Scott corrected, turning his head for an instant to cast a disapproving look at the driver.

In that instant, almost faster than the human eye could see, Richard stood, crossed the distance between him and Scott, and disarmed him of all three weapons, a feat he couldn't have even hoped for before.

Erica screamed, and Scott went from stunned to angry to scared-shitless in the space of two heart beats.

Hanna tried to see what was going on, taking her eyes off the road momentarily and causing the mobile lab to swerve a bit.

"Keep your eyes on the road please, Hanna," Richard said. "There are bad things out in the dark places, and I'd really rather not have to walk if you crash."

"Ok," Hanna said with a tremble in her voice as she nodded.

Richard walked backwards to the table and sat facing them again. He deliberately kept himself from bringing a hand up to rub his ears which were ringing now thanks to Erica's scream and his enhanced hearing.

The ringing subsided and then disappeared just a few seconds later, and Richard smiled, marveling at how quickly the Harper series nanos repaired his damaged internal ear.

"So, your name is Erica. Is that correct?" Richard asked.

Roof girl nodded in fear.

"Just Erica? No last name?"

"E-e-erica Bliss," she stuttered.

"Erica Bliss," Richard repeated. "Lovely name. So tell me about yourself, Erica."

"You first," she replied.

Richard laughed.

Brave girl, he thought.

"Touché," he said. "I knew as soon as you dropped off that roof and ran that you had a pair of balls on you, figuratively speaking of course.

"Ok, me first. My name is Philip Quinio. My acquaintances here knew me as Richard up until recently because, as I told them earlier, I infiltrated DARPA on assignment from the U.S. D.I.A. See, the DARPA office in Spokane hadn't been following the rules, so I was sent in to find out why. I was undercover to answer legitimate legal questions posed by certain government officials whose sole job is oversight for some of the government's most secret secrets.

"I had to leave my fiancé in the dark without telling her where I would be going or when I would be coming back. I had to put up with petty, know-it-all scientists who believed they were better than everyone else because they were educated at schools like Harvard or Yale or MIT. And I had to watch my case officer have his head cut off for protecting me from the assholes associated with Joshua Harper, creator of the Zombie Series Three, with which most of the rest of the rest of the world is now either infected or desperately trying to stay away from for their very survival."

While Richard had directed his conversation at Erica, he had drilled holes with his eyes through Scott's face. His voice had gotten louder as he went and sharper in tone.

"So that's me, Erica, in a nutshell. Oh, and I like puppy dogs, romantic walks on the beach, and friends that don't turn on you at the first sign of trouble!"

Erica withered into her seat.

Scott looked like he would rather be out with the zombies than face Richard's wrath.

"So, Scott," Richard said, in his pseudo-sweet voice again. "How did you break my cover anyway?"

Scott's Adams apple bounced a few times before he could answer.

"I ran your photo through a facial recognition program after I saw that your background info was pretty thin as Richard. Philip has a much more dense and believable file."

Richard nodded.

"Ok," he said. "Now that we've had the chance for me to vent my…disappointment, let's talk.

"Erica, I'm sorry for including you in my little bitch session. That was rather impolite of me. I apologize."

Erica nodded but still looked like she was trying to hide in front of the seat.

Richard took a deep breath and slowly blew it back out.

"So what are your concerns, Scott?" he asked.

"Both you and Jason were bit by one of those zombies. How can you be so sure you won't turn into one and infect the rest of us?"

"At first I wasn't. Even now I am not one hundred percent sure, but Harper designed the ZS3, and he designed the watches that I put on Jason to countermand the ZS3. Time will tell just how effective they are.

"As for me, Harper accidentally infected me back at DARPA with a new nano series he so egotistically called the Harper Series. It is supposed to provide complete immunity from not only the ZS3 as an 'infection,' for want of a better word, but also from the ZS3 hosts, the zombies themselves. I could walk right through a pack of those festering things, and they wouldn't even see me, or so Harper claims in his diary. I'd still rather not put it to the test if I can help it.

"Anything else?"

"How did you do that super-fast ninja stuff earlier?"

Now that he had disarmed Scott, Richard didn't mind answering that particular question.

"It's the Harper Series. It has enhanced my body in some surprising, but, so far, beneficial ways."

"Then you don't need us anymore," Scott replied. "Why even bother with us?"

Richard cleared his throat.

"It's not about needing you or not needing you, Scott. It's about doing the right thing and helping each other out. It is the right thing for me to help all of you survive this zombie apocalypse. Each of you has helped me, just as I have helped you. Going it alone is a lot harder than you could possibly know. Even with these nanos in me, there are plenty of things I don't know or can't do alone. So, in actuality, I do need you. We need each other.

"All this suspicion that you've had against me because I used a different name before, well, none of that matters now. The world had irreversibly changed from what it was even a week ago.

"Jason and Hanna and I decided to go to Wyoming, each for our own reasons. Me? I want to make it back out to my fiancé, before travelling long distance becomes impossible and before she turns into a walking corpse.

"Jason and Hanna are coming with me because they want to right some of the wrongs that have been done with some of their work—which had a totally different intended purpose than the zombie creator it has become. They know I have Harper's 'cure' inside of me, so they are coming with me in order to run their tests and hopefully duplicate the good part of Harper's work, to hopefully save lives.

"Erica came off that roof to join a group of total strangers because she saw that her long term survival options up there were severely limited,—and we offered her a better looking alternative.

"And, Erica, I promise you I will do everything in my power to keep you from regretting that decision."

Erica nodded. She seemed less frightened than she had earlier. She no longer seemed to be trying to hide behind her seat. She was listening.

"Scott," Richard continued. "I'm guessing you came with us because you saw our leaving as the better long term survival option as well. You could have stayed at DARPA for a while safely, I'm sure. But it wouldn't have lasted. Besides, there really is safety in numbers."

"Until someone in the group becomes infected and threatens the rest of the group," Scott replied, with a renewed touch of strength and conviction in his voice.

"You're right," Richard said, as he nodded agreement. "But our situation is a little different than in the movies you've seen. We've already got a cure," He pointed to himself. "We just have to find a way to replicate it and distribute it."

"All right," Scott said, breaking eye contact. "I'm sorry."

"Forgiven," Richard said quickly. "Here," he added, passing the shotgun back. "I'm sure you'll need this before everything is put right."

Scott nodded and took the gun.

"Now," Richard said, sitting back down and folding his hands on the table in front of him. "I am dying to hear Miss Erica Bliss's story."

Chapter 27: Bliss

Erica sat a little taller and brought a hand up to brush a stray lock of her hair to the side from in front of her eyes.

"Oh, ok," she said. She looked at a point on the ceiling while she gathered her thoughts.

Oh boy, Richard thought, as she caught Scott steal a look at her somewhat well-padded chest and then look away.

Erica looked back down and sighed then began telling her story.

"Almost a week ago I dumped my boyfriend. I caught him with a blonde bimbo on the cheerleading squad. I should have seen it coming. He was always looking at other girls when we were out together. He was always...ah, never mind. He's a jerk.

"Let me start over. I've been in the Coeur D'Alene area for most of my life. I wanted to go to college somewhere else, but Dad couldn't afford it. He was an auto mechanic and just couldn't. So I started college here at the University of Idaho. I've been studying photography.

"Well, I dumped my boyfriend after he cheated on me, and I took it a little rough. My dad found out and said maybe I should just get away from the campus for a day or two, so I could get my head on right again.

"So I did. I came back home, and Dad let me cry on his shoulder. He couldn't afford to take time off from work though, so he went back to the station the next morning. I went too, to keep my mind off of things. I took my camera and gear.

"Behind the station there's a nice trail through the trees that ends at a beautiful lake with the mountains as a backdrop. I hiked out there and took some sunrise photos and messed around, experimenting with different settings on my equipment.

"Around mid-morning I started getting bored, mostly because I didn't bring enough memory cards and had already filled up what I had brought with me. Dad and I were planning on having lunch together, so I headed back to the station.

"Dad was still working on a car when I got back, so I went inside and chatted with Gus. He's the owner of the gas station. He was filling in because his normal cashier called out sick.

"Anyway, we were sitting there talking when this big silver SUV pulls up outside, its horn blaring, and almost smashes into the station after just missing the fuel truck that was filling the pump reservoirs. It scared the crap out of Gus. We looked at the guy who was driving, and he's freaking out, hitting at his passenger and trying to keep her off of him because she's up out of her seat trying to strangle him, it looked like.

"My dad heard the horn and went out to see what was going on, and Gus went out too. I stayed inside.

"Gus went up to the guy's door and opened it. The driver fell out and the woman right after him. The guy got back up, and Gus tried to stop the woman from going after him again because she was still freaking out and growling. She had blood all over her face and in her hair.

"Then she started going after Gus. He must not have been expecting that because she got him pretty good; she bit him on the hand."

Richard winced. He could guess the rest but let her continue without interruption.

She had tears in her eyes, but her voice had strength to it and anger.

"Dad smacked her in the back of the head with one of the folding signs that was out on the sidewalk. It distracted her enough that Gus could get away from her, but otherwise it didn't seem to hurt her.

"I saw her eyes when she turned to go after Dad. She was out of her mind crazy looking. Dad smacked her again, but she kept coming, so he ran back inside and locked the door.

"Gus scuttled off and came in through the garage entrance. He was bleeding pretty bad and cursing up a storm. The woman kept trying to pound her way in through the glass, but then she saw the guy that had been driving the car, and she started running after him. I don't think she saw the fuel truck driver because he was hiding around the other side of the truck, or maybe she would have gone after him instead. I don't know. I didn't see her or the guy she was chasing again after that.

"Gus washed his hand off pretty good in the bathroom, and Dad brought out the first aid kit. I helped disinfect and bandage it up, but it looked pretty bad, and Dad convinced him to go have it looked at in the city at the hospital. Dad drove him, while I stayed and watched after the station."

Erica huffed and shook her head.

"They couldn't get into the city though. The military had put up a road block and wouldn't let them through. Dad kept telling them they had to get to the hospital, but they were turned away.

"Post Falls never needed a clinic before because we had Coeur D'Alene right there, just a short drive away."

"So what did they do?" Scott asked.

Erica looked at him and breathed out heavily then looked away and raised a hand to wipe away a tear that was threatening to slide down her cheek. Her hand trembled, and she brought it back to her lap.

"Ah, Honey," Hanna said, reaching over to pat Erica's shoulder. "You don't have to say anymore. We understand."

"No, no, it's ok," Erica said and wiped her other eye. She blinked a few times to clear her vision. "I haven't had anyone to talk to in days. I'll finish telling it. I don't want to be the only one that knows.

Hanna nodded and put her hand back on the steering wheel.

"They came back to the gas station," she continued. "Dad didn't have a cellphone, and in the flurry of trying to get fixed up, Gus left his there with me. So when they got back they came inside and began making phone calls. Gus wasn't feeling well by then and without the hospital we weren't sure how to help him. He was moaning, and Dad started talking about making the long drive to Spokane. Gus didn't seem to like that idea, but there wasn't much else that made any sense.

"The fuel delivery guy came up and said he was done pumping, but Gus was getting worse, so Dad signed for the fuel and then got back on the phone. The fuel man said he just had to clean the hoses and then he'd be on his way to Coeur D'Alene. I told him about the military road block, and he wasn't too happy. He went back out and started packing it up.

"I didn't think it could get any worse at that point," she said, getting a distant look in her eyes. "But then it did.

"I went into the bathroom to moisten some washcloths in cool water for Gus because he was burning up, and I heard Dad yell 'Oh, shit!' I had never heard my dad say a profane word in my life, so that really got my attention. I ran out to see what had happened.

"Just up the street a Greyhound bus had crashed into the church on the corner. People started piling out of the bus in a hurry. Some of them were running away from us, but a lot of them came in our direction. All of them had blood on them—so much blood—and on their faces and arms. Some of them were fast, and they acted crazed just like the woman that bit Gus.

"Dad jumped over the counter and locked the front door. After the crazy lady from earlier had left, we unlocked it to deal with the fuel guy, so he had to lock it again. Then Dad ran and locked the garage door. I had already closed the bay doors when Dad and Gus left earlier because I didn't want anyone walking up and stealing any of Dad's tools while I was inside minding the station. Dad locked the garage door anyway in case any of the crazies decided to lift the bay doors."

Erica shook her head before continuing.

"The fuel delivery guy didn't even try to run to the station. I think he knew he wouldn't make it in time. He was too far away. He tried to climb up on his truck instead. He tried. But the top of his boot got caught on one of the levers, and they got him before he could shake it loose. Even from inside the station I could hear him howl in pain.

"They got him right here," she said, pointing to her own lower calf. "Right on the leg above his boot. It looked like they could almost get to him even on top of his truck, so he jumped up and grabbed the edge of the roof over the pumps and climbed up on top of there."

She looked at Richard and cried as she shook her head.

"I didn't know he was still alive when you were down there getting gas," she said. "I swear I didn't or I would have warned you. He hadn't moved for days."

She broke down and sobbed some more.

"Hey, it's ok," Richard said, as he got up and moved closer. He sat down on his haunches a few feet away from the seat and reached out to grab the seat back. "It's ok. I believe you. All this stuff that's going on is like nothing anyone has ever seen before. Don't blame yourself."

She shook her head.

"I'm so sorry."

"All right," Richard replied softly. "Jason is going to be fine. No one here blames you, ok? Ok?"

Erica nodded and wiped the tears away then cleared her throat.

Richard nodded and stood then went back to his seat at the table.

"While the crazies were going after the fuel guy," Erica said, after a few hard swallows and several seconds of silence. "My dad went to the back room and brought out a lock and chain. He wrapped it around the front doors and said the lock wasn't strong enough if enough of them pushed on it all at once.

"Gus started groaning again and then I remembered the washcloths in the bathroom. I went to get them for him, and when I came back he was on his feet kind of slow walking towards my dad.

"'Are you ok, Gus?' I asked. He didn't answer and then Dad turned around from locking the chain and saw him. I couldn't see Gus's face, but I know my dad did because he froze with this stunned look on his face.

"Then Gus shook, his whole body, like he was having a seizure or something, and then it stopped, and he growled and jumped on my dad. They both fell on the ground with my dad underneath.

"I panicked and ran over and started kicking Gus. And then Gus looked up and saw me. His mouth was all bloody and his eyes—they had these dark lines spider-webbed through them. They were horrible."

Erica shivered, and Richard knew she was reliving the moment in her head.

"Gus tried coming after me then, but Dad yelled at him and grabbed his hair. He attacked Dad again. Then I saw Dad's wrench sitting on the counter by the cash machine, one of those big heavy adjustable wrenches. I grabbed it and then I hit Gus on the head, and I didn't stop hitting him until there was blood everywhere and Gus wasn't moving anymore."

She blew out a heavy breath then continued.

"Before he turned into one of those things, Dad got me cleaned up and filled up some bags with food and water, as much as we could before he really started feeling it take over, and he forced me up onto the roof. He knew he was going to turn, so the last thing he did as a man was make sure he couldn't hurt me after."

She paused to wipe some more tears out of her eyes.

"I opened the hatch one time to look down and check on him, but he *had* changed. His eyes were like Gus's with the spider web thing. Then for the rest of the time that I was up there I could hear him growling and groaning right under the hatch. It didn't go away. I thought it would drive me nuts.

"Those things must have gotten everyone in town after that because before long they were all over the place—a lot more than what came off of the bus that had crashed. I stayed as low on the roof as I could whenever I knew they were around.

"Until you guys came to the station I hadn't seen a normal person since I had been on the roof."

"Wow," Scott said after a few moments of quiet. "You have got to be the bravest woman I know."

Erica caught his eyes then looked down with the barest hint of a smile.

PART 3 – Going Home

Chapter 1: Spooky Dude

The deep percussion of the helicopter's rotors outside, combined with the high-pitched whine of the engine inside, was like music to Allen Taylor's ears. It was a familiar tune to which he had created so many intimate memories. It relaxed him, and out of habit he willed himself to sleep just a few minutes after taking off from the ranch in Jackson Hole, Wyoming.

The bumps and jolts of the turbulence as the helicopter skimmed the tree tops couldn't compete with his music, so the crew chief had, reluctantly, been forced to wake him with a little tap on the shoulder.

"Two minutes!" the crew chief yelled from about a yard away while holding up two fingers.

Allen nodded his head and gave a thumbs up.

The crew chief walked back up to the side door by the cockpit where he manned an M134 D-H minigun.

The ramp had been lowered at the back of the helicopter, and outside was pitch black. The sun had gone down while he napped. The inside of the helicopter was dimly illuminated with red light.

Taking a deep breath and then slowly releasing it, he mentally centered himself for the mission he was to perform. Then, feeling full of energy, he brought his three-day pack out from under his seat, stood, and strapped it to his back. He charged the handle on his HK 416 rifle then did a quick brass check to make sure a round had gone into the chamber. Lastly, he swiveled the four-tube panoramic night vision goggles attached to his helmet down to eye level and turned it on.

"One minute!" the crew chief yelled, holding up one finger.

"One minute," Allen repeated with a smile and held up his middle finger.

The crew chief shook his head and went back to looking outside over the barrel of his machine gun.

For thirty seconds Allen looked off into the distance out the back ramp. There was a soft glow right on the horizon. Spokane was burning.

When the helicopter descended, it was quick with a flare at the end of the motion that left the aft end of the chopper angled down. Allen could feel his stomach float up to the bottom of his throat like what a person feels on that first big drop on a roller coaster ride. As the chopper flared, he found himself looking out the ramp, almost straight down at the ground.

"Go! Go! Go!" yelled the crew chief.

Allen ran and jumped, bending his knees to absorb the inevitable impact with the ground. When his feet hit the soil he did a sort of spinning roll to his side that slowed his momentum and then he was up again, running a few meters into the cover and concealment of the trees.

Already the helicopter was a distant noise disappearing into the darkness.

He took a knee, opened his mouth to aid listening, and looked into the green-tinted night for threats. After a few minutes the night noises came back. Crickets and other insects. Small scurrying animals. And the predators that hunted them all.

"Creeper, Dwarf. Wonderbra, over," he said, giving the brevity code for a successful insert.

Using predetermined brevity codes allowed him to communicate with the control center without giving away any information to anyone who managed to intercept his transmission and break the comm. encryption. It also made transmissions quick, to cut down the likelihood of an enemy force being able to triangulate his position from the radio signal point of origin.

"Copy, Wonderbra, out," the control center replied.

If anything happened between now and arrival at the objective, at least follow on forces would have an initial location from which to begin their search if they needed to come looking for him.

He had picked that particular clearing in the forest to be his landing zone because it was large enough to accommodate his ride, it was far enough away from his objective to not draw attention from human or zombie, and it was close enough to his objective for him to walk to in only a few hours at most.

As he walked, his conscious thoughts jumped between focus on patrolling quietly and on questions about what he potentially faced at the Spokane DARPA facility, his objective.

He had lost five of his men in the Spokane area. Keyser and Davies had died, possibly taking Richard with them, in the safe house raid. He had been able to get that much out of Wagner and Brock. Then Mercer had disappeared at the DARPA facility with no forthcoming explanation other than the possibility that the zombies had done it, but Harper, his protectee, had gone missing too, and Benson had been furious about that. So Allen had sent

Wagner and Brock with some heavy firepower, and then they'd disappeared too just a few hours ago.

Instead of facing Benson's wrath again, Allen had taken it upon himself to find out just what the fuck was going on and to fix the situation before it spiraled completely out of control.

Benson wanted Harper's hybrid nano series. His plan wasn't a complete wash without it, but the Group would be so much better off if they did recover it— assuming it worked as well as Harper had hinted that it might. Possible immortality—and physical enhancements that made his own EWES-7 look like an antiquated Chevy Bel Air next to a brand new Ferrari.

He climbed over a large fallen tree and avoided stepping on the dry branches on the other side. Ferns and low scrub bushes brushed against his olive-colored pants.

Several times the trees and undergrowth vegetation thinned out into grassy clearings. He skirted around these areas, staying well under the trees.

The stench of rotting corpses assaulted his nostrils at about the same time he detected a bit of a glow of illumination ahead of him through the forest.

He slowed his pace and took extra care looking around for mobile corpses. He had been there for Harper's briefing to Benson a month ago, so he knew that noise drew them and that the nanos could sense bioelectric activity produced by an uninfected human body. He also knew his EWES-7 nanos would not stave off the ZS3 nanos should they find their way into his body.

As he crested the hill above the compound, his night vision optics became unnecessary. At the bottom of the hill the DARPA facility illuminated everything around it. It was its own little self-contained city with electricity still running and water still flowing. The only real problem that he could see was that there didn't appear to be any people.

He removed a pair of binoculars from his pack and began glassing the facility. Most of the streets were empty, but along one particular avenue there were corpses littered all over the place. In some places the corpses appeared to be in piles three or four deep. Then he saw some that were still on their feet, walking around somewhat aimlessly. They didn't have anything to hunt.

Doing a quick count of the mobile threats, he determined that there were at least thirty visible, not visible—no idea, maybe fifty percent more, maybe one thousand percent more. There was no telling yet from his position how many more were in the dead space behind the buildings and on streets that he couldn't see.

"Creeper, Dwarf. Where's my eye in the sky? Over," he said into his throat mic.

"Dwarf, Creeper. Reaper—Oscar Sierra. Over."

"Creeper, Dwarf. Solid copy. Tango Update."

A few seconds passed, and Allen continued to watch the avenue with the pile of bodies. The control center had confirmed that a UAV surveillance drone was on station, and now they were running a count of enemy forces in the objective area.

"Dwarf, Creeper with your tango update. Over."

"Send it, Creeper."

"Quadrant One—zero, Quadrant Two—thirty-seven in southeast corner, Quadrant Three—one five four northeast corner, Quadrant Four—one three northwest corner. Over"

"Good copy. Out."

Allen sighed.

There were close to two hundred threats pretty much right in the center of the facility, which, of course, was exactly where he needed to go to investigate Harper's lab.

Thinking back to what he recalled of the facility from the few times he had been there before for participation in the Elite Warriors Enhancement Program, he matched up the memories in his head with what he saw before him and configured a mental picture of what the compound looked like in the dead spaces that he couldn't see from his hilltop position. Ideas flowed through his head, and before long he knew how to proceed.

"Creeper, Dwarf. Kilo Oscar. Quadrant Three, southwest corner. I need a loud distraction. Negative target. Follow with Tango Update. Over."

"Dwarf, Creeper. I copy Kilo Oscar, Quadrant Three, southwest corner. Deploy payload without target. Over"

"Creeper, Dwarf. Solid copy. Follow with Tango Update. Over."

"Dwarf, Creeper. Tango Update. Out."

Allen watched the southwest corner of the DARPA facility. That area was largely an open field where the Hellfire missiles fired from the Reaper UAV drone would make a big noise without doing much damage to the facility. He just needed the zombies to go towards the noise, so he could access Harper's lab. This was his first time giving a kill order without actually having a target.

A few minutes later he heard a Hellfire launched from the Reaper. The missile impacted the ground a good hundred yards short of the fence. It made a beautiful flash and quite the thunderous explosion.

Looking through the binoculars, he shifted his gaze back to Quadrant Two. The thirty-something zombies he had first spied had definitely heard the explosion. They were moving in the direction he wanted them to.

"Dwarf, Creeper. Tango update. Over."

"Send it. Over."

"Dwarf, Creeper. Quadrants One, Two, Four—Zero tangos; Quadrant three—Two-zero-four tangos."

"Solid copy, Creeper. Dwarf out."

His distraction had worked. Now he just needed to get through the broken section of the fence and into the lab without making any noise and drawing them back.

He threw the binoculars into an empty pouch on the side of his pack. Then he half ran, half slid down the hill. At the bottom, he stepped through the torn section of the chain link and transitioned to a smooth combat glide, a fast heel-to-toe walk that lowered his center of gravity for balance and stability and enabled him to fire his rifle, if needed, from a steady, moving position.

Signs of a previous battle were everywhere. Brass casings littered the asphalt, some stuck in place in puddles of congealed blood. Here and there a few extendable batons lay on the ground, fully extended, some stained with blood. Clear plastic police shields, a few riot helmets, a few gas masks, even a pair of scuffed handcuffs lay strewn about.

Keeping to the shadows cast by the squat perimeter buildings, he moved quickly, with sure feet, his rifle sweeping with his eyes: left, front, right, front, up, front, and every so often behind as well.

The building he needed lay ahead, across a clear street, the only obstacle being a police cruiser that had crashed into the corner of the building on his side of the street. He skirted around the police car, which turned out to be empty but bloody, its red and blue take-down lights still flashing, and ran across the street.

The door to the building was locked, as he had expected it to be, and he could tell from a quick glance that the ground and second floor windows were not designed to be opened at all let alone from outside.

The third floor had balconies and, he assumed, doors that led out onto those balconies. Being a government building, he knew it would have a sturdy drain pipe, a veritable ladder for SEALs on their way up in the world.

Shimmying up the drain pipe and climbing across to a third floor balcony was easy. He had climbed hundreds like them before. On the balcony he brought his HK416 back around to the front and then inspected the door to the building.

Someone had left it unlocked he was surprised to discover. Well, not all that surprised. How many people walk in through a third floor balcony door with access only from inside? Still, there had been plenty in past experience who had, and in each instance he had had to take the time to pick the lock. He was glad it wasn't necessary this time.

Walking into the building, he found himself in an office. It belonged to someone who had a high opinion of himself, judging by the size of the desk. He could fit a small inflatable boat on the damned thing. And it had a nice humidor resting atop it.

Allen remembered Harper telling Benson that his zombie creations couldn't smell anymore once they'd been infected, so he opened the humidor and took out a handful of cigars. He opened a few desk drawers until he found a cutter and a lighter.

Clipping one end and lighting the other, he clamped a Davidoff Maduro between his teeth and puffed away. The smoke smelled and tasted wonderful. It had been a long while since he had taken the time to smoke a decent cigar.

A damned shame there won't be many left to smoke now that we've come to the end of the world, he thought, as he left the office and entered an inner hallway.

He found the stairs at the end of the building and quietly walked down four flights. The door at each floor had an inset wire mesh and glass window which he used to spy in on the floor for any signs of life—or undead.

Nothing.

Everyone had walked away but had left on all of the lights. It was an eerie sight.

At the basement level he left the stairwell and entered a familiar hallway. He walked down the corridor and made several turns before he found Harper's home away from home.

He blew out a few puffs of smoke from the cigar as he looked at the entrance to the lab. He didn't have an access card and hadn't had the time before leaving the ranch to have one wrangled up. There was no mechanical bypass, no lock to try to pick, and the glass was bullet resistant.

And on the seventh day God created high explosives, Allen thought with a smile.

He shrugged out of his pack and set it on the floor then opened the main compartment. He pulled out several rectangular packages sealed in green Mylar wrap and a black plastic case about the size of child's lunch box. These he set off to the side. Digging deeper, he pulled out a zippered green nylon pouch and some rolls of cord.

Using tools out of the nylon pouch, he clipped some det cord from the first roll and connected it to a blasting cap from the black plastic case. Then he connected the blasting cap to a length of time fuse from the second roll. Finally, he connected an initiator to the time fuse.

The last item he took from his pack was a roll of OD green duct tape. He used pieces of tape to connect his length of det cord to the lab window in a rectangular coil shape that was about four feet long and three feet tall at its narrowest, the bottom edge of which rested where the glass met the waist-high wall/frame. Inspecting the three loops in the rectangle, he puffed out some cigar smoke then kneeled down to replace the items he had taken from his pack.

After making the pack comfortable on his back, he pulled the ring on the initiator attached to the time fuse and then walked down the hall. He made a quick left turn and knelt next the corner of the cinder block wall with his mouth open, eyes closed, and hands pressed hard against his ears.

Half a minute later there was a loud boom and a wave of pressure squeezed the breath out of him. It passed over him in an instant. He stood, unfazed, and walked back to the glass.

There was a clean hole where the coil of detonation cord had been.

He rolled over the wall through the hole in the glass and stepped down onto a million tiny shards of pulverized glass that crunched underfoot. For just a second he thought about the damage being done to the sensitive tissues of his eyes, nose, and lungs by the suspended particulates of glass dust that now hung in the air, but he thrust those thoughts aside when he also thought about the millions of EWES-7 nanos that were in his body repairing the damage.

A second wall of glass was his last obstacle to the general lab. This glass was also bullet resistant, so he repeated the process of setting up an explosive breaching charge then climbed out and waited for the second blast.

After it detonated, he returned and entered the lab through the new opening.

The first thing he noticed was a steel table on its side and a missing leg. The second was the body of a security guard with the missing table leg through his chest and a head that was completely caved in from the sides, rendering the face unrecognizable. Someone had really done a number on him.

It looked the like the work of one of his EWES-7 brothers.

Allen searched the lab for Harper's new project. He found a few vials labeled EWES-7A which he would bet was an upgrade to his own nano series, but nothing else that looked like it could be Harper's most recent work. This didn't surprise him because he knew the McIntyres were not knowingly involved in the Infinity Goup.

He hadn't really expected to find anything useful in the McIntyre lab, but it wouldn't have been thorough of him to skip their section of the lab. Satisfied that there wasn't anything else mission oriented to find there, he moved on to Harper's lab, where he was presented with another obstacle.

Harper's door was locked, and this time there wasn't a window large enough for him to blast through.

Inspecting as much as he could of the door, he found that it was just as big and heavy as the very first door to the lab, which he had been able to bypass. He wouldn't be bypassing this beast.

The door was warm to the touch.

Interesting, he thought.

As he was running the numbers in his head for how much explosives to use for a heavy duty breaching charge, he saw the body of the dead security guard on the floor and thought of an idea.

He stepped over and rifled through the pockets of the dead man, looking for a security access card. He found one and was about to hold it up to the card reader when he spotted something poking out from under the dead man's t-shirt that looked familiar. He pulled down the t-shirt to reveal the rest of a tattoo that he immediately recognized.

He snarled.

The tattoo was of a king cobra loosely coiled around a Navy SEAL trident.

There was only one man that he knew of with that tattoo.

Mercer.

He yanked on the t-shirt, ripping it down the center and found a pair of military dog tags on a breakaway metal chain. He grabbed the tag and confirmed. Mercer, Timothy.

Snarling again, he yanked the dog tags free and began kicking the wall.

When he calmed down, he put the dog tags in his front pocket and dropped his pack. He noticed a security camera mounted to the ceiling in the corner and decided to find the recording for the lab after he had finished his task.

Someone was going to have hell to pay.

Locking his emotions away where they could fester, he brought himself back on mission and held the access card up to the card reader.

"Enter Security PIN," appeared on the small display screen.

Allen entered four numbers.

"Incorrect PIN," appeared.

He swept the card again and tried a different combination of numbers with the same effect. Several times he tried, each time using easy number combinations like 1-2-3-4 that people aren't supposed to use but sometimes do, and each time the PIN was denied.

"Fuck it," he muttered and flung the access card to the ground.

Digging into his pack, he brought out the C4, det cord, and blasting caps. He tore the Mylar film off of the C4 then connected three bricks of the explosive with a length of det cord. Then he prepared another charge just like the first.

He wasn't positive which side of the door had the hinges, so he placed a charge vertically on both sides. When the charges were securely in place, he crimped blasting caps to time fuse, using enough length to give himself plenty of time to leave the lab before it should detonate. Finally, he pushed the blasting caps into the C4.

He double and triple checked his work then put his gear away and shouldered his pack.

Giving one last look to his fallen comrade, he pulled the ring on the initiator and climbed out of the lab. This time, just to be safe, he went around the corner and a little bit further down the hall before taking a knee and waiting.

The blast shook the building.

He retraced his steps to the lab and found the door to Harper's lab on the floor, right where he wanted it. Its buckled mass shifted under his feet as he stepped inside.

Harper's lab was a burned out husk. Someone had taken all of the equipment that could possibly hold even a drop of any nano series and had turned it into a pool of slag in the middle of the floor. There were vials, no beakers, no computer; there wasn't even any blood. Ash covered every surface. The room felt uncomfortably warm from the molten pool of metal that was still cooling.

Allen stepped back and tried putting the pieces together in his head.

Keyser and Davies were assumed to have taken out Richard. But what if they didn't? What if Richard had set a trap then gone back to DARPA and gone to Harper's lab? And killed Mercer? No freaking way. Could Wagner and Brock have come here? Would they have turned against us to get Harper's nanos—even kill one of their own to get it?

Then they kill Harper and use thermite grenades to destroy his lab, so they'll have the only available cure to ZS3?

Nobody had seen them since they'd come back here, after all. That was partly why Allen had come here in the first place. He didn't want Benson getting any ideas.

Allen shook his head. His men could be bastards at times, but they wouldn't turn on each other any more than they'd bite the hand that fed them. They knew damn well Benson could put any of them down in an instant. And they had to know that if they tried to bargain using Harper's new nano series as leverage, Benson would still win.

No, it made more sense that Richard had ghosted Mercer, but how could he have done that? Richard was a nobody, a D.I.A. nobody, but still a nobody; while Mercer was a bad-ass EWES-7 enhanced Super SEAL.

He considered the McIntyres briefly but ignored that line of reasoning as laughable. Jason and Hanna were geeks who knew their place in the food chain. No way would either one of them, or even both of them acting together, be able to effect what had happened to Mercer. No way.

Is there somebody else at work here? Some unknown adversary that found out about us that we haven't factored into the equation?

Four possibilities, each more unlikely than the one before it.

He didn't know the answer, but he knew of at least one place that he could go look for it.

The DARPA control center.

Chapter 2: Password

The DARPA control center had the footage from all of the CCTV cameras in the facility. As long as the video memory was being stored, not overwritten, he had a distinct probability of finding out who was responsible for this mess and for Mercer. More importantly, he might be able to find out if Harper's new series was still in play.

Allen left the lab and climbed a flight of stairs. The first floor was lights on just like the rest of the building he had seen.

Instead of rushing out into an open hallway and then back out into the night air for an uninformed jaunt towards the control center, he took a knee around the corner next to the hallway that led to the outside and called for a tango update for Quadrant One.

"Dwarf, Creeper. Quadrant One still negative on tangos. They're singing 'Koombaya' by the crater in Quadrant Three. Over."

"Creeper, Dwarf. Moving Pos. to Alpha-Niner. Over."

"Dwarf, Creeper copies moving to Alpha-Niner. Out."

Allen walked down the hallway to the front door and nudged it open a crack and then more and more, looking for threats as it swung slowly open, until he could step out knowing that there was nothing close by. It was all well and good to get a report from someone watching your back, but still, it was a good idea to verify. Stepping out, he reached back and let the door close quietly with just a little click.

Bringing his rifle up, he transitioned to a combat glide and started moving towards the control center. The further he got from the center of the facility, the less destruction was evident.

By the time he made it to the building he was looking for, the streets looked the same as they had when he had been indoctrinated into the EWES Program—minus the people, of course, but with the night sky still visible beyond the bright street lights that bathed the facility, it was easy to imagine everyone else was quietly sleeping in their beds, leaving the night to predators like him.

Walking around the corner of the building from the back, he moved up its side in the grass to soften the sound of his footsteps. The entrance was around one more corner, and even if it were locked, he'd have a chance to pick the lock with all of the zombies at the opposite corner of the facility.

That's what his thoughts were working on when he rounded the corner and saw three zombies in security uniforms, smacking bloody hands against the glass of the front door. He hadn't been expecting them after Creeper's report, and a touch of annoyance sparked through him for making assumptions.

Trust but verify! He told himself yet again.

One of them turned towards him as he thought of sneaking away and finding another entrance. It started to moan and walk towards him.

Too late to back away now.

He continued gliding forward heel-to-toe and centered his red dot sight on the meatbag's head. He pressed the trigger and the suppressor on the end of his HK

416 coughed out a round. Then he sent two more at the others, and in the space of as many seconds, three truly dead zombies cluttered the sidewalk. As he walked past them he saw that each had evidence of chest and abdominal wounds where someone had already tried to kill them with center mass shots. Clearly those hadn't worked.

The front entrance had a roughly twenty foot covered awning that ended at the driveway in front of it. The three had been under the walkway.

Allen guessed that was why the UAV flying surveillance for him had missed them.

Lesson learned.

He moved to the front door and pushed the corpses aside with his foot. Looking up, he saw that someone inside had moved a couch in front of the doors and then draped a gray blanket to hang over it, probably so they wouldn't have to look at their former comrades walking around in various states of decomposition.

Reaching down to one of his pants cargo pockets, he pulled out his lock pick set then paused and put it back.

Better not make the mistake of assuming again, he thought and brought his rifle back up. He walked across the front and checked the one side of the building he hadn't yet cleared. *Nothing. Good.*

He went back to the front door, took out his lock pick kit, and crouched down to work on the lock.

The door was splattered with gelatinized blood, but the lock was clean, having been below the level of where the zombies' raised hands had been smacking the glass. It was a standard five pin tumbler dead bolt and took him only two minutes to defeat. Swiveling the cylinder in the lock took some effort, as the torsion bar he was using was fairly small against the much larger bolt it was dragging, but the bolt did finally slide home with a nice metal on metal thwack.

Allen pushed gently on the door until it touched the couch and then he pushed a little harder. The couch began to slide inch by inch across the floor and then there was a loud explosion like a gunshot.

What the hell? He fell backwards in surprise. He brought his rifle up to his shoulder and looked for whoever had shot.

He didn't have a target, so he didn't shoot. That damned blanket was in the way.

Just as he started to roll off his back to stand up, he heard boots running down a hallway inside coming his way, and it clicked in his head. Pushing the couch had tripped an early warning device the people inside had jury rigged at the entrance so they could focus their manpower on other things. The boots slapping the floor was likely a little reactive force coming to quell a small invasion or block off the rest of the building if it were more than they could handle.

Not a bad idea, Gents, he thought.

He decided to stay in place outside lest he surprise the response crew and get shot for it, but he did roll back up to a crouched position. Raising his left hand as if to wave hello, he put on his best smile, puffed on his cigar, and waited for the blanket to move out of the way.

And it did just seconds later.

"Hello there," he said, as he stared down the barrel of a shotgun.

"What the hell?" the black clad security officer said.

"Master Chief Allen Taylor, US Navy SEALs. Mind if I come in?"

By then there was another shotgun and an M16 pointed at him as well.

All three had plastic police shields and riot batons slung across their backs.

Their point man blinked as he processed that he was looking at a live human and then he lowered the barrel.

"Yeah, come on in, Master Chief," he said. "Geez, that scared the piss out of us. We thought they got through."

"Nope, just me stopping by to say hello."

The others chuckled nervously then stepped off the couch and opened the door the rest of the way to let him in.

As soon as he was inside, one of the men closed the door and turned the dead bolt back to the "locked" position. Allen watched as they shoved the couch back in place then replaced the shotgun shell in the early-warning device with a fresh shell from the butt stock of one of the guns they carried.

"We've been trying to figure out what the hell is going on," the point man said. The name tape on his uniform read: Niland. "We've been hearing and feeling explosions inside the facility. We haven't been able to tell if the facility is under attack by an outside force other than the zombies or if parts of the facility are malfunctioning. We've been trying to call for help since—"

"Hold on, Niland," Allen interrupted, holding up a finger and then pressing it against his ear.

"Creeper, Dwarf. Say again. Over"

"Dwarf, Creeper. Tango update. Tangos from Quadrant Three now moving North East into Quadrant One. Looks like they're headed right towards you. Over."

"Solid copy, Creeper. Keep me updated. Dwarf Out."

The security men looked at him with concern in their eyes.

Allen sighed.

"Well," he began. "One of the explosions you heard was a missile hitting the empty Southwest corner of the base. It did what I intended it to do and drew all—most, I should say, of the infected to that area. Unfortunately, that little early-warning device I just tripped back there was pretty loud, and now they're headed this way."

"Ah, shoot, man! What are we going to do?" another asked. His name tape read: Sweeney.

"You're going to hide inside like you have been, Sweeney," Allen said. "I'll take care of it."

Sweeney looked a little angry but then he looked down and nodded his head.

Oh, you coward, Allen thought, but he kept his opinion to himself and gestured for Niland to lead on.

In just a few turns down the hallway and up a small set of steps, they arrived at the door to the control center, which Niland promptly unlocked with his key before leading the group inside.

An older man in the same security uniform waited atop a platform, raised a few feet above the rest of the room, where he could supervise all the goings on in the control center. He stood in front of a desk with his back straight and his arms crossed in front of his chest. He was staring at them from the moment they entered the room, a stern look emblazoned on his face.

Ah, yes, the leader, Allen thought.

"Master Chief," Niland said. "This is Mr. McNeil. He is in charge of security here at DARPA."

Allen nodded and walked forward.

"McNeil," Allen said, offering his hand. "Master Chief Allen Taylor, US Navy SEALs. You've been calling for help right?"

McNeil looked him up and down without answering. His stern look hadn't softened. If anything it looked more severe.

Allen lowered his hand and cocked his head a fraction.

"I've seen you here before," McNeil finally said.

"That's possible," Allen replied after a short pause.

"You're one of those super soldiers Harper has been working up," McNeil said. "I know all about you new guys."

Allen nodded and looked around the room. There were three security personnel behind him, four more off to his left, a hand full of people in civilian clothes seated in front of surveillance camera monitors, and then McNeil right in front of him.

"Two of your guys were here four or five hours ago with miniguns shooting the shit out of my base," he continued. "They caused some real problems for us in here. They took out our communications array in their little Tombstone style standoff with those things outside, and then they got themselves killed and caused even more problems."

"You're sure they were killed?" Allen asked. He still didn't know what had happened to Brock and Wagner after he sent them back here to collect Harper and his work.

"Damn right I am. We watched the whole thing on camera right here."

Allen narrowed his eyes and studied McNeil for any signs of dishonesty. He didn't find any.

"And how did they cause trouble *after* they were dead?" he asked.

McNeil's face turned red and his body was shaking.

This guy's pissed, Allen thought. *What did Wagner and Brock get into?*

"Whatever the hell Harper did to them to make them 'super soldiers' passed on to the zombie things out there after your boys went down in the middle of them. Now some of those things are faster and stronger."

Oh shit, Allen thought. *Not good.*

"I sent some of my boys out there to give you guys a hand, and those new ones tore them to bits. Now the guys I sent out there are just like them."

Oh fuck me, Allen thought.

McNeil stared at him, apparently waiting for some kind of response.

"Have you told anyone about this?" Allen asked.

"We've been trying to, damn it," McNeil replied before gesturing towards one of the civilian work stations. "Our comms are out; your guys…"

Allen cut him off with a suppressed gunshot to the face.

As McNeil collapsed to the floor, Allen turned and put shots into each of the four security guards to the left

400

then ducked, turned, stepped to the side, and took out the three men that had been behind him. Only the civilians remained.

"What the hell did you do that for?" One of them asked, before Allen turned back and put a bullet through his chest.

The others looked stunned. They didn't move, didn't speak.

Allen pointed his rifle at the next civilian in line and said, "Pull up the video footage from Harper's lab. Run it back to four days ago."

"I don't know how," the civilian replied. "That's not my j…"

Allen shot him dead and turned to the next one in line.

"All right, all right; I'll get it for you," the next civilian squeaked in terror.

The room was beginning to reek of piss and shit and blood.

"Don't move," Allen said at the other two civilians who had so far been silent.

They nodded with quick, jerky movements and kept their hands up in the air.

Allen moved closer to get a better view of the television screen in front of his unwilling helper and positioned himself so that he could keep all three of them in plain view.

"Start there," he said, when he saw Mercer step into the frame with Harper. After a few seconds it was clear no one else was with them. They were in Harper's private lab typing at Harper's computer keyboard.

"Pause it."

The image froze with the tap of a key.

"Now bring up the rest of the lab on this monitor, same time sequence. I want to see what happens in both labs at the same time."

The civilian nodded and rolled the chair over to use the other keyboard. Soon both monitors showed where he wanted to see.

"Now scroll forward in time until there's more activity."

The civilian complied, and before long, Allen had seen Harper and Mercer leave the lab then return hours later with Brock as well. By then, the McIntyres were at work in their section of the lab. Brock left some time later. Then Mercer left after taking some of Harper's things out of the drawers under the lab counter.

Shortly after Mercer left the lab, someone else arrived, and the McIntyres looked first annoyed then frightened. At first, only the person's back was visible, but then he turned.

"Pause them."

It was definitely Richard, he saw as he looked closer.

"Son of a bitch," Allen said. "All right, continue."

He watched Richard cuff the McIntyres to the table then surprise Harper, fight Harper, be stabbed by Harper, kill Harper. He watched him pass out, it looked like, then recover. He watched him ambush Mercer when he returned, watched him break the leg off of the table and kill Mercer then crush his skull in his hands.

"Holy shit," the civilian said.

Allen had seen a lot of fights in his time, but he'd never seen anyone move as fast as Richard had against Mercer.

"Rewind it to the fight in the adjacent lab," Allen ordered, blinking quickly several times.

He watched the fight again and saw the pain enunciated on Richard's face, as the hypodermic needle Harper wielded punctured his upper trapezius muscle.

That's it, Allen thought.

The final piece of the puzzle fell into place.

Harper had stabbed Richard with his new nano series without even thinking some of it would transfer—or thinking he'd be able to eliminate Richard before it had any positive effect. That was how Richard had had the ability to take out Mercer. Now Richard's enhancements were better than those of the elite super soldiers.

Allen backed away from the civilians and sat in a chair still looking in their direction, though his thoughts were far away. He didn't notice how nervous they were or even anything about them, actually, other than that they were occupying space.

"Sir?" the one who had been helping him said, interrupting his thoughts.

Allen's eyes gained focus, his thousand yard stare disappearing.

"Sir, please don't kill us. I have a wife and two kids. I haven't been able to talk to them since this all started. I just want to go home and see them again. Please don't kill us."

He looked on the verge of tears, and the other two tripped over themselves to put in their own desperate pleas for mercy.

"Shush-ush-ush-ush-ush," Allen said, with a hand outstretched to quiet them. "People," he said, shaking his head. "I don't care."

And then he shot each of them twice in the chest. After they had fallen to the floor, he walked closer and put an extra shot into each head. When he was finished dead-checking the bodies, he dropped the magazine from his rifle and checked how many rounds remained. There were only a few, so he replaced the magazine with a fresh, full mag.

While the civilian had been moving through the video data backups, Allen had been learning the controls to the system by watching. He knew that the tech experts back at the ranch had been having trouble accessing the data on Harper's computer because they had neither Harper nor Harper's BIOS or OS passwords. The only other people who had known Harper's passwords were dead as well. So far, all they had accomplished was reassembling some of the files that Richard had sent to the D.I.A. website he and Guddemi had set up.

The program hidden in Harper's hard drive had digitally shredded most of the electronic data, but some of it had been recoverable. Unfortunately, the Harper series tracking frequency had not been one of those files. If they could find out the frequency, they could track down Richard and recover Harper's new series.

Allen thought he had found a way to recover that elusive data on Harper's drive, but, first, he needed to see where the McIntyres had gone after the lab. That was the last place they'd been seen before they disappeared, and he needed to recover them too.

He used the controls to move the video footage forward again to where Richard had fought Mercer in the lab. There were the McIntyres, cuffed to the lab table. Skipping forward past Mercer's death, he watched Richard set them loose and then pass out. Jason and Hanna appeared to have a fairly heated discussion about Richard before, to Allen's surprise, they picked up Richard's unconscious form and carried him out of the lab.

Hmm, the nerds have chosen which side to play for, Allen thought. *All right, they're helping Richard. My mission remains the same then. Find Richard, and I'll have the McIntyres as well. So let's see if we can get a bead on Richard.*

He began skipping back through the footage until he found the night Mercer and Harper had first gone to Harper's lab—just a few hours before the failed hit on Richard. Harper's computer was on the counter top, as was the keyboard. The camera had a side view from above. He watched Mercer go to the keyboard and slowly type in the password at Harper's direction. There was no audio to the recording, so Allen was forced to zoom in on the keyboard.

Fortunately, Mercer was bad at typing. He used two fingers to peck away at the keyboard, and it was clear when he used the "shift" key to capitalize letters or use different symbols.

Allen wrote the first password down, one slow digit at a time, as he watched and paused the video. Then he moved on to the second password and did the same. Each was a long-string, pseudo-word, so he could see how it would take a long time for the techno-geeks to crack without knowing the password.

"Dwarf, Creeper."

"Send it, Creeper," Allen answered.

"Tango update. Two-zero-four tangos approaching pos Alpha-Niner from the southwest. ETA two minutes."

"Creeper, Dwarf. I copy. Two hundred plus from the southwest with two minutes remaining. Out."

Allen stood and looked at the control center. The room was bound to be a tomb for a long time. He walked out the same door he had entered through and went looking for the stairs.

Someone else might have opted to take the elevator, but he knew that even though the facility had its power supply, technology tends to fail without constant human monitoring and maintenance. The last place he wanted to be stuck was in a dead elevator, in a dead building, with only the dead for company.

The stairs couldn't malfunction and trap him.

When he found them, he raced upwards two and three steps at a time, until he made it to the top floor. A short while later, he found the roof access ladder and climbed up.

The stench on the roof was even worse than what he had sensed from up on the hill from which he had come. Walking to the edge of the wall, he looked down at the walking corpses. They looked disgusting and smelled worse. He walked around the perimeter of the roof, watching the ground for gaps in the crowd below.

There were a few here and there, but they were rather small, not large enough to jump and run through before the nearest zombies could be attacking, especially these supposedly faster, stronger zombies McNeil had mentioned.

But that wasn't the only reason he had gone to the roof.

Shrugging out of his pack, he opened an outer compartment and pulled out a green, semi-rigid pouch from which he extracted an extendable parabolic dish antenna array. Turning the power on, he connected the array to a Secure Telephone Unit, put an earpiece in place, and dialed an area code (307) phone number. After one ring the line went active, and he placed the phone in a pocket so he could be hands-free.

"Authenticate"

"Echo-whiskey-echo-sierra-seven-zero-one," Allen replied.

"Proceed"

"Request transfer to echo-whiskey-echo-sierra-seven-zero-two."

"Standby"

The phone rang again, this time for several cycles.

"Come on Jax. Pick up."

"Jax"

"Hey, Buddy, I've got something for you."

"Allen?"

"Did I catch you sleeping, you lazy piece of shit?"

"Oh, fuck you. I've been babysitting this damned computer, waiting for it to blossom, so we can extract its sweet virgin nectar."

"Ah, listen to you. I didn't know you were so sweet. Now wake the fuck up. I've got the goods to open your flower petal or spread your legs or whatever the fuck you want to call it. Got a pen and paper handy?"

"I love it when you talk dirty to me. Yeah, go ahead. Send it."

"All right, for BIOS use: 'B-u-c-k-m-1-n-5-t-3-r-f-u-l-l-e-r-e-n-3' and for the DARPA O.S. use: '3-n-d-o-h-e-d-r-@-l-F-u-l-l-3-R-e-n-e'."

"Geez," Jax replied, after he had repeated them back. "Those are some kick ass long string passwords. No wonder the system's been taking so damned long to crack entry."

"All right. Now, Jax, here's the important part," Allen said. "Harper's new nano series has an operating frequency just like ours does, so we can track it. Do a system wide search on Harper's drive and find me that damned frequency. Harper is sure to have documented it somewhere."

"Ok, will do."

"I'll stay on the line."

Allen heard rapid-fire keyboard strokes over the earpiece and then Jax started whistling a fairly high-pitched tune. Allen rolled his eyes and shook his head.

"Would you cut that shit out? I'm surrounded by the fucking walking dead here. I don't need any distractions whistling in my ear."

"Oh, right. Sorry," Jax said.

There were a few seconds of whistle free key tapping and then he began to hum.

Oh come on, Allen thought, walking over to the edge of the wall around the roof.

Several of the undead below raised their heads. They knew he was there. They started moaning, and it began drawing others towards them, towards him.

He unzipped his pants and began to piss on them.

They didn't react.

When he was finished, he zipped his pants back up and did a round count through his gear. He had six three-magazine pouches that made up his chest rig and an additional three-mag pouch on his belt at his left hip. Doing the math and accounting for the rounds that he had already fired, he came up with an estimated five hundred and sixty rounds left.

That should be plenty, he thought.

Bringing his HK416 up to his shoulder, he lined up his sights on the nose of a zombie below.

Exhale. Squeeze.

A bullet flew out of the suppressor and shot straight through the zombie's head and into the abdomen of another behind it. The first zombie fell limp. The second didn't appear to react at all.

From his position of safety, he shot one after another through the head, dropping them permanently to the lawn with the same detached focus he had used against the control center personnel.

There were fewer standing than fallen when Jax interrupted.

"Got it. Freq (pronounced 'freak') is 10387875 hertz."

"Excellent," Allen replied. "Now get that out to the monitoring stations with highest priority response. If

Benson gets his shit, maybe we can have our poppers removed."

"Man, I hope so," Jax said. "All right, I'll get right on this and then I'm goin to scour Harper's drive for anything useful."

"Good. I'm out."

"Later"

Allen disconnected the call then raised hand to touch the back of his skull. His fingers felt the smooth, bulbous scar tissue where his popper had been implanted. He hated Benson for being his leash holder, but the man could end his life with the push of a button. He wasn't ready to die.

He should have known the man would have a sure fire way to control him once he got him and his men out of the Leavenworth Federal Penitentiary. It had been a sweet offer. Avoid the firing squad. Free from prison. A complete pardon from the President of the United States. A fresh start. All he had to do was submit to some military experiments in human enhancement. He should have fucking known.

Shaking his head, he lowered his hand and began shooting the rest of the zombies, reloading as needed.

"Creeper, Dwarf. Tango update. Over."

"Dwarf, Creeper. Standby for Tango update. Over."

A few seconds passed and Allen began walking around the perimeter of the roof again. Before he had walked a full length of one side, he had his answer."

"Dwarf, Creeper. Tango update: zero tangos Quadrants One through Four. Over."

"I copy, Creeper. Zero Tangos. Go topless. Over"

"Dwarf, Creeper copies. Go topless. Over."

"A-firm. Out."

Allen reached over to the small IR strobe attached to the shoulder strap of his pack and turned it on. Then he packed away the antenna array and his empty magazines and shouldered his pack.

He had twenty minutes to reach the LZ for extract, or he'd be walking back to the ranch.

Chapter 3: The Phone

Allen ran. He knew, as he had seen earlier, that it was possible that the UAV had missed a zombie in its count and that one could be waiting for him around any of the corners he turned as he wended his way through the facility streets and alleys, but his speed should easily make the possibility a nonissue.

The ground cleared before him, and the fence loomed ahead of him. Using his momentum and enhanced strength, he was over in seconds and ran into the forest on the south side of the facility. He spooked a deer as he ran down into the valley between the facility and the next hill. He took that as a good sign that he was alone in the area.

There was a fair number of trees to move through, but quickly and quietly, he put them behind him. His night vision device was back in front of his eyes ever since having left the illuminated area in and around DARPA.

A mile or so later, after he had descended into another valley and then crested another hill, the trees thinned out and opened up into a football field sized clearing. This was his exfiltration LZ.

Looking at his watch, he saw that he had about five minutes remaining before the helo should arrive to take him out of there.

As he rummaged in an outside pouch for IR chemlights to use to mark the LZ, he noticed something unusual in the periphery of his NVG enhanced vision. He looked closer and saw a dark-colored automobile sitting partially in the shadows of the trees off to his left.

Immediately, he stopped digging in his pack, brought his rifle up into the ready position, and began a combat glide towards the car, looking this way and that for anything living or undead. He did a complete sweep around the car. Nothing alive or pretending to be alive was inside the car or in the immediate area.

What is this doing out here? He thought. *It almost looks new.*

It seemed like too much of a coincidence for the car to be out in the middle of nowhere with only the DARPA facility around unless someone was either spying on DARPA or stargazing in the middle of the field, and he didn't see any telescopes around.

I wouldn't be surprised if this were Richard's, he thought. *Come in from the south while DARPA security is preoccupied with activists in the north? Maybe.*

He looked in the car again, this time for information not just bodies.

It was mostly empty, but a gym bag in the front seat held a set of civilian clothes with shoes and a hat and a cellphone. The phone looked cheap, like an older prepaid model some foreign intelligence services liked to use as burn phones for anonymity.

Allen nodded his head and smiled, liking the probability that the phone had belonged to his quarry. He pocketed the phone and began walking back to his pack. He looked back at the car one last time and memorized the license plate number.

More for Jax to break his teeth on.

He heard rotor blades in the distance and rushed to prep the LZ.

Chapter 4: Roadblock

They were on the road for hours longer than they'd expected to be. Helena, Montana had become a death trap of zombies and burning buildings, forcing them to leave the main highway for smaller back-roads around the outskirts of the capitol city, many of which had been blocked by derelict vehicles left in the road by their drivers when hordes of zombies had swept through attacking any uninfected people they could find.

They'd had to backtrack often to find alternate passable roads. In the end they'd driven through quite a few front and back yards, smashing through picket fences and gardens and even a few clothes lines and children's swing sets.

The children...Hanna couldn't stop thinking about the children they had seen. *The poor darlings...*

The steering wheel shook in her hands, sending vibrations all the way up her arms as she fought to keep the large vehicle from swerving off the road.

"Hold on!" She yelled, as they went off onto the highway shoulder. She kept her foot mashed down hard against the brake pedal. Thoughts of the zombie children finally fled her mind, as she was forced to face a new situation.

As they came to a stop, the headlights shone off the side of the road, past a gulley, and up a tree-covered hill that rose before them.

"What the hell was that all about?" Scott asked.

"We blew a tire," Hanna replied. "And it looks like there's something in the road ahead."

Richard went to the front and looked out through Hanna's driver's side window, which now face up the road.

"Not good," he said, his enhanced vision showing him what Hanna had seen, what was still hidden from the others in darkness.

"What is it?" Scott asked, before any of the others could.

"Looks like a truck is blocking the road about fifty yards just in front of us."

If someone had blocked the road intentionally, they couldn't have picked a better spot for it. It was just a little beyond a curve in the road, where drivers headed east, as their group was, wouldn't see it, until they were practically right on top of it, giving potential ambushers an easy target. Timbered hills to either side guaranteed nobody would be driving around it.

Richard hushed the others to silence when they barraged him with variations of what, why, who, and how. He continued to look out Hanna's window for any signs of movement.

"Scott, get me the NVGs please," he said. "Hanna, turn off the headlights."

Both followed directions, and soon the night was dark again to everyone except Richard, who fitted the night vision goggles into the head harness and then slipped them down over his eyes.

Though the night opened even more to him in shades of electronic green, he detected no signs of movement near the obstacle, which he could now see was most definitely an eighteen-wheeler truck with a large, white trailer hitched in tow. For five minutes he merely sat and watched and listened, waiting for anything to move, to make noise, to draw his attention; but nothing did.

"What is going on?" Scott asked, when he could contain himself no longer.

Richard looked over at him, huddling close to Erica's seat and saw that the young man was itching at a scab just above his ear. The anger he had felt at the breach of noise discipline faded away as he saw Scott for what he was, a scared little boy in a grown up's body. He sighed.

What the hell? He thought. *Since when did I get all emotional and sentimental? Could this be a side effect of the new nanos? I'll have to talk to Hanna and Jason about it later when there's time.*

"Are we going to just sit here in the dark?" Erica asked, bringing Richard's mind back on task.

He cleared his throat.

"There's a semi blocking the road just ahead," Richard replied, "But I'm beginning to think to think it might have been abandoned. Nothing is moving around. No one is talking. No one is shooting at us. If it were an intentional road block, I would think there would be people manning it, but so far I haven't seen anyone out there.

"Someone is going to have to go out there and look around. I would, but now I can't. I took Harper's watches off and put them on Jason to keep him from turning. If I go out, the Infinity Group will be able to track me, and that would lead them right to the rest of you as well."

"Come on, Scott," Erica said. "You and me then. How about it?"

Scott nodded.

"Yeah…yeah. Ok. I'll go out with you," he said.

Thank you, Erica, Richard thought.

"Here," Richard said, offering Scott the pair of night vision goggles. "You'll need these. And I'll get the other pair out of the lab for you, Erica."

"What about a gun?" Erica asked.

"Scott has a shotgun," Richard replied.

"Well, what about me? And don't tell me I can't have one because I'm a girl."

"It's not because you're a girl," Richard replied. "Have you ever even touched a gun before?"

"As a matter of fact, I have," she replied. "I've shot my dad's shotgun, my uncle's hunting rifle, and an ex-boyfriend's hand gun before. This is Idaho. Hello."

"Actually, this is Montana," Richard replied. "We crossed the state line a little while ago while you were telling us how you ended up on a gas station roof, but I get your point. All right. You think you can handle a shotgun then?"

"Yes"

"Scott, give her the shotgun. You wanted the MP5 anyway."

"Yeaahh, Baby," Scott said, nodding his head with a big grin and handing over the shotgun. "There's one in the chamber. Tube's full. All you gotta do is push the safety off, aim, and pull the trigger."

"If you can't see the safety in the dark," Richard added. "Just feel it with your trigger finger and remember: 'Flat on the right—ready to fight'."

"Flat on the right, ready to fight. Got it," Erica replied.

Richard walked back into the lab. While he was retrieving the other pair of NVGs, he checked on Jason.

Jason still slept. His breathing was deep and slow, and he no longer felt hot to the touch.

All good signs. It looked like Harper's watches were working.

Closing the lab door, Richard stepped over to Erica and handed her the NVGs.

"Here's how you work them," Richard said before letting go.

"Scott already showed me with his," Erica said, as she turned them on and them up to her eyes.

"Ok," Richard replied, looking at Scott and giving him a good nod.

Scott smiled and shrugged his shoulders.

"All right then. When you go out, I would suggest going back down the road a bit, keeping our vehicle between you and the road block. Do this until you get into the curve in the road, where anyone at the semi and anyone watching the semi won't be able to see you."

"Then climb the hill and sneak up on the road block from the side?" Scott asked, to finish Richard's advice.

"Yes, and try to keep a solid object between you and the road block at all times."

"So we'll have something to hide behind if someone starts shooting at us right?" Erica asked.

"Yes," Richard replied. "But preferably so they won't see you in the first place. And stay together. You don't want to get separated and end up shooting each other."

"Friendly fire isn't friendly," Scott said.

"Exactly. And watch out for traps."

"Traps?" Erica asked.

"Yes, traps. I'm pretty sure tire spikes in the road is what caused us to blow a tire."

"Like the kind cops swish out into the road?" Erica asked.

"Yeah, swish," Richard said, making a playfully mocking swinging gesture like the one Erica had just used.

She shook her head.

"Got it," Scott said.

"Be careful," Hanna offered.

"We will," Erica said.

Scott moved to open the door.

"Hold on," Richard said. "A few last things. One: watch out for zombies. I can smell something rotting. You never know. Two: we won't be able to identify you coming back since you have both set of NVGs, so knock three times, pause, then once, pause, then four times. Three plus one equals four."

"All right," Scott replied. "Three plus one equals four."

"Good luck," Richard said.

Scott nodded and opened the door. He and Erica stepped out into darkness.

Richard closed the door and locked it.

"And now we wait," he said.

"Again," Hanna added, with a fatigued sigh.

Chapter 5: Nano Nano

"How is Jason?" Hanna asked a few minutes after they were alone together.

"He seems to be doing fine," Richard replied. "He was sleeping when I checked on him. No fever. Regular breathing, but you should know that he does have those black lines in his eyes like the zombies. The watches seems to be working the way they're supposed to, though. He still has his wits about him, and he hasn't gone homicidal."

"I don't know what I'll do if I lose him."

"You're not going to lose him. He's going to be just fine. He's doing much better now that he's got Harper's watches on."

"Harper," Hanna spat. "What an asshole he turned out to be."

"Yeah, you could say that."

"You, know, for the last month before all of this happened, Jason kept saying something didn't seem right with him lately."

Richard nodded but then realized that she couldn't see him in the dark. When he looked into her eyes he saw that they were unfocused and drifted a bit as she tried to see with her ears.

"Mm-hmm," he grunted.

"Well, he was definitely right. There's something wrong in someone's head if they would be willing to unleash these monsters on the world."

"You're right," Richard agreed quickly. He had something else on his mind that was bothering him. "Hanna, I understand that Harper's nanos, his new ones, are supposed to enhance my body's functions and senses. What about my mental functions though? Are they supposed to enhance my emotions and thought process, do you think? I mean, I know you don't know much at all about the new series, but your guess would be better than mine."

"Hmm, well, I could definitely see them affecting your emotions and emotional triggers. One of the things we noticed in the Elite Warrior Enhancement Series was that the volunteers' aggression levels ramped up considerably. Many of the volunteers for the first four series either had rejection issues where their bodies just didn't accept the nano presence, or they were hyper-aggressive to the point that they actually self-destructed during post-injection physical testing."

"Self-destructed?"

"They ended up pushing themselves beyond limits even the nanos could handle, and they basically died of either internal hemorrhaging or heat stroke.

"That was before Harper made a few new types of nanos to add to the series. There are actually several hundred different nanotech designs actively operating inside the series."

"Holy crap," Richard replied. "Several hundred types in one series. Man, I thought it was just one kind of bug replicating and making things happen."

"Nope. There are all kinds of different nanos in the cocktail. Each nano is specialized for one or a few connected tasks. Some act as command and control for the other nanos. Some repair damages cells. Some turn blood into gel to speed coagulation. Some trap oxygen until the body needs extra. Some are even specialized to remove body waste faster and to remove expended nanos. And, of course, there are some that their entire job is replicating more nanos. Then there are nanos that make sure the replicating nanos don't make too many. They keep everything in balance."

"Wow. There's a lot more going on in there than I would have even thought about."

"Well, Harper was a huge part of the thought process, and Jason and I contributed our share to the EWES Program, but there were quite a few others that were involved too. A few of the other DARPA facilities around the country have their own nanotech research labs, and they routinely sent us specs on various types of nanos that their people came up with towards EWES for making a more efficient system."

"Is it possible that Harper sent his work to any of these other facilities? Maybe another star in the community thought like he did."

"Two months ago, I would have easily said 'No'. Harper was pretty egotistic and didn't like to share with others unless he had to. But now, I don't know," Hanna said, shaking her head. "I wouldn't have believed two months ago that he would create something to turn most of the human population into flesh-eating zombies. But we've seen the zombies, and his own diary entries claim it was his intent. So now I don't know if he would have shared that with someone else at DARPA. I suppose anything is possible at this point."

It grew quiet inside as Richard let his thoughts wander, and Hanna was content to do the same. He could hear her breathing in a way he could only attribute to his newly keen senses. If he listened closely he could even hear the soft pitter patter of her heart beating and the start-stop swish of blood through her arteries and veins.

"There's something that I still don't get," Richard said, blocking out all of the little sounds of Hanna's working anatomy. "Why would the EWES Super Soldiers side with the Infinity Group? I've known a lot of guys in the Special Forces community, and I can't think of any of them that would go along with this save-the-earth-by-killing-all-the-people bullshit."

He saw Hanna slump lower in her seat and sigh.

"In the beginning, when EWES started, all of our subjects were volunteers, all of them in the Special Forces community," she said. "But they kept dying or losing their minds. Word got around, and by EWE-S5, unit commanders wouldn't even let us talk to their men. Series five, six, and seven were all convicts, lifers out of Leavenworth."

"What!" Richard exclaimed. "That's freaking insane."

Hanna nodded.

"I know. We were told that we could take or leave the offer. 'We,' meaning: DARPA. Jason and I would have been fine if EWES had been shut down. Most of what we did would easily carry over into the medical field.

"DARPA took the deal and damn the consequences. Their super soldier program apparently trumped good sense. We stayed on after they put controls in place because we believed that once we had a well-tested, working enhancement series, with all of the bugs worked out of it,

423

that it would be put into service with the military to save troops' lives. I guess now we'll never know."

Richard sat shaking his head.

"You said there were controls. What controls?" he asked after a few moments of listening to her breathe.

Hanna looked down and closed her eyes, clenched her jaw.

"When the military inmates arrived, they were sedated and rendered unconscious. Then a team of doctors performed a surgical procedure in which they implanted a small explosive device at the base of their skulls. At the push of a button, from anywhere in the world, the charge could be detonated. It would instantly sever the medulla oblongata from the rest of the brain. Instant death."

"So they either obey orders immediately and completely, or it's lights out," Richard said.

"Yes," Hanna whispered. "They're murderers and rapists and thieves; and DARPA's been using them as guinea pigs."

"And thanks to someone inside DARPA, presumably Harper, now the Infinity Group has control of them."

Hanna nodded.

"As if zombies weren't bad enough," Richard commented, shaking his head.

After a moment of quiet, he tilted his head to the side and strained to listen beyond the immediate area.

"Someone's coming," he said, standing and drawing his handgun.

Chapter 6: What They Saw

"Three plus one equals four," Richard said, listening to the knocks on the door. "It's them."

Taking no chances, he opened the door with his gun pointed towards them.

"Ow," Erica said when she bumped into Scott.

He had frozen in the doorway as soon as he saw the gun pointed at him.

"It's us," Scott said. "You said 'three plus one equals four'."

"Sorry," Richard replied, as he lowered the gun. "I had to be sure."

He stepped out of the way and allowed them to enter then shut the door behind them as they sat opposite each other at the table.

"Well?" he asked.

"You were right about it being a roadblock. It is definitely positioned just right for it," Scott said, nodding. "There was plenty of blood and a whole lot of shell casings from a fire fight, and quite a few dead bodies. You were right about that too. The stench was horrible. Flies everywhere. We didn't see anything moving, human or zombie though."

"It all looks abandoned," Erica added. "Or overrun."

"Maybe overrun and then abandoned," Scott replied. "And there were a few cars crashed together on the other side."

Erica nodded.

"Can we get through?" Hanna asked.

425

"I'm not sure," Scott said, shrugging. "That depends on whether or not Philip here can drive a big rig. I can't, and Erica said she doesn't know how to either. If he can't then we've got a long way to back track and find another route."

"I'll take a look," Richard said, a little annoyed at how Scott was still throwing his real name around as if to remind everyone of his subterfuge. "What about the tire?"

"You were right about that too," Erica said. "Tire spikes—hollow ones too."

"OK, do either of you know how to change a tire?"

"No," Scott said at the same time Erica said, "Yes."

Erica looked at Scott with a questioning look.

"What? I'm a computer geek not a grease monkey."

She smiled and shook her head.

Hanna laughed.

"All right," Richard said. "Scott, if you would, please help Erica change the tire. I'll go try to start the truck that's blocking the road. I'll need to do this fast to limit my exposure time outside. We don't want pissed off super soldiers catching up to us."

"About that," Scott said. "I was thinking about it while we were outside. According to the message I intercepted back at DARPA, they didn't even know Harper was dead yet. I don't think you have to worry about being tracked for a while. It's only been, what? Six or seven hours. They're probably still trying to find their missing scientist."

Richard nodded.

"Well, that is encouraging, but still, it'd be better if we keep our risks to a minimum. Better safe than sorry."

"You're right," Scott said. "I just thought you'd like to know, so you're not freaking out the whole time, you know?"

Richard nodded. "Thanks."

"So where are the spare tire and tools?" Erica asked.

"Honestly, I don't know," Richard replied. "Best guess, I'd say, either on the back or underneath."

"All right. Come on, Scott," she said and flipped the NVGs back down over her eyes.

The three of them stepped out. Richard was last.

"Yell if you need anything," he said to Hanna before closing the door.

"I will," she replied to the empty compartment. "Hurry please," she whispered.

She sat there in the quiet darkness for a few seconds before deciding to go see her husband for herself.

Chapter 7: A Familiar Name

The smell of pine filled the air, just barely covering the undertones of dried blood, until the wind changed, bringing back the smell of death.

Richard walked quietly towards the truck, his senses hyper alert. Just because the others hadn't seen anyone in the area didn't mean they were actually alone. The abundance of corpses littering the area led him to believe that there could be zombies still remaining in the area; but there were shell casings scattered all over the place. It was possible that everyone involved could have been living, breathing humans who had been shooting at each other and that there had been no survivors. Or maybe there were survivors, and they had fled. Or maybe they were still out there and just hadn't been seen by Scott or Erica.

At this point, Richard didn't care, as long as nothing slowed him down any further. He just wanted to be gone from there, so he could be home with Linda.

He shook his head.

So maybe the Infinity Group *didn't* have his frequency yet. Sooner or later they'd get their hands on it. What then? If he stayed in the open he'd endanger the others, maybe even Linda. Or he could consign himself to life in a faraday cage. Neither option was very palatable, but he knew which one he'd choose when it came down to it.

He already had.

He was only outside the faraday cage they were driving around in because he had to be. Because the dangers of the road right here, right now, were greater than the distant threat of the Infinity Group and its super soldiers.

With gun in hand, Richard walked past the big trailer and climbed up to look in the cab of the truck. The window was up, but he could see inside. No one there. He looked but couldn't see if the keys were in the ignition, so he looked up to the visor.

Bingo

The door was unlocked, so he climbed in, retrieved the key from the visor, and turned it in the ignition.

It didn't start.

He turned the key again. He could hear the starter sparking, but the lights didn't come on in the dash, and the engine didn't turn over.

Great! The battery is dead, he thought. *But how can that be? It would only have been sitting here for a few days at most. Certainly not even a week.*

He checked the headlights. The switch was in the off position.

A sneaking suspicion began to grow in his head, so he climbed out of the cab, went around to the front, and raised the hood.

Sure enough, the battery cables had been disconnected from the battery terminals.

He reconnected the cables then went back to try again.

The engine purred to life, eliciting a grin.

That explains why someone would leave the keys so readily accessible in a road block vehicle. It also suggests that someone was likely planning on coming back for it at some point. If that's the case, it's probably carrying something valuable.

Putting the truck into reverse, he eased into the gas. He didn't know what was in the trailer in haul, so he didn't know what to expect as far as handling went. But the truck didn't have any trouble rolling backwards. The back of the trailer smashed into some trees with a loud crash.

Oops

He changed gears and pulled forward. There wasn't much room to maneuver such a large vehicle, and he was a little rusty at operating a big truck, so it took a number of times backing up and going forward before he was able to drive it forward in a single lane, leaving the way home clear at last.

He turned off the engine and took the keys from the ignition. Planning to disconnect the battery cables just as he had found them, he stuck the keys back up in the visor and froze for several heart beats as he caught sight of something unexpected. The dome light came on as he removed the keys from the ignition, which was why, with the battery disconnected, he hadn't noticed earlier. A small silver clip had been slipped onto the side of the driver's visor to hold some paperwork in place.

Etched into the clip was a figure eight on its side, the symbol for infinity.

Holy shit, he thought, remembering the resource pods he had ordered for Linda to be delivered from the Infinity Group's own supplies. He wondered if that was what was in the trailer.

Sliding the clip and paperwork off of the visor, he began to read.

The papers were transport manifests and delivery receipts. None of the addresses for delivery were the Cody, Wyoming address he had sent his order to, for which he was grateful. Hopefully his orders had already been delivered.

That would be just too weird if this were my order...and it would mean Linda didn't get the pods.

As he flipped through the receipts, he did see a few things that caught his attention. First were the dates. The driver had been on the road nearly every day for weeks prior to the outbreak except for his final completed delivery to an address in Jackson Hole, Wyoming. That one had been delivered two days after the outbreak had gone public in the news. What was interesting about that particular receipt was the name and signature of the person accepting delivery of the cargo.

Shelley Benson, billionaire Bruce Benson's daughter.

Chapter 8: Cargo

Richard slid the entire stack of papers, clip and all, into one of his pants cargo pockets. He suddenly knew with certainty that the information he could glean from them would be extremely valuable sometime in the not so distant future.

He searched the rest of the cab for any more papers or log books, anything that could be useful about the Infinity Group or the Bensons later. The only things he found were a three years old spiral bound map book of the United States and a large metal Maglite that had been plugged into a mobile charger. There was also a dash-mounted carrier for holding a cell phone or GPS device, but it was empty.

Now that he knew the truck had been used by one of the Infinity Group's minions, he decided to check the trailer's cargo, even though it meant more time that he would be outside risking being tracked. He grabbed the keys and flashlight and walked to the back, noticing several holes in the side of the trailer that looked like they had been made by bullets.

There was only one other key on the ring, and it slid smoothly into the heavy-duty padlock that secured the trailer doors. Before he unlatched the doors he stopped to unholster his handgun. According to the delivery receipts, the contents had already been delivered in Jackson Hole, but the driver had a new destination once he had left, and the new contents weren't listed in his paperwork. For all Richard knew, there could be a horde of zombies in the back that Benson wanted delivered to a lab for study or to spread the infection somewhere that wasn't dying fast enough for his liking. Or it could be empty, and the driver had just been sent back to one of the Infinity Group's cache warehouses for another assignment.

He didn't know, but he wasn't going to take chances.

He turned on the flashlight and, holding it in one hand and his gun in the other like a policeman would, he slid the latch up and pulled the door open a few inches.

Having psyched himself up to put a bullet in anything that jumped out at him, he flinched a little when he saw boxes stacked on a pallet and bound up tight with plastic shrink wrap. Without lowering the gun or light he swung the door fully open. Then he worked the latch on the second door and swung it open as well.

Another pallet, stacked tall with boxes, filled the other side.

Between the two rows of pallets, a narrow aisle ran to the front of the trailer. He could see that each row was made up of more of the same pallets with some variation in the size and color of the boxes under the plastic.

He looked closer at the pallets closest to him and saw through the multiple layers of plastic that they contained potatoes and broccoli. The next one back held more potatoes and a mixture of peppers over boxes of cauliflower.

There was a lot of food here. He began to think of ways to bring some of it with them. He knew that as much as he would like to drive the truck himself, there was no way he was going to go home outside of the radio frequency-blocking mobile lab. Scott and Erica already said they didn't know how to drive the truck, so that was out. Maybe Jason? As long as he wore the watches, he should be ok now.

I'll have to go see if he has ever had a commercial driver's license because it would be a shame to let all of this food go to waste, especially with the hard time that are sure to be co...

The sound of something dropping and breaking towards the front of the trailer interrupted his thought. Reflexively he raised the gun and flashlight to point down the narrow aisle while also moving behind one of the rows of pallets so his body wouldn't be visible to whoever—or whatever—was back there.

"I know you're back there!" he yelled. "Show yourself right now!"

Nothing came out into the aisle, but he could hear a little movement and then soft whispering. It sounded like a female's voice. Before he could concentrate on the sound with his enhanced hearing, Scott and Erica ran over to join him, clearly having heard him yell, their rushed footsteps drowning out the whispers he had heard.

Then he heard whispering again, definitely female, and at the same time, he saw a face peek around the pallet farthest from him, up towards the front of the truck. It was a man's face. So there were at least two of them in there.

"Come on out. I'm not going to hurt you," Richard said.

The man slowly stepped sideways into the aisle to come forward, but a hand from behind the pallet tried pulling him back. He shrugged it off and spoke softly into his shoulder. Richard didn't recognize the language, but he knew it definitely wasn't English, Spanish, or French.

Richard checked the man's hands, as he came closer. He carried no weapons in hand, or anything else for that matter.

"The girl too," Richard said. "There's no point in hiding back there anymore."

As the man slid out to the edge of the trailer, Richard saw that it wasn't a man after all. It was a teen-aged boy. He was dressed kind of weird for a teen though. He had on black slacks, a long-sleeved blue shirt, and suspenders.

And he was surprisingly muscular.

Richard saw that he had been mistaken about him being empty-handed too. In the hand that had been hidden behind the boy's body as he side-stepped between the pallets was a wide-brimmed black felt hat.

"Hi, you ok?" Richard asked.

The boy nodded, worry clearly visible in his eyes.

Richard still had his gun out and realized that this appeared to be the source of the boy's unease. He put it away and shifted the flashlight to his right hand.

Offering his left hand, he said, "Here, come on down from there."

The boy took it and stepped down to the pavement.

His grip was strong.

When he let go, the boy looked around to see where they were.

Richard shone the light down the aisle, but no one else had followed the boy.

"What is your name, young man?" Richard asked.

"Samuel. Samuel Miller."

"Ok, Samuel, you have nothing to worry about from us. We were travelling along the highway when we found this truck blocking our way. We don't know who you are or why you are here."

Samuel was silent, but his gaze was steady.

"Does this food belong to you?" Richard asked, knowing the question had an obvious answer.

"No"

"Then you won't mind of we take some?"

"It's not mine to say either way."

Richard nodded.

"How long have you been locked in the back there?"

"A few days, I think."

Richard paused. The boy seemed hesitant to talk much, even though, so far, he had answered all of the questions he had been asked. He prolonged the silence a few more seconds, giving Samuel a chance to say something, anything; but he was disappointed. The boy said nothing.

"All right, Samuel," Richard continued, opting for the apparently necessary direct approach. "Why were you in the trailer?"

"My father was only trying to protect us," the boy said, after a few seconds, his face and voice wracked with anguish. "Please don't hurt him. He was only trying to protect us."

"Whoa, hey, hold on," Richard said, holding up his hands in a warding gesture. "We're not going to hurt anyone. Is he back there with you?"

A puzzled look crossed Samuel's face.

"No, he…who are you?"

Richard debated what to tell him and after a second decided to tell him the truth, but he was losing patience.

"I'm Philip," he said. "And this is Scott and Erica, and we, along with a few other friends in the vehicle over there, are on our way to Wyoming, where there is safety. Now I don't know who you thought we were, or why they would be after you, or why you thought we would want to hurt your dad, but that's not us.

"We didn't expect to find this truck blocking the road, and we certainly didn't expect to find anyone hiding in the back of it. We just want to know what is going on before we take some of this food and go back on our way. But if you aren't quick about it, we'll just take the food that we want and then we'll go because it isn't safe to be out in the open like this for very long, even out here in the middle of nowhere. So speak up, or go back there and hide with your girlfriend."

He finally got a rise out of the boy.

"She's not my girlfriend," Samuel said, a corner of his mouth drawn inward and upward for just a fraction of a second. "She's my sister."

Then, turning to look into the dark of the trailer, he spoke in the other language Richard had heard whispered earlier. A timid reply in the same language prompted another burst of speech from Samuel.

Even without knowing the language, Richard could tell he was giving orders from the tone of voice that he used.

Once again he shone the flashlight down the narrow aisle. But it wasn't a girl Richard saw coming towards them. It was another teenaged boy.

"How many of you are back there?" Richard asked.

"We are four," Samuel said. "This is my brother, David."

David jumped down to stand by Samuel. He was dressed almost identically to his older brother, but he was a few inches shorter and wasn't as muscular.

"My sisters, Ruth and Rachel."

Richard offered his hand to the young ladies who had trailed behind David, and they climbed down to stand by their brothers.

"They're Amish," Scott blurted in surprise.

Erica just stood there, eyebrows up, biting here her lower lip.

"Yes," Richard said, also surprised but trying not to show it.

The girls were dressed in blue calf-length, plain-cut dresses with white aprons. They wore white capes in the back that tied into their aprons, and on their heads they wore bonnets. Rachel, the younger girl, had a white bonnet; and Ruth's was black.

All four of the young people wore simple black shoes without any visible consumer product labels displayed.

"How old are you?" Richard asked Rachel, the shortest of the quartet.

"Nine," she whispered.

"Nine," Richard repeated, nodding his head. "Well, I can see that there is a long story to be told here, but we are running out of time.

"Samuel, would you and your siblings like to join us? As I said, we are on our way to my family's place in Wyoming. It's safe there. Here you'll be exposed, even if you do have all of this food."

Samuel looked to Ruth, the next oldest of the four. She looked unsure. He looked back into the trailer and then out into the darkness that covered the road and the trees on either side.

"Yes," he said, returning his gaze to meet Richard's eyes. "I believe it is what our father would want us to do. We will travel with you."

Chapter 9: Trace Alert 3

In the last few days Deron's attitude toward his job had taken a serious plunge. He shared his workstation, and thus the workload, with only one other person now, since his supervisor and three of his coworkers had somehow gotten themselves turned into zombies, he'd been told. Two others had been transferred out to who knows where.

What the hell? A zombie apocalypse? And here I am still watching monitors like a trained monkey, he thought.

What pissed him off more than doing twelve hours on and twelve hours off with no days off in sight was the fact that he had volunteered for the schedule back before the apocalypse had kicked off and surprised everyone, back when he wanted the extra money, so he could afford a Harley Davidson Sportster, customized by Rough Crafts, all black and thunderously loud. But now there was no way he'd be able to get one. Civilization had taken a dump, and what fun is it to ride if you have to spend your time dodging zombies instead of cruising and taking in the sights, enjoying the freedom of the open road and the attention from hot women?

He shook his head. He couldn't even leave the ranch. Well, he could if he really wanted to. Benson had made that clear, but he had also made it clear that no one would be allowed back if there was even a hint that they were a risk of infecting anyone at the ranch. Why chance it?

So Deron had stayed. At least here he was safe and had guaranteed food and water and medical attention if needed. Benson was a billionaire with enough food-producing land and cattle to feed his entire staff of employees at the ranch plus the battalion or more of mercenaries that were paid by his Black Tower Tactics Corporation. So why leave the security of the ranch?

Maybe someday when the zombies have died off, I'll get my chance to cruise cross-country all the way from California to Maine then down to Florida and then across and up to Seattle. Find a place close to other survivors and start to rebuild.

He sighed again.

Sometimes it really sucked being a dreamer, especially since he knew he needed to work on being patient. He hated having to wait.

Speaking of which, he had to wait three more hours before Johnny came to relieve him from this cramped box that they called a work station.

And why Johnny of all people? He thought. *Why couldn't it have been Sharon?* He imagined her dyed auburn hair framing that smooth creamy face with long flowing eye lashes batting over emerald eyes and blood-red lips. A gothic dream girl. And she had liked the photos of the Harley he had shown her, said she might even go for a ride with him if he got it. *Uhm, and those tits.*

He shook his head.

Instead, he had to work with Johnny, who always wore that shit-eating grin and rarely seemed to have showered and had the perpetual smell of garlic and B.O. about him.

He looked down at the print off on the desk in front of him and read his most recent instructions again. Another end of the world number to call if such and such alarm goes off.

Fitting since it is the end of the world. Oh joy, I'll get to talk to Spooky Dude again and hope he doesn't choke me out for not picking up the phone fast enough.

Yesterday, Johnny had said Spooky Dude had chewed him out for taking a piss during an emergency, like he could have known an alert was going to go off while he was in draining the bladder. He'd said he'd thought Spooky Dude was going to kill him. He'd seen the fire in his eyes he'd said. The dead soul.

Well, yeah, Johnny, we call him Spooky Dude for a reason, but you're still a stinky, smelly...turd? Damn, I need to get some sleep. I can't even come up with a good insult, my brain is so fried.

The computer screen above the desk refreshed and a list of command codes began cascading down the screen. The printer came to life and began spitting out paper.

Deron grabbed the top sheet as soon as it hit the holding tray and began skimming the contents. His eyebrows rose. This was the fourth new entry for high priority alerts just this week. He watched as the cascade on the screen slowed and then stopped.

The damage control guys somewhere else in the building had finished entering it into the system.

Almost immediately a two-tone alarm went off, ratcheting his heart rate into overdrive.

"Damn it!" he swore, when he saw the instructions on the screen. Picking up the phone, he punched in the number for the third time this week that his supervisor had sworn he'd probably never need to call. He didn't even need to look it up in the binder anymore.

As the phone rang, he silenced the annoying alarm.

"Hello," someone said when the line connected. It wasn't Spooky Dude and that disconcerted him. "Hello," the man repeated.

"Ah, yes, Sir. The entry that was just put into the system alerted."

"That was fast. A lot faster than I expected."

Wow, this guy is totally different than Spooky Dude. He actually spoke more than two words at a time.

"Excellent. Someone will be right down. Get the information ready."

Click

"Yes, Sir," Deron said into the dead phone. He set it down in its cradle and began tapping away at his computer.

The door opened five minutes later, and in walked Spooky Dude.

Deron's breath caught in his chest.

He'd never seen Spooky Dude in anything but civilian attire as you'd expect from a private security mercenary in a dressed down environment. Now he was in full combat dress: chest rig, thigh holster, and all. And his blouse sported one of the most respected patches found anywhere: the Navy SEAL Trident.

Holy shit, Deron thought. *No wonder he's so spooky.*

Spooky Dude walked up to the computer and looked at the screen over Deron's shoulder.

"Good. The mouse has come out of hiding," he said, as he reached over and grabbed Deron's phone.

"Jax, Allen. This is our boy. Is BrownOtter back with the blackhawks? Good. Scramble the duty react team. I'm going with them. Tell them it's a snatch and grab but no tasers. I don't want to risk shorting out our golden ticket tech upgrade. I'll meet them on the tarmac in ten minutes. Yeah, yeah, I will. All right, get on that."

Allen hung up the phone.

Deron's eyes were wide and focused on Allen's forearm, which looked like it was as big around as one of Deron's scrawny legs. Allen laughed when he saw that Deron was looking at his forearm tattoo and trying to figure out what it said.

"No Mercy; No Remorse," Deron whispered.

Allen smiled. "Can you read the rest?"

Deron shook his head.

"It's Latin," Allen replied. *"Vivo Ego, Ut Interficeret*—it means 'I live to kill'." He laughed again when Deron cringed and drew back. Then he turned serious again. "I'm going out there to catch this son of a bitch. Keep Jax informed of the location. Keep the information flowing. This bastard slipped away twice before. This time I want him bad. You got me?"

Deron nodded, his eyes wide and locked on Allen's.

"Good," Allen said then turned and left.

"Sweet baby Jesus save me," Deron whispered, when he had the room to himself.

Benson was generous enough to let each of the EWES men stay in their own cabin at the ranch. Or maybe he was just smart enough to realize that if he didn't keep

444

the Alpha males separate they would butt heads, rather violently given their backgrounds.

Allen's cabin didn't seem to get much use, since he was always out running ops for the boss. When he crossed the threshold this time, as usual, it was to go up to his weapons locker. He had told Jax they needed to use a nonlethal show of force tonight, and he had meant it. For two reasons: one, he needed to recover Harper's new nano series, and two, he wanted Richard in good health when he tortured him to death for what he'd done to Mercer and Keyser and Davies and Wagner and Brock.

He looked down at the tattoo that had so enthralled young Deron.

"I live to kill."

And kill I will, he thought, as he opened the locker and removed a Remington 870 shotgun. *But not Richard, not tonight. Time enough for that later.* He grabbed a case of rubber 12 gauge rounds and loaded up.

He ditched the HK416 and dropped the chest rig with its bunch of magazines. He opted for chest armor, remembering the shot Richard had gotten on Wagner that first day. *I wear this out of respect,* he thought as he strapped it on. *Not out of fear. You are a worthy opponent, but I will defeat you.*

He slipped his hand through a bandoleer of less lethal shotgun rounds so that it rested across his chest. Then he switched out the old batteries for new to his personal comm and topped off his handgun magazines. He was just about to head for the door when he remembered his prize from earlier tonight, so he climbed the steps back up to his bedroom loft.

Picking up his chest rig, he retrieved the EWES-7A vial. He didn't know what the upgrades were supposed to be, but since Richard had the Harper series, he decided to take it and hope for the best. He filled a hypo from his med pack and injected the 7A into the meat of his opposite bicep. The needle went deep enough to prick against the bone under his muscle, but he ignored the pain. His nanos would fix any damage it caused.

Remembering the fatigue the first series caused him as the nanos stole from Peter to pay Paul within his body, he mixed some vials of metal into a Dixie cup of water and gulped it down.

Ammo for the bugs, he thought. *But I'll have bloody shit tomorrow if they don't need it.*

He grabbed a few more items he had a feeling he might need to keep Richard restrained, including a hypo of tranquilizer, and then left for the tarmac.

The blackhawks were waiting, their rotors already spun up and glowing in his night vision. The react team came running up about twenty seconds after he did.

"Line up!" Allen ordered, yelling to be heard over the deafening helicopters.

Fourteen men, seven to a stick, just like he'd grown accustomed to in the Teams. Seven because that's how many men fit into the inflatable boats SEALs so commonly used on missions.

These men were not EWES candidates, now were they SEALs, and he'd only trained with the briefly before Benson had forced them all into the apocalypse. So he inspected their gear to make sure they were prepared for a snatch and grab mission with nonlethals and backups in case all hell broke loose and killing became necessary.

They didn't let him down.

Benson does pay for the best toys and people.

"All right, let's go!" Allen shouted. "I'll brief you in the air!"

They loaded up, and the birds took off into darkness.

When he could see in the dim light that they had each put on the comm headsets, he told them everything they needed to know. Where they were headed. Who their target was and his known capabilities. That he carried something Benson wanted. That they needed to take him alive. That he probably had two scientists with him that Benson would want as well. When none of them, on either chopper, had questions, he sat back and closed his eyes and resumed thinking about how he would punish Richard once he'd recovered the new nano series and how the scientists might be able to free him from Benson's control.

A clicking in his ear roused him from his pleasant thoughts, and he toggled a switch on his radio.

"Dwarf"

"We lost the signal." It was Jax.

"Say again, Creeper."

"I said we lost the damn signal. But listen. That doesn't necessarily mean he's gone. I found a passage in Harper's diary where he mentions some special watches that he made to block the signal. And he mentioned that he hadn't told Benson about them. So he may still be there if he took them off of Harper."

"I copy. Keep me updated."

Clever, Harper, Allen thought. *Not very trusting though, considering you were about to get hitched to the boss's daughter.*

For the next several hours of flight time, his thoughts lingered on possibilities. Perhaps having one of the McIntyres remove the small bomb they had planted in his skull while one of his men held the other hostage. That might work. It seemed like the best option at the moment, assuming he could find them first.

"We're two minutes out," the crew chief notified him finally over the comm channel. This one was far less timid than the other one he had dealt with earlier tonight.

Or maybe he's just better at hiding his fear.

Allen like that the others feared him. It gave him a sense of power over them. Their own fear defeated them in his eyes. He would be victorious against any man he faced because he didn't experience any of the fear that he instilled in them.

He nodded to the crew chief and watched the man turn and walk away. He caught the man shiver, almost imperceptibly but it was there.

Allen smiled and breathed in deep, imagining he could smell the man's fear, even closely held as it was.

"Damn, would you look at that!" the pilot said.

Allen looked into the cockpit.

Pilot and Copilot were shaking their heads.

"Son of a bitch; you're right."

Soon he knew exactly what they were talking about. He'd been here just a few days previous rescuing one of the Infinity Group's truck drivers who had been set upon by bandits. A few of the local cops had been there too, trying to keep outsiders out but not unwilling to take anything, like a truck load of food, for their people. Allen and his men had killed them all and retrieved the driver before being called to handle another similar incident elsewhere. They'd been forced to abandon the truck where it was.

The truck had been moved, not by much but enough to notice.

"Negative hostiles on FLIR," he heard the copilot announce through the headset.

If nothing was showing up on the Forward Looking InfraRed the Richard and the McIntyres had probably left the area. Otherwise their body heat would have been picked up. He still needed to go down and see for himself.

The crew chief was on the ball. He was already attaching the fast rope to the boom that stuck out over the side hatch. The Blackhawk helicopters couldn't land on the road or anywhere nearby because of how close the trees were to the road. So Allen and his men would have to take the rope.

The helicopter stopped in a hover. He was a firm believer in leading from the front, so Allen was the first to reach out and grab the thick rope then jump out and slide down to the asphalt, using his boots to apply enough pressure to slow him down at the bottom. He bent his knees to absorb the shock of landing then stepped away to give the man above him room to land.

As soon as he had two other sets of boots on the ground with him, he began advancing on the truck, his shotgun up and ready for business. On the opposite side of the truck, men from the other helicopter would be doing same. They'd meet at the truck in the middle.

It didn't take long to confirm that there wasn't another living soul in the area. Richard truly had moved on.

"Creeper, Dwarf. We've secured the objective but the package isn't here."

"Copy, Dwarf. Standby for an update," Jax replied.

While he waited, Allen walked around the truck looking at the scene. The corpses he and his men had left a few days ago lay pretty much where they'd fallen. Flies were everywhere, feeding and laying eggs, and a few carrions that hadn't been scared away by the choppers still pecked at their feast. Bloody tire tracks cut a path through some of the bodies.

Along the side of the road, he spotted one of the new NAIS road marker posts with cattle-tracking RFID chip readers. He remembered them being installed shortly after the most recent mad cow disease or bird flu scare.

One of those, he thought. *Waste of fucking money.*

"Dwarf, Creeper," the radio interrupted.

"Send it."

"Dwarf, Creeper. I've sent your pilots the coordinates to a cabin in Bozeman that we previously extracted from Guddemi. He said it was where Richard would eventually go to ground."

"Why am I just now finding out about this?" Allen demanded.

"Look, I'm sorry, Buddy," Jax replied, throwing military radio etiquette to the wind. "We thought Richard was K-I-A in Spokane. When you gave the word that he was still active and that he's got what we need, I started reviewing the files of Guddemi's interrogation and everything we know about Richard. I just found it."

"Fine," Allen growled. "Review faster. I want to know everything about this asshole."

"Will do, Dwarf."

Allen ground his teeth and imagined choking the life out of Jax, but then reined in his emotions and reminded himself that Richard was the focus of his anger, not his teammate.

"Creeper, Dwarf," he said when he was calm again.

"Go ahead."

"Deploy a reaper over the new objective area. I want to know what we're going into before we get there."

"I copy. Standby."

Allen sighed.

"Dwarf, Creeper. That's a negative. Your position is approximately an hour out from the objective. Soonest a reaper can be on station is at least two hours. Do you still want to task a reaper?"

Allen ground his teeth again and then sighed. *What the hell? I was doing this shit before they even had reapers. I'll just have to go old school.*

"Negative, Creeper. Disregard the reaper. We'll go in blind."

"Roger that, Dwarf. I'll send you what you need. Creeper out."

"Dwarf out"

Allen took a brief moment to gather his thoughts and get a firm grip on his composure before gathering the men and explaining the new turn of situation.

They had to hoof it up the road half a mile to a scenic overlook to reload into the choppers since it was faster than trying to climb a rope against the rotor downdraft or be hoisted up individually by the helo's winches.

As they were flying, Allen ran the numbers in his head. They had flown for a little over two hours after having lost Richard's signal. Then they had spent about half an hour on the ground searching the area. And Jax said it would be an hour in the air to their next objective. That came up to just over three and a half hours total since they'd last had a bead on Richard.

Unless Richard's group ran into trouble on the ground, it was likely that they would reach the cabin before Allen's group did. That wasn't optimal, but they'd make do. Maybe just being at the cabin would convince Richard he could relax his guard, making Allen's job easier.

And I've got surprise on my side, he thought. *Plus I outnumber him by four to one.*

The nonstop mission to mission action was beginning to catch up to him. *Or is it just the new nano series making me tired?* Looking at his watch, he saw that he had a good forty-five minutes before they'd be in striking distance of the cabin, so he leaned back to grab a quick power nap and re-energize. He willed himself to drift off with the chop of the rotors his lullaby.

"Master Chief"

"Master Chief"

Allen opened his eyes. He wanted more sleep, but he remembered what was next and fought to banish the cobwebs from his mind.

"Master Chief, we're five minutes out from the LZ," the crew chief said. "Creeper said to give you this."

Allen nodded and took the tablet that was offered then removed the comm headset. He flexed his abs and lats then the muscles in his arms and breathed out a sigh that was also half a yawn. When he relaxed he felt more awake.

Jax had sent the pilots instructions on where to take Allen and his men for insert into the objective area, taking into account a number of different variables: the local terrain, vegetation, weather, lunar illumination, air density, and distance among others to determine if the helos would fit in the landing zone, landing conditions, how easily they'd be to see or hear from the objective, how long it would take to reach the cabin from the LZ, etc.

The tablet the crew chief had handed him was the latest iPad with milspec security features and some upgrades that had never hit the civilian market and now probably never would. As soon as the screen came on, illuminated in a way that didn't destroy an operator's natural night vision, Allen saw a four square grid. The upper left square expanded to a document that described the cabin and surrounding area. The lower left square expanded to a video of Guddemi's interrogation in case Allen wanted to review it for himself.

He decided not to for now. He'd trust Jax's findings. Maybe later he'd indulge.

The upper right square was the most up to date compilation of data that they had found on Richard. It really wasn't much actually, which was surprising.

Allen scanned the contents.

Holy shit, a red raider? He thought, when he read Richard's resume. He narrowed his eyes and tried to remember the faces of red raiders he had known and had interacted with. Richard's face wasn't attached to any of the raiders he remembered. He wondered how accurate the file was. It wouldn't be the first time some dickhead had made a false claim about Special Forces experience. But if the file was correct, that would certainly explain a lot about Richard's being alive after confronting most of the EWES-7 candidates.

Respect—not fear, Allen reminded himself, as he tapped the lower right square.

The lower right square expanded to display a topographic map of the area with the option to change the display to a satellite photographic view or even a 3-D model view. Allen chose the 3-D view and tapped an icon on the screen. The LZ Jax had chosen for them began to glow in green, and a black line traced out a primary patrol route through draws and valleys to his objective, the cabin, which blinked and glowed red. An alternate route showed up as a gray line, with a pink line as a tertiary route in case either of the first two didn't work.

Allen analyzed the tactical data Jax had worked out for them and had to admit it was pretty close to how he would have planned the operation had their roles been reversed.

The choppers dropped them a little over a mile away from the cabin where the chop of their rotors wouldn't be heard by those in the cabin. It could have taken him and his men through the forested hills between the LZ and the cabin, but he preferred to sneak up on them and attain complete surprise instead of rushing in and having Richard or one of the McIntyres potentially escaping into the woods and then taking an equally long time or longer trying to find and apprehend them.

The night air was cool and crisp with the pleasant aroma of pine trees and musty earth drifting about on the occasional breeze, a far sight better than the putrid rot and buzzing flies of their last stop.

One thing he appreciated about being in the mountains was being able to look up and see the stars without the smothering glow of city lights to steal their glory. When Benson had his way, this would be the new norm.

Pine needles underfoot dampened the sounds of their steps. Allen stopped the patrol every so often to check that they were navigating correctly. Moving at night through the mountains quietly, in the dark, without getting lost or walking off the side of a cliff requires skill and practice, something Benson's men were showing Allen that they had.

Allen consulted the iPad 3-D map and kept them on course.

A few minutes after they resumed their patrol from a short security halt, the iPad vibrated against his chest. He called another halt. His men took a knee and scanned their overlapping sectors of fire. There wasn't much to see, but they'd be ready to engage if anything showed up.

Allen brought the iPad out and woke it from sleep mode. An email from Jax awaited.

I was able to divert some time from one of the ISIS blimps and get you a quick peek with thermals, so you wouldn't have to go in blind. Don't count on it happening again. You know how hard it is getting into the queue. Looks like heat signatures from three adults, two children, and one medium-sized dog—all inside the cabin. No sentries. Happy Hunting.

—Jax

I take back everything bad I've ever said about you, Jax, Allen thought. *Well, almost everything.*

He was thoroughly impressed with Jax's ingenuity. A reaper drone hadn't been available, so the man had used sensors from the Air Force/DARPA Integrated Sensor Is Structure (ISIS) Stratospheric Airship Program to get him some imagery of the cabin. The modern day upgraded blimps hovered over the continent in the stratosphere and stayed aloft 24/7, 365 days a year, for upwards of ten years at a time, the whole time just watching.

They were usually assigned to high priority missions and access to anyone else was pretty much unheard of. For Jax to have used one to get Allen what he needed...well, it warmed his heart.

Allen smiled. Jax wanted the poppers out of their heads as much as Allen did. They needed Benson to be happy.

The warm and tingly moment passed, and Allen focused back on the task at hand. He studied the thermal images.

Jax was right. There did appear to be three adults and two children with a pet inside the cabin. That's what they were looking for, though where the kids came from Allen couldn't even guess. No one else was outside, but a large vehicle was parked outside. It looked big enough to

456

be a moving truck or an RV, and its engine compartment was still radiating heat, indicating that it had been used recently.

The time stamp on the image showed that it was only fifteen minutes old.

Allen checked the navigation route again. The cabin was just over the rise and down the hill from his location.

He motioned for the men to rally on him then waited for them to pass the signal up the line. A few minutes later they huddled around him, and he gave them the good news.

Half the men set up a perimeter behind the cabin, an anvil to the hammer of the other half, who would break in through the front (since the cabin didn't have a back door) and subdue everyone inside. Just to be safe, Allen assigned a pair of men to the RV parked out front.

Allen and his men remained downwind of the cabin, taking into account that the dog was inside with their targets. They approached with quiet, guarded footsteps.

The front of the cabin was sheltered by a porch that stretched the length of the building. They inched across the porch and stacked for entry beside the door. Dim light from candles and the fireplace leaked in fits from the front windows.

Allen, as point man, would enter first. He waited until he felt the tap on his shoulder from the man behind him then he held up three fingers and did a silent countdown. On zero, the man positioned two steps back rushed forward and kicked the door just to the side of the door handle.

The door burst inward with a loud crash, and with a surge of adrenaline, Allen was in the cabin, shotgun up, before the door could rebound off of anything. His men came in behind him, button-hooking towards the corners of the room and fanning out.

The dog's bark turned into a yelp when one of the men shot it with a rubber bullet.

A man and woman at the table jumped to their feet with yells, and Allen shot each of them in the chest with the rubber slugs. They went down in pain, and another woman threw her hands up and started screaming. Allen shot her in the chest as well just to shut her up.

No threats appeared. Only the man had a gun, a huge cowboy action revolver that had been in a holster, the leather belt on which it rested slung on the chair he'd just vacated.

Aiming the shotgun at the man, Allen provided security while his men cinched zip ties around their wrists. Another of the entry team came back into the room from the hallway he and another had cleared. He carried two kids. One was a boy, one a girl. The girl was crying, and the boy was kicking and hitting, trying to break free. They looked like they were about eight or nine years old.

"Aarghh!" the man yelled, as Allen lifted him from the floor with one hand and dragged him towards the fireplace where there was more light.

His men brought the two women and lined them up next to the man.

"Dad!" one of the women called, as Allen slammed him to his knees.

The man shook his head at her and she quieted.

"Damn it!" Allen yelled, when he had a good look at them. He had his flashlight out and shone it into each of their faces in turn. These were not Richard or the McIntyres. He kicked a couch, and it scraped backwards a few inches on the hardwood floor.

The kids hugged their mother and cried. She tried to shield them, but one of Allen's men smacked her across the head and told her not to move.

Allen paced the room thinking. *Where the hell is Richard? He was supposed to be here. Guddemi said...*

It clicked.

Of course Guddemi said. He had been tortured while being interrogated to speed up the process of getting information on Richard. But Guddemi had been a trained intelligence officer. Of course he'd have a believable cover story worked out ahead of time.

Allen looked at the man on the ground. These people had some horrible luck, either that or Guddemi had a grudge against them. No, had to be bad luck. The cabin didn't look like it was a year-round home. Maybe a hunting cabin? It might have been a good place to hide from zombies but not from him.

Allen sighed and wiped sweat off of his forehead.

The only easy day was yesterday, he thought, quoting a SEAL mantra.

Benson's men were silent, waiting for a decision from him. They kept their weapons pointed at the prisoners, but their eyes kept going back to him, as if asking for directions.

He looked back down at the prisoners.

The man looked like he was in his fifties, his hair graying, facial wrinkles in all of the right places. He wore cowboy boots and jeans, a flannel shirt with folded reading glasses in the breast pocket. He was stoic, betraying no fear, but he clearly didn't enjoy being at their mercy.

The women looked like sisters in their late twenties. They shared the same dirty blonde hair, though the heavier of the two had curls, while the other kept her hair straight.

The skinny one's kinda hot, Allen thought and suppressed a shiver and the animalistic urge that shot through his loins. *Hmm, haven't felt that in a while. Interesting.* He walked closer.

The kids clung to the plump sister. Their shivers of fear spoke to Allen. They were so honest, so emotionally transparent. He felt a moment of compassion, when, for the kids' sake, he thought he might just leave this family be and walk away with his scary men.

But just for a moment. Skinny Blonde had his attention again. She made his balls tingle.

Plump Mama Curls threw herself against Allen's leg as soon as he was within reach and yelled "Run!"

The two kids obeyed immediately. Allen was impressed.

Benson's men were not.

They dropped the kids with rubber bullets to the back.

The old man tried to take advantage of the moment to kick out against the man closest to him.

Allen shot him through the head with his handgun then fired a shot down into the back of Plump mama's curls.

Skinny Blonde barely had time to register what had happened to the rest of her family, when Allen stuck the hypodermic needle of tranquilizer into her neck and plunged about a third of the contents into her blood stream. She dropped to the floor unconscious. He had intended to use it on Richard, but Richard clearly wasn't here, and Allen was out of leads.

He pulled the needle out her neck, looked at how much remained, and nodded, satisfied that he hadn't given her too much. He tossed the needle into the fire, where it sizzled and the plastic began to deform.

The little girl had fallen at a bad angle, her head clipping the base of a free standing cabinet. The rubber bullet had added enough energy to her own momentum that her neck had snapped on impact. She was dead.

Her brother was not.

The brown-haired little boy wheezed as he tried to drag himself away on his stomach. He was clearly in pain. Tears ran down his cheeks, and he grimaced with each labored breath.

Allen shot him in the back of the head, stopping his slow progress.

He had never killed a child before tonight.

He stopped to think if it felt any different.

Nope, not really, he decided.

"Call for extract," he ordered before walking back over to Blondie.

He felt another stirring in his groin, as he picked her up and tossed her limp form over his shoulder.

You're coming with me, bitch. I'm going to have to be careful with you. You're very distracting.

461

He ushered the men out of the cabin then turned and looked at their handiwork. He shook his head. They'd missed Richard and the McIntyres. The whole night was wasted.

Well, mostly, he thought, as he shifted his captive's weight.

Keeping her in place, he propped his shotgun against the outside wall of the cabin and pulled a gray canister out of a pouch behind his hip. Purple markings indicated that it was a thermite incendiary grenade. He brought it up to the hand holding the woman in place and removed the safety pin. He tossed the grenade to the juncture where the hallway joined the main room then picked up his shotgun and walked away.

Already he could hear the choppers approaching.

By the time he and Benson's men were on the Blackhawks headed for the ranch, the cabin was nothing but flames reaching to those distant stars he had admired earlier.

Skinny Blonde lay on the floor at his feet, her hair splayed out in the shape of a fan. The tranquilizer he had used would leave her unconscious for hours. He used flexicuffs to ziptie her hands together anyway. He was going to have fun with her.

A chirping sounded in his ear, an incoming call, and he reached up to activate his bluetooth receiver.

"Send it."

"Allen, we gotta talk."

"No shit, Jax"

"Look, man, I'm sorry the cabin was a bust. You know I don't make this shit up. I just pass on what I find."

"I know. Doesn't mean I have to like it. Do you have any actionable intel for me? Anything. Did you find anything on that phone I gave you?"

"Yeah. That's actually one of the reasons I called you. There were only three calls made from that phone for its entire history, and two of the calls were to one number. All in the same day too, by the way."

"Ok, and…"

"And the first and last number dialed is registered to a group of animal rights activists that operates out of Spokane."

"Ok, well, Spokane is history. The other one?"

"The other is registered to *Rogue Paladin LLC* with a mailing address in Cheyenne, Wyoming. *Rogue Paladin*, in turn, is property of *Kochen Bahls LLC*, a holding company also registered in Cheyenne."

"Cock and Balls? Seriously?"

"No, not cock and balls. Kochen—like H&K, Heckler and Koch."

"Whatever. What can you tell me about *Cock and Balls*?"

He could hear Jax sigh.

"Not much, unfortunately. It is registered anonymously. Not many States allow anonymous company registration anymore because of the tax evasion possibilities, but apparently Wyoming still does."

"So we can't trace it back and get a physical location for whoever received the phone call? Maybe you can check which cell tower the call went through?"

"I can't access the actual company records online. Someone can get the info out of the sealed court records,

463

the actual paper that was filed, but that's only if they go to Cheyenne. As far as tracing the call through a tower—well, I can try, but cell towers have been going down all over the place."

"Do what you can. Damn it," Allen cursed, and breathed out heavily. "Have you seen Benson lately?"

"Just in passing. He looked pissed. He was going on about some missing kids and liabilities."

"All right. Look—find out everything you can about *Rogue Paladin* and *Cock and Balls*. I'd prefer not to go to Cheyenne if I don't have to. The place has got to be a mess with these fucking dead-heads everywhere. I also need to know if Harper said anything about how to disable the poppers. I have this growing feeling Benson isn't going to take them out even if we get him his upgraded nanos."

"You got it, Buddy. I'll be in touch."

Chapter 10: Obstacle

Hanna and Erica saw to it that the four new additions to their growing travel group were comfortable at the table Richard had previously claimed. The children were quick to accept water to drink, since they hadn't had any available to them in days.

When they were finished changing the tire, Richard and Scott put the tools away and began carrying boxes of produce into the lab. Samuel offered to help and volunteered David as well, but Richard turned them both down. He knew they had been without water for a few days, and that was no way to start heavy lifting.

Instead, Richard drove the lab up next to the back of the truck, so he could pass boxes directly from the trailer into Scott's waiting arms at the lab's side door. The whole time, he imagined the nanos inside of him sending a beacon to the Infinity Group, and it made him uncomfortable.

Jason seemed to be doing better. Richard checked on him alone to prevent any of the others from being in danger if he had turned. Jason's vital signs were in normal range, and his fever had diminished, so Richard woke him, and they packed more boxes of produce in where he had been resting. He said his head didn't feel fuzzy anymore. The zombie nanos didn't appear to have progressed at all since the watches had gone on and the power had been shut off in the lab. The black lines in his eyes looked slightly larger but not by much. Everyone hoped it would stay that way. In such tight quarters, it would be a mess if the watches failed or if the nanos began to duplicate again after exposure to the electromagnetic waves put off by the electronics in the passenger area.

Hanna promised to keep a close eye on his condition. Erica said she would do the same.

Before long the lab was full with nowhere else to stack the food safely, so they made room at the tables by the children and stacked a few crates of honey there. It was all they could hold, so they closed the door to the trailer and left, resuming their trek to Cody.

Hanna still drove, but Erica gave up her seat in the front so the married couple could have some time together. She went and sat on the couch with Scott. The vehicle was beginning to feel cramped, but no one complained. They were glad to be alive and on the move again.

The only spot left for Richard to sit was in the reclining chair behind the driver's seat, so that was where he parked himself. He didn't mind; he was feeling fantastic. Without the watches keeping them in check, the Harper Series nanos were hard at work in his system, and he felt stronger and more energized than he ever had before in his life. He was also hungrier, since the nanos, miraculous as they were, still needed fuel and raw materials to work their magic, so he began chewing on a power bar from his pack.

Across from him Erica and Scott shared the couch. Scott looked nervous. One of his legs was bouncing, and Richard could tell he was struggling not to start scratching. He had a crush on her. That was clear from how he kept glancing over at her, and she didn't really seem to notice. She was sitting with her legs up underneath her as she leaned away from Scort to rest on the arm of the couch.

Hanna and Jason were holding hands, and it felt invasive to watch, but he watched anyway. Even though he knew how they must feel after Jason's near brush with death, Jason wasn't out of the woods yet, and Richard was the only one who had guaranteed immunity from the zombie nanos. If Jason turned, it would be up to Richard to protect everyone else.

But watching them made him think of Linda back home. He really missed holding her in his arms, smelling the clean floral scent of the shampoo in her hair, and seeing her smile. He thought he'd give anything right then to have exactly that. He wondered if she had been able to go into town and stock up on everything he had recommended the last time they had talked. He wondered if the Infinity Group supply pods had been delivered.

Thinking about the Infinity Group led him to wonder about the truck at the roadblock and where it may have been headed—*and how were those kids planning on getting away once it reached its destination?*

Clearly they had been able to sneak onto the truck when no one was looking, unless someone else had helped them, but how had they planned to stay hidden when the truck was being unloaded? Did they have someone else at the final destination that was planning on helping them? *No, that can't be it; they acted like they didn't know where the truck was going.* What if they had just been heading for another Infinity Group outpost? As soon as the last pallet was unloaded they'd have had nowhere to hide and probably nowhere to run.

He cleared his throat as he stood and turned to the children.

"I'm sorry, Samuel," he said. "I've been thinking. I just...I couldn't help wondering...how were you planning on getting away once they started unloading the truck at their final destination?"

Samuel sat a little straighter on the bench and made eye contact with his siblings before turning to Richard.

"We didn't know how we were going to escape," he replied. "My father just told us to get into the truck and hide, and the Lord Father would guide and protect us."

Richard nodded and considered.

Either your God was looking out for you, or you were extremely lucky, he thought.

"So *your father* told you to hide on the truck," Richard repeated.

Samuel nodded.

"Why?"

The youngest sibling, *Rachel*, Richard remembered, spoke quietly in their not-English language to Samuel, who hushed her with a hand gesture and a not-English response.

Samuel turned back to Richard.

"I will tell you what we know," he said. His voice sounded wooden, as if he were not used to speaking this much.

Richard nodded and leaned back against the wall, crossing his arms in front of him.

"It started one week ago," Samuel began. "We were sleeping in our house in Berlin, Ohio. We were woken in our beds by men with guns and herded outside, where we were loaded into a bus.

Holy shit, Richard thought, remembering the news story that had been on the TV while he was uploading

468

Harper's hard drive. *The town where all of the people disappeared, all of the Amish.* He had joked about it to himself then, but it didn't seem very funny now.

Samuel continued, oblivious of Richard's thoughts.

"They filled the buses with everyone in town and then drove for hours. They kept men with guns on the buses with us so that we could not open the curtains in the front to speak to the driver nor remove the blinds that covered the windows. They beat anyone who was not quiet or who tried to stand up.

"We did not know where they were taking us or why.

"When the buses stopped, the sun had been up for several hours. We were told to get off of the bus."

Samuel paused and clenched his jaw. He suddenly looked older than his seventeen years.

"We were in the mountains. There were houses close together, one for each family we would soon find out.

"As soon as we stepped off of the bus, the men with guns began pulling people aside while forcing others forward. They took all of the married women and some of the older unmarried women as well. A few small children, like my brother Amos and sister Ezra, were also taken."

His voice quavered, and he was silent for a moment before clearing his throat, clenching his jaw, and continuing.

"They took the rest of us past the houses to a big building with glass walls, five stories tall, like a big city building. It is a medical clinic.

"They sent in small groups at a time and forced their medical injections on us and took our blood. My father and most of the other men protested because we consider most of your medicine to be sinful, but they had guns and told us they would hurt our women, our mothers and wives, if we did not comply. A few still tried to argue, but the men beat them into silence with their rifles.

"My father was one of those who still resisted and was beaten," Samuel said after a pause. "My father is a big man, very strong. He is a blacksmith."

Ah, so that explains why you are so big yourself, Richard thought. *Your father had you working the forge right there with him, passing his trade down to you just like in the old, old days.*

"But those men were even stronger," Samuel continued. "They beat my father until he was bloody and stopped fighting back. They broke him," Samuel said, looking up meet Richard's eyes again. They were moist and hard.

It made Richard uncomfortable to see so much raw emotion, and he grew even angrier at the Infinity Group people for how the Amish had been treated.

"And then they put their drugs into him anyway and took his blood. They said it was for our own good."

Samuel wiped his eyes and sniffed.

"They would," Richard whispered, afraid his own voice would crack if he spoke any louder.

"When we finished their tests, we were told to gather into family groups, so we could be led to our new living quarters. That was when we found out that our mother and two youngest siblings would not be rejoining us."

Richard frowned and shook his head slowly.

"The men claimed that they needed to be quarantined because of a contagious illness that was discovered during their medical tests, but Father says they were taken hostage to keep the rest of us in line."

"That makes sense," Scott said.

"That's horrible," Erica added, shaking her head.

Richard nodded but kept his thoughts to himself.

"Every family had at least one person missing for quarantine," Samuel continued.

"Were any of these hostages men?" Richard asked.

Samuel thought about it before shaking his head and saying, "No, not that I can think of. Mostly they took the women and some small children."

Richard nodded. "So they didn't take many, if any, of those they expect to work."

Samuel nodded slowly.

"I think I see what's going on," Richard said.

"You do?" Scott asked.

Richard nodded as he looked at the couple on the couch. His nano-enhanced brain was alive, making connections he might not have otherwise made so quickly.

"Think about it. According to Harper, the nanotech in the zombie series is powered by ambient electromagnetic waves. The Infinity Group plans to release an EMP in the upper atmosphere that will knock out the power, all of the communications, basically anything and everything that emits any E. M. waves."

"Which will turn off the zombies," Scott said.

"Right, just like flipping a switch. But what happens to the Infinity Group when they no longer have all of these modern conveniences at their fingertips?"

471

Samuel frowned but kept silent.

"Well, I'm sure they have to have shielded technology. Look at this lab on wheels. It's shielded. Why would they turn off their own power?" Scott asked. "They'd have so much more of an advantage by keeping it."

"Certainly," Richard replied. "But even if they do have that advantage, their technology won't last forever. They'll be killing so many people that they can't possibly hope to have enough people alive to keep finding raw materials, processing the materials, manufacturing the materials into useable goods, powering the usable goods reliably—the whole production chain for every consumable in the world, let alone keep what they have running indefinitely. A long time, sure. But not forever. And they want to live forever. So what then?"

"When today's tech is breaking down and they still want to live like kings. Then," he said, without giving anyone the chance to answer him. "They will already have a large group of slaves who are used to working, growing food, storing the food for later, caring for and butchering livestock, everything it takes to live off-grid without modern technology.

"They keep a few hostages from each family working in a separate area to keep them from rebelling and to keep them productive, and they survive. The rest of the world is either dead or fighting and struggling to survive."

"Right, because without modern infrastructure the world, by then, is back to the Stone Age, and hardly anyone has the skills needed to survive like that. We've let it all go," Scott said.

Richard nodded.

"The Amish can do it," he replied. "And there are a select few others that live primitively, but, yes, overall society is screwed now that the lights and phones have gone out for good. Some will survive the zombies, but the vast majority of them are going to die. The grid is gone."

"That totally makes sense," Erica said. "That is so scary."

Scott nodded agreement.

Richard turned back to the children.

"So why would your father have you run away from safety and risk being attacked by zombies?" he asked.

Samuel hushed his sibling who chose that moment to talk over each other in their private language.

"What language is that?" Scott asked.

Richard held up a hand to ward off additional questions that might get them off topic.

Samuel sighed.

"We do not know about zombies," he said. "We've never heard of them. You keep using this word, but we do not know what you are talking about."

"Zombies," Scott said. "Like in the movies, zombies—walking dead people."

"I think I might have seen something moving outside when you had your computer on, something strange, but that doesn't mean I understand what you are talking about. You may have noticed that we do not know much about the world outside of our culture, but don't for an instant think that we are completely ignorant. The dead do not walk. That is not possible. "

473

"I doubt they've seen very many movies, Scott," Richard replied. "They're Amish. I'd be surprised if any of them even have a television."

"Right," Scott said, pursing his lips.

"Zombies," Richard said, turning back to the siblings, "are basically mindless, psychopathic …creatures…that used to be human people before they became what they are. They run around trying to bite people, turning those people into zombies as well.

"They were fictitious monsters in boogie man stories and horror movies, but now, thanks to advances in science and a particularly devious and deranged scientist, they are real, and they're all over the place. We are not trying to insult your intelligence by telling you that the dead walk.

"Under other circumstances I would agree with you that it just isn't possible, but things have changed. The 'zombies' as we are calling them are really just humans who have been hijacked by microscopic robots that can keep the body working even after the body's brain has died. These zombies are a blunt force weapon of attrition conjured by a group of people who want to destroy humanity and claim the world for their own."

Samuel looked down at his hands, which were clasped and resting on the table.

"Well, we didn't know anything about zombies or world domination when we left," he said, before looking back up. "We were just trying to reach the authorities and hope they could rescue our family and friends. And it's Dutch."

"What?"

"Dutch. We speak Dutch to each other and English to outsiders."

"I see," Richard replied, nodding his head. "I'm surprised your father risked upsetting your captors. After all, they still have your mother and siblings hostage. When they find out you are missing there are sure to be repercussions."

"My father is a blacksmith, one of the most important men in town. They will not harm him. He is too valuable."

"And you think that protects the rest of your family?" he asked.

"Sending us away was the right thing to do," Samuel said. "We can bring help."

Richard nodded. "Well, I hope your father made the right choice, for everyone's sake."

Richard slid along the wall and stumbled forward, as the lab slowed to a stop rather quickly.

Everyone looked to the front.

"Oh my gosh," Scott said.

Off in the distance, a huge fire lit the sky and all of the land around it for miles. Smaller fires surrounded it.

"What happened?" Erica asked.

"It looks like the oil refinery caught fire," Richard replied, looking over Jason's shoulder. "That could be trouble, since we need to drive right by it."

"Look," Hanna said and pointed.

Elongated lights zipped away from a point ahead on the road and arced off into the distance, looking very much like laser beams from Star Wars.

475

"Tracers," Richard said. "Best guess—the military is up ahead, and it looks like they've got a lot of targets. Samuel, turn off those lights."

Soon the interior of the lab was darker than the night outside.

"Holy sh—cow," Richard said, remembering the religious children behind him. Now that the lights were off, his vision wasn't impeded by the glare that had been reflecting off of the windshield. Now he could see more than just the fire and tracers.

"What do you see?" Jason asked.

The tracers stopped flying.

"Looks like a military roadblock, say, three miles ahead, right on the highway. They're surrounded by zombies. They're starting to be overrun. Why don't they just back up?" He squinted as he looked closer. "Ah, they can't. They're tangled up in the wire perimeter."

"You can see that from three miles away?" Erica asked.

"Yes," Richard replied, a little surprised as well. "Harper's enhancements, I guess."

"What should we do?" Hanna asked.

"Well," Richard replied. "We could…"

A bright fireball flashed into blossom right where the armored personnel carrier had been spewing machinegun fire.

Jason flinched back at the flash.

A second later the ground shook.

"Poor bastards," Richard said, wincing as he analyzed the unfolding scene. "But I guess it's better than turning into one of them." He sighed. "We won't make it through there. The road is well and truly fu…ugh…fudged up. That was a thousand pounder, at least. The road ahead is a crater."

"What is a thousand pounder?" Erica asked.

"A great big bomb," Richard replied. "Dropped by a great big bastard of a warplane, an A10 Warthog."

"Tank killer," Scott said, shaking his head. "Man, they just killed their own guys. That is not cool."

Richard nodded, his face grim.

"I guess we'll just have to find a way around Billings like we did Helena."

The other groaned. None of them looked forward to doing that again, least of all Hanna who was still driving. She'd had a time of it seeing the little zombie children in Helena, and she didn't know if she could stand to see sights like that again.

"I know," Richard said. "But cheer up; once we find a way around the oil refinery, we'll be less than two hours away from our new home. You ready, Scott?"

"Yeah, let me just get connected again."

While Scott brought his laptop back to the docking station between Hanna and Jason, Richard took the time to better observe the area around the mobile lab. The highway they had been driving on was fairly open. He guessed the reason for that was that most of the cars that would have been on the road were stopped by the now dead roadblock ahead. All of the people that had been in those cars were likely part of the mob of zombies that even now wandered around near the flaming ruins of shattered armored vehicles.

He knew that as soon as Scott engaged the antenna array for an internet signal, the zombies would be drawn towards them like a starving wolf to bleating sheep. With the distance between them, they should have plenty of time to get the directions they needed and move off before the zombies could impede them, if Scott was quick about it.

Richard knew immediately when Scott started broadcasting a signal because even from miles away, the disposition of the zombies changed. They went from slowly wandering around in the jumbled mess of derelict cars to focusing on and moving towards the lab. It was a frightening sight to see, knowing that every one of those infected biters was coming to tear them apart.

"Here they come," he said.

"No worries," Scott replied, as he tapped away at his keyboard. "All right, got it. A quarter mile ahead is an off ramp. Take it and then take the immediate right turn."

Hanna nodded and began driving.

"Hmm, that's strange," Scott said, as he entered commands on the laptop.

"What is it?" Richard asked.

Scott shook his head and furrowed his eyebrows. He tapped away and shook his head some more.

"What's up?" Richard asked.

"I don't know," Scott replied. "The antenna array doesn't seem to want to disengage, so we're still broadcasting."

"Well, keep trying. There are a few towns ahead that are pretty small with no good route around. We don't need a crowd of zombies stopping us in our tracks...or following us home. This beast is pretty solid, but it won't mean diddly squat if there are so many zombies under the tires that we lose contact with the pavement."

Scott sighed. "Yeah, I know."

He went back to typing, and Richard watched from the reclining chair behind Hanna.

Forty-five minutes later Scott was still working on the problem with Jason and Erica throwing in their thoughts on what the problem might be. He had started scratching at the scab above his ear and was mumbling curses at all things electronic.

Richard had to quiet him several times, since his blaspheming was beginning to annoy Samuel and the other kids who weren't used to regular profanity, let alone the litany of creative and colorful words Scott managed to come up with. Richard was even a little surprised; he hadn't heard such choice swearing since he'd served in the Corps.

"Guys," Hanna called, as she slowed the lab and brought it to a stop. "We've got a problem."

She wasn't exaggerating.

The narrow bridge into the town of Belfry was blocked by a pickup truck that had hit one of the sides of the bridge and had gotten stuck with its front wheels caught over the concrete handrail. It completely blocked the bridge. Scattered around the truck were the zombified bodies of what looked like everyone in town.

"Crap," Richard muttered when he saw it. He immediately thought about the likely viability of just ramming the truck out of the way, but the more he thought about it, the less he liked the option. They were already beginning to have malfunctions in the lab, and they really didn't need any more, especially anything that might slow or prevent the McIntyres from studying the zombie nanos and the Harper nanos and hopefully being able to replicate a cure.

"What should I do?" Hanna asked. "Is there somewhere to go around this bridge?"

"No, there isn't," Richard replied. "Not for quite a way anyway. Hold on, let me think."

The zombies began their walk towards the lab and were smacking up against the outer skin by the time Scott started cursing at the antenna array again. They looked gruesome crossing through the headlight beams with limbs dangling and bloody and nearly all of them sporting bloody evidence around their mouths that they had done their part to spread ZS3 nano infection to their neighbors.

"How much ammo do we have left?" Richard asked, when Scott began to annoy him.

Scott mumbled a last litany then gathered up the guns and began counting bullets.

"About two hundred rounds of nine mil for the MP5, fifty for the shotguns, then whatever you have left for your handgun."

Richard nodded and then sighed.

"Not enough," he said. "I counted upwards of four hundred and fifty zombies out there. Damn."

"Why don't we just back up, get a good head start, and ram it?" Erica asked, mirroring Richard's earlier thoughts.

Richard shook his head.

"We can't risk the damage it might do to the lab equipment."

Despite the mood, Richard smiled at how cute she looked when she sat back and started to pout.

Well, she's not really pouting, he thought, *but I bet that's how she would look if she did.*

He thought about having to go out there and move the truck and didn't like what outcomes played out in his head. He wasn't so much worried about the zombies, since he had already seen for himself that he was immune to their bites. But the idea of being tracked by the Infinity Group, especially this close to home, really gave him pause.

"What if some of us got up on the roof like we did back at DARPA and just brain them with shovels?" Jason suggested. "An' I've still got my trusty baseball bat."

Richard chuckled.

"We may just have to, but I think that will be one of our last choices." He sighed then turned to Hanna. "I need to know how the electromagnetic signal put off by these nanos is tracked."

"You're not thinking about going out there are you?" she asked.

"Maybe but I need to know how I can be tracked."

Hanna looked into his eyes and saw the seriousness there then nodded.

"Ok," she said. "I have to assume the process would be the same for you as it is for the EWES candidates."

"Naturally," Richard replied.

"It's the RFID readers. You remember right after the turn of the century when there was a big debate in Congress over the National Animal Identification System and how the public didn't want the mandated RFID readers installed all over the country because the REAL ID Act was introduced at the same time, and the civil rights groups went nuts, saying the government was trying to track everyone, and the people wanted their privacy?"

"Uh, no," Richard replied. I spent most of that time over in the deserts of Iraq and Afghanistan protecting America's oil interests, but I have seen the cattle trackers along the highway, if that's what you're talking about."

Scott began typing at his keyboard.

Jason nodded. "Yes, and don't get her started on oil interests. If you haven't noticed, she's got a mean libertarian streak in her, and she loves to talk about it."

Hanna gave her husband a mock punch to the shoulder, but she smiled.

"And look at who I married," she replied. "Anyway, the cattle trackers were mandated in the NAIS legislation to track the RFID cattle tags, but they can pick up the signals made by the EWES nanos—and probably the Harper Series as well."

"Is there any way I can mask the signal like I did before with the watches?"

"Um, I don't know," Hanna said, before biting her lower lip.

"I don't think so," Jason replied. "Not with what we have here."

"Great," Richard muttered.

"The RFID chip readers the N.A.I.S. installed to track cattle in case of mad cow disease or avian flu are the same readers that are used to track Harper's various nano series?" Scott asked.

"Yes," Hanna said. "That's what I said."

"N.A.I.S. as in the National Animal Identification System, overseen by the U.S. Department of Agriculture?"

"Yes, Scott. That's what I said. What is the point of these questions when you already know the answers?"

"Oh, just that I am now hacked into the U.S.D.A. N.A.I.S. website, where I can power down certain RFID chip readers with the push of a button," Scott replied nonchalantly.

"No way," Richard said.

"Way," Scott said with a grin.

"Well then, shut them down."

"What kind of radius around you do you want?"

"Let me see the screen."

Scott turned the laptop so Richard could see the map for himself.

"Hmm, no kidding," Richard commented. "All right, shut down everything here, here, here, and here in Park County as well."

"Four counties—well, you do think big."

"I have to now," Richard replied. "My woman is waiting for me at home, and I'm not going to let anything hurt her."

"All right, just give me another minute to make sure my tracks are covered, so it all looks legit."

A rapid fire assault on the keyboard followed, and Richard left him to it, so he could look at the scene outside again. More and more zombies were crossing the bridge. It seemed like half of the town was already around the lab, beating on any surface they could reach, trying to get in. Fortunately, they weren't much for climbing, and the bottom windows were just above the natural extension of those bloody, deadly hands.

The lab shuddered slightly under their assault.

Samuel and Rachel held hands and said prayers in Dutch with their younger brother and sister, who had their heads bowed and their eyes shut tight in fear.

"All right, Philip, you've got your blackout," Scott said.

"Thank you," Richard replied, before turning back to the front. "Jason, you mind letting me borrow your prize baseball bat?"

"I don't know," Jason said, smiling. "It's gotta be one of the last autographed Barry Bonds bats in existence. It must be worth a fortune now."

"Sure, go buy yourself a mansion with it."

Jason laughed. "Here, take it. Our lives are worth it."

Richard smiled as he took the wooden slugger.

"All right, here I go," Richard said, as he went over by the Amish kids and stepped on the bench to reach up and unlatch the cover to the roof access. He used the bat to push the hatch up then jumped and grabbed the edge. He pulled himself up into the cool dark night air and took a deep breath.

Which he regretted immediately.

Half of the dead town was surrounding the lab, and they smelled horrible. Having enhanced senses suddenly wasn't such a blessing he decided, as he pinched his nose and blinked away tears that had come unbidden to his eyes. Even breathing through his mouth was difficult, as he could literally taste the putrid rot on the back of his tongue.

He closed the roof hatch then walked forward far enough to see the crowd below and find an aiming point. Then he retreated back a few body lengths, ran forward, and jumped. He was in the air above a crowd of zombies intent on eating his friends.

And then he crashed down right into them.

As he had intended.

Landing on the outskirts of the crowd, several shambling meatbags broke his fall. Even as he pushed himself off of them, they were oblivious to his presence and only had eyes for the lab, which was still transmitting from the damaged antenna array.

He looked down at the blood and gore on his clothes.

Ugh, I'll never wear this outfit again. Won't even bother washing it. I should just burn it, he thought.

He felt a flash of fear that the nanos inside his body might somehow not work on a few, or even one, of the zombies while he was in their midst.

The zombies ignored him.

His nanos were working. He hurried across the bridge unseen and unmolested. He didn't even want to imagine how it would be different for any of the others if they tried this stunt.

The cab of the obstructing truck was empty with the passenger's side door open. He stood on his toe tips to see what gear it was in.

He noticed that it was in "Drive," as he had expected, at the same time that he noticed something was brushing against his shins. Jumping back, he raised the bat to swing.

It was a zombie.

He side-stepped and tensed to swing at the zombie's head, but then he realized that the zombie wasn't tracking. It didn't see him. It was trying to go towards the lab, but its legs were trapped under the truck's rear driver's side tire.

He lowered the bat and breathed out a sigh of relief.

He couldn't reach the gear shift handle from outside the passenger's side, so he closed the door and walked around behind the truck, stepping out of the way of two shamblers, to get to the driver's side. The gear shift popped easily into neutral. He worried that the truck might roll back off the guard rail, which could be beneficial as long as it wasn't onto him, but it didn't budge.

Kneeling down, he inspected the truck's under carriage where it was caught up. It just didn't seem possible that it had made it up that high to get caught as it was. There wasn't even a sidewalk curb that it might have otherwise bounced up off of.

Richard shook his head and sighed.

Whether it seemed possible or not, it was there, and he just had to deal with it.

He entertained the thought of using the lab to slowly but steadily push against the back corner of the truck's bed to dislodge it, but realized that even if it did come down, it would unfortunately come down onto the bridge right beside the lab. Two fairly large vehicles on a bridge with two tiny lanes—it would be like a double-feed in a gun. It would jam the action, and neither would be very mobile afterward. The zombies cluttering the bridge wouldn't much help the situation either.

Pulling the truck down was out too. There was no way for him to get the leverage.

I wish I could just push the damn thing over the side, he thought then chuckled. *Why not? It's not like the owner is going to complain.*

He looked at the snagged undercarriage again and smiled. If he could get something with enough force to push it over, there didn't look to be any reason why it wouldn't work.

Behind the truck the bridge opened to the wide road which had a few derelict vehicles sitting at the impasse. Only the pickup truck stuck in line a few cars away looked like it would have enough muscle to budge this truck, so Richard went towards it.

The driver's door was open with blood splatter on both sides of the window. More blood decorated the upholstery. The battery was dead, and the fuel gauge was on empty. This truck wouldn't be pushing anything any time soon.

Great. Now what? He thought, as he leaned against the truck with a sigh and looked back at the lab on the other side of the bridge, surrounded by zombies.

A thought popped into his head, and he laughed.

It just might work.

Chapter 11: Glorious Shower

"It must be nice to be invisible to those things," Hanna said, as she squeezed Jason's hand.

Jason nodded his head but was silent.

He and she were watching as much as they could see by the lab's headlights, while the kids were in the back, still praying in Dutch, and while Scott and Erica talked quietly to each other on the couch behind him.

He squeezed her hand in return and looked down at some of the gruesome faces outside. He couldn't help but think that he would be just like any one of them if Richard hadn't put these watches on him when he had. He looked at the watches and sighed then turned back to look out the front. They'd come so far, and yet here they were, stopped by a single truck on a narrow bridge. He doubted they'd be stuck there for very long because Richard was a pretty smart guy, and he'd gone out to deal with it.

What he saw next caused him to wonder just how smart Richard really was though.

Richard had walked back onto the bridge and bear-hugged a zombie from behind.

"What is that man doing?" Hanna asked.

They saw him walk towards the side of the bridge then toss the zombie over the side.

"What the hell?" Jason asked, in a drawn out voice, when Richard grabbed another and tossed it too off the side of the bridge.

The zombies weren't resisting. They still only had eyes for the mobile lab.

For the next half hour, they watched him toss zombies off the bridge, one at a time, until there were none left to be seen. The sun began to lighten the sky from black to deep blue with hints of orange and red following at the distant horizon.

Finally, when there were no more zombies to be seen, Richard knocked at the door.

Scott opened it half a foot and looked at him without speaking, just raising his eyebrows.

"Everyone come on out," Richard said. "It's mostly safe."

"Mostly?" Jason asked from over Scott's shoulder.

"Yeah. It's fairly safe, but I'd still like the ladies to bring out the shotguns to watch our backs."

Scott opened the door the rest of the way and looked to either side before stepping out.

Ugh, it stinks—bad," Scott said. "And you look a mess," he said, looking Richard up and down.

"Yeah, believe me, I know. Come on."

Jason followed Scott then Erica. Hanna poked her head out.

"Me too?" She asked.

"Yes," Richard replied. "And bring a shotgun."

He was pleased to see that Erica had heard him talking to the men and had already brought one with her.

"Samuel, we could use your help," Richard called. "Your siblings can stay in the lab if you like. I mostly need some muscle."

Samuel nodded from the doorway then stepped out after telling his family to stay put.

"All right," Richard said. "Ladies, one of you at either end of the bridge with a shotgun to watch our backs, please. Gents, we're going to push this Chevy into the river."

Jason went to the rail and looked over. It was only a ten or twelve foot drop to the river running below. A small pile of corpses made an island where some of the zombies had snagged on something underwater and then drowned as one after another piled up on them. Many had been swept away with the current. Only a few looked like they were in any condition to attempt to swim, but even they stayed where they were. For reasons Jason didn't understand, they appeared averse to going into the water from their corpse island.

Perhaps the ZS3 nanos in the drowned zombies had sent some kind of distress signal to warn the others above water.

He shrugged his shoulders and followed Richard.

As long as they couldn't come back up out of the water, he really couldn't care less.

"Samuel, take this corner, if you would," Richard said, pointing to the driver's side rear of the bed. "I'll take this corner, and, Jason and Scott, the middle please."

"On three," Scott offered and then counted.

They pushed together and grunted with effort. The truck's undercarriage made loud metallic screeching sounds and then began moving. They pushed even harder, and the truck lurched forward, balanced precariously out over the edge for a second, then tipped forward and crashed over the side.

There was a loud splash, and, looking over the rail, they saw the truck sink to the bottom of the river and shift a few feet down the stream. Silt clouded the water, but they could see the last few feet of the back of the truck bed sticking up out of the water at an angle along with the very back edge of the cab.

Jason guessed it must have landed on a submerged rock to be sticking out like it was instead of being swallowed whole. It seemed to have dislodged the little island of corpses because they were now being swept away with the current and sinking.

Good riddance, he thought.

"Why didn't you just push it over yourself?" Scott asked, after he had caught his breath and noticed that Richard hadn't even broken a sweat. "I mean, you've got the enhanced strength now, right?"

Richard paused and then grinned sheepishly. "I guess it's going to take some getting used to. I didn't even think about it."

The sun peeked over the edge of the hills to the east and began to shine daylight on the town of Belfry.

"I hope you're not planning on getting back in like that," Hanna said, gesturing towards Richard's blood and gore covered clothes and arms, as he and the others walked back from the far side of the bridge. "You'll stink us all out."

"I know," Richard replied. "What do you think? Maybe I should ride up top? It's not too cold out. An' the sun's out. It will get warmer?"

Hanna shook her head and looked down at the decomposed human flesh that covered him. She couldn't help but curl her lips in disgust."

"I was going to suggest you break into one of the houses in town and take a shower," she said. "But if you think your fiancé would appreciate this more then who am I to judge?"

Richard laughed and shook his head.

"I think I like your idea better," he replied. He looked down at his clothes and body. "Ugh—much better. Yes. Hot shower it is...if there's any hot water left."

The others climbed in to the lab, and Richard climbed up onto the roof for a short ride across the bridge and into town.

Hanna turned onto the first residential street she found, and Richard jumped down in front of a single story ranch style house with no cars in the driveway.

The front door was wide open as he approached. He climbed the steps to the door and peeked inside. Other than some leaves that lay on the carpet close to the door, nothing looked out of place or broken. No blood. No stench, other than his own. No zombies.

"Hello?" he called. "Anyone home?"

Silence

Walking through the house, he found no people, though he did find signs of hasty packing: cupboards open with mostly empty shelves and a few cans on their sides, dresser drawers open and clothes hanging from them and on the floor, an empty box of handgun bullets and some scattered bullets around it, dust tracks where it looked like several other boxes of the same size had rested for a while on top of the dresser.

In one room there were knives and swords and battle axes hanging on display, taking up nearly an entire wall. Judging by the swimsuit model poster hanging on one of the other walls, the high school text books on a small desk in the corner, and the overall messiness of the room, Richard figured it must have belonged to a teenaged boy. There was an empty gun rack against the wall too.

Took the guns but left the swords and knives. You guys must have really been in a hurry to get out of here. This kid was proud of his collection. It is pretty impressive. Especially this one, he thought, lifting and taking down the katana sword that served as the display's center piece. It wasn't new-looking like the others, and that's what drew the eye to it. It was definitely older, with the scratches and chips in the scabbard that hung separately above it. But the metal. *Look at the beautiful pattern,* he thought, admiring the fold pattern that had been created when the sword had been forged.

He remembered seeing a documentary about the Japanese process of forging a katana. The video had said that very few swords were made the old way, the right way. Many of the owners of the original samurai swords had been killed in World War II, and their swords had been taken by American soldiers as trophies of war. He wondered if maybe the kid's grandfather had brought this sword home from the battlefield.

I'll take care of it for you, kid, he thought, sliding the sword home into its scabbard and taking it with him. It would come in handy when ammunition for the guns became scarce.

Richard finished clearing the house then went back to the master bathroom. The water was still flowing, for which he was grateful, and best of all, it was warm. He washed his hands with profound pleasure. Then he washed them again. He had had blood on his hands before, years ago in Iraq, but he hadn't been sickened by it then like he was beginning to be now. He used an abandoned tooth brush to scrape away the gunk that had dried under his fingernails.

When his hands were clean enough to handle fresh clothes, he pulled a plush towel from the linen closet and hung it next to the shower. Then he raided the previous owner's dresser. Fortunately, it had been a man whose waistline was only a few inches larger than his own.

He grabbed clean clothes but left the underwear, deciding that it would just be too weird for him to wear another dude's skivvies. Free balling it for an hour until he got home would be manageable.

Undressing was a task, one unsuitable for the close confines of the bathroom. Some of the blood that had soaked through his clothes had dried and stuck to his skin. He had to peel them off, and knowing that it was blood, not water, touching his face just made his skin crawl. He felt bad for leaving them in a pile on the bedroom floor, even though the owners were long gone…hopefully, and would likely never be back to see the stains his clothes were making in the carpet.

He stepped into the hot shower. The soap smelled like heaven after his earlier activities, and he was tempted to stay longer than was absolutely necessary. But his longing to get home to Linda won out, and soon he was toweling himself dry and dressing in another man's abandoned clothes.

God bless you and best of luck, he thought to the family that had left so much behind. He slipped into clean, dry socks. *Oh, that feels so good.*

He cinched his new belt down tight to keep the pants from slipping down over his butt gangsta style and maneuvered his pistol holster to its customary spot just behind his right hip.

Lastly, he looked at his boots. There was surprisingly little zombie residue on them, but there was some, mostly on the bottom surface. The only other shoes he found in the house were smaller than would fit, so he used that toothbrush again, this time to scrub the bottoms of his boots. He masked any lingering smell with a few squirts of aftershave cologne.

When he stepped outside again, the morning was bright and a little bit of heat had come back to the world. Birds were chirping from their perches in trees and on telephone lines.

He walked back to the lab and tapped "Pop Goes the Weasel" on the door. This time Jason opened it.

"We were about to go looking for you. We were getting worried." He looked down and smiled at the sword Richard carried.

"I see," Richard said, looking around. Everyone but Jason and Hanna were sleeping; the kids were at the table and Scott and Erica on the couch. "Well…yeah, I've got nothing. It's been a long day," he said, shaking his head.

"Here I am. I found this inside," he said, holding up the sword. "I figured it might come in handy later."

"Well, it won't run out of ammo, that's for sure," Jason replied.

Richard closed the door and locked it.

"I tell you what," he continued. "I'll drive. Why don't you two try to catch some Z's? We should have open road the rest of the way home. This part of Wyoming is sparsely populated. I'll wake you when we get there."

"That sounds wonderful," Jason said, grabbing his wife's hand and pulling her over to join him in front of the reclining chair behind the driver's seat. She nodded and muttered something unintelligible then plopped down in the chair. Jason snuggled in next to her and closed his eyes as she laid her head against his shoulder.

Richard smiled as he sat in the driver's seat and rested the sword against the center console next to him.

Almost home.

He turned the key in the ignition, shifted into gear, and pulled the lumbering vehicle back out onto the interstate.

Chapter 12: The Sleeping Captive (This chapter is rated NC-17. Graphic sex/rape scene)

Author's Warning – This chapter is intended for adults only, and even adults might want to skip past it. A graphic rape scene is included. I didn't really want to write it, and in the editing process I toned down the details, but the result is important to the end of the story and a future story line.

When Allen walked down the helicopter ramp and crossed the tarmac towards his cabin with an unconscious blonde over his shoulder, a few of the other men in the area looked on with a little more interest but quickly went back to minding their own business when they saw that it was him. Allen was the top alpha of the group, and they knew not to interfere or show too much interest in what was now, essentially, his property, his business.

They'd seen him fight in Benson's private gladiator games arena. He was a killer, like most of them, but he made his enemies suffer before he finished them off. They didn't want his attention.

He saw their looks and was unperturbed. Walking confidently past them, he thought of the fun he had planned for his new little pet. He felt a familiar pressure growing in him, pushing for release, an impulse he hadn't had the opportunity to satisfy in a long time, not since before Leavenworth.

He stepped onto the covered porch and unlocked his door.

The cabin had an open floor plan with a loft bedroom that overlooked the living room and dining room. At its heart was a live cedar tree that stretched up through the roof. The small kitchen sufficed for the little cooking he did for himself. A buffalo skin rug covered the hardwood floor between the live cedar and the fireplace.

He had limited furniture downstairs with only the couch and a round table suitable for two with chairs. He had plenty of open space.

Upstairs was more crowded. He had his bed; a footlocker, which ironically rested at the head of his bed; a dresser for most of his clothes; and a large upright locker for his weapons and equipment.

She was still unconscious as he laid her down on his small couch, her hair swishing out over the edge of the cushion, her clothes rumpled from being crushed between her body and Allen's shoulder.

He didn't know her name, but that didn't really matter. He would call her Emily. She looked like an Emily.

The urge to take her right then and there was strong, almost overpowering, but he reined himself in. The anticipation would make this conquest that much more delicious. Besides, before she gained her wits again he needed to find a way to keep her contained when he wasn't there to watch her.

He wanted to hear her scream and cry when he had his fun.

He remembered the setup he had used in the past before he had been caught and court martialed, and judged the layout of the cabin to be suitable to his needs for now.

A proper kennel for his bitch would come later. For now, a leash would suffice.

He put the shotgun in the weapons locker upstairs and stowed his gear, glancing over his shoulder every few seconds to look down at his captive. He knew she would likely be out cold for at least the next hour, but he also knew the danger of making assumptions. Having an assumption turn out to be inaccurate could really come back and bite him in the ass.

Besides, he liked to look at her. She wore fitted denim pants that accentuated every glorious curve of her legs. She'd lost one of her boots somewhere on the trip to the ranch, but that was ok. She wouldn't need it. She wasn't going anywhere any time soon.

Allen dragged the footlocker away from the head of his bed and spun the dial on the combination lock that kept it securely private. A few quick turns had it open, and he swung open the lid.

Inside were black, heavy leather restraints, for wrists and ankles, each several inches wide with multiple layers of leather stitched together and outfitted with a locking steel buckle and D rings. A matching collar and four foot leash finished out the ensemble, and he lifted each with reverence. He'd made quite a few memories with these, and he so looked forward to making more.

He glanced down and watched Emily's ample chest rise and fall with each breath.

Yes, many more.

Taking up most of the bottom of the foot locker were some steel bolts and other accessories and lengths of ¼" stainless steel chain, heavy duty enough to be unbreakable by any man or woman but light enough that the weight wouldn't be unbearable in a relaxed position.

He felt his hands shake with anticipation. He felt like he was losing control. He didn't like losing control. Closing his eyes, he deliberately shook his hands and then balled them into fists, flexing his forearms and lats until they burned. Opening his eyes, he relaxed and embraced the calm, picked up the footlocker, and carried it downstairs.

It was a little chilly inside now that he didn't have his gear on, so he went to the fireplace, stacked some wood in the hearth, and lit a fire. Once the flames were happily crackling away, he looked at the room and visualized what he wanted.

With the design firmly in mind, he quickly began measuring the distance between the live cedar in the living room and the corner log pillar. He drilled deep holes in each, several feet higher than average person could reach. Then he took eye bolts and screwed them into the holes he had drilled. Next he took the longest chain he had and fed it through the loops in the bolts. A heavy duty bolt snap, similar to but stronger than those used on dog leashes, was welded at each end of the chain.

The chain was about six feet longer than he wanted it to be, so he folded it in the center a few times, until it was closer to the length that he wanted. Then he fed the shackles of two padlocks through the chain links at the folds and closed each lock.

Grabbing both ends of the chain, one in each hand, his arms were stretched out to his sides. They weren't much past half extension, but that would be ok. Emily wasn't as tall as he was, so her arms wouldn't have the reach his did, meaning her arms would be more extended than his currently were once she was in the restraints. He stepped forward until he was stretched to the max then pulled—hard.

The chain snapped taut, and he felt his muscles strain with effort. The chain, the eye bolts, the wooden anchors: they all held, though he felt a little more effort on his part might have snapped a bolt. This didn't worry him because there was no way Shelly could match his EWES7A-enhanced strength.

Looking around the immediate area to see if he could reach or pull anything towards him that could be used to aid escape, he found nothing. He did the same backwards and to each side with the same results.

When he shuffled to the sides, the chain slid through the eye bolts until the tension on the opposite arm made more movement to that side impossible.

Still holding the ends of the chain, he tried to reach down to touch his left foot. Stretching one hand down resulted in the chain shifting through the eye bolts and pulling the other arm higher. He couldn't even reach his knee. Nor could he bring his hands together or even get them close enough to be within a foot of each other, even if he stretched himself up to stand on the tips of his toes to give the chain some slack.

Perfect

Satisfied with the upper half of the restraint system, he went to the cedar and drilled another hole, this time down by the floor, and screwed another eye bolt into it. He measured out a shorter section of chain and fixed it to the eye bolt with another padlock. He did the same at the corner log pillar. He performed a strength test on these as well and found them also to be secure.

It was ready.

He now had potentially two restraint systems he could use.

The first system included the top chain, which would keep her upright with her hands in the air; and one of the bottom chains, probably the one anchored at the cedar; which would keep her in one small area in front of the fireplace.

If she got feisty enough to try to kick him with the other leg that wasn't anchored to the tree or log, despite the four foot length of chain that would connect the two leather ankle restraints; he could always completely immobilize her by securing both ankles to the corner chains. Then she'd be spread eagle and completely vulnerable, but he didn't think that would be as much fun. He needed her to have the ability to resist.

The second system used only the two bottom chains. One would attach to one of her ankles while the other attached to one of her wrists. This would keep her lying down on the buffalo skin rug near the fireplace. He could still have his way with her. She'd be able to fight back a little more, which he kind of hoped she would. But she would still be unable to escape. He would use this system to allow her to sleep lying down—as long as she behaved.

Emily was still drugged and didn't respond when he tapped her cheek a few times.

Smiling, he clipped and removed the flexi-cuff/zip tie restraints and replaced them, almost reverently, with the leather. He fitted them to be tight enough to keep her where he wanted her but not so tight that they cut off the circulation of blood in her arms. Then he secured them with small padlocks.

He slid off her one boot and both socks then slipped the restraints onto her ankles. He adjusted the fit then added the four foot section of chain between them, padlocking an end to each restraint.

Lastly, he gently moved her hair out of the way and lifted her head enough to slide the collar around her neck. It was loose enough that she could swallow and breathe without discomfort but tight enough that looking up at the ceiling would put uncomfortable pressure on her esophagus. He secured this in place with a padlock as well. He left the leash attached to the D ring at the front.

Let her grow accustomed to the weight of it, he thought. He imagined the leash hanging down between her beautiful big tits, the leather soaking up the beads of sweat and tears she would shed for him.

One of his hands shook again, and he quickly stopped it by clenching it tight into a fist. For several more minutes he sat there just looking at her, breathing in her feminine scent without touching her, just to prove to himself that he did have control.

He noticed a subtle change in the darkness outside and realized that morning nautical twilight had begun. The sun would be rising in less than an hour.

Damn, it's been a long day, he thought, yawning.

He considered getting some shut-eye, but decided that since he'd shown enough control, he would have a little fun before getting some sleep. Sex always helped him sleep better anyways.

"Now, which system do I want to use first?" He wondered aloud. *Hmm, I think I'll start her training with a gentler hand*, he thought. *She did just lose her family after all.* "Bottom set it is," he muttered, feeling some small measure of regret, not so much for killing the family but for getting angry and reacting with less than complete control over his failure to find Richard and the Harper Series.

Fuck it. What's done is done. I'll still get him and the new bugs. I just need to look more. He's out there. I'll find him.

Turning his attention back to Emily, he lifted her off of the couch and carried her over by the fireplace. He set her down on her back on the buffalo skin rug. Using padlocks as connectors, he attached the cedar-anchored chain to her left ankle restraint and the other bottom chain to both of her wrist restraints.

There was a little too much slack for his liking, so he tightened the chain by a few links over at the corner pillar.

Kneeling by her feet again, he took one more look at her before taking out his folding knife and flicking the blade open. He turned the edge away from her and cut through the denim up the length of each pant leg. Closing

504

the knife, he put it back into his pocket then grabbed the destroyed pants and jerked them out from under her.

He pulled on her white cotton panties, lifting her butt enough to get them down past those curves, until they were hanging on the chain. He pushed them a little further down the chain towards the cedar then turned his attention completely to her.

Her legs were mesmerizing, now that he could see them without the pants hiding them. He traced a finger from the top of her foot, around her one unshackled ankle, up her calf to behind her knee, and up her thigh, crossing her waist line and feeling the smooth skin of her lower abdomen. He flattened his hand and caressed a small circle around her belly button, luxuriating in the silky texture of her cool skin, and then brought it down to just above her mound of Venus.

She was one who had shaved her bikini area before the world went to hell, but now she had a week's worth of stubble. He brushed his fingertips through the new growth, enjoying the rough contrast to her smooth skin.

It will be fun shaving this off, he thought. *Not today though. Maybe tomorrow.*

He repositioned himself between her legs and spread them a little wider. Lying down on his belly, he propped himself up on his elbows and tilted his head down to breathe in the scent of her private femininity.

A little musty, he thought; but it had been so long since he'd last tasted it. He went for it anyway.

She tasted a little salty because she had been sweating, but it was heaven for him. It brought back accelerated memories of before: the women he had turned

505

into slaves and abused, broken their minds until they would do anything he told them, anything to avoid the pain he inflicted on them. Torture. The blood, the bruises, the screams and resigned whimpers. The tears, the spasms, complete and utter submission at last. The shame he saw in their eyes when they were forced to orgasm and enjoy the pleasure he brought them after the pain.

The memories made him swell and become erect, but still he denied himself quick gratification. He wanted to enjoy it for a while longer.

A small part of him also realized that he wouldn't have the luxury of using the women until he broke them and then discarding them to find another like he had before. The end of the world as they had known it was upon them. Women would become much rarer; they would become a valuable resource to whoever had them. He would have to take care of his women now. He might eventually be able to let them roam around within the confines of the compound, if he were able to come up with some kind of control, like what Benson had on him with the popper.

But he still planned on having his fun for now.

He played with her girl parts for a little while, remembering more and more of what he had done to other women in the past. Her body began responding to the stimulation even if her mind was still oblivious.

Allen dropped his pants, moved her one free leg open a bit more, and then rubbed some spit on his target. Disappearing into her, he tilted his head back and basked in the pleasure that radiated up his body.

The heat from the fire was no competition for the heat that flared inside of him as he moved in and out of her.

When the initial thrill of forcibly violating an attractive female after having endured prison enforced abstinence for so long began to where off, he found himself wishing she were more involved. It was just too quiet without whimpers or moans or shouts of pleasure or pain. He began to contemplate waking her with smelling salts or water.

Then his phone rang.

And he missed the quiet.

"Your timing sucks, Jax," he said, after fishing his phone out of the pants pocket down by his ankles and seeing the caller ID. "What is it?"

"You weren't sleeping were you? You don't sound like you were sleeping. You sound like..."

"What. Do. You. Want, Jax?" he repeated slowly to let his associate know he was running out of patience.

"Ok, moving on," Jax replied. "Well, I already told you about how I couldn't get any useful information out of the electronic files on this holding company out of Cheyenne. Well, I did a little more digging on the company it is holding: Rogue Paladin LLC.

"It turns out that Rogue Paladin LLC has an office in Cody, Wyoming; and that's a lot closer than Cheyenne, about two hours by chopper instead of six. Plus, one of the numbers that was listed for Rogue Paladin was none other than the number your throw away phone called. I tried calling the number, but the phone lines out that way are down. I wasn't even getting an answering machine. They're in the dark."

"Good work, Jax," Allen said. "Get me the address and as much intel as you can on the surrounding areas. I'm going to assemble the men and go get whatever the hell I can find. We need leverage with Benson, and I want Richard."

"What, you're going now, like right now, now? You need to get some sleep, man. You've been running mission after mission for days. "

"Yes, right now; the sooner we have Harper's series the sooner we can rid ourselves of Benson. An immortality serum that he would almost die for—leverage doesn't get much better than that. I can sleep when I'm back."

"Or when you're dead."

"Hmm, that is a possibility," Allen admitted. "I'll take that chance—but if for some reason I'm not back and you don't hear from me for, say, two days, go over to my cabin and feed my new pet, would you?"

"You got a dog? It better not be a cat, man. I'm allergic to cats. They make me break out, and my face swells up, and I start dripping like gallons of snot all over the…"

"Just come over and take care of things if I'm not back in a few days, and you can enjoy a little bit of whatever you find, all right? Just don't abuse the offer."

"Ok, I don't know what you're talking about, but I hope you're talking about those Cuban cigars we stole from Castro back in 2014 after we kicked the shit out of his…"

Allen shook his head and broke the connection. Jax could go on all night like this if he didn't have someone to shut him up. The guy could talk up a storm at a blank wall if given half a chance. He was an asset for his hacking and surveillance skills, as well as his command and control abilities, but holy hell he was annoying when you were busy.

The tempo of his thrusts had slowed to just what he needed to keep himself erect while he was on the phone.

I don't have time to really enjoy this, he thought, looking down at his sleeping captive. *Every minute that Richard is out there is another minute that I don't have the leverage I need to get out from under Benson's thumb.*

He imagined the small explosive device having been removed from inside the back of his cranium and then the thrust of his knife right into Benson's taint just before he cut the man's balls off and sliced outward to sever his femoral artery and watch him bleed out. With Benson gone, Allen could run the Infinity Group and take over Benson's harem. He knew enough about the inner workings of the IG to be confident that he could control Benson's lackeys, and he sure as shit had the libido to manage his bitches.

Allen smiled as he sped up his thrusts until he was pounding away at her and sweating.

Less than a minute after he had hung up on Jax, he reached his peak and shot his sperm into the unconscious woman on the floor.

He let out a deep sigh and his shoulders sagged. He was spent, wished he could sleep, but knew he had to get to Richard fast.

Reaching back, he grabbed her panties from where they dangled on the chain and used them to wipe the mess off of him. Then he stood, pulled up his pants, and tucked in his shirt. He looked at the mess he had left in her, that was even now beginning to drip out and run down her thighs to the buffalo rug.

He laughed.

You're mine, Bitch. Get used to it.

He went back up to the loft to grab his gear. This time he was going to take his usual weapons of war, but he brought the shotgun with the less lethal ammunition as well, just in case he did have a chance to get Richard. That would make all of the bullshit he'd had to endure from the arrogant, condescending prick worth it.

On the way out, he looked at Emily and decided to adjust her restraints. If for some reason he was delayed in getting back to the ranch, whether from injury or following additional leads that would take him elsewhere or just being re-tasked to something else, it would be better for her if she had a little more maneuverability, for her health.

Not too much.

She would need water, and she would need food. She would need one of her arms free so that she could get to the water and the food.

He freed one of the wrist restraints from the chain, leaving the leather restraint still securely attached to her wrist. Then he left a bottle of water, its lid unscrewed, by her side, close enough that she'd be able to see and reach with her free hand but not so close that she wouldn't see them and accidentally knock them over when she inevitably woke up and freaked out, wondering where she was and wondering why she felt like she'd been fucked.

He smiled at the thought. He wished he could see that, but he doubted he'd be back that soon. He double checked that she would be ok then closed and locked the door. Before trotting off to get the other EWES-7 men ready for the mission, he checked to make sure a spare key was on top of the porch light fixture where it was supposed to be, just in case Jax decided to swing by and "feed his pet."

The sun was beginning to peek over the horizon.

Chapter 13: Another Dammed Bridge

Though the northwest corner of Wyoming was sparsely populated, they were still driving past a fair number of vehicles on the road, many of them tangled wrecks, all of them either abandoned or occupied by the dead. More dead bodies littered the road, and the flies and vultures were already feasting, as were the coyotes and some domestic dogs that already looked to have turned feral. Black smoke rose in various places from behind the hills on the horizon.

Sights that they had been passing in the night without seeing or seeing only as a distant glow were now glaringly visible in the bright light of day. It was a far grittier scene than anything he'd ever seen before in America, and it scared him that this was the new reality. The only thing in his memory that compared to the current view was seeing the hell fire and smoke from burning oil fields during the war in Iraq and all of the burned dead bodies that had littered the highway there, but back then there hadn't been corpses walking around trying to eat his loved ones.

I hope you're ok, Linda.

While everyone else slept, he kept the vehicle moving ever onward, ever homeward. He tried to ignore the heavy breathing that made such loud noise to his enhanced hearing. Jason in particular had an annoyingly loud whistle through his nose hairs with each exhale.

Almost there, Phil. Keep it together. We're almost home, he told himself.

As he scanned the horizon, his eyes swept across the decorative CD hanging above the center console, catching his own reflection.

What the hell? He thought, reaching up to stop it from spinning and then looking closer.

Now that there was daylight he could clearly see his eyes. They had metallic flecks crisscrossing each orb in a spider web pattern just like the zombies had but shiny gold instead of black.

He looked closer.

It was definitely noticeable even without his enhanced senses.

Oh, man, what is Linda going to think? I hope this isn't a complete turn off for her.

Looking at the rest of his face, he couldn't see any other obvious changes. The nanos were healing his body, if Harper could be believed, though apparently they weren't very good at making hair grow back on top of his head.

Oh, well, he thought. *I've still got plenty of razors and a hat.* He looked back down. *But, Man, my eyes are just weird now.*

He forced his eyes away from the reflective surface and back onto the road. The more he drove, the more he worried about what Linda would think when she saw his eyes. He decided it would be better if he could tell her about them before she saw them on her own so that the shock wouldn't be as sudden or as bad. He would have to hide them.

He needed sunglasses.

There weren't any gas stations left on the road between where they were and the edge of Cody, where they were headed, but he remembered a small mom and pop diner just this side of town. He'd stop there and buy a pair if they were still open, which he doubted, or he'd acquire a pair if they were closed for zombies.

It felt good to crest the final hill before the descent down into Cody, at least, until he saw what was on the other side. Columns of black smoke rose high into the sky. The entire valley looked like it had caught fire. It looked like hell. His heart grew suddenly heavy.

He brought the lab to a stop and stared at the carnage. His first thought was of Linda. He looked to the South Fork Road and just barely saw the castle's crenelated walls sticking up above the forested horizon, the tall Medieval Kingdom flags flapping soundly in a breeze likely boosted by the nearby oxygen-sucking fires. He couldn't see lower than the battlements, but the fact that there didn't appear to be any black smoke coming from the vicinity of the amusement park gave him hope that his fiancé had survived whatever hell this town had experienced in the last few days.

I'm coming, Linda. Just hold on a little longer, he thought.

Putting the lab back in gear, he started coasting down the hill until the road leveled out, and he was forced to drive more carefully to bypass more and more derelict trucks and cars that were piled up between him and his fiancé. There were far more vehicles on the road here than there had been for most of the last few hours or even when he had left town six months ago. This time of year was the tail end of the season for tourists that came to see Yellowstone National Park, so it made sense that there would be more people in and around town than when he had left.

But where are all of the people? I see a lot of cars but not a lot of people.

He brought the lab to a halt again on the approach to the bridge into town.

Of course, it's blocked, he thought, shaking his head. All he wanted was to get home.

"Jason, Scott, nap time is over. I need your help," he said, gently shaking each of them in turn. "Come on."

The men grumbled but did climb out of their cozy positions. Hanna and Erica were roused by movements of their men, and they stood up as well.

"What's going on?" Hanna asked, bleary-eyed. "Are we there yet?"

"Not quite," Richard replied. "We're maybe two miles away, but this bridge is blocked too, and it's the only way into town."

"Ahh, again?" Erica asked, her tone more whiny than Hanna's had been. Somebody didn't like being woken up.

"Yes, again," Richard replied. "But don't worry; we'll handle it. You might want to be awake though to help if anyone gets hurt, and once we clear the bridge you ought to look around. This is the town we'll be scavenging from in the near future. It will help if you get accustomed to what is around the area."

"All right," Erica said, this time without whining. She sat up and began checking on Scott to make sure he was ready to go out into danger.

Richard drew his handgun from the holster and dropped the magazine. It was full. He pushed it back into the magazine well and pulled back slightly on the slide. He checked to see that a round was chambered; it was so he released the slide and holstered. He checked that his spare magazines were filled to capacity as well.

Next he checked the shotgun and the MP5 and made sure they were ready to go should they have to fight.

"Here you go, Scott," he said, handing off the MP5. "And Jason," he added, passing off the shotgun. "Make sure you are careful with those watches."

Jason nodded solemnly and took the shotgun. He racked the slide and a live round popped out of the ejection port and fell to the floor.

"Oops," Jason said then bent down and picked up the round.

"Yeah," Richard replied, reminding himself that Jason was not combat trained and fighting the impulse to roll his eyes. "It's already ready for you."

"Thanks," Jason said, feeling a little embarrassed. He pushed the round back into the magazine tube.

Richard nodded then turned back to the front where he had left his newly acquired sword. The wooden black scabbard had the wear and tear one would expect on an antique. The handle appeared to be covered in an authentic manta ray skin wrap, though the skin was dry and cracked. He took a moment to admire it, despite the neglect the former owner had shown in its care.

The kid probably admired this as a family heirloom, but someone should have shown him how to preserve it better. This manta skin is more cracked than should have ever been allowed, Richard thought. *Something to fix later when there's more time, I guess.*

The scabbard had some cord tied into it. It was a little flimsier than he would have liked, so he quickly cut it off and tied some 550 parachute cord in its place in a way that would allow him to carry the sword diagonally across his back. Carrying at the waist would be more traditional, and more practical if he were a samurai, but he wasn't and didn't want the sword swinging around and bouncing off of anything or getting caught up on anything should he need to move quickly later. He slipped it on over his back and checked that the handle was in easy reach over his shoulder.

"Wow, that's pretty cool," Scott said, seeing it for the first time. He had already been sleeping when Richard had first brought it out.

"Yeah, guaranteed to never run out of ammunition. I found it back when I went in for a shower. Some kid had a collection."

"You didn't get everyone else one?"

"Well, the rest of the collection was junk. Don't worry, if you want a sword, there will be plenty of them where we're going," Richard replied, pushing past Scott and going to the door. "If you guys are ready, let's go clear the bridge."

"Almost," Jason replied. He walked over to his wife and wrapped her in his arms. "I love you, Babe"

Richard turned away. Watching would only make him miss Linda more, and his heart was aching to be with her enough as it was.

"What is happening?" Samuel asked quietly. His siblings still slept.

"The three of us are going to go out and clear the bridge," Richard replied. "We're almost home, but the way is blocked. It's ok; you can stay here with your family. Rest."

Samuel looked like he was going to argue, but Richard shook his head and motioned for him to stay seated.

"If we need more help, we'll call you. Ok?"

Samuel nodded and eased back into the bench seat, let out a deep breath, and closed his eyes.

Take it easy while you can, kid, Richard thought. *You've been through enough lately. And I'm afraid there is going to be so much more to come.*

"All right," Jason said. "Let's go."

Richard put his hand on the door handle then thought better about going out and turned to the others.

"Let's stay close together when we go out there," he said. "I didn't see any movement on the bridge, but that doesn't mean there isn't anything lurking. I want to do a quick walk up to the other end of the bridge, so we can get a big picture view of just what we're looking at.

"If all goes well, we'll be able to clear enough of these cars out of the way to make the bridge passable without having to fire a single shot. Just remember, the more noise we make, the more hostiles, whether human or zombie, we'll likely have to face. So let's keep it quiet, and let's get it done."

Scott and Jason nodded in unison when they saw that Richard was done.

"All right then. Let's go," Richard said, as he open the door and stepped outside.

Scott followed right behind him. Jason stepped out and blew his wife a kiss and a wink then closed the door.

Richard took a few steps away from the lab then took a knee and began listening to everything around him. So much of the other end of the bridge was in dead space thanks to the taller vehicles in the middle that blocked his view. He didn't smell the overwhelming stench of death that was so typically prevalent when zombies were near, but that was only an indication of what was upwind, which unfortunately was behind them.

Even though the fires in town were mostly downwind, the smell of smoke was still a strong acrid stench on the bridge, thanks to a number of vehicles that had burned after crashing nearby. They had finished burning out, leaving only their charred remains and a haze that stung their eyes.

The wind whistled through the husks of dead vehicles on the bridge and through trees along the river banks below the bridge. The river rushed over rocks and gurgled around tree branches that dipped low enough into the water. Flies swarmed on dead bodies somewhere nearby. All of this he heard, just as he heard the controlled breathing of the men behind him and their hearts beating a little faster than they had inside the lab. The lab's engine, now off, ticked as the metal cooled. Hanna and Erica spoke quietly inside. Distantly he could hear the flames consuming buildings in town with crackles and pops.

What he didn't hear were footsteps, dragged appendages, moans, whispers, or any other sound that would indicate other people nearby or zombies on the bridge.

Looking back over his shoulder at the other men, he nodded then stood and began walking towards the opposite side, sticking close to the side rail.

"What do you think he's doing?" Erica asked, when they saw Richard pause and take a knee.

"I think he's taking in the surroundings, getting a feel for what is happening around him," Hanna replied. "He's done this every time he's left the lab."

They saw Richard turn and look their way then give a slight head nod before turning back to look towards the opposite end of the bridge.

"Oh my gosh, he can hear us?" Erica asked.

"It sure looks like it. I think we are going to see a few more surprises from him," Hanna replied. "The enhancements he got from the Harper Series nanos are amazing. He is so much more advanced than we had any idea Harper was capable of. It's downright scary if you really think about it. Sure, Harper made this really great series that could really take humanity to super-human status, but then he also gave us the zombies, and who knows how hard it is going to be to rid the earth of those monsters?"

Erica nodded.

"It will never go back to the way it was."

"No," Hanna agreed.

They watched the men disappear from view as they moved around a van that had jumped the sidewalk and smashed against the sidewall.

"Do you happen to have binoculars in here?" Erica asked.

"You know what, I think we do," Hanna replied. "I think I saw some in that cabinet over there earlier when Richard had us taking inventory of the food that was already here."

"Good call," Erica said, pulling the lens caps off a pair of military-issued eight power Steiners and looping the strap over her head. "Give me a hand, will you?"

"Ok...what do you need?"

"A lift," Erica said, pointing up to the skylight window.

Hanna nodded and smiled.

"Good idea."

She walked over, put her hands together with her fingers interlaced, and gave Erica a boost.

Erica was athletic enough that pulling herself up through the opening was not overly challenging.

"Thanks," she whispered from above when she had her feet under her and was sure she wouldn't fall back in.

Hanna gave her a thumb's up then went back to the front of the lab.

Erica walked forward as well and crouched behind the large antenna array that had so aggravated Scott recently. The wind changed direction suddenly and came in from the downriver side, blowing wisps of smoke towards the lab. She coughed and bit back her gag reflex as she pulled her shirt up to cover her mouth and nose.

The wind changed again bringing her the relief of fresher air. The combination of sunlight and the breeze felt good on her back. She brought the binoculars up to her eyes

521

and began scanning the bridge for the men. When she found them she began looking forward of their position to scout the way ahead. From her vantage she could see more than Hanna would be able to, but she still couldn't see much beyond the taller derelict vehicles in the center of the bridge. That didn't stop her from trying.

As they crept forward down the center of the bridge, the men took note of the key vehicles that were blocking the lab's route forward. Mostly there were vehicles that had slammed into the backs of the vehicles that had swerved out to the sides. Most of them looked like they could be put into neutral and rolled out of the way. A few were smashed beyond that simple fix, but Richard thought he could probably flip them over on their sides and roll them out of the middle that way with his enhanced strength. He looked forward to testing his strength's new limits.

They saw dead bodies in a few of the vehicles, people that had died upon or shortly after impact. Several were merely charred remains, having been caught inside as their car caught fire and roasted them alive. A few bodies were lying on the bridge itself with crows and flies picking at their flesh.

The birds squawked and took flight at their approach. The flies became a nuisance as they investigated the fresh meat that walked amongst them.

Richard covered his nose with one hand and kept his mouth closed, so he wouldn't have any fly up into his facial orifices. Jason and Scott swatted at them and shook their heads. They moved a little faster to put the swarms behind them, and soon the flies went back to the easy meat.

It wasn't until they made it to the opposite side of the bridge that they found something that might truly be a problem for them to move or bypass. They hadn't been able to see it from their side because of the jumble of trucks and moving vans that had blocked it from view.

"A freaking tour bus," Scott mumbled.

A full size tour bus lay diagonally across the road on its side. There was barely enough room for them to walk between it and a Toyota pickup truck on one side and around its roof at the edge of one of the bridge's side rails on the other.

"Yellowstone Tours," Jason said, reading the stylish paint on the front.

Richard studied the scene and sighed. The road beyond the bridge was clear enough, but this bus was going to be a problem.

What a pain, he thought, shaking his head. *Damn it, this is going to take hours.*

Moans began to assault their ears, moans that were definitely coming from inside the bus.

"You hear that?" Scott asked.

Richard nodded.

"Relax," he said. "As long as the bus stays on its side, those poor bastards should stay trapped inside. Keep an eye out anyway, though. Just in case."

Walking around the bus, he examined its positioning and was thinking of the best way to move it out of their way. He was just reflecting on the irony of needing engineering skills more than combat skills, when two sounds caught his attention almost simultaneously, though from opposite directions.

The second was Erica, yelling at the top of her lungs. "Look out!"

From a quick glance at Scott and Jason, he could tell that neither of the other men could hear her over the sounds of the rushing river below them. He didn't need to look back at her to wonder where she was trying to focus their attention. She was alerting them to the other sound he had heard first, and it was coming from town.

He first noticed it as a low rumble, just barely discernible as separate from the river. Then he heard Erica and knew he had to investigate further, even as the rumble grew in volume and proximity.

The other men were as oblivious to this other sound as they were to Erica yelling at them from on top of the lab. Richard moved to the edge of the bus to peer around a corner, and what he saw chilled him to the core.

"Go to the lab! Now! Run!" he yelled.

Both Scott and Jason had a deer in the headlights look, as they processed the sudden warning, but they started moving to obey too, just slower than Richard would have liked. They weren't slow he realized. His perceptions had sped up.

"Go!" he yelled again, hoping to encourage them to move faster.

Looking back towards town, he took in the scene with an eye for details. Coming down the hill, running down the road was a mass of zombies. Like most of the zombies he had seen so far, these ones were a mess with blood and dirt smeared over their bodies and soaked into their clothes. There were hundreds of them, and they were moving fast.

Zombie marathon, he thought. *A race to see who can eat first.*

But they weren't pacing themselves like a distance runner would. They were sprinting.

Time to see just how strong the Harper Series has made me, he thought, backing up against the side rail farther away from the bus. He looked at the undercarriage and picked a spot to aim for while taking several quick breaths. *Here goes nothing.*

He ran forward in a blur of speed and slammed his shoulder into a flat sturdy section of the bus. He pumped his legs and kept pushing as if he wanted to push the bus over into the river.

And it moved. Miraculously, it moved the width of an entire lane.

He pushed some more, until he felt it hit something on the other side. When he stopped, he was sweating and breathing hard. Leaning over, he placed his hands on his knees and took a few deep breaths and willed himself to calm down. His heart rate felt like it was off the charts, and he knew he needed to slow it down, so he'd be able to shoot accurately.

The door to the back of the bus slammed down to the ground, and the moans that he had heard earlier became even louder.

Great, must have dislodged something inside that freed the door when I slammed into the bus.

Zombies tumbled out to the bridge and turned to stumble towards the lab.

Richard tensed for a fight at first then smiled.

That's right. They can't see me. And they're moving slow.

He let out a deep breath as he brought out his handgun, cocking it on the draw; closed his eyes; breathed deep again; and counted off seconds in his head while listening to the cacophony of footsteps beating their way closer and closer.

Still too far away. Gotta go for sure headshots or the shot is just wasted ammo and time.

He breathed out slowly and opened his eyes, smoothly bringing the gun up in front of him in a solid two-handed grip. The front sight came into sharp focus and his sights aligned with a bouncing head attached to a charging enemy in the front of the crowd.

He pulled the trigger, absorbed the recoil, and aligned the next shot, taking satisfaction in the back corner of his mind at seeing his first threat drop dead, tripping several more sprinters in the process. Second shot, more down.

His ears were ringing with each shot, seriously diminishing his ability to hear what was going on around him.

One after another in quick succession he shot down the lead zombies until his slide locked to the rear. He did a speed reload with a fresh magazine and began again. At the end of his third and final magazine he reassessed the situation.

Over a hundred sprinters remained, and they were quickly closing the gap. He had to go. Without taking the time to gather the handgun magazines he had dropped during his reloads, he thrust the empty gun into its holster, drew his sword, and began running towards the lab.

He quickly caught up with the slower zombies from the bus and swung the sword at the first few. They dropped when their heads were cut clean from their rotting bodies, but there were plenty more ahead of them.

As he was winding his way through the maze of cars, he drew abreast of one of the zombies by the railing. Without even slowing he gave it a quick push that tossed it into and over the railing to fall down into the rapids below.

He smiled. That one had felt good.

The ringing in his ears tapered off as he ran, the nanos rebuilding his damaged inner ear, and by the time he was close to the lab, it was gone altogether. He could hear again.

He lopped off a few more heads in passing and then he was ahead of them all. Feeling confident in his strength, he ran faster, judged the distance, then ran up the hood of a car onto the roof and leapt.

Glancing down, he saw Hanna behind the windshield of the lab, her jaw dropped in shock at what she was seeing him do. And then he landed on the roof of the lab next to Erica, who had quickly ducked behind the antenna array when she saw him coming.

"I can't believe you just did that!" she exclaimed. "That was awesome."

Richard chuckled.

"That was fun, but now we've got trouble. Scott and Jason are back?"

"Yeah, they just came in a minute ago."

Richard nodded and walked over to the roof access skylight.

"Hey, Jason"

"Yeah?" the other man replied, walking over to where he could look up and see Richard.

"Watches still in good shape?"

"Yeah," Jason said after a quick glance down at his wrists.

"Good. Now do me a favor. Pass me the MP5 and a shotgun with all of the spare bandoleers we've got."

"Ok"

"And one other thing," Richard added, after looking down at the blood on the sword. "A washcloth or some paper towels or something like that."

"Sure," Jason replied and ducked out of view.

A few seconds later he reappeared with a wet washcloth and tossed it up through the hole.

"Thanks," Richard said, as he caught it and carefully wiped the blood off of the sword's blade. He tossed the soiled cloth down onto the bridge and slid the sword back into its scabbard.

"MP5," Scott called, passing the weapon up, butt-stock first. "And shotgun."

Richard took both firearms and set them down on the roof.

"And the bandoleers," Jason added, tossing up the bands of extra ammunition.

He slung the bandoleers across his chest and stood, a gun in each hand.

"Head shots only," he said, handing the MP5 to Erica. "Take your time and make each shot count. This is the last of our ammo."

"Got it," she replied, nodding.

Richard checked to make sure the shotgun was loaded to capacity with one in the chamber as well then looked back to the bridge just in time to see the first of the sprinting zombies approach through the jumble of cars.

The first zombie to get close ran up the hood of the car Richard had just used as a springboard and launched itself towards the lab.

This surprised both of them on the roof, but Richard reacted instinctively and pulled the trigger. Nine .38 caliber steel balls left the barrel and tore right through the zombie's forehead and out through the base of the back of its skull, killing it and some of its forward momentum.

Instead of landing on the roof, it slapped into the lab's windshield, causing Hanna to scream.

Richard pumped the action and lined up the sights for another shot, his ears ringing painfully again.

Erica's shots were much quieter thanks to the lighter round and the improvised suppressor still attached at the other end of the barrel. She took her time and aimed carefully, dropping a zombie with nearly every shot.

The lab rocked under them as zombies massed around them and beat and pushed against the lab's exterior.

They were able to speed up their shots now that the zombies were not moving around as much or as quickly.

Now Erica understood the age old phrase, "Like shooting fish in a barrel." The shooting was easy, and there were so many of them.

But the stench was horrible.

Erica ran out of ammunition before Richard did.

Richard's rate of fire was slower since he had to reload after every five shots, but soon he was out of ammunition as well. He unslung the empty bandoleers and dropped them to the roof.

A handful of zombies were still coming towards the lab. They moved slower, so Richard guessed they were probably from the overturned tour bus.

He jumped down onto the car's roof and then down to the ground, which was littered with corpses. Bodies were stacked on bodies. Some were draped over car hoods or caught in the jambs of open doors. They were everywhere, and already the flies were coming in to start feeding.

Drawing the sword again, he walked to a cleared spot on the bridge where he would have room to swing.

Moans filled the air.

As he waited for the zombies to arrive, he realized that he felt hungry.

Now, of all times, I feel hungry? He thought, shaking his head. *It must be the nanos. I need to give them fuel, or they'll start stealing from healthy cells again, which will make me tired.*

A shambler came around a car and into range. Richard swiped the sword through its skull, and the zombie dropped to the ground. Congealed blood stuck to the blade like jelly.

Stop thinking about food, he told himself.

The rest came, and the rest went down for good. The last had been a male in a polo shirt. The back of its shirt was surprisingly clean. Richard fixed that by using it to wipe the blood off of the sword's blade before returning it to its scabbard.

Walking back to the door to the lab was messy. Corpses and blood with chunks of rotten flesh and decomposed internal organs littered the pavement.

Richard waved at Hanna and motioned her to back up.

Hanna gave him a thumbs up sign and began driving the lab backwards. When a few car lengths of black pavement had opened up in front of the vehicle, she stopped and turned off the engine.

"Thank you," Richard said when he stepped inside. "Oh man, what a mess."

"You ok?" Scott asked. "You're looking a little off."

"Yeah, I'll be fine. I think I just need to eat something."

"Seriously?" Erica asked, disgusted. "After what we just did out there and the horrible smell, you want to eat?"

Richard gave her a slight smile.

"Not really," he admitted. "But I think my nanos need fuel. I'm starting to feel…diminished."

"Yes," Jason said, getting up from the seat next to Hanna and walking over. "You need to eat and soon. Come over here."

Richard followed him to the lab and helped him move produce boxes out of the way to get to a cupboard full of science nerd odds and ends and a tray of vials full of some kind of granules.

"Are those metal shavings?" Richard asked, as he lifted one up and looked at it a little closer.

"Yes," Jason replied. "Trace metals, carbon-based matter, and some organic materials: these are what your nanos need to replicate to replace the nanos you've been burning through. This is just a quick fix though. They work best when you are able to replace your body's stores naturally with a healthy diet."

"I see."

"If you don't replace what they use by eating, they'll start stealing what they need from healthy cells..."

"And that would not be good," Richard finished.

Jason nodded.

Richard grabbed an apple from one of the boxes on the counter then took them back out to the front. He grabbed a bottle of water from the refrigerator and popped the top.

"I can't believe I'm doing this," he said, shaking his head. He took a large mouthful of water, swallowed half, and downed the vial from the back with the rest of the water. He wanted to gag, not from the taste, which was negligible, but from the grainy texture of grit sliding down the back of his throat.

"Agghhh," he complained, and followed it with several more swallows of water. "Note to self: eat lots and lots of food."

The others either smiled or laughed at him.

"All right, shows over," he said. "Come on, we've got cars to move, so we can go home. Samuel, I'd appreciate your help this time."

"Yes, I would like to help," Samuel replied, standing.

"You pair up with Erica. Scott, you and Jason. Erica and Jason can each steer, while you two can push for them. If we move two vehicles at a time, this will go much quicker. If you get one you can't move with just one pusher, we'll all tackle that one together."

"What about you?" Hanna asked. "You're not going to push one all by yourself are you?"

"No," Richard said. "I would be pushing too if it weren't for the fact that we just used up all of the rest of our ammunition. We need someone to stand guard while the others work. I've got the sword, and as you've all seen, the ability to use it; so I'll keep our people safe while they clear the path. And I already moved the bus at the end of the bridge."

They couldn't argue with that, and no one wanted to go out there without a measure of safety, so they got themselves ready and followed Richard.

He was the first one out the door, and the stench hit him again. Not the best thing to experience after what he'd just swallowed. The others made retching noises as they stepped out too.

He led them around the pile of bodies then pointed them towards the first few vehicles that needed to be moved. As they stepped to it, he climbed up on one of the trucks that was smashed up against the railing and began scanning the area for anything that could hurt his friends.

They made quick work of clearing the bridge. Each team moved a vehicle, and they leap-frogged past each other to the next, only once having to combine three pushers with one to steer a truck that was just overly big.

Richard only had to hop down a few times to deal with zombies straggling from the bus or coming from town. He could see that more were coming, but they were moving slowly, and the bridge was almost clear.

"Last one," Jason called, wiping sweat from his brow with the back of his hand.

It was a Dodge van, and it smelled pretty bad. The windows in the back had curtains that shaded the interior. The front door was already propped open.

The four of them approached it with caution.

Richard looked towards town and gauged the distance to the nearest of the approaching zombies. They would be a while longer in getting to the bridge. He spit off of the side of the bridge then slid the sword into the scabbard across his back and hopped down off of the roof of a Ford Explorer he had been roosting on.

"All right then, let's do this," he said, brushing past Jason and Erica to go towards the driver's side door. "You guys take the back."

Jason sat in the driver's seat and put the van into neutral.

"Ready?" Richard asked over his shoulder while getting ready to push against the van's frame at the front door. "Push!"

The van moved a foot then two.

They leaned into it, their legs burning after so much physical exertion on the previous cars.

There was a growl from inside the van and Jason screamed just prior to jumping out of the van, as if his pants were on fire, effectively pushing Richard out of his way.

A zombie crawled forward over the driver's seat, grabbing where Jason had just been and growling as it pulled itself forward.

As the van continued to move forward with the momentum of the pushers at the rear, Richard grabbed the driver's door and tried to slam it shut.

The timing couldn't have been better. The zombie was just about to slide out and to the ground. The force of Richard's slam was fueled by a sudden surge of adrenaline and his nano-enhanced strength. The edge of the door impacted the zombie's head, squishing it against the van's frame.

Blood sprayed the side of the van and the ground, and the zombie crumpled to the pavement, all semblance of its previous life extinguished.

The pushers at the back had stopped pushing by then, afraid of what might be happening, but the van slid forward a few more feet.

"I guess we should look in the back and make sure there aren't any more waiting for a meal," Richard said, smiling at Jason who was leaning over and trying to stop shaking.

"It grabbed my shoulder," Jason said. "Holy crap, I thought it was going to get me."

"Quick reflexes you've got there," Richard added before leaning into the van and taking a peek into the back. "I wonder if it actually sensed you or if it sensed the others at the back and was just trying to get out to go after them. Maybe you just happened to be in its path. Harper's watches are supposed to make them blind to your presence."

Jason looked thoughtful as he nodded.

"Unless they're broken...or don't work the way he thought they would," he replied.

"A possibility," Richard said. "But the ZS3 inside of you hasn't shown any more progression. I think it was after them," he said, pointing his chin towards the others.

Jason laughed and grinned sheepishly.

"Man, I hope so. Either way, it scared the crap out of me."

Richards chuckled.

"No worries there. I've got clean underwear just up that hill, through the town, and up another hill. Almost home. Come on, let's get this out of the way, so we can go."

Jason laughed at himself again then climbed back into the driver's seat, this time looking in the back before steering as the others pushed.

Hanna brought the lab to them when she saw that the way was clear, so they didn't even have to walk back down across the bridge again.

The lab's tires crunched over the bloated bodies of zombies that were walking down the hill, drawn towards the still broadcasting antenna on top of the vehicle.

Richard started whistling an old Willie Nelson song, "On the Road Again."

Hanna laughed.

"I think I'm about done with being on the road again. I would love to settle down and not have to drive for a while."

"She's never really been much into road trips," Jason said, putting his hand on his wife's leg.

She patted his hand then put both hands back on the steering wheel.

"Let alone a road trip where we're dodging zombies at every turn," Jason finished.

"Or being chased by the bunch of genocidal whackos that unleashed the zombies in the first place," Scott added.

Richard nodded as he said, "Well, it's almost over. We're only about two miles away from the castle now."

"A castle?" Erica asked.

"Yep, a genuine, medieval-style castle with a moat and drawbridge and knights in armor," Richard replied. "We finished building it just about one year ago from last month."

Then he proceeded to tell them about how he came to have a castle.

Chapter 14: SkyFall

Two Blackhawk helicopters chopped their way low through the sky, their pilots using the surrounding tree-covered mountains to partially dampen the noise and keep their visual signature to a minimum.

Allen nodded at the crew chief when he informed them that they were about ten minutes out from Cody, Wyoming.

Jax had given him the street address for the local Rogue Paladin LLC corporate office. He looked back down at the new iPad and studied the street layout around where Jax said he might find the answers they needed to find Richard and the new nano series.

The other EWES-7 super soldiers that were with him each had their own tablets and were mostly going over technical details of the mission ahead of them. It was a spur of the moment mission, so they hadn't had time for in depth mission planning or rehearsals.

But they were professionals. They'd done missions like this day in and day out in operational theaters around the globe. They'd manage.

They were going to fast rope on to the roof of the target building and clear it room by room from the top down. Then they were going to pour over whatever information could be found there, to include interrogating anyone they found inside, if any unfortunate souls were even around. Allen didn't really expect to find anyone still there. After all, who reports in to work after the zombie apocalypse kicks off?

If they were exceptionally lucky, Richard would be there or someone who could tell them where Richard would be.

If not, well, they'd work on that once they knew more.

The valley they flew through opened up to the plains, and up ahead, the town of Cody spread before them. Like many other towns and cities they had flown over, Cody was in complete disarray. Buildings burned unchecked, the local volunteer fire department having scattered to the wind who knew how long before. Zombies roamed the streets. There didn't appear to be any looters, but with so many zombies out and about, it would be pretty foolish to risk going after anything but maybe food or medicine.

Allen located the local airport, Yellowstone Regional, and used it as a reference point to begin looking for the corporate building that housed Rogue Paladin LLC.

"Master Chief Taylor, you're going to want to see this, Sir," one of the pilots said over the comm. headset.

Allen looked up towards the cockpit at hearing his name.

The pilot was looking back towards him and was making a "come hither" gesture with his free hand.

Allen stood and slid the iPad into the space between his chest and chest rig and walked up towards the cockpit.

"I'm not sure what to make of this, but that's one of ours isn't it?" the pilot asked, pointing down at a large gray vehicle that was driving uphill on the road down below. On the roof of the vehicle was the infinity sign in black.

"It sure looks like it, but I wasn't told of any friendlies operating in this area," Allen replied. "Observe, but do not engage. I'll call home and find out what the hell is going on."

"Roger that, observe but do not engage," the pilot said.

Allen continued to watch the new object of interest below as he turned off the throat mic connected to his radio and hit the speed dial on his phone.

"House of Beauty, This is Cutie."

Allen growled.

"Hey, it was either that or 'Bridgeport Sperm Bank: you squeeze it, we freeze it.'"

"Cut the shit, Jax. You're not funny, and I need answers."

Jax sighed over the phone, irritating Allen further.

"All right, what have you got?"

"I need to know if there are any I-G assets in the area. We're almost to the objective, and we've got a large vehicle, looks like a communications platform, with an I-G infinity marking on top."

"Hmm, that's strange," Jax replied. "I didn't see anything on the intranet about another operation in that area. I would have told you if I had. You know I would, but, yeah, I'm seeing it now on the feed from the Predator drone I've got on station above you."

"Well, look again at the ops schedule."

"All right. Give me a minute."

The vehicle below crossed town, drawing zombies towards it. It easily outpaced them, but the zombies didn't stop following. Then it made it up another hill and stopped.

Ahead of it was an open plain for about half a mile, open as in: no houses or trees.

But there were zombies everywhere.

It looked like most of the town and then a whole bunch more people-turned zombies covered the ground between the vehicle and the one building in the area, a castle, complete with exterior wall, moat, and drawbridge, backed up against the Buffalo Bill Reservoir. Something was out of place up in the corner turrets, something distinctly more modern, but they were covered and he couldn't quite make them out.

What the fuck? Allen thought. It didn't feel right.

"Are you seeing this?" he asked over the phone.

"Oh, wow," Jax replied. "Where did they all come from?"

"Not them, you idiot. The castle. Why isn't there a castle on my map, when there is clearly a castle on the fucking ground?"

"Chill, man. The maps are a few years old. Either it's a newer structure than the maps, or it's a black site or something."

"Black site, my ass. It's right out in plain view in the middle of a fucking tourist town," Allen snapped. "And what are they hiding on the walls?"

"Well, I don't freakin' know, Dude. I just load the info I get from…whoa! Wait a second," Jax said. "Holy crap, you're not going to believe this. Hold on."

"What?" Allen asked. "I'm not going to believe what?"

"Hold on, this is...I gotta check something...there's...wow, yeah," Jax said, not making any sense, clearly completely distracted.

"Are you going to tell me what the fuck is going on?" Allen asked after a few seconds.

"Ok," Jax replied. "Our eye in the sky is showing three...nope, make that four, four I-G trailer beds in the courtyard of yonder castle and a whole lot of hardware that looks... And, yeah, I've got a verified transfer order here on the intranet for delivery of said trailers to this Medieval Kingdom amusement park. You don't think Benson had another site and didn't tell us or the rest of the I-G about it, do you? I mean, I wouldn't put it past him. He *is* the boss. He does whatever the hell he wants, when he wants, so sure why not build and stock a castle; and it's fairly close to the ranch, so maybe he felt he need a bolt hole away from home in case the rest of the I-G decided it didn't want to follow..."

"Jax, you're rambling," Allen said, as the helicopter flew close enough to the castle for him to see over the wall. "I hate it when you just talk, talk, talk, talk, talk. So it's one of ours? Yes or no."

"It looks like it is. I see the order from..."

Allen didn't hear the rest. Alarms began blaring inside the helicopter, and his stomach jumped into his throat as the pilot took evasive action. Through the window, the world spun, and he caught sight of white smoke that cut across the sky in an instant. Then a distant but close, freakishly loud explosion added chaos to the blaring alarms and spinning feeling inside the cabin.

The pilots began yelling.

Someone was shooting at them.

The other Blackhawk was hit and going down.

The EWES super soldiers clenched their gear tight and waited to deploy the instant the helicopter touched down.

Another explosion drowned out the alarms and the yelling. The world shifted, and Allen found himself flying backwards away from the helicopter. He hardly felt the communications headset rip off of his head as he was ejected out of the helo. He knew he was moving very fast, but the world seemed to have slowed down.

He could see clearly now. The helicopter had been hit by a missile. It was burning as it disintegrated and fell out of the big—no, huge, baby blue sky. His vision tightened back in. Pieces of the helo's fuselage were travelling in every direction. Some of the metal shrapnel was going to hit him.

White hot pain flared in his gut as a slice of aircraft aluminum embedded itself in his abdomen after piercing straight through a pouch full of spare M16 magazines in his chest rig and then through the iPad he had stuffed in there. His leg was on fire too, as several large pieces, and probably some smaller pieces, of shrapnel punctured the muscle in several places.

Then his back slammed against the ground. He couldn't breathe. Dirt, debris, and smoke pelted him, drifted over him, blotted out the sky. His guts felt like they were sliding back and forth between his throat and his asshole, and he knew he had at least a few broken bones.

Pain paralyzed him.

The world went black.

Chapter 15: Dilemma

Jax watched in horror from several hundred miles away as the scene unfolded on his monitor. The bird's-eye view from the Predator drone captured everything— everything except the sound.

But he heard the radio traffic, pilot's yelling with alarms in the background.

He watched as first one, then a second missile shot across the sky from the castle wall and impacted on each of the Blackhawk helicopters in quick succession. The radio traffic went to static for a brief second then went completely quiet.

And he could do nothing.

He was in shock. He couldn't comprehend how or why this was happening. I-G shooting on I-G. Unheard of. Was this really happening?

The helicopters broke up and fell out of the sky. They were already burning before they hit the ground, but bright flames flared up as soon as they impacted.

He stared at the screen, not sure what to do. There was no one else to call. No reinforcements waiting in the wings.

Movement.

Men were scrambling out of the wreckage, their clothes on fire.

Impossible.

He shook his head. It broke his malaise. He reached for the phone. Then stopped.

A massive wave of zombies crashed over the wreckage. The men that had emerged from the downed helicopter broke under the wave, their brief flashes of gunfire far too ineffectual to stop the undead that swamped over them.

The zombies tore them to pieces.

Jax shook his head again.

No, this can't be happening.

But it had happened.

His eyes burned with dryness, and he blinked.

He suddenly felt numb and disjointed, separated from reality.

He glanced over at the RFID markers that each of them carried for tracking purposes. None of them were active except his own.

A realization washed over him. He was the last of the EWES.

And Benson was going to kill him. What good was a lone super soldier? Even with their enhanced strength and endurance, super soldiers were really only an effective force multiplier when operating in teams. And they had uncovered one of Benson's secrets; a secret so closely held that he hadn't even shared it with the rest of the Infinity Group, that den of sneaky, genocidal murdering bastards.

It didn't matter if he tried running away from them. Benson could activate the explosive device embedded in his skull from the other side of the planet, at least for a few more years until the signal relay satellites began falling out of orbit. Could he last that long in Benson's, maybe not good graces, but tolerant graces? If he were going to, he'd need one hell of a good explanation ready to present to Benson for why every other super soldier had just died and why they had been near one of Benson's secret bases in the first place.

Would he believe that they had been after Richard? That the facts led them there?

Then another thought hit him.

Was Richard working for Benson?

Was Richard a fall back plan to get the new nano series if Harper went off the reservation? It could make sense. Why else would all of this have happened? How else to explain that Richard's trail led straight back to a secret base that Benson had told no one else about?

Holy crap, he thought, as the pieces fell into place in his reeling mind.

Chapter 16: Lucy, I'm Home

But Jax was wrong.

"I was a Marine sergeant at the time," Richard said. "We'd been in Iraq for close to four months when my squad and I were assigned to provide security for this hush-hush DIA operative who was going to set up shop in Baghdad and coordinate missions that were tailored to eventually have the big shots in the Iraqi army working for us. His name was Jeff Guddemi. He was a pretty quiet guy, super smart, kept to himself—at least at first.

"After we'd been with him for a while, he did open up a bit. He just had to get comfortable with us first. We'd have conversations that gave us mental escape from all of the bullshit we were seeing over there.

"He must have seen something in me because, subtly at first, he started feeling me out about joining the intelligence community. I was open to the idea, so I let him lead me in that direction. We spent a lot of time together—that's just the nature of the work, and we ended up getting pretty close, close enough that he even introduced me to his sister, Linda, who, as it turns out, is the same Linda waiting to marry me in that castle I'm about to tell you about.

"Anyway, Jeff had heard that Saddam's palace was being looted and wanted us to help him secure it. More than just the monetary treasure Saddam was rumored to have, there was the military intelligence treasure that Jeff believed to be there.

"My men and I cleared the palace and surrounding grounds. The place was a mess, trash and treasures and historical artifacts all mixed together and strewn all over the place. And after all of the crap we had been through fighting those loyal to Saddam, I didn't say shit to the guys who pocketed a few gold pieces here and there. We were supposed to be there for the military intel anyway. And there was gold everywhere. You may have heard rumors of Saddam's gold toilets? Yeah, sat on one.

"After we cleared Saddam's palace, Jeff and I went looking for a place inside the palace to set up shop for his DIA investigation. Well, while we were poking around, we found Saddam's stash of American dollars. He had billions. The looters hadn't been able to get through the locks on the vault, but they didn't have access to the tools and toys we had. Well, we found it and talked about how we were going to handle the situation.

"Long story short, we decided to keep some of it for ourselves, spoils of war you might call it. We liberated a few million, well, more than *just a few* million. We packed up a pretty good amount and hid it in some of the DIA equipment boxes. Then we brought in a few of the other troops and 'found' the stash in front of them.

"Jeff called in the find, and the intelligence agencies' ghosts were quick to swoop in and snatch up the money and make sure it came back to America. They never knew that we had separated a bit for ourselves."

The others looked at Richard in shock.

"We brought the loot back with us in a CONEX box that only Jeff, as the lone DIA representative there at the time, had access to, and we kept it off the books.

"We knew that if we straight up spent the money, it would run out eventually, if we didn't get in trouble for having it in the first place. We needed to invest the bulk of it, live off of the proceeds, but we didn't want to risk losing it in a stock market crash or a downturned economy. We decided to invest it in real estate and business, so we came up with a plan then formed a few companies here in Wyoming, where it is still legal to own trusts and corporations anonymously.

"A holding company owns the land and the park, which, in turn, is its own company; and the park leases the land and facilities. Everything operates in the clear. It creates a tax haven that doesn't trace back to us. The money we invested in the park brings in some pretty significant cash flow. We own nothing, technically, but control everything. We use the facilities without actually having an income, so we don't pay our life away in taxes. This was our path to eventual retirement, at least it was until all of this happened...And besides, who doesn't want a castle?"

He looked down and was silent as he thought about his friend, the first casualty that he personally knew in this new war.

"So when you found out the zombie apocalypse couldn't be stopped, you called home and told your fiancé to get ready for it?" Jason asked, ignoring the questionable legal assumptions Richard was making and the whole stealing from a dictator situation.

"Yep," Richard replied, nodding. "It's a secure location with its own water supply and plenty of room for small livestock. It has productive year-round gardens and greenhouses. I had her take the rest of our liberated cash and get things from town, and I used the Infinity Group's own system to arm and supply the castle. As long as Linda stays inside and keeps trusted friends and family close, she should be completely safe inside until the zombies rot away to manure."

"Or this Infinity Group wises up and tries tracking down their supplies," Jason suggested.

Richard frowned.

"Oh…my…gosh," Hanna said, stepping on the brakes when they crested the hill and came in view of the castle.

Zombies were everywhere…and already they were turning to take notice of the lab.

"Of course," Richard muttered, thinking about how much he would love to have a few million rounds of ammunition for their now useless firearms.

Then he heard the helicopters too.

"Oh, great!"

"What's wrong?" Scott asked.

"Helicopters," Richard said, looking up and behind them as if he could see through the roof of the lab.

"What?" Jason asked. "Are you sure? I don't hear anything."

Richard nodded.

"I thought I heard something a minute ago, but it was too far away, and I wasn't sure. Now I'm sure. And they're getting closer. If I had to guess, I'd say they've already spotted us."

He turned, as if following their progress through the sky, which he was, and pointed through the window.

"There"

First one, then a second helicopter came into view, flying low enough to be intimidating to the group in the lab but high enough to be out of range of small arms fire. They were military and laden for war. They circled around the castle.

"What do we do?" Hanna asked.

Richard shook his head.

"I don't..."

A ripping, buzzing sound cut off his reply, and everyone turned to look at the castle, where the sound was coming from.

A heavy machine gun was blasting off rounds at one of the helicopters, and just as they turned, they saw a battery of anti-air missiles join the salvo.

Both helicopters were shot down and crashed nearby. Shrapnel pelted the lab.

Richard saw the zombies swarm the wreckage, leaving an opening to the castle walls, and knew he had to do something fast to take advantage of it. He had thought of a solution to their uncontrolled broadcasting problem before but had been hesitant to take action because of its destructive nature and the uncertainty of whether or not they would need the array in the future. But the situation had changed, and in an instant, he opened the roof hatch and launched himself up and out of the lab.

He found the antenna that Scott couldn't turn off and ripped its wire connection out of the back of its array.

"Scott, are we still broadcasting?" he half yelled.

Before Scott replied with a loud "No, we're not," Richard already had his answer. The zombies that had been approaching the lab, changed direction towards the helicopter wreckage the instant he separated the wires from the antenna.

"Hanna, go for the gate!" he called.

"All right!" she replied, and the lab lurched forward, forcing Richard to lower his center of gravity and grab onto the antenna array to keep from falling off of the roof.

The lab's wheels crushed several zombies that were plodding along towards the helicopter wreckage. Bloody tracks lay behind them as they moved forward towards the main entrance to the park.

"What do I do?" Hanna yelled when she saw the portcullis down in the archway, blocking the way in.

"They'll let us in," Richard replied, poking his head down into the cabin from the skylight. "Just pull up close, and let me talk to them."

As they drove closer, there was yelling from inside the castle. Richard looked up at the parapets and saw men running along the wall to confront him and the lab. They carried machine guns and a few had shoulder-fired anti-tank rockets, but otherwise they looked like they could have been extras on a Lord of the Rings movie set, all decked out in medieval garb and some armor.

"Stop right there!" someone yelled.

Richard raised his hands and hoped they had enough discipline to at least find out who he was.

As the lab stopped just short of the portcullis, Richard looked up at the men, his heart sinking as he realized that he didn't recognize any of them, and they clearly didn't recognize him, their guns pointed at him and the lab.

Please don't shoot.

He felt even more apprehensive when he saw that there were several bodies hanging by rope at the neck from the tops of the walls. The bottoms of their feet and legs looked to have been eaten away by the zombies below, and one or two of them twitched, having become zombies themselves.

"Linda! Get Linda!" Richard yelled. "Linda, it's Philip! I'm home!"

The men didn't drop their aim, and no one looked to be leaving to get his fiancé, but some of them did look at him with new curiosity.

"Make way!" a booming voice echoed from above.

A few at a time, like a rolling wave, the gun carriers on the wall glanced back at the person coming to the scene before focusing back on Richard.

"Make way!"

Richard smiled. He recognized that voice.

Sure enough, who poked his head over the wall but David Skiles, one of Medieval Kingdom's celebrity jousters and a trustworthy man who knew Richard back when "Richard" was Philip Quinio.

"Dave," Richard called. "Good to see you're not stumbling around in this crowd down here," he said, gesturing back to the flesh eaters that mobbed around outside.

"Phil? My God, you are alive! Lady Linda has been most distraught. Put your guns down, men; this here is the lord of the castle. You, there," Dave said, pointing at one of the men. "Run along and fetch the Lady. Tell her King Philip has returned. She will be most pleased."

Richard chuckled and shook his head as footsteps echoed away with the messenger.

The end of the world was upon them, and zombies walked the earth, but Dave Skiles still couldn't bring himself to go out of role.

The men raised their weapons away from Richard, and he breathed a little easier.

"You mind raising the portcullis so we can come in, Sir Dave?"

"Ah, I would, My Liege, but it's not to be raised without Lady Linda's explicit direction—new rules with dire punishments attached, I'm afraid," he said, jerking a hand over towards the bodies hanging from the walls. "A lot has changed."

"I see," Richard replied, a little disappointed that he wasn't immediately admitted inside but pleased at the same time that his fiancé had taken charge of her protection and the protection of everyone else inside the castle. At least he hoped that was why there were people hanging from the walls.

"Is she well?"

Dave nodded and smiled.

"She is well indeed; and she has really come into her own, keeping us all alive and safe, for the most part."

"Good," Richard replied.

The loud ripping sound of the machine gun opened up startling everyone, including Richard.

He followed the line of tracer rounds from the gun barrels to the target and saw a reconnaissance drone falling from the sky. He thought he knew who was watching from the other end, and it bothered him that the Infinity Group most likely now knew where he and his friends and family were hiding.

"Philip!" Linda yelled.

Richard looked up at his fiancé and smiled.

Finally, he thought.

"You sure are a sight for sore eyes," he said. "You mind letting us in, my Lady?" He half bowed theatrically.

She was all smiles as she ordered her men to let them in.

"I'll meet you down there," she said, before dashing away to go to the entrance.

Richard noticed she had a group of men that tagged along with her and wondered if they were meant to be bodyguards or advisors.

I'll know soon enough, he thought.

The inner portcullis began to rise up into the wall.

Richard breathed a sigh of relief then dropped back down into the lab.

"They're raising it," Scott said.

Richard nodded and smiled, thinking: *You have an undeniable talent for pointing out the obvious*, but he kept his mouth shut instead of being sarcastic and rude.

When the inner portcullis was up enough, a group of men crowded into the entrance archway. They carried clear plastic shields with police markings and long wooden batons and wore ballistic helmets with clear plastic face shields and disposable white medical face masks underneath. They were dressed in black BDU's with riot control protective gear. Forming up in ranks, they faced the outer portcullis and the lab and waited, poised to push back any zombies that tried to enter the castle or attack.

Looking into their eyes, Richard sensed that these were hard men, nonplussed by being on the front line of this new battle. They looked intimidating, however much good that would do them facing off with fearless zombies. Still, he was glad they were protecting his fiancé.

He looked beyond these men and saw into the castle courtyard. More men waited, dressed similarly to the frontline troops, but instead of riot batons, they held rifles and shotguns. Clearly, if the frontline troops were overrun, these men would have to end the threat to the castle, even if it meant shooting into the midst of their own vanguard.

The realization caused Richard to respect the front line even more. They didn't stand there in ignorance. They knew quite well what was expected of them.

The outer portcullis began to rise. The men pushed forward baby steps at a time.

Inside the lab, Richard and the others could hear the police shields scraping down the length of the lab.

"They are keeping it tight," Jason said.

Richard nodded. "Yeah, they don't want any zombies to make it in through a gap."

As the front rank push forward enough, men from the deeper ranks began filling in to the sides, maintaining an unbroken wall of body and shield between the entrance to the castle and the zombie horde that were still more attuned to the downed helicopter occupants than to the castle entrance. The final rank of men pushed forward to back the center.

One man remained inside the archway. He watched the men form up and shouted orders, adjusting their positions. As soon as his men were where he wanted them, he grabbed Hanna's attention and waved her forward.

"Here we go," Hanna said, as she drove the lab forward.

The man stepped out of the way, and suddenly their view was dominated by ranks of men aiming rifles in their direction. The others must have just been seeing this for the first time because there several gasps of surprise and worry.

Richard ignored the men in front of them. He knew they were a necessary precaution. He was more interested in the men now behind them.

As soon as the lab had pulled forward through the men, a gap was created. The men that had been reinforcing the center sidestepped to fill the gap, even as the inner portcullis lowered, cutting them off from the inner castle.

Now their leader was marching them backwards towards the archway.

A few zombies finally took notice and charged. They impacted the shields but were jarred to a halt. Then the men behind the shields brought their batons down to crack them across the heads.

And still they marched backwards, giving ground but not giving up their tight shell of protection.

Shortly they were inside the archway and stopped, still facing outward. They repelled several more lunging zombies as the outer portcullis lowered to protect them.

Only when the outer portcullis was completely lowered was the inner portcullis once again raised, admitting the men back into the comfort and protection of the castle courtyard.

Richard breathed a sigh of relief. They'd made it in with no lives lost, a good day by anyone's definition. He turned his attention back to the front to see Linda running towards the lab, a huge smile on her face. He couldn't help but smile himself.

"We're home," he said. "If you'll excuse me."

Richard opened the door and stepped out. Linda jumped into his arms without slowing, and they both fell backwards against the side of the lab.

She hugged him tight while saying, "Oh, Philip, you had me worried sick. I thought something had happened to you. I haven't been able to sleep or eat...oh, but you're here. Wait, what happened to your eyes?"

Before Richard could really say anything, Linda's entourage arrived and gathered off to one side. They looked to be a mixture of well-armed bodyguards and advisors, to Richard, and some of them didn't look too pleased to see him.

At about the same time, the other lab occupants began filing out into the sunlight. Scott and Erica stepped out first, followed by Samuel and his siblings, with Hanna and Jason bringing up the rear.

"I have a lot to explain," Richard said. "But first let me introduce my new crew. They all played a part in getting me home. This is Scott Lewis; he was a computer programmer for DARPA before all of this happened."

Linda nodded and offered her hand for a handshake. "Pleased to meet you, Scott."

"Thank you," Scott replied, shaking her hand then quickly pulled away and scratched at a scab on his neck.

"This is Erica," Richard said.

"Infected!" one of Linda's guards yelled, jerking her away from the group by her belt and drawing his pistol from his side holster.

Time slowed down for Richard, and he saw that the man was focused intently on Jason, specifically Jason's black-line-infused eyes—his gun was coming up to aim at Jason's head.

Just like he had in the lab when Scott had had a gun pointed at him, Richard moved so fast it was hard for the others to follow. In the blink of an eye he was in front of the man with the gun and actually helped him bring the gun up faster. But he continued to lift the gun with that momentum, until it was no longer on target or pointed at himself either.

The gun went off, the bullet flying safely out over the castle walls without impacting anyone.

Richard shifted his grip from being on the man's wrist up to the gun itself. While the slide was still rocking back from the shot, he shifted the slide catch lever up, locking the slide back as it began its forward return. Then he pushed the magazine release at the same time he gave the gun a bit of a downward pull. Another quick push back up on the gun dislodged the magazine, and it began falling to the ground. Finally, he pulled down on the take-down lever with one hand and pulled the slide towards him with the other, effectively removing the upper half of the gun and making it impossible to shoot without reassembling first.

He knew several handgun disarms that would leave the attacker on the ground with broken fingers at a minimum, but he knew this guy was only trying to protect the castle and everyone in it, so he chose not to hurt him. After disassembling the gun faster than the man or anyone else could react, he gave the man a gentle push, which still was enough to cause the man to lose his balance and fall to the ground.

Linda's other bodyguards drew their weapons and began to circle up around her, aiming towards Jason and now Richard.

"Stop," Richard ordered. "He is infected, but it's contained. He isn't a threat."

"Stop!" Linda screamed, when she saw them aiming at her fiancé.

Her men lowered their guns but kept them in hand, ready to bring back to bear should things change.

"I admit," Richard said. "There is a bit going on here that you are not going to like right now if you just look at it for face value, but there's more to everything than meets the eye—so much more."

Richard stepped forward and reached his hand out to the man on the ground.

"My apologies," he said, "For making you fall. I need this infected man alive. I could not allow you to kill him. I promise you he will not infect anyone else, and you will not regret his presence when you see what he will help us with."

The man clenched his jaw and squinted his eyes at Richard, clear sign that he was not only angry but was unlikely to forget what had just happened, but he grabbed Richard's offered hand and accepted the help to his feet.

He dusted himself off without taking his eyes off of Richard.

"You're infected too," the man said, looking him in the eyes, "But yours is different, isn't it? That's why you can do what you just did."

It was stated as a question, an inference.

"What is your name, Sir?" Richard asked.

"Dave—Dave Cummings."

"No kidding. The same Dave Cummings that led the Cody Broncs to the State Champions back in what—oh nine?"

"Yeah, one and the same, but that was a long time ago."

"Yes, it was," Richard replied, with a nod. Then he sighed. "You're right; I am 'infected' so to speak, but what I've got is the cure to all of that out there," he said, pointing out beyond the walls. "What I've got was designed by the same asshole that made the zombies. It was intended as something for him and his mega-rich asshole buddies, so they could rule the world after they eliminate most of humanity with the zombie apocalypse. But I got it away from them, even though I couldn't stop all of this from happening.

"Those helicopters you all just shot down were theirs, I think, which means they know where we are now. Things are going to get worse before they get better."

Dave looked down and shook his head.

Richard extended the man's upper half of his pistol.

Dave took it.

"That was unbelievably fast. That shouldn't be humanly possible."

"It's not humanly possible," Richard replied. "My 'infection' is a collection of nanotechnology enhancements that make my body and mind more than human. Jason there," he said, pointing back at Dave's previous target, "Is going to help us figure out how to replicate it and turn the tide against the zombies and these Infinity Group assholes."

Linda stepped forward and tilted Richard's chin down towards her, so she could look into his eyes. She shook her head, and Richard suddenly worried again that she wouldn't be able to accept him with his differences.

"How do I know this won't destroy you?" She asked.

"We'll just have to have faith," Richard whispered. "I can't honestly assure you that nothing bad will come of this, but I believe things will work out. I have to, or what the hell am I doing anything for?"

She gave the slightest nod of acceptance, and Richard knew they would have to talk more in private later.

"And my brother?" she said, before her voice cracked and she went quiet.

Richard was silent for a moment. How to explain what had happened without making her pain even worse? How to explain without possibly making her hate him for partially being the cause of Jeff being murdered? If only he had considered the possibility of a trace program hidden in the hard drive before he had uploaded it. He sighed.

"Jeff died protecting me," he said. "It wasn't his fault that we were found out, and it wasn't pretty what happened. He...I..." Richard shook his head and clenched his fists. "I'm sorry, Linda. I fucked up, and it got your brother killed."

She turned away from him, her head down, and he saw her suppress overwhelming emotions.

Straightening her back, she turned back to him.

"Before you left on this mission of yours, my brother spoke to me in private. He told me it would be dangerous—dangerous for you and dangerous for him. He knew the risks just like you did. I had to sit on the sidelines in the dark and hope you both made it through whatever it was that was so important that he brought you back out of retirement. I wanted to hate both of you. Him for taking you away from me before we could even get married and you for agreeing to go. But the world has gone to hell, and life is too short for me to hold that hate. I love you both, and I'm not about to lose the one man I have left."

She stepped into his embrace and hugged him with all of her strength.

"Just promise me you won't leave me again," she whispered.

"Yes, Ma'am," Richard replied, holding her tight, and he hated himself for making a promise he had a feeling he wouldn't be able to keep, not if he were going to ensure her safety.

Fucking Joshua Harper, he thought, as he squeezed her a little tighter to himself.

Linda cleared her throat and wiped her eyes.

"Well, I think that's enough excitement for now. Let's get everybody settled in, and we'll finish introductions later. We'll feast tonight," she said, raising her voice and turning to all of the men that had just put their lives on the line to bring the lab into the castle. "And then we'll bring our new guests up to speed on the rules and requirements of life at Medieval Kingdom."

"Hurrah!" they shouted.

A feast meant the food wouldn't be rationed for this one night as it had been for the last week.

Scott squeezed in close and whispered into Richard's ear, just loud enough to be heard over the cheers of the surrounding crowd.

Richard listened then looked at him with some concern, weighing some private thoughts. Finally he seemed to make up his mind, nodded, and leaned in close to whisper in Scott's ear.

Scott looked up at the tower central to the castle and nodded back.

Then Richard stepped in closer and whispered again.

Scott listened closely, trying to be sure he heard each word correctly over the still cheering crowd, until Richard finished. He smiled and nodded, and Richard gave him a final nod of approval before turning back to the lady of the castle.

As the crowd pulled the happily reunited couple towards the castle, Scott slipped unnoticed through them and returned to the lab.

Only Erika saw him leave and thought anything of it.

Chapter 17: Licked Wounds

Allen woke and lay still as the zombies crowded around his fallen fellows and feasted just a few yards away from him. Out of the corner of his eye, he saw a jagged piece of shrapnel sticking up out of the ground. He moved his hand toward it ever so slowly, not wanting to draw zombie attention. Pushing and pulling an inch at a time, he worked it up out of the ground and held it in hand. Now he had a weapon. He waited for a zombie to get close, so he could end it before he was torn to pieces.

But the zombies ignored him.

He was covered in dust and blood. His whole body ached. He'd been able to remove the big pieces of shrapnel from his leg, but after the pain involved with that little operation, he still hadn't made the effort to remove the piece of aircraft aluminum that jutted out of his gut. He coughed, couldn't hold it back. His throat was so dry, and his nose was blocked up with grit.

A zombie nearby turned towards the sound but quickly lost interest and went back to chewing on EWES-7 Captain Forester, a former Seabee engineer that had been kicked out of the Navy for stealing munitions and selling them to gang bangers associated with Mexican drug cartels.

Allen remembered Forester saying that if the US Attorney General could do it with Operation Furiously Fast then so could he.

Never mind that some of the explosives he had sold ended up being used in a bank robbery that killed seven civilians and an off duty cop who had been working a day off as bank security. That was how he'd come under scrutiny by investigators and eventually caught.

Dumb ass.

And now a zombie was chewing on Forester's lips and part of his cheek.

Allen curled his own lips in a silent snarl.

Why aren't they attacking me? He wondered.

He gathered a painful breath and exhaled slowly.

It's gotta be the 7-Alpha upgrade.

He knew the zombies had been keen on him before he took the 7A upgrade. He had taunted them a few times, drawing them in close before ending them, just like on the roof of the DARPA control center back in Spokane.

And now they ignored him.

But it had been in the McIntyre's section of the lab not Harper's. Had Harper given it to them without explaining to them just what it was or what it did? Or had the McIntyres unknowingly made something that counteracted Harper's doomsday nano-plague? Had they known? Too many possibilities.

Allen closed his eyes as a wave of pain rolled through his body. His head dropped back to the ground, and he let out a tight breath.

Those fucking bastards in the castle. Took us completely off guard. A perfectly executed ambush. Fucking hell, that hurts.

Smoke still drifted between him and the clear blue sky he saw when he opened his eyes. Rolling his head a little to the side, he saw a distant sliver of water, the reservoir, and next to it the beginning of a mountain slope, Spirit Mountain if he remembered the map correctly.

If he could make it to the mountain, he could get out of the kill zone and call home to the ranch. If he couldn't establish comms, he could still use the mountain as the start point for an evasive trek back to the ranch for reinforcements.

He was going to kill every last mother fucker in that castle.

He swore it over and over as he bent the knee of his good leg slightly, brought that foot a little closer to his butt, and pushed, extending his leg completely and progressing inches at a time towards the mountain.

I'm going to kill them all.

Push

I live *to kill.*

Push

I live to kill.

Push

You can't stop me. *I'll kill* all *you motherfuckers.*

The sun had gone down, and it was dark before he'd made it even half way to Spirit Mountain. He was parched. His bleeding had stopped, but he was still losing strength. He needed water, and he needed nano-fuel. His pockets came up empty when he searched for a vial of the metal granules for the nanos to tear apart and construct more of themselves with. He still recited his kill-them-all mantra but less now out of actual conviction than out of pain-dampening repetition.

Stopping to rest, he looked back past his feet at the castle walls. They seemed to glow slightly in the moonlight, but when clouds crossed in front of the moon, the castle was lost in shadow.

Fuck! He thought. *How did Benson keep this hidden from me? I'm ass deep in everything he's got going on, and I didn't know about this? What else do I not know about?*

He wheezed out a tight breath and just barely managed to not cough.

The clouds let the moonlight back at the walls, bringing back the illusion of glowing. That's when he noticed that the piece of aluminum that had been sticking out of his abdomen was no longer there. Bringing a hand up from where it rested in the dirt, he gingerly touched around the wounded area. It was still painful to the touch, but, miracle of miracles, it was sealed and no longer bleeding. He couldn't remember when it had happened. He knew a few times during the day he had passed out.

He smiled. The nanos in his blood had found the shrapnel and taken it apart a little at a time to generate more nanos which then accelerated the process. They'd partially healed some of his wounds. He probed the areas where he had taken shrapnel in the leg.

His smile grew even wider.

Hot damn, he thought, realizing that he might not have to limp home to the ranch. He'd be able to use both legs.

His smile disappeared, though, as the pain in his chest reminded him that several of his ribs were broken. Now that he knew his nanos worked just fine with other forms of metal that entered his body, he looked around for more scrap.

He didn't immediately find any, but he resolved to find some as soon as he was out of the area. And now that more clouds were moving in to blot out the moon, he decided to use the concealment of darkness to try getting up off of his back and walk for faster progress.

His back felt raw from all of the scraping on the ground it had been submitted to with his slow push towards the mountain. He needed more metal, and he needed to drink some water.

Walking with a hunched over gait brought him to the shore of the reservoir in about twenty minutes. Shaking his head, he wondered if he might have been able to walk during day light, maybe blend in with the walking corpses that still shambled around farther from the water.

The cool water felt so good going down his throat. He had a hard time not taking in a deep refreshing breath after a few swallows. His fractured ribs precluded that luxury.

He took a few minutes to wash some of the dirt and grime from his face, arms, and hands. Being somewhat cleaner felt heavenly by comparison. It made him feel energized.

Feeling recharged, he thought about calling home. Maybe Jax could have a ride meet him for extract somewhere outside of town and away from the castle. But what if Benson had it out for him, now that he knew about the hidden castle?

It still didn't make sense. Why would Benson have him hunting down Richard if Richard was working for Benson? Why else would Richard be coming here, to an I-G stronghold? Did Richard betray Benson? What if Richard could help Allen and Jax get the poppers out of their skulls so that Benson couldn't control them anymore? If it meant hurting Benson more, would Richard be willing to do it?

Fuck! I've got to know what the fuck is going on.

I'm still going to kill him after what he did to Tony, though, he told himself. *Damn it, why hasn't Jax sent me reinforcements?*

Maybe Benson took him out when he found out we know about his secret castle. Maybe Benson thinks I'm dead.

Now there was a happy thought. He pondered that one for a while.

He shook his head.

I need to know. I'll make the call. I'll let them talk first. If it isn't Jax that answers, I'll go off grid, totally dark. If Jax answers, he can tell me what is going on. And if Benson thinks I'm dead, I can get Jax to keep it secret that I'm alive. I'll be able to take out Benson myself, and then we won't let anyone control us again.

This time he nodded.

Yes, that will work.

He'd get the best signal from up on top of the mountain, so he started walking, again hunched over to be less visible to anyone watching from the castle. He clutched his side for most of the way. The pressure eased some of the pain.

While making the air smell somewhat fresher and cleaner, the wind also caused the mountain to moan. That's what it sounded like at first anyway.

I guess that's why it's called Spirit *Mountain.*

It wasn't until he stumbled across the opening to a small cave that he realized the real cause of the mountain sounds. He wondered what he would find if he went in, but decided finding a ride home was higher priority than exploring.

Before he made it to the top of the mountain he found another three cave openings. He left them alone as well, opting to call home as soon as possible. ·

When he reached the top, he found a clearing in the trees. Nestled in the clearing were a log cabin and a tall radio tower. Not wanting to risk discovery if the cabin was still occupied, he kept to the shadows in the tree line.

He just about exploded in a cursing tirade when he took his radio from its pouch on his Load Bearing Vest. Its antenna was broken, and the body itself was smashed beyond repair. He cursed himself for not checking before he'd just spent the last few hours climbing this mountain. He'd just wasted time climbing when he could have used that time to go down to town. Hell, he could have been on the other side of town by now, hot wiring a car or maybe even a small plane from the local airport.

He felt like throwing his radio off the side of the mountain, but the shiny antenna gave him another idea. Within minutes he had the outer plastic shell off, and he pried out bits of metal that made up the internal working pieces. A few of these he popped into his mouth and started sucking on. His nanos could use the fuel. He'd heal faster that way. The rest of the metal pieces he put in his pocket.

Still disgusted at how much time he'd lost, as well as the loss of his radio, he began to think about what he should do next. He didn't have comm. He didn't have transportation. He didn't even have a weapon anymore other than a small folding knife he had in his pocket. The walk into town would be long and tedious with his still-injured leg.

The cabin in the clearing beckoned to him. What could he find in and around the building that he might be able to use to improve his situation?

Well, let's just look and find out, he thought.

Instead of crossing the clearing, which would make him visible to anyone inside who happened to look outside at the wrong moment or to any sentries posted in the shadows on the other side, he kept to the tree line and the concealment of shadows. He kept his knife handy in case he had to kill a sentry.

The radio tower in the center of the clearing was silent, no buzzing, no flashing lights, just a hulking metal structure piercing the sky.

As he came closer to the cabin, the air began to once again carry the smell of rot. Something nearby was dead. He found that this didn't bother him as much as it used to, now that the zombies seemed to not see him.

The stench grew steadily stronger until he found the source of the smell on the most shadowed side of the cabin. A white Jeep Cherokee, with the driver side window down just a crack, absolutely reeked, and the mass of flies buzzing around it was off-putting.

Allen squinted and tried to see through the windshield. It looked like the driver was still inside, but whether he was dead or undead was unclear. The foul smell was horrible and made Allen's eyes water.

As much as he didn't look forward to a trek down the mountain on foot, he decided he'd rather hoof it than use the jeep with the guaranteed linger of the smell and flies.

Leaving the jeep behind, he circled the cabin, looking for signs of habitation, security, and resources. Signs of habitation and security turned out to be slim, but, should he decide to stay, there were plenty of resources.

Around back there was a nice sized generator for powering the house and a stand-alone fuel tank that smelled like it held gasoline. A shed held plenty of assorted tools, some of which he grabbed for his trip. A flashlight lay on the table. He took that. He also grabbed a small bucket of nails. He popped one into his mouth and held it between his lips like a tooth pick.

More fuel for the little buggers inside.

Already he was feeling better internally, though the ribs, he knew, would be an issue for a while.

He checked through the cabin windows without seeing anyone alive or dead. The front porch didn't creak as he crossed the wooden planks, a pleasant surprise. Someone had taken good care of this cabin.

He set the bucket of nails down on a rocking chair.

Using the light on the face of his digital watch, he studied the lock on the front door. It looked to be a standard 5-pin tumbler lock like on most residential doors. It should only take him a minute or two to pick through. There wasn't a dead bolt to accompany it.

He visualized picking the lock, a mental rehearsal of the task, but then a thought struck him. He remembered a prisoner in Leavenworth that had had the cell next to his own—he couldn't remember the guy's name—who had been bragging about his own sexual exploits after he found out why Allen was in prison. Story aside, the dude had claimed that when he had raped his baby mama it was in a small town out in the country where people didn't even lock their front doors. Anyone could just walk right in. They didn't lock their doors because crime was so low in those areas, and they just didn't see the need.

Allen had never experienced life in a small town, so he wondered how accurate the other inmate's story could be.

I'll be damned, he thought, when the door swung open an inch after just turning the door handle. He shook his head. *What the hell kind of person leaves their front door unlocked?* It just made no sense to him, but he wasn't going to complain. An easy way in was a lot better than a tough way.

Once inside, his first priority was to clear the building, one room at a time, and make sure there were no threats waiting for him. This went fairly quickly, as it was a small cabin and he was well trained in CQB. Having the flashlight helped immensely.

There were the usual furnishings, though done in a style he was unfamiliar with—very rustic and earthy. There weren't many knick knacks, which surprised him. What surprised him even more was the quantity of books in the place. There were books everywhere. Not just on shelves. They were on the kitchen counters, in the bathroom, on the dresser and nightstand in the main bedroom. A smaller room was nothing but bookshelves covered in even more books.

When does a person have time to read all of this? He wondered.

It was in the basement that he hit something useful.

A tall upright safe—the kind guys use to lock up their guns, and on the door, a Browning bumper sticker, a clue to the contents inside.

Unfortunately, the safe was closed and locked. Fortunately, he knew a thing or two about breaking and entering from his special operations training.

This one was a SentrySafe brand safe with a push-button combination lock set in the door. While your standard, uninitiated criminal might either leave the safe alone or try a brute force attempt at cracking the safe, Allen knew a trick to open this particular brand of safe quickly, provided he could find the right tool.

He walked back outside to the shed, hoping to find something useful. He turned on the flashlight while covering most of the bulb area with his thumb to cast a smaller beam of light around the shed. He didn't want anyone at the castle to see a stray beam of light or glow up on the mountain that they would possibly come investigate. Even though the clearing up here was surrounded by trees, he wasn't going to risk discovery.

The shed was well organized, just like the cabin, so it was quick work to find what he needed. There were thin strips of metal about four or five feet long, hanging over a metal peg in the wall. What they were supposed to be for he didn't know, but it didn't matter because he had an application they were well suited for. Unfortunately, they were too long. He only needed about a one foot length.

He took down one strip and found some bolt cutters. After cutting off a foot length, he went back into the cabin and down to the basement.

Now, let's see if I've still got the touch, he thought.

The safe's door handle was on the left, so he knew the door would be hinged to swing outward on the right. Starting with one corner of the metal strip, he pushed and wiggled it into the seam between the door and the safe itself, about a foot down from the upper right corner. The metal strip was a little stiff, so he ended up having to bend it multiple times, but after a bit, he was able to maneuver it to where he needed it.

The inner edge of the door on the hinge side had a little push button to reset the electronic combination lock on the front. He knew right away when he found the reset button because it sounded an audible beep. Then all he had to do was hold the pressure on the strip and wait for the light on the combination to flash red.

The lock gave another beep indicating that it was ready for a new combination to be entered.

Allen pressed 1-1-2-2-2, a random combination, and saw the light turn green. He reentered the same combination and heard a small mechanical shifting inside the lock. He pressed down on the safe door handle and it opened. Smiling, he opened the door and looked inside.

Guns

Mostly guns designed for hunting, but there were several, and plenty of ammunition for each one, as well as for the two handguns sitting on the inner shelf, both 1911 style Kimber .45s.

Hell, yeah. Not just a bookworm were you? He directed at the dead driver outside.

One of the rifles stood out from the others. It didn't have a large scope on it like most of the others, and it wasn't a bolt-action like the others either.

He picked it up with a smile and inspected it as well as he could in the limited light. A Springfield M1A Scout, National Match iron sights, sling, three—no four ten-round magazines—fully loaded, .308 caliber, well-lubricated action.

Excellent

The .223 magazines he carried were no good now that he didn't have an M16, so he pulled them out of his chest pouches and replaced them with the magazines for the Scout. Then he pocketed a few extra boxes of .308 ammo.

Next, he inspected the Kimbers. Both were .45 caliber with a few extra magazines each. Both were well lubricated with smooth, tight actions, and both fit comfortably into his waistband. He took a few boxes of ammunition for them as well.

He was running out of pockets.

Looking at the other guns in the safe, he felt a longing to bring them with him but knew that they'd be more of a hindrance at this point. Maybe if he got the Jeep cleaned up inside…

No, I'm not going to put up with that smell, not even for a small drive down into town, let alone a drive all the way out to the ranch.

He turned to leave then thought better of it and grabbed another box of ammunition for the Scout before walking up the stairs and out of the basement.

Carrying the Scout, he was reluctant to carry anything else in his hands, so he left the bucket of nails on the porch, though he did grab a few more nails to carry in a spare pouch on his kit. While his legs were healing, he still walked with a pronounced limp.

Smiling at the thought of the old saying about the guy who's so tough that he eats nails for breakfast, he put a nail in his mouth and began sucking on it.

Now I do eat nails for breakfast.

It was still dark, and he hadn't seen his own reflection in days. If he had, he might have noticed the spider webs of silver beginning to arc across each of his eyes.

He began descending the mountain, one painful step at time. He thought about all of the messy ways he could kill first Benson and then the castle occupants, one at a time as the others watched, waiting their turn. The fear he imagined seeing on their faces gave him a tingle of sexually charged energy and his thoughts soon drifted to his captive, little Miss Emily, back at the ranch in his cabin, stretched out and waiting for him. He'd been in too much of a hurry with her before he left. Next time was going to be exquisitely drawn out.

Chapter 18: Sleeper Awakens

"Little Miss Emily's" real name was actually Holly—Holly Burke.

She had woken in confusion and pain just as Allen had fantasized. She ached all over but especially down between her legs, and she was woozy enough that the room felt like it was spinning. She'd never felt so weak, and her tongue felt like sandpaper in her dry mouth. Her thirst for water was almost unbearable. She felt dehydrated, almost to the point of delirium.

It took her a few moments to realize through her blurry vision that she was looking up at a ceiling and that she couldn't move because she was held down in chains and restraints. She was naked, and she couldn't move much more than one arm and one leg. She burst into tears when her situation hit her, but she kept quiet as well. She could see a light on in the loft bedroom above her, and she didn't want to attract her captor's attention if he was up there.

Light shined in through the living room window, and she could hear the distant sounds of work being done somewhere outside. She thought about calling out for help, but until she knew where she was and who had taken her, she didn't know if calling out would do more harm than good. She wasn't in a position, or in any condition, to defend herself.

When she reached down between her legs with her one free hand, her panties were stiff with dried blood. She pulled them aside to assess the damage that had been done to her, and she gasped at how sore and tender she was. When she brought her hand back up to look at it, she found it speckled with dried flecks of blood. She closed her eyes tight and wished she were just caught in a dream.

But she was in too much pain for this not to be real. She was just thankful that she had been unconscious for the act.

She knew her time was limited if she couldn't get free. Her father had warned her and her sister before they'd even left the city that men would be a danger now that society was crumbling. Law and order was out the window. Now, only the strong and the smart would survive. Her abuser would be back before long or might wake up soon, if he was upstairs.

Thinking of her father's admonitions of caution around other people brought back the memories of the cabin being broken into and her father, sister, nephew, and niece being killed right there in front of her. She felt hollow inside, and guilt for not being with them strangled her thoughts.

Her body's need for water was what ultimately forced her mind off of her loss and made her think about how to fix her situation.

She began to take stock of her surroundings and look for a tool that she could use to break free of her bonds. It was then that she noticed the bottle of water off to the side and just within reach of her free arm. She downed the bottle immediately in gulps. It helped take away the gritty feeling in her mouth, but she needed more.

Thirst momentarily sated, she turned her attention to the problem of her restraints. She jerked and pulled at them, but they were solid, and she made no progress.

She lay there, panting with exertion, and tears threatened to spill again as she found hope of escape dimming.

No! she screamed in her thoughts. *I will not accept this! Come on, damn it!* She tested her restraints over and over, but they did not yield.

She couldn't understand why she felt so weak. Even though she had been drugged and raped and chained, she had been well fed, healthy, and used to a full day of activity before all of this. It had only been last night that she had been taken. She'd slept, but she felt exhausted.

Before long, she found herself wanting more water to drink and cursed herself for drinking the bottle she'd had too quickly. As if to torment her thoughts, the sky darkened and rain began to drum at the roof. So much water only a few feet away, and she couldn't sate herself with any of it.

And then she had to pee. It was humiliating, but she ended up letting loose right there. It had a pungent smell to it. She was dehydrated.

She noticed something metallic and shiny on the floor to her right. The first thought that flashed through her mind was that it was something she could use to scrape and cut with. She could use it to slice away at the leather wrist restraints. Her right arm was the one stretched out over head by the chain. She reached across her body with her left hand and turned over on her side. It was just out of reach.

She stopped straining and relaxed completely, taking a few calming breaths. Then she pointed her left hand up at the ceiling, expelled her breath quickly, and jerked her body and hand towards the metal. She couldn't grab it because it was flat on the floor and still too far out of reach for that, but her efforts were rewarded when it scraped across the floor towards her as she was jerked back by the tension of the chain.

It disappeared from view, and for a second she panicked, thinking she had lost it, but it had merely slipped under the edge of the buffalo skin rug. She could see it in a slight bulge. Breathing out in relief, she tugged at the rug, and there it was again. Just barely able to reach it now without straining at the chain, she scraped it a little closer across the floor and then picked it up.

A quarter

Really? A quarter?

She almost started crying again. What was she going to do with a quarter? It didn't have a sharp edge to it. She tried scraping it against the leather restraint of her chained hand. She could hardly reach the restraint, stretched out as she was, let alone scrape at it. She wanted to throw the coin in frustration, but after the effort she had just put into getting it, she just put it on the floor next to her head where she could look at it.

A 1962 Kennedy quarter, scratched up some but still some shine to it. She knew it was ninety percent silver. Her father had been a bit of a prepper and collected silver and gold for when the government pushed the dollar to a hyperinflationary economy-down scenario. He'd been keen on teaching his girls how to prepare for the worst.

Tears came to her eyes as she saw the memory of him being shot in cold blood all over again.

Lying on her side, looking at the quarter, it didn't take long to become uncomfortable, and her body screamed for water again. She chided herself for wasting water in tears for something that couldn't be changed. She embraced the pain, embraced the memory of her father, embraced his love, but resolved not to shed any more tears until she could afford to.

The rain outside came down even harder, reminding her that the water that could quench her thirst was just feet away.

With her father fresh in her mind, she remembered a trick he had shown her and her sister on one of their camping/outdoor training trips. He'd shown her to put a small pebble in her mouth when she was thirsty, to trick her body into thinking she had food in her mouth. She'd make saliva, and her mouth being wet would help curb some of the mind numbing thirst for a little while, hopefully until water became available.

She wondered if putting the quarter in her mouth would do the same thing as sucking on a pebble. She thought of how many times the quarter must have changed hands over the course of its life and how many of those oily hands had left their residue on it, and she almost decided not to try her dad's trick.

A pain in her stomach decided it for her though. She put it in her mouth and closed her eyes, trying to ignore the metallic and, sure enough—oily taste. She thought about sucking on a butterscotch candy and pretended as hard as she could that that was what she had put in her mouth.

A few seconds later, saliva did begin to coat her mouth. She swallowed, sending some of it to her stomach, and waited for more to come. She knew she was robbing from Peter to pay Paul, but the pain in her stomach did seem to diminish some.

A crash of thunder startled her sometime later, and she realized she had dozed off. Her eyes flashed open, and she frantically search the room to see if her captor was there yet.

The living room and kitchen were empty. The door next to the kitchen was still closed with no light coming from under the edge. The light was still on in the loft. There didn't appear to be anybody in the house with her.

The light coming in from outside had dimmed considerably, and she wondered if it was just the cloud cover from the storm blocking the sun, or if the sun was going down for the evening.

There was something in her mouth. She remembered putting the quarter in to generate some saliva, but the thing in her mouth was too small and oblong and uneven to be the quarter. She pinched it against the roof of her mouth, swallowed the saliva, and then spit out the...

Quarter?

It used to be the quarter anyway. That much was clear when she picked it up and held it up to the dimming light. She saw part of Kennedy's stamped profile and a smidgen of the date left on the face of it.

What the hell?

Without understanding why, she knew all of a sudden that her body craved for her to put this partially...*dissolved?*...quarter back in her mouth.

So she did.

And she fell back to sleep a little later.

Chapter 19: The Pet

Jax watched the drone recording over and over again. He couldn't believe it. The most technologically advanced and bio-enhanced warriors the world had ever know had gone down in smoke and had then been torn to shreds by zero-intelligence zombies.

What the hell?

And while he wouldn't have called any of them friends, he had gotten to know most of them pretty well. They had tended to make fun of him behind his back when they thought he couldn't hear because he was the runt of the gang, the brain to their brawn, the hack, the control center guy—not an *operator*.

And he didn't even hold that against them. He knew in his bones that he wasn't an alpha type personality like they were. But for his own sins he'd been thrown in with their lot. He'd faced execution in military prison same as them, and he'd been offered the same deal as them: a pardon and redemption. All he had to do was sign on the line and agree to some top secret testing that would likely save lives someday.

He'd felt the need for redemption then. After one of his hacks had shut down critical electrical and medical systems, hundreds of innocent people had died. He'd felt horrible for that and still did. He hadn't wanted anyone to die. He'd had no criminal intent.

But the lawyers had argued otherwise. He knew what he was doing was illegal they had said. He intended to hack those systems. Knowledge and Intent.

Doom On You, Jax.

And even though Jax hadn't been in the special operations community, Allen, bad-ass Navy SEAL of all people, had taken him under his wing and protected him in Leavenworth.

Allen was the only reason he was still alive, and now Allen was dead.

He watched the recording for the hundredth time.

There was confusion in the radio chatter. Something about the people below being friendlies, even though Jax had never heard of the Infinity Group having a base there. But the video clearly showed the IG emblem emblazoned on the tops of the trailers.

And then guns opened fire from the castle walls, followed shortly by surface to air missiles. The helicopters exploded.

Jax even saw someone get flung away from the main debris before everything impacted with the ground in an even larger fireball. He'd watched that particular bit several times over and over to see if it was anyone he could identify and to see if they had survived the fall. But he lost them in the smoke from the fiery crash, and the video feed cut out a few minutes later when the drone lost contact.

Zombies swarmed the scene…so many of them. What were they all doing there? Wasn't Cody supposed to be a *small* town?

He'd told Allen to go there. It was his fault they had gone, and he hadn't done a good enough recon with the drone to know about the castle fortifications. Nor had he filed an op plan on the IG intranet, like he was supposed to. Allen had thought it better not to wait in case they could get their hands on Richard and the Harper series. Have a

587

bargaining chip against Benson. But it was still his responsibility to make sure the way was clear for Allen and the others before they got there, to give them a heads-up at least. Once again he couldn't fix his own fuck-up. Allen wouldn't be coming back.

Jax closed his eyes.

He dreaded the meeting with Benson that would surely come. As soon as the boss found out what had happened, Jax was history. Frankly, he was surprised he hadn't been dragged in front of him already. If the castle was one of Benson's many secrets, things could go very badly for Jax. Very badly indeed. Benson wasn't the type that fired people. He was the type that killed people...slowly, and enjoyed every second of it.

One of Benson's men walked by with a leashed combat dog.

Oh, shit, Jax thought, just before he sneezed. *Allen said he needed me to feed his pet. Crap, I'll be sneezing all night if I can't find an antihistamine. I'd better get going. It probably hasn't eaten all day.*

Even though Allen's cat or dog wouldn't be able to appreciate Jax's feelings of indebtedness to their master, it made him feel better to be doing one last kind act for the man he owed his life to.

He was about to sign out of the system when he paused and thought better of it. He decided to take a risk, after all what did he have to lose?—and created a new hidden folder on the hard drive. Then he selected all of the mission files for the disastrous op at Benson's secret base and placed them in the new folder. Next, he used an NSA encryption program to make himself the only person able to access any of those files.

It wouldn't stop those at the base from reporting an attack to Benson, but maybe they wouldn't know who it was that had flown in on them. The helos were burned out shells now, and all of the men were either zombies or dead.

He could play dumb for a little while, and Benson wouldn't have any way to prove that he knew anything about anything. Maybe he could survive this after all.

He left the control center with a furtive look over his shoulder. How long before Benson ordered one of his men to snatch up Jax and present him for questioning? That was one meeting he'd feel good dodging for a while.

Opening the door to exit, he was pelted in the face with a brisk wind full of rain, and he sputtered. The weather was unexpected. He'd been watching the skies over Cody, just a few hours away, and there had been no signs of a torrential downpour like what they were getting here.

He shook his head and muttered under his breath. He didn't have a rain coat with him or an umbrella, and, of course, Allen had to pick a cabin over by the chopper pad which would take longer to walk to than to his own cabin by the control center, and, of course, none of the walk was under cover. He didn't even bother trying to stay dry. That just wasn't an option.

Lightning flashed in the distance.

He replayed the image in his head of the person getting thrown from the helicopter with the explosion.

Even if that was Allen, there is no way he could have survived the fall or the close proximity to the blast. No way.

But he wondered.

Thunder shook the world.

When he walked up the porch steps at Allen's cabin, it hit him again that his buddy wasn't coming home. He stopped and closed his eyes, resting one hand on a pillar support and holding the other at his temples and forehead.

More lightning flashed and thunder followed three seconds later.

Breathing out a heavy sigh, he opened his eyes and reached up to take down the spare key that Allen had secreted on top of the outside porch light. The cover that protected the light slipped loose and fell to the planks. Shards of glass scattered across the porch.

"Son of a bitch!" he cursed.

He stepped over to the door, glass crunching under foot, and put the key in the lock, turned it, and made kissing sounds.

"Here, boy. Come here. It's time to eat."

Chapter 20: F—You

Holly woke feeling uncharacteristically strong. Darkness had fallen. She yawned and realized that the pain that had infused her earlier was now mostly a memory. She was still a little sore, but the pain didn't dominate her physical feelings anymore. The quarter that had been in her mouth had curiously disappeared.

She was still thirsty as all get out though.

As good as she felt, especially compared to before, she almost forgot that she was naked and chained.

Time to fix that, she thought.

Lightning flashed through the darkness outside, outlining the window frame and the table and chairs below it. She reached up with her free hand to grab the chain where it held her other wrist and curled her free leg around the restrained leg then tightened her core muscles. She pulled towards her center with every ounce of her being, exhaling slowly, as her muscles and the chain strained against the chain's anchor.

Perspiration beaded on her body and dripped down her sides, tickling her as she pulled harder. She began to feel like she was running out of air. Her arms screamed for relief, but she refused to stop.

The corner log to which her hand was chained groaned and creaked. With a loud cry she pulled even harder, not even realizing she even had any more to give, but giving it anyway.

Then suddenly a sharp snap sounded, the chain fell to the floor, and her hands jerked downwards, dragging the chain towards her. She panted, trying to catch her breath, and rolled around on the floor. Her muscles ached, but it felt glorious to be able to curl in on herself a bit instead of her body being stretched out to the limit.

When she had her breath, she looked over at the end of the chain. The eye bolt that had anchored the chain into the log had snapped. A smile turned into a laugh, and she lay there for a few moments longer. She'd had no idea she was so strong.

Now she needed to free herself from the chain that held her to the tree that grew in the center of the cabin.

Thunder rumbled in the distance.

Only the light up in the loft let her see what she was doing. The night outside was as black as could be save for the occasional flash of distant lightning.

She crawled over to the live tree and studied the chain's anchor. It was another eye bolt. She didn't know if she could break another. She still felt strong, but the energy she had just expended had cost her.

She found herself craving a number of things to eat, another quarter, strangely, being one of them. The picture that flashed through her mind of a great big, juicy steak was also especially appealing at the moment.

Instead of trying to break the eye bolt with brute force, she applied some torque to see if she could unscrew it. It was in there pretty tight, but it did move.

Lefty-loosey; righty-tighty, she thought, as she turned the eye bolt to the left.

With each quarter turn, the bolt moved out of the tree a little more. But the chain twisted as well. She found it applying some uncomfortable pressure to her ankle. To relieve the constant and growing tension on the chain she ended up standing and turning in circles to her left. The chain uncurled, but she felt a little dizzy.

When the room stopped spinning, she went back to turning the chain.

The eye bolt popped free as a bolt of lightning lit up the window frame. Three seconds later the thunder shook the window pane.

Another three seconds later and a crash sounded on the porch.

Holly jerked towards the sound, and fear spiked inside of her.

Her captor was back. He was cursing on the porch.

No way was she going to allow him to rape her again. She would rather die.

Better yet, I'd rather kill, she thought.

She darted over to the wall by the front window where she would be in a blind spot when the door opened. The section of chain attached to her ankle rattled across the floor, and she worried that it would alert her captor, but there was really nothing she could do about that. He'd be inside in seconds. She just didn't have time to be sneaky quiet. She hoped the thunder outside would work in her favor.

Gathering up the chain that was attached to her wrist, she grabbed the end then let some slide through her hand until the doubled up length was short enough to use as an impact weapon. She eased the chain over her shoulder and prepared to swing.

She heard glass crunching underfoot right on the other side of the door. Then the key being pushed into the lock, the locking mechanism disengaging the bolt, the door swinging open.

Air kisses

"Here, boy. Come here. It's time to eat."

She didn't recognize the voice—no surprise there, really; and she was a little taken back at what the dude was saying. It didn't matter. This was her captor. He had to be destroyed.

Her adrenaline was through the roof, and she had a little bit of fear flowing through her veins, along with an unhealthy dose of anger.

Unhealthy for him.

As soon as he stepped in and cleared the door frame, he started to swing the door shut, and she started to swing the chain.

She yelled with effort as she brought the chain down.

Her yell drew his attention, and the look of surprise on his face embedded itself forever in her brain as she connected with the steel that had held her prisoner. The chain crashed into the base of his neck instantly severing its connection with his lower body. Additional trauma was inflicted to the muscles surrounding and underlying the chain's impact area.

He crumpled to the ground at her feet, paralyzed though not quite dead. Tears were in his eyes, and his breath was merely air escaping his uncontrolled and unresponsive lungs. He'd be dead from asphyxiation within minutes, unconscious with seconds.

Holly didn't let that happen. Instead, she used the chain to beat his head and shoulders to bloody pulp. All of the rage she felt at having been violated at the hands of this monster went into each successive swing of the chain.

She stopped swinging only when she realized that the man's head was gone and her efforts were merely tearing up the floor. That's when she dropped the end of the chain, fell to her knees, and began sobbing uncontrollably.

Wiping the tears from her eyes with the back of her hand a few minutes later, she accidentally scratched her forehead with the leather restraint she still hadn't gotten out of. She felt at the wound and her palm came away with a smear of blood.

Looking down she saw that her knees were planted in a pool of blood that was still spilling from his body and spreading across the floor. When she stood up the blood trickled down her legs in rivulets, which then smeared across her ankles at the restraints.

With steadier nerves than she thought she'd have, having just killed another human for the first time, she walked over to the front door and locked the deadbolt. That's when she noticed that the door had an internal cross bar that braced the door to the walls like the cathedral had in the black and white Hunchback of Notredame movie she had watched recently with her niece and nephew.

Her niece and nephew.

She slammed the cross bar down into the brackets, turned and leaned her back against the door, and let the tears stream down again. She cried for her father, for her niece and nephew, for her sister—for herself. The tears flowed even though she was dehydrated, her mind surrendering to the grief and allowing her body to give up its precious water. In letting it all go, she slid down with her back still against the door and hugged herself.

Sometime later she realized that she was no longer crying and that the blood that clung to her legs and that coated the floor was beginning to really smell bad. It didn't help that her captive had pissed and shit himself when he had died. She needed to clean it off of her, but first she needed to remove these chains.

She struggled to her feet and went to the kitchen. A block of kitchen knives rested on the counter. She pulled a paring knife out of its slot and began sawing away at the leather restraints at her wrists. When they fell away, she massaged the skin they had covered. Then she went to work on removing the restraints at her ankles.

She stopped in front of the bathroom door.

She was somewhat hesitant to see what was on the other side. She could imagine some decked out ninja psycho killer on the other side. But there was no light coming from under the door, and why would a psycho ninja killer still sit in the dark with everything else that had happened out here in the last hour?

More lightning flashed through the windows.

Still holding the paring knife in hand, she steeled herself for the possibility of a fight and opened the door. Inside she found a sink, a toilet, a shower with an open vinyl curtain, and a night light. No psychos. No ninjas.

She closed the door and turned on the light. A towel already hung on the rack. She crossed in front of the mirror above the sink and quickly turned away from it without looking. She didn't want to see herself, not yet, not until she felt clean again.

The water ran hot and quickly steamed up everything in the small room. Holly let her mind go blank as she stood under the hot water. She let the water run over every part of her, let it wash away the blood; let it wash away any residual uncleanliness inflicted on her by her rapist. She found herself swallowing some of the water. Yes, she was pretty thirsty. Even hot, the water felt good going down her throat.

She reached for the soap and saw that she still held the knife. She forced herself to set it down on the ledge and grab the soap instead. As she lathered up, she began thinking about her future and began worrying.

She knew she had been raped, and even though she focused on doing an overly thorough job of cleaning herself down there, she worried that she might become pregnant with her rapist's child. It wasn't a thought she wanted to have, but ignoring the possibility wouldn't make it go away.

A more pressing worry though was: what would her captor's colleagues do when they found him dead with his head bashed in? It was unlikely they'd think it was suicide. They'd know someone else had killed him and, they'd try to find the killer.

They'd try to find her.

Whether or not they'd be sympathetic to her being kidnapped and raped she didn't know, but she did know she didn't want to trust them enough to give them the chance.

Which meant she needed to find a way to escape this place. Then she needed to go somewhere these people couldn't find her and where the zombies couldn't reach her.

She wondered how long it would take before someone came looking for the man she'd just killed.

It was time to take stock of what she had available to her. Then she could come up with a plan for running and hiding.

She rinsed off the soap then turned off the water and toweled herself dry. She looked at the mirror's steam-fogged surface and found that now she wanted to see herself. She wanted to see herself as others saw her.

She wiped away some of the condensation and looked at the reflection of her face.

She looked like she had dropped a few pounds in the last twenty-four hours, and, with her hair wet and pulled back a bit it, she looked harder, more serious. She looked downright mean when she set her jaw and scowled.

Something was different though.

It took her a moment to realize what it was, and then she focused in on her eyes. She moved her face to just a few inches away from the mirror's surface and alternately squinted and opened her eyes as wide as she could.

Lines of shiny silver stretched through and just under the convex surface of each of her eyes. She gasped and covered her mouth as she pulled away from the mirror.

What the hell is this? She thought.

Moving in close again she looked at the gossamer threads interwoven through the surface of her orbs. She'd seen the black lines in the zombie eyes, but this was something different.

What did he do to me?

She was still wondering just what was going on, when she carefully walked up to the loft bedroom after glancing around downstairs looking for her clothes. She had found her panties, but with the dried blood in them she didn't want to wear them ever again. They would just remind her of what she had been through, and it wasn't something she cared to remember. She found one of her boots along with her socks on the floor at one end of the couch but couldn't find the other.

I hope this asshole has extra shoes, she thought.

The dresser held plenty of clothes, but they were for a large man. She'd fit in them, they'd just be very loose and baggy, even the fitted spandex-like Under Armour brand clothes.

Fortunately, she found a military riggers belt that could be cinched down though a large ring with a sliding tension bar, instead of worrying with a buckle that would be much too large for her. She was able to keep the dark green colored cargo pants securely on her hips, though she did have to roll up the pant legs. She found a matching BDU blouse, but she practically swam in it, it was so large. She shook her head as she took it off and dropped it on the floor.

She found boots upstairs as well, but they were much too large for her feet. She tried stuffing extra socks into the toe end, but they still felt very awkward and loose.

Oh well, beggars can't be choosers, she thought, as she tied the laces and then tucked the pant legs into the top of the boots.

So confident was her captor in the restraints he had locked her in, that he had left his weapons locker unlocked. She saw the rifles, shotgun, handguns, with ammo galore as well as smoke and incendiary and fragmentation grenades. She didn't know what all she should take.

Her dad had taught her how to shoot. She hadn't shot much or very often, but she did know how to aim, pull the trigger, and reload, and had shot each class of firearm. She also knew that if she was going to move quickly, a rifle or shotgun would be too much weight. They'd slow her down, and then being re-captured was a risk.

She decided to take a handgun. Even though she had never shot an HK USP-45, she chose that one because it had a suppressor threaded onto the end of the barrel, and she knew that if she had to shoot someone, her chances of escape would be best if she could do it quietly. She grabbed the boxes of ammo that were next to it as well as a fixed blade knife in a kydex sheath that, when she inspected the edge, found to be razor sharp.

She was tempted to take some fragmentation grenades but was afraid that one of them might explode on accident, since she didn't know how to use them. An extra backpack was next to the locker, so she packed some smoke grenades and extra ammo boxes into this.

When she rifled through the drawers of the locker next to the weapons, she found unopened MRE cases. She opened a box and took out four then stuffed them into the pack.

She also found some papers. She didn't know what most of them were and didn't care, but she found one that looked like it was a map of something. Hoping it was a map of where she was, she stuffed it into the pack to study later.

Looking at the clock on the dresser, she saw that it was getting close to midnight. She knew she needed to put some distance between her and the cabin before morning, when someone might come looking for the dead man downstairs.

I don't have any water, she realized, but she remembered seeing a few canteens in pouches on a load bearing vest that hung on the side of the weapons locker. She took them out of the pouches and threw them in the pack along with a metal cup, contoured to hold a canteen, which was also down in one of the pouches, a canteen cup.

The canteens were empty, so she took the pack down to the kitchen and filled the canteens from the tap then put them back in the pack.

She was worried that the pack was going to be too heavy with everything that she was adding to it, but when she put it on her back and cinched down on the shoulder straps, she found it easily manageable.

As she was about to open the front door to leave, she noticed that the boots on the dead body appeared to be smaller than the ones she had commandeered from upstairs. So she looked a little closer.

She was correct.

Which meant this guy, whoever he was, was not her captor. This wasn't his cabin. He was a visitor.

Oh shit, she thought, realizing that her captor, her rapist, could step onto the porch at any moment. She was glad she had added the crossbar to the door. At least that would slow him down if he did arrive. *I have to go—now!*

She still took the time to change into the dead man's boots.

Much more comfortable.

They were also a lot less likely to trip her up.

It was still raining as she looked outside. She saw the coat rack by the door. It held three jackets and a ball cap. She put the ball cap on her head and pulled the bill down low. Then she grabbed a Gore-Tex jacket and put it on before putting the pack back on over it.

Can't wait any longer. I have to go before he gets back.

She opened the door and stepped out onto the porch, looked around to see if anyone was around, and stepped off towards a stand of trees that didn't look to have any other buildings around. The rain hushed her foot steps and soon her foot prints blended in with all of the other signs of foot traffic through the area.

Chapter 21: Suicidal

Blood and brain matter splattered against the wall and ceiling. A massive groove cut into the rock wall of the castle bedroom by high velocity lead. Little particulates of ZS3 nano-laced blood floating in the still air, freshly propelled out of the top of his skull, just waiting to be inhaled by the clean-up crew or maybe first by Hanna.

Enough to infect?

He didn't know, and ultimately the not knowing was what led Jason to take his thumb off the trigger and move the barrel of the shotgun out from under his chin. Looking down at the gaping tube of destruction made him sick to his stomach. He ejected the one unused shotgun slug he had found wedged between the front seat and center console of the lab. Rolling the round across the palm of his hand, he wondered just how much of the ZS3 it took to spread the zombie infection.

Suicide was not something he had ever contemplated, not before he'd become infected. Now he'd begun thinking about it and the possible after effects constantly, and only for one reason: Hanna.

They'd been happily married long enough that he couldn't remember off the top of his head just how many years it had been, not without stopping to count up the years. He loved her more now than he had when he had joined her at the altar, but even though he was still there for her in a limited emotional capacity, he knew deep in his soul that he could never again be there for her physically, as a husband, not without infecting her too.

603

There was only one set of watches that could keep ZS3 in check.

Sex was completely off the table now, even with a condom because the nanos were so much smaller than the pores of latex or even PVC rubbers. They'd still pass through the membrane and infect her. Worse, he couldn't even risk kissing her. His saliva, by design, was sure to have the highest concentration of ZS3 of anywhere else in his body.

A walking dead man: that's what I am.

He knew he could bring down every single person in this sanctuary with ZS3 infection without even meaning to, and that scared him. He couldn't live with himself if he caused Hanna to turn into one of those walking cadavers. Was it worth the risk to stay, even working on a way to replicate the possible cure that was inside of Richard?...*actually, Philip*, he reminded himself. *That's going to take some getting used to.*

Sighing, he set the shotgun down on the floor and shifted it under the bed with his foot. He bounced the one round he had for it in his hand then gripped it tight and dropped it into his front pocket. He'd gotten his wife to safety. He'd almost convinced himself to pull the trigger.

Not yet. Gotta get Hanna settled. Then I'll end the threat. Though, I might have to hang myself instead of spreading my blood all over the place.

But then he thought about what would happen when someone took the watches from his dead wrists. That might just have the same effect he was trying to avoid.

Maybe a jump off the wall would do it. A jump to the outside. I'll have to make sure I explain everything in a letter before I go.

The door to the room swung inward.

"Hey, Babe," Jason said, with a tired smile, at least he hoped she thought it was tired and not sad.

Hanna smiled and closed the door.

"I'm so glad we're not driving anymore," she said by way of reply. "Look, I found someone who was willing to give away a few towels. We can finally take a shower."

This time Jason's smile was genuine. Even if he was contemplating ending his earthly existence, he would certainly feel better washing the grime of the road off of him before taking that last step into oblivion.

"You wanna go first?" he asked.

"Mmm, how about we take one together?"

A deep feeling of sadness pierced his soul, but he smiled through the pain.

"Ok," he replied. "But no hanky panky. I'm so tired I could die. I just want to get cleaned up and go to sleep."

"I know, Jace. Me too. Come on," she said, opening the door to the adjoining bathroom and turning on the light.

With a heavy heart, Jason stood and walked to the bathroom.

Killing himself was going to be hard on both of them.

Enjoy these last few hours with her, Jason, he told himself. *She'll need some good memories to hold on to after you're gone.*

The steam from the shower was already clouding up the mirror, so he didn't have to see the black lines that webbed the inside of his eyes.

Chapter 22: Tower

The tower steps seemed to climb up forever, even though Scott knew that the tower was really only about five stories tall, having seen it from the courtyard when they first came out of the lab. It was just a sign that he needed to exercise more.

After the embarrassing incident with Jason being almost gunned down by castle security, Scott had whispered a request to Philip for a quiet room away from everyone else where he could set up his electronics.

Philip offered the tower.

It was perfect, even with the long steep climb. That should prevent everyone else from coming around, annoying him. Just so long as it didn't keep Erika away. *Would it?* Maybe he should request another room closer to hers, where he could sleep and just go to the tower for his work. Then she couldn't use distance as an excuse for staying away from him.

Who am I kidding? What reason could she possibly have for wanting to be close to me? He thought, as he paused his climb and scratched furiously at his forehead with the back of his hand.

Then he remembered how she had cozied up next to him and snuggled against him on the couch in the lab. How she had stayed close to him when they went out into the dark on the road at the roadblock. How she smiled at him when she talked.

Was it because they had rescued her from the top of that gas station? *No, that was Philip, not me.* Maybe because he tried to protect her and the rest of them before Phil had taken the gun away from him in the lab? *Maybe.*

She liked him. He could see it. But self-doubt crept in as usual. What if she was just being nice? What if she was only acting that way because she wanted something from him? Maybe fix her broken camera? What if…?

Stop thinking about her, he told himself. *Focus on Philip's project. The Infinity Group is out there, and they are coming for us. But I'll know when they do.*

Breathing out a huge sigh of relief, he topped the last step and set his things down. He leaned over and put his hands on his knees as he tried to catch his breath. Sweat dripped down and stung his eyes.

I really wish there were an elevator, he thought.

Before he'd even finished thinking it, he heard a "Ding!" around the curve of the wall to his right, the unmistakable alert that elevator doors were opening.

You gotta be freaking kidding me.

Scott stepped over to see Richard, *No—Philip,* stepping off the elevator.

"Hey, Scott," Philip said. "I wanted to check on you real quick, and help you get situated up here…why didn't you take the elevator? Oh my gosh, you look exhausted. That's my fault. I should have said something before you took off. I'm sorry; I thought you would see the elevator sign."

Scott clenched his jaw and willed himself not to burst out with an angry retort that he knew he would regret later. He also forced himself not to scratch at his forehead or his ear, even though they felt like they had a million ants crawling on them at the moment. Instead, he nodded and looked down at the stone floor, hoping Philip would think he was still trying to catch his breath.

A moment later he was glad he had kept his mouth shut because Erika came off the elevator.

"Here, let me help you," she said, stepping around him to grab the handle of a wheeled suitcase from behind him. She was so close he could smell her. It was wonderful. "I'm sure it is going to take a few days to learn the ins and outs of our new home, so don't feel bad that you didn't know there was an elevator. I started going up the steps too, until Phil stopped me and told me the elevator was faster."

Scott's anger was gone. He smiled, content to just look into her eyes and breathe her in. He wasn't sure if it was from the climb, or from her suddenly being there unexpectedly, but his heart suddenly felt like it was working extra hard.

"You're a lucky guy, Scott," Philip said. "Erika said she wants to room close to you. Of course, with a quarter of the town harbored up behind these walls, there wasn't going to be much choice about that. Most of the living space was already taken a week ago...And I'll shut up because you aren't paying any attention to me anyway."

Scott didn't hear Philip talking to him other than as a buzz of noise in the background. He was intent on Erika as he followed her into the single circular room at the top of the tower. She was commenting on what a great view it was from there, and he agreed wholeheartedly, though he wasn't looking beyond her.

"Oh, where did Phil go?" Erika asked.

That snapped Scott out of his almost trance-like stupor, and he mumbled a reply that didn't even make sense to his own ears. Then he felt embarrassed and withdrew into himself a little more.

"Is that everything?" Erika asked, looking past him to see another large suitcase at the top of the steps. She walked to get it as Scott put his hard cases down on a table that looked ancient but on closer inspection was actually fairly new.

That's when he finally looked around to see the room instead of it all being a blur while he focused on her.

The room looked like it had been transported straight out of a fantasy novel. A wizard's tower. It was cluttered-looking, without actually being cluttered. *Clever.*

Stacks of dusty-looking books looked to be in danger of falling over at any moment, some on the tables, some on the floor. More books were packed into the available bookshelves than there was space for. Scrolls littered a bench near a window that looked out over the reservoir and a mountain.

Specimen jars lined a series of shelves that were spread around the wall. Some held aromatic herbs and spices, and others contained very realistic-looking creatures, some ordinary and others fantastical. There were snakes, bats, some kind of bird. One even looked like a baby dragon that might have just hatched.

A king size bed sat off to the right from the entrance. It was the one piece of furniture in the entire room that didn't look cluttered or in some way unorganized.

Instead of modern lights there were candles spaced around the room, not real candles, he saw upon closer inspection. *LED bulbs.*

I bet this place looks plenty freaky after dark, Scott thought, with a slight feeling of trepidation. *It will definitely take some getting used to.*

"Here is the last one," Erika said, parking the large suitcase below the cases Scott had placed on the table.

"Thank you," he replied. "This place is kind of creepy, if you really think about it," he added, looking up at the rafters, where it was darker with shadow.

"It's nothing compared to what is out there beyond the walls, trying to get in and either eat us or turn us into one of them; but before all of this started, yeah, it would be a little creepy in here, especially at night. Phil said some of the guests like it like that, and rent this room especially for the effect. Weird, if you ask me."

Scott smiled, and she smiled back.

He'd thought his heart felt heavy earlier. Now it felt like it was melting.

"So where are you staying?" he asked.

"Well," she answered hesitantly. "I was offered a room downstairs that I would have to share with a family of five, three of them being little kids—noisy little kids. Don't get me wrong, I love kids; I'm just not sure I'm ready to live with them full time right now. So, I was hoping— maybe I could share a room with you? Phil said there is plenty of room up here, and I already know you—kind of."

She paused, and Scott didn't fill the silence.

"Or, nevermind, I guess I shouldn't have asked. You're not used to being around other people, and I'd probably make you too nervous or interfere with whatever it is Phil asked you to do up here. I'll just go."

Scott's mind had gone blank as soon as she asked to share a room with him, *with him*, a scabbed up, pasty-looking, socially-awkward if not downright anti-social, well, nerd. And then she was withdrawing the request.

"No! Stay!" he blurted. "I'm sorry," he whispered, realizing he'd been a little louder than was probably polite. "You can absolutely share the room," he said, in a more conversational tone. "Sorry, I was just surprised you…you know."

Erika smiled.

"Ok, then," she replied. "I claim the bed."

Scott opened his mouth to speak, but nothing came out, and he looked stunned again.

She laughed. "I'm kidding. The bed is huge. There's no reason either of us should have to be uncomfortable on the floor—since, I don't see any couches."

"Wizards don't have couches," Scott said.

She laughed again.

"Come on, let's unpack, and you can tell me what is so important that Phil has you up here away from everyone else."

Scott smiled.

"Ok," he said. "I'm a bit of a whiz with computers. I'm a programmer and hacker. That's what I did for DARPA before all of this."

"A computer wizard in a wizard's tower. How appropriate," Erika said with a smirk. "So what does Phil want you to do with your super powers?"

Scott smiled and caught the twinkle in her eyes.

"He wants me to set up an early detection system for him, so hopefully we'll know when the Infinity Group makes a move on us; and set up a response plan for fighting back. I'm going to give him some eyes in the sky and some teeth on the ground," he replied. "The last thing I did before I left my place to join Philip's little group was set myself up for this in case I ever needed some real firepower against the zombies. I'm going to bring him the drones I still have access to at DARPA."

Erika's eye brows arched toward her hairline.

"Impressive," she said.

Chapter 23: Smoochy

"Come here," Linda said, sinking onto their bed and holding her arms open.

Philip could see that she was exhausted. They'd spent most of the first few hours after their arrival getting his travel companions settled into their new home and seeing that they had what they needed.

That had taken longer than he would have thought. The castle was already full before they made it home. Linda had done a good job of getting the word out to the locals and some of the tourists in town that there would be safety for them behind the walls.

Having Scott take the tower was a no-brainer. Most of the other guests were too freaked out by the room anyway. Erika being with Scott made things a little less complicated as far as finding space went.

The McIntyres were going to be a problem though. They didn't take up much room, but the other people around them were scared. Word traveled fast that Jason was infected, and those that didn't know, found out as soon as they saw his eyes. No one but Hanna wanted to be anywhere near him, and he knew fear could turn to violence quickly if things weren't handled well. But that was an issue for later. He'd given them the small room attached to the library to use for now. It was away from everyone else, and it included the three necessities: a toilet, a shower, and a bed. That would have to suffice until he could drum up something better for them.

He breathed out a sigh.

It was good to finally be able to have some alone time with his fiancé.

He set the sword down against the wall by the door and dropped his small bag of personal belongings to the floor then crossed the room to her embrace.

"I missed you," he said, holding her tight to his chest.

She looked up into his golden eyes and tears sprang to hers.

"I've tried not to show it in front of the others because they needed someone to project strength to get them through this, but you really had me worried," she said.

He brushed the tears away from the corners of her eyes with his thumbs and smiled.

"Well, I'm here for you now," he said, "And I'm stronger than I ever have been before. There's a cure to this abomination, and it is inside of me. I won't let anything happen to you. I promise."

She hugged him even tighter and buried her head in his chest.

"We've only got a little time to get ready," Philip said, stroking his hands down through her silky hair. It still smelled of her usual shampoo. "Some very bad people are going to try to come after me, more of the same people, I think, that were in the helicopters out there that got shot down. They may already know where we are.

"I noticed that the delivery trucks that I ordered have arrived, and that's a good thing. We're going to need the supplies and the heavy weapons. As bad as it is now, it is going to get worse, much worse. Food is going to run out. So will the medicine and the ammunition. We'll still be in survival mode long after these zombies have turned to dust. Those people have set us back to the Stone Age."

"Shhh," Linda whispered. "Not right now. Let me just enjoy the moment. Like you said, we've only got a little time. Let's make the most of it."

Philip nodded and held her close, breathing her in.

Enjoy the moment...because tomorrow the war begins. No more running. It's time to fight.

Chapter 24: Surrounded

Standing behind his desk, President Edward Nelson looked out the through the Oval Office windows at the fence line that surrounded the White House's south lawn.

Normally, uniformed Secret Service officers stood watch outside the fence, guarding against threats to the President and his four to eight year home. No longer. Over the last few days, hordes of zombies had arrived from Maryland and Virginia to join those already in the District of Columbia and surrounded the entire White House complex, forcing the Secret Service to fall back to positions inside the fence.

It was not a problem unique to the south side.

Sensing the live meat just feet away, the zombies lingered, doing their mindless best to attack through the bars. Fortunately, they were no longer smart enough to try climbing over the fence.

Enough of his uniformed guardians had begun to abandon him and his staff to go protect their own families that he had been forced to follow Dunwoody's advice to invite the Secret Service's families to stay within the protective barrier of the White House grounds and give them living area in the Old Executive Office Building. Many had taken him up on the offer. Where else was there to go?

Now that the Secret Service had their own families there to protect, they were more vigilant than ever before in their duties, despite the growing mass of walking corpses and the accompanying stench around them; but by being close to the fence, they attracted more and more of the infected towards them and their protectees.

Worse than the stench were the swollen clouds of flies that were busy feeding and laying eggs on the decomposing bodies of the infected, prompting the Secret Service to wear face masks and protective eye wear that were normally reserved for the cold, windy months of winter.

This was one of the few places inside the city where anyone was brave enough, or foolish enough, to stand outside in close proximity to the zombies. It drove the zombies into a frenzy. The press of rotting flesh against the steel bars caused more than a few of the zombies to be squished through into the secure area. The bars were close enough together that this effectively crushed their skulls in most cases. In the few instances when the zombies survived the squeeze through, a Secret Service officer was there to dispatch the crushed but moving corpse with a shot through the head.

Despite the crush against the steel bar, the fence remained sturdy—for now.

Nelson blew out an exasperated sigh. This wasn't how he had imagined his last days in office would be spent. Benson had insisted he remain at the White House for as long as there was enough of a human presence in America that warranted needing leadership from the President.

As long as the people looked to the President to save them from the zombie threat, they wouldn't be taking steps to save themselves. Most would die when the promised help never came, which was fine with Benson. That just meant there would be fewer to resist in the war

Benson's private army would wage against the apocalypse survivors. He would be Master of the World, and Nelson would be one of his most trusted subjects.

At least, Nelson told himself, *I will be until I get my hands on Harper's life extension nano series.*

The only reason Nelson obeyed Benson's order to stay at the White House, surrounded by a walking graveyard, instead of hopping on his helicopter, Marine One, and flying away from the putrid stench around him, was the fear that in doing so, he would forfeit the future of wealth and health that he deserved.

Someday Benson won't be calling the shots, he thought. *I will, and then Diane really will be the First Lady—First Lady of the whole world. We'll see how Benson likes being surrounded by these stink-bags. Someday soon, if I have my way.*

Marlon stepped in through the side door without knocking.

"We've got the latest satellite photos," he said to the President's back. "It looks like we'll only have to stay here for another week—two at the most. Almost every major city in the U.S. is overrun. The rest of the world is in the same boat, if not worse. Project Wildlands is working every bit as well as we had hoped."

Nelson turned to face his assistant and forced a smile, never forgetting for even a moment that Marlon Dunwoody was first and foremost Benson's man.

"Now we just need the life extension series we were promised."

Marlon smiled.

"Soon, but we still have work to do."

To Be Continued

Thank you for reading *The Zombie Conspiracy Parts 1-3 The Population Control Bundle*. If you enjoyed the story, please do me a favor. Go back to Amazon.com, find the page for this book, and leave me an honest review. I read every one of them. I hope you'll come back and read the rest when it is ready. The conclusion of this story arc has Richard and company taking the fight to the bad guys. You don't want to miss it. Sign up to my email alert list by emailing me at Jeremy8541@zapsgear.com and tell me you want to know when the rest is available. I promise not to spam you or give/sell your info to anyone.

About The Author

Jeremy McIlroy lives a private life with his family in Virginia.
He likes to tinker with outdoor and urban survival gear. He created the original Z.A.P.S. Gear Survival Grenade, a versatile survival kit wrapped in parachute cord. They are available at www.zapsgear.com, along with other creations made of parachute cord.
Z.A.P.S. Gear = Zombie Apocalypse Paracord Survival Gear

Friend him on Facebook:
https://www.facebook.com/jeremy.mcilroy.73

Follow him on Pinterest: Username – zapsgear

Follow him on Instagram: Username: zaps_gear

You can email him with questions, comments, concerns:
Jeremy8541@zapsgear.com

Made in the USA
Middletown, DE
02 November 2023

41835644R00348